Praise for *Becoming Sarah*

"Lyrically and meticulously composed, Botnick's novel plumbs the emotional depths of the Vogel women, from childhood through adulthood. Not a traditional Holocaust story, Botnick's narrative examines the effects of the detritus left behind by the great atrocity on those who survived as well as their offspring. The novel is rich with early postwar historical detail, spotlighting the lingering virulent antisemitism in both Europe and America."

—*Kirkus Reviews*

"A prism-like gaze at the jewel of motherhood, with its sharp edges and smooth, opaque surfaces, *Becoming Sarah* keeps churning through several generations of Jewish women, who strive to understand each other and themselves beneath the shadows of the Holocaust. Every sentence is meticulously written, not a word wasted."

—Suzzy Roche, founding member of The Roches
and author of *The Town Crazy*

"*Becoming Sarah* is the rare book I finished and wanted to immediately start reading all over again. Lush with figurative language but spare in mood, this finely written novel mines the depths of an identity forged in deprivation but redeemed through resilience, love, and the lessons of loss. An impressive debut!"

—Barbara Stark-Nemon, author of *Even in Darkness* and *Hard Cider*

"From Sarah's birth in Auschwitz through many generations of daughters stretching into the future, Botnick shows us the slowly uncoiling effects of motherlessness, persecution, and displacement—and how love weaves, struggles, and sometimes triumphs through it all."

—Helen Benedict, author of *The Good Deed* and *Wolf Season*

"Botnick masterfully weaves the 'bundle of loose threads, each with its own beginning' as she carries the reader through decades, deep inside a world of survivors and strivers. Full, fresh, and often startlingly funny, every page of this novel offers a new way of looking at the world, and just in time."

—Amy Friedman, author *Desperado's Wife*

"How does a survivor of unspeakable acts survive? And how does their trauma affect future generations? Botnick takes on these questions with great skill in a style that is witty, downright funny at times, and wonderfully hopeful. *Becoming Sarah* offers a brilliant quartet of unforgettable women who each crave a love that has been stifled but never destroyed."

—Gloria Jacobs, former executive director of The Feminist Press and executive editor of *Ms. Magazine*

". . . an unusual and deeply moving peek into the aftermath of the Nazi Holocaust—leavened with occasional humor—about a flawed but believably-human protagonist and the positive and negative influence she cast on subsequent generations of family members."

—*Newpages Blog*

BECOMING SARAH

BECOMING SARAH

A Novel

DIANE BOTNICK

SHE WRITES PRESS

Published in 2025 by
She Writes Press, an imprint of The Stable Book Group

32 Court Street, Suite 2109
Brooklyn, NY 11201
https://shewritespress.com
Library of Congress Control Number: 2025909643
ISBN: 979-8-89636-000-1
eISBN: 979-8-89636-001-8

Interior Designer: Andrea Reider

Printed in the United States

For my mother Dee, her mother Dora,

Dore and Olivia,

my love and partner Hass—

and to all those who survive in life and in memory

TABLE OF CONTENTS

In March of 1957, Stanisława Leszczyńska, known as the Midwife of Auschwitz, attended a gathering of her colleagues in Łódź, Poland, where she reported that in the two years of her imprisonment at the camp, she delivered 3,000 babies. Despite her aid and prayers, most were immediately and brutally murdered. Thirty survived.

Sarah Vogel was not one of them. Though the world she travels is founded in history, she and her story are fictional. Any resemblance to a real person is unintentional.

PROLOGUE

Deep into the twenty-first century, change is everywhere. But when the days are fine, scents assail her garden same as they ever did. Winter witch hazel. Springtime pear. Summer honeysuckle, so heady at dusk. When praised for her green thumb she says, "You live this long and see what color your thumb turns."

A boy from down the block is sent by his mother to see if she needs help around the yard. Unwilling to pay for work she can still do, she sends him back to his mother. "Your phone is ringing," he snarls at her.

"Let it," she snarls back.

Worms tunnel beneath her feet. She rakes the stones out of her way. She digs. Dirt cakes the moons of her fingernails. She claps the dust from her hands and the squirrels riot. A round of pre-sliced bologna on two slices of pumpernickel is lunch. Nowadays, everything is pre-sliced. It's nearly impossible to find a whole loaf of bread. A whole of anything. The sandwich draws bees. Occasionally, one forgets itself and stings, but there are still plasters for that. The gnats swarm at sunset, and then there's nothing to be done but go indoors. She remembers when summer evenings still brought bats to sup on them, but because remembering doesn't always allow for good endings, the bat crisis gets filed away with everything else.

Some things need remembering, like the way home from the drugstore or how to coax a chicken into falling apart in the pot, but everything else is served up in dreams, events harvested from life, whether they happened or not. Like this one where a man sits parked by her bed in a straight-backed chair, feet square on the floor, reading aloud from her favorite bedtime story, a pamphlet entitled "Definitions You Should Know to Assist You in Determining Your Zipper Needs." The pamphlet's hers. He is, too. Both stolen from the same friend.

Her hair, not yet gray, covers her face.

"Number one. Chain," he reads. "The continuous piece that is formed when both halves of a zipper are meshed together.

"Two. Chain size: the specific gauge of the chain, i.e., size of the teeth.

"Three. Teeth . . ." He stares longingly at her, then drops his eyes to the page. "Teeth . . . the individual elements that make up the chain."

His is now the face of another, the brooding, soulfully sunken, rabble-rousing, chain-smoking love of her life, but from the neck down, it's clearly what's-his-name, the one from the shop, in uniform. White shirt buttoned to the Adam's apple, tails loose; black wool jacket snug at the shoulders, long in the arms. His work trousers, dark, bagging in the rear, and showing too much white sock. His feet don't make it into the frame. She presumes they are shod. In oxfords, if it's him. And it seems to be. His hair is thinning, but he's still only a boy. Boy-ish, anyway. Soft. Almost fat. He wears spectacles with lenses thick as bottle bottoms, and still he squints. The shoes, though, that would settle it.

"Number four. Slider," he continues. "The device that moves up and down the chain to open or close the zipper.

"Five. Pull tab." He looks up through his bottle-bottom glasses and recites by heart: "The part of the slider that you hold to move the slider up or down."

She rises from the bed. The room is unlit, unfamiliar. She feels his breath. Nutty from his smokes. She slips the nightgown off her shoulders and tells him to close his eyes.

"I can't even see with the lights on." He laughs.

She turns her back to him. Lowers herself onto his lap.

He mumbles a weak protest.

"Shush," she shushes, and he does, arms hanging limp, jacket sleeves hiding his knuckles.

Her back rests against his chest. They both look in the same direction, he through closed eyes. He shifts under the weight, her legs atop his.

"Give me your hand."

"Which one?" he asks.

"Both," she tells him.

He raises them, palms up.

She takes them and guides his left hand under her nightgown to her left breast, over which it forms a warm shield. She wants to know what it feels like. "Tell me," she says.

His fingers explore, stop, continue, tentative. They do all the thinking.

"It's smooth," he says once his words catch up. "And soft. So . . . soft."

His fingers fan, groping in the dark, but don't find what they're looking for because the dream has taken a dreamlike turn, time leapfrogging over itself, carts rolling ahead of their horses, only somewhat accounting for how the diagnosis, cancer, has already been delivered, the treatment come and gone, though this man, this lover, should be loving her long before they'd come for her breasts. Before they gave her the new ones. Nice ones, too, though the skin there is numb even now so it's his surprise she feels, not his touch. Feels it turn to curiosity, and then, there, he's discovered it. Or the lack of it. In place of the little bump that would have been so appreciative of his attention, there's only a horizontal seam, a patch on a busted tire his fingers trace.

"And that's the good one," she says, guiding his right hand to cover the other, a lumpy little mess.

"Go on," she says.

She can't feel that one, either, but looks down in the dark and through her shirt watches the hand moving under her shirt, a reader of Braille, a kneader of bread.

But now it's her turn to be surprised. The twill pleat covering his trousers' zipper has nosed its way up between her legs. *That* she can feel, and she rocks back and forth, riding its ridge. She's tempted but doesn't go down on her knees to take the brass pull tab in her teeth and guide it down the zipper's length, the boxy little shoe releasing one at a time each of the chain's brass teeth and knitting them together on its slide up, and repeating: down, then up; down, then up. Down. Then up.

What she does is cover his hands with hers and press them tight to the bald, lumpen, emptied-restuffed-and-stitched, titless tits that have made him hard.

"Open your eyes," she says to no one, the dream most probably over, a spring wind replacing the heat of his breath on her neck, clues that she's back in the garden, a place what's-his-name could never have been. But who knows, with the scent of paperwhites souring to the smell of bad electrical wiring. The smell of old. Maybe old is a dream, too.

BEFORE

Beginnings

A baby is born inside a war. From one unfriendly womb to another she goes. It's like living in a fishbowl. The view is panoramic, but the glass won't give. It's she who must.

1942

It happened in winter, this birth, this unlikely, uncelebrated event. A winter that so efficiently branded her with its cold, she was never not cold again. So cold that of all the things she might have wished to do over, chief among them was to have been born in summer.

It happened in Auschwitz, this birth. Auschwitz. Winter. Impossible for a grown-up to wake, work, sleep, and wake again. For a newborn, miraculous. The cramped barracks, the sparse water—not enough to touch an inmate's thirst let alone fill a pot for boiling, and even if anyone could have afforded anything so dear as a pot, there would've been no fire for it to boil on, nothing to warm an infant. Forget the mother. Which she did. The mother, the face, the roughened hands she fell into, the random tits she suckled until they gave out or she was cut off.

But in March, the women of Auschwitz were twice blessed as the waning of winter brought with it a midnight move to Birkenau. Their own little suburb built of wood. As promised, work had set them free. Free as birds. A thousand in a cage built for hundreds. A month, two months old, they brought the child along. What else to bring? And though they were all well-defended against miracles, one stepped forward and volunteered the last corner of the slice of bread she'd stood so long in line for, chewing before spitting it into her hand and putting the pasty wad into the tiny mouth puckered like her own because it, too, wanted more. Tough luck. The woman was good but no saint. It cost her nothing, though, to stick a pinkie into the baby's mouth, so she did, and then miraculously, when that first nurturing soul disappeared, another stepped in. And because in night's meat locker a baby took up little room and gave off much heat, soon there was a queue of women.

That the guards never learned of this baby's existence was only one of the miracles at play. There was that she survived the winter of '42 to see another and another and another. That there were women enough who pooled their paltry resources and bartered rag and needle for thread and buttons, a bit of wire, a pair of shoes, and stood for a while in a cement-block room, holding her, rocking under a sprinkle as ephemeral as spring rain, pretending the water ran hot and clear instead of cold and murky, a chant, *loo la loo-loo-loo*, rising from them, these women stripped down to their mourning-dove gray. Normal babies don't see the world in Technicolor for five months. For this one, it would be years.

1945

Winter. Sixty thousand followed their German protectors away from the Eastern barbarians' offensive. Five thousand didn't. Their choice. Those whose feet felt the treads of boots and tanks grinding toward them, left; those with feet too numb to feel anything, stayed.

Another self-selected mother lashed the child to her chest with great care and no less ingenuity, considering the materials at her disposal. A three-year-old barely big enough to budge a scale was still a grievous weight to a woman herself no more than bones and air, but it wasn't so dumb to have a little ballast and a hot knaidel to cozy up to on the trek. While two-thirds of their parade slept forever in the snowbanks where they fell, this mother and child made it in mostly one piece to the train cars waiting at the border. The woman swayed with the train burrowing deeper into the Fatherland, cradling her marginally expanded girth, the burden within, her lucky charm, the girl licking ropes of snot streaming from her still-bridgeless nose as she slipped through another camp's gates, an undetectable error.

A timorous spring. In Bergen-Belsen, the trees insisted on budding before being told. How should they know they were prisoners, too? The inmates, less rooted, suffered the cruelest time yet, every breeze torturing them with rumors of Salvation, the earth beneath their feet rousing from its coma while more and more campers lapsed into their own. Auschwitz was kaput. This was no rumor. This was fact. One that didn't send all hearts soaring. *Remember when we were only two or three to a bunk, not five, how much better the food, in that there was some? Remember?* And because grass is never as green as it looks through barbed wire, some did.

On the night of the fourteenth, everyone fell asleep as usual to the sound of the rough-hewn giants barking duets with their hounds. But the next morning, there were no usuals, no crack of billy clubs, no infernal howling. Only a disturbing silence awakened them. They didn't know it was the sound of Liberation. They didn't know they'd turned from prisoners awaiting their fate to displaced persons awaiting theirs. They knew only that the giants and hounds no longer cared what they did and by afternoon were replaced by men in belted, brass-buttoned khakis, clean-shaven, voices sharp as whistles, aiming cameras instead of guns, eyes popping with the surprise of hanged men who should've known what would happen once the noose tightened and they started kicking. The *A*nglish, they were told, were soldiers too, there to nurse the sick, bury the dead, identify the living, and not a stitch more. And the inmates found pity for the fine-mannered Brits, *menschen* to the core, who felt obliged to add a little oomph to the protein-deficient diet they observed, searching the German larders, war-emptied to near subsistence levels, as well as their own government-issued dopp kits for a bit of salt, a little sugar. Treats, they thought, and who could blame them for failing to anticipate how such treats would eat like acid into those unseasoned tongues? Higher-ups warned against offering ham to *those people*, yet ham was all those people wanted. They clamored for it, along with toothpowder and shoes not made of wood. Heaven's merchandise.

Soon, the inhuman proportion of the campers' needs was cut down to size only to be replaced by their wants. They *wanted* to gather and dance and kibbitz and drink and marry and cut the foreskins of newborns and wail thanks to God or curse His name and dress up and organize and be bad with no music to face and dance to music in the minor key of their souls. And they did.

1947

In Bergen-Belsen, when summer came out of cold storage, the *kinder* wandered about, little ghosts freckling in the sun. Fall followed, its stink of memory rising from piles of rusting leaves.

Somewhere along this path of shortening days, she became Sarah, one of many. In this camp, there were more Sarahs than a five-year-old could count. Oh, there were plenty of Ruchels, Channahs, and Rivkas, too—they'd been welcome to keep their shtetl names—but the girls from Krakow and Minsk, Prague and even Paris, whose mamas thought a pretty name would save them, the Floras and Bellas and Veroniques, soon learned their mothers had been wrong. A name was just another thing to forget. And now, not even in this newest camp—free of padlocks, barbed wire, Germans, and *A*nglish—could they conjure pictures of their precious Krakow or Minsk, Prague or Paris. Only *this* Sarah, this accident, this curse of a baby girl, Auschwitz born and bred, who'd never known an elsewhere, had the gall to imagine there might be one.

Ten men in hats, the camp's new leaders, wanted to see Sarah find a proper home, but she didn't make it easy. Like she thought she was so special she deserved their attention, what with all the plumbing to fix, the mealtimes to negotiate, and the squabbles—both legal and personal—only they could settle, not to mention the running of the schools, hospitals, newspapers, and shops, all built around the organizing principle that while no one should starve, they shouldn't get too comfortable, either, that city-sized stew of tattered souls, the ten thousand, *their* ten thousand, who trembled as if it were the edge of a cliff they were being pushed to when it was only The World, which had, in fact, continued to exist—contrary to popular opinion—but which, God knows, was hardly holding its breath waiting for them.

The one called Yitzchak, the leader of the leaders, shook his head. Only two days before, she'd been reported for stealing bread from another child's plate. This time, the cook had her by the ear, having caught her elbow-deep in the bucket of chicken fat it had taken days to render.

"The little gonif, she's yours," said the cook, releasing Sarah's ear to swipe one palm against the other three times and spit on the ground.

The men in hats called themselves the Committee. The campers called them Big Shots. Or self-appointed messiahs. They were not Germans, they were not *A*nglish; they were only campers, no better than the rest. If anything, a little *meshuggana* for sticking their skinny necks out so soon After. They joked but whispered the word "After" as if there still might be a Before to rile up, as if their prepositions hadn't vanished, absorbed by the mongrel language they'd picked up in the camps, words born in the throat and spat more than uttered, as if anger was the only thing they understood. Even the angriest agreed, Committee men did for their people, even for the little *teivel*, who by God's Grace had not wound up as bird food and by *their* grace now received nourishment enough to outpace the growth of many small mammals. And how did she thank them? By getting caught elbow-deep in a tin of cooking fat. Not a mortal sin, but bad enough.

Flummoxed, they solemnly debated what consequences the five-year-old's actions required, the little gonif offering neither defense nor contrition.

"A crime yearns for its rightful punishment, no?" Leader Yitzchak asked his men.

"But who has been harmed?" one of a different nature wondered.

"Without order what are we but animals?" the leader said.

"We had order with the Germans. What were we then?" they answered.

Complicating the matter was how few punishments remained, thanks to the new laws banning spanking, slapping, knuckle-rapping, ear-pinching (dining hall cooks exempted), shackling, any sort of hand or foot binding, dousings of cold water, force-feeding, food deprivation, sleep deprivation, or any other corporal retribution the more creative might have devised. They themselves had forgotten nearly every quality of mercy in the book, but thankfully, the world was quick to remind them. *You of all people* this, *You of all people* that. There were landmines everywhere. "Tread lightly," they now said in place of "good night."

"So, what are we to do with you?" the Committee men asked.

Sarah said nothing. If they'd truly wanted to hear what *she* thought they should do, she'd have told them to give her more, more of what they also wanted—everything—but especially more of that lovely oleo, white as snow but for the golden threads of pullet schmaltz running through it. She'd have told them to fill a whole room with it, lock her in, hide the key, and leave her to lick her way to the top, because she wanted not just to eat it but to savor every mouthful, to swim in and through it, emerging iced as a wedding cake, or be left alone in the quiet of its sluggish depths. But lacking the words to impress upon them the nature of its butteriness, that tasteless jam as bland as kindness, she was dismissed as incorrigible and sent off to contemplate her behavior while they contemplated her sentence.

Standing on her cot, Sarah stared out a window in the empty dormitory, watching the young campers laughing and singing through chores. Only from this distance could she laugh and sing with them. When among them, she became the sourpuss nobody wanted on their team, the flat note disturbing their harmony, the annoyance kicking the seat in front of her.

It was another Sunday before punishment was meted out. As always, she made her way to the dining hall for breakfast and announcements. A man with a bullhorn shouted that for the first time ever, and for their eyes only, a motion picture was coming to Bergen-Belsen. The ten thousand campers might as well have been twenty, they were all so beside themselves with anticipation. Sarah, too. By the end of her morning at Juden school, she had dug eight little moons of excitement into the heels of her palms. But before she could skip away with her classmates, she was headed off by the Committee. She would *not* be among the moviegoers, they informed her. And Sarah said nothing.

The movie was hardly appropriate for little ones, the leader said. In fact, calling a newsreel about the liberation of Auschwitz a movie was, in his opinion, an overstatement. There were no hoodwinks to laugh at, no dreamboats to swoon over. And everyone already knew how it ended. What mattered most was that her crime had been justly punished, a point had been made, and no scars had been left. *Alles gut*, no?

Alles gut, yes, for she was like water, a mosquito, a mouse. There was no keeping her out of anything or anywhere. She slid through a crack in a door. She fit under a chair. She did everything she could to be one with the other children, her round eyes raised to the muddy images stuttering across the makeshift screen—a wall cleared and whitewashed—at twenty-four frames per second. While the rest marveled over this thing called the movies, the steady thumping inside her chest quickened to a flutter as she stared up into the face of a Russian soldier, his smile so wide it spread across two walls, his eyes transparent as glass, his arms so strong they didn't notice the weight of the hundred children they held.

Winter came with its own axe to grind. Around the country, Germans were brought to their knees by record lows. In Bergen-Belsen, they said *boo-hoo*. Some of the older children, those lucky enough to be entrusted with brooms, made music by sweeping the paths clean. It was called work, but the way they waltzed across the endlessly renewing snow cover followed by the younger, broomless horde wrapped head-to-toe in wool, made it look like a game, one with no losers, for at the end they were all rewarded with a cup of steaming Marmite.

All but Sarah, who was alone in the dormitory, standing on her cot, ear cupped to the icy window for the sounds of the children's progress, their brittle straw brushing the ground, *whoosh* two three, *whoosh* two three, and the quiet thuds of well-aimed snowballs. She picked at a sliver of wood that had sewn itself into the pad under her third finger. She'd been told to use the afternoon to think her way into a new story, one that didn't start with a broom. But with no broom, what was there to think about, for if the girl whose broom it was hadn't laughed at her for lacking one or called her Bupkis, a name that clung like a bad smell, Sarah, too, would be dancing in the snow, awaiting her cup of Marmite. Instead she'd *become* Bupkis, a nothing, a nit, smaller than all the rest who grew so fast they couldn't wait for the crates that came from England and America, full of mismatched mittens, mufflers, caps and coats, leggings and boots, brassieres the boys strapped over their clothes and strutted about in, smoking jackets with satin collars. All that, yet never anything for anyone who outgrew nothing.

And who could have blamed her? Such a darling little broom, whittled for a child by a man who knew what to do with a piece of wood, who had once healed the sick but now wanted only to carve and whittle and bury his feet in shavings, all for his daughter, a girl who called herself Charlotte Berger, who should have been content counting her own blessings—a first name, a last name, *and* a father—but who insisted everyone else count them, too. And if Sarah could've stood on her own two feet when she was dropped at the Displaced Persons office by a woman whose name she didn't know but whose breasts were so familiar she could still trace in her sleep their lacework of veins, a woman who'd pinned to Sarah's shirt a scrap of paper with a message the child couldn't yet read but knew it described what she was, or what she would be, provided she made it that far, before bidding her *gei gezunt* and then vanishing. And if she'd known the investment caring requires, and how under-financed she'd been from the start, and that campers are not always good, and wanting something doesn't make it yours. And if Charlotte Berger hadn't dared them, *Just try to pull it apart*, and Sarah hadn't reached for it, only to have it yanked away, the others chanting, *Bupkis, Bupkis* . . . and if vile tears hadn't sprung from Sarah's eyes, watering her craving until it exploded into a want that whispered in her ear, *Why shouldn't you have it?*, making her grab the broom and hold fast, its owner taunting, *Why don't you get your papa to make you one? Oh, I forgot, Bupkis doesn't have a papa.* And if the others hadn't laughed, short on fathers themselves, Sarah wouldn't have cried that she had a papa, all right, and not a skinny old man with broken glasses who spent his days carving broom handles—*her* papa was as tall as a house and big as a mountain, a soldier who would save her from this stupid, stupid place and take her home, which made Charlotte howl because a proper father, a *real* one, would have told her a *Yiddishe meydl* should never lie, and if Sarah had not wrenched the broom from Charlotte's nasty grip, if she'd run instead of letting her tears turn to words, *I'm no Yiddishe nothing, you dirty Jude,* she might have been able to think her way into a story with a better ending.

1948

In Bergen-Belsen, the motherless were a dime a dozen and depreciating by the day. For three years, the people had been leaving. The bright, the fit, those with a brother in London, a wife's uncle in Brooklyn. Bergen-Belsen was now a pound full of strays. Which the Committee had to empty. Quickly. There were still few who could look upon them without weeping, but how much longer could that last, they asked each other whenever they met. Which they now did daily, reviewing the list of leftovers. The stubborn ones, the lazy ones, the sick, those with no connection to the world beyond their gates . . . and oy, the children. Because even if Palestine could have opened its doors to all those ready to make aliyah, it wasn't orphans they needed. And so every meeting ended the same, all of them shaking their heads over how they'd finish the job, until a man who knew a man called them to a different sort of meeting and told them how. It was a way the good were loath to go. But it was a way.

"Where *are* the Schvarts?" Sarah asked on her way to inspection, her third that week. She'd heard the place was crawling with them, cellar rats in black-brimmed hats. The Schvarts Mark. The Black Market. Puppet masters working everyone's strings. *You got a foot, they got a shoe,* was what she'd heard. *You got two, it'll cost you triple.* The man in charge of inspections wore a black hat but was pale and did not look at all like a rat. He was called Teacher, though Sarah had never seen him in the classroom. "Don't speak of things you know nothing about," he told her. "Hurry now. Pick up your feet when you walk. No one wants a girl with dirty soles." She didn't ask about all the other times when her shoes and turned-down socks and shins and even her knees were clean as soup bones and still they hadn't wanted her.

Teacher took a lightly trafficked route along the camp's outer perimeter to the showing area, a derelict warehouse, where Sarah and the others were cautioned not to trip on the debris littering the crumbling concrete floor—tires and carburetors, fan belts and bumpers that had refurbished the vehicles of first one then another army. Though the place was well-ventilated, the walls held the smell of old oil and let in so little light that Teacher always brought a candle. Other men came, each with his own candle, bringing more children to fill out the line.

They were all girls that day, wearing the blue frocks and white aprons brought out of storage on special occasions. Arranged by height and standing at attention with the breeze ruffling their skirts, they looked like little banners at a parade.

"Well done, children. Tell me again: what is your job?" Teacher asked, pointing to one of the girls in the lineup.

She answered without hesitation. "To be good."

"And?" He pointed to another.

"Smart."

"But not too smart," Teacher added with a finger wag.

"And we don't ask for seconds and never talk back," another child volunteered.

"Yes. And?"

And nothing. The girls' faces went blank.

"And?" Teacher repeated, pacing the length of their line, forcing every eye to the floor.

"Oy, are those *kops* made of wood? For *your* sake . . ."

"We forget," Sarah said, nearly inaudibly.

Teacher bent down to her. "We can't hear you," he sang.

"WE FORGET," she bellowed.

Satisfied, he straightened.

"And for the sake of us all?"

"WE REMEMBER!" they chimed in unison.

In the last-minute fluffing, some got their hair pinned back, some got their cheeks pinched, some—the ones with no tattoos to frighten the customers—got their sleeves rolled up. And finally, they were told to smile. "Like this," Teacher said, pulling his mouth wide with two fingers, as if the children didn't know how to smile, as if children hadn't invented the smile.

Sarah, her hair a bird's nest, mimicked Teacher, pulling at the edges of her mouth with not-so-clean fingers, showing off her jagged little teeth. Feeling mocked, he huddled briefly with his helpers but decided against yanking her from the line. At this point, even the rottenest apple had to find a new barrel.

Teacher pushed open the corrugated doors to welcome the people of Celle, Bergen-Belsen's neighboring town, but his face collapsed when he saw the pitiful turnout: a single couple, Herr and Frau Vogelmann, both breathing hard, arms looped together in support. Teacher tried to put them at ease, his greeting respectfully formal. And then, with great flourish, he announced the winning number of the day's lottery drawing. The couple looked on anxiously. How could they have known that no one ever went home empty-handed? They looked nice, the Vogelmanns. At least they dressed nice. A watch fob's gold chain swooped across the gentleman's vest, and a crocheted scarf wrapped the woman's neck. Their boots were worn at the heels, though, and needed a good polish. On the ground by the man's foot, something bright and red tickled Sarah's eye. Teacher saw it, too, but Sarah got there first. Like a stealth hawk, she dove for it and was back in line with the bright red thing dampening in her fist, the Vogelmanns none the wiser.

Teacher stared disapprovingly at the spot where the ticket had fallen. Seeming to think it was their dusty shoes he found displeasing, the woman's face turned pink. The bus never came, her husband interjected. They'd had to walk. It was twenty kilometers, but what could they do?

"We had the fare. Money for the ticket, too. Go on, Helmut, show him," the woman said, spearing her husband with her elbow. His pockets held nothing but lint. He frowned. Her chin trembled.

"No worries," Teacher said. "Anyone can see you are honest folk." Not needing a pair of crying customers on his hands, he promised to look for the ticket while they decided which of Bergen-Belsen's lovely girls might suit them. "But choose wisely," he said, wagging his finger. "There are no returns."

It was always the same with Teacher when one of his jokes fell flat. He'd puff up his chest and disappear into the shadows where he and the others would place bets on the likeliest winner. No one ever bet on Sarah, but the Vogelmanns knew none of this and turned their attention to the line of girls standing before them, stepping from one to the other, looking long and hard at each.

To Sarah's left and right, the children mugged. Some were older and more capable, others were younger and more adorable, but only she had a red ticket to wave high in the air and make the couple want only her. The man's smile warmed Sarah. But when he reached for her ticket, she turned cold and held fast.

"Helmut," the woman said, her voice scolding but gentle. "Can't you see what a determined little one we have here?"

The two kept talking. The words coming from their throats didn't sound angry. Maybe they were considering the prettiness that touched all the girls but her. The hair no brush could penetrate. The sallow skin the sun never sweetened. The dark, blank eyes. Sarah didn't understand what they said but wanted it to be about her, good or bad, and when Frau Vogelmann got down on her knees, she knew it was.

"Do you want to be my little girl?" The woman's eyes were camper-dress blue.

Sarah nodded.

"How much?" the woman whispered.

Sarah's fist opened. Teacher returned just in time for the woman to hand him the wilted ticket.

"We'll have her," Herr Vogelmann and his wife said together.

Teacher and his pals, men who thought they'd seen everything, couldn't hide their surprise.

"*If* it's all right," Herr Vogelmann said, glancing at his wife. "We are Christian people."

"*Ja, ja.*" Teacher shrugged.

"We would not know how to raise her Jewish."

"You are today's winners. Raise her any way you like," Teacher said, handing them the girl's ration card plus a stack of Deutsche Marks for their troubles. "She's not the best of the lot, but she will be of great use to you cleaning the house and minding the children."

"But she's only a child herself," the frau remarked.

"This one?" Teacher said. "This one was never a child."

1950

Celle, Germany. Sarah was eight by the time she saw her first telephone, Vater wrapping his beefy hand around the black receiver as if it were a club or a revolver. It was among the first in town and precious to him. *Vater* was what they called Herr Vogelmann, husband to Frau Vogelmann, their *Mutter*. Vater was a working man with no work to do. In the morning, he took tea with his newspaper and then talked on his telephone about what he'd read to the other men with no work to do. Mutter called this his passion. Sarah sat at the kitchen table while Mutter's smooth, white fingers twisted her hair into braids. There had been a time when she'd feared Mutter's touch, but now she stayed still as stone, fearing the merest breath might cut short the woman's daily assault on her tangles. When finished, Mutter inspected her work.

"What do you think, Helmut?" she asked Vater.

"She's no beauty, but there's time," said Vater, who had known Mutter since they were in nappies. They had two sons. Sarah wasn't much older than either boy, but enough so to be entrusted with their care. Now that she was one of them, Vater and Mutter wanted her to add their name to her own. They got no argument from her. Sarah Vogelmann she'd be. The chosen of The Chosen. She looked puzzled, so the Vogelmanns explained. "You know, the Chosen People, like you Juden say."

"But I'm not Juden," she said. "I'm Auschwitz."

They laughed. "Whatever you were, you are Vogelmann now." They were proud that under their roof, two sides of a world war had come together. At the table Sarah had set for the dinner she'd made, they all joined hands and bowed their heads while Vater thanked their one God for the miracle of a second chance at grace and for the miracle of the additional bread they now broke, manna straight from heaven, thanks to Sarah, who'd been added to their family portrait, proving the Vogelmanns were not like those who'd done her wrong. Though there were good ones among those, too, they wanted her to know. People now shunned by neighbors and friends, some merely for the sin of turning their heads, as if anyone could've looked at a thing like that straight on. "And shouldn't you of all people be able to forgive?" Mutter asked as she passed a tureen of dumplings. "You did win, after all."

Sarah guessed they thought it was them that she'd won. The Vogelmanns, both Herr and Frau, were decent people. Above and beyond what was required, they'd given her a name, a home, and a seat at the family table. They'd taught her to read German and encouraged her to explore with the boys they called "the brothers," who always came home with pockets full of bits and bobs, like the set of false teeth Sarah had put right into her own mouth, delighting the little ones for the rest of the night. And why shouldn't she have had a bit of fun, considering all she contributed, freeing Mutter to spend her days working for the neighborhood grocer and her nights bringing in laundry, tending to Vater, standing on a stool to reach the stove and cook his dinner with the rations she earned them, and, on those evenings when Mutter was too tired to tuck the boys in, stumbling through the family's great book of Grimm until the brothers' eyes grew heavy. They were dear, these Vogelmanns, perhaps not the saviors they fashioned themselves to be, but what did an eight-year-old need saving from?

1957

At fifteen, she was done with pigtails. Mutter gave her a tortoiseshell barrette to secure the end of her single braid. The brothers were mostly left to amuse themselves, except when Sarah played school with them. She was always Teacher. She no longer needed to run her finger under the words while reading them fairy tales. She was still no beauty but her face had character, Vater told her. "And you are lucky, *liebling*. Character lasts far longer than beauty."

It was true. She was indeed a lucky little *liebling*. Proof? The distinguished gentleman with the clean fingernails, hands folded across the second button of his long, dark coat, who'd come to inspect the goods: her. Meeting in the parlor, she curtsied, kept her eyes on the floor, and remained dutifully silent until the man lifted her chin and demanded she sing. It wouldn't do to embarrass Vater, so she sang, loo la loo, over and over until the man nodded his approval. The choir at his church had lost its soprano and she'd do just fine, he told her. She didn't know any other songs, she confessed. He told her not to worry, he would teach her. With the same sonorous voice, he congratulated Herr Vogelmann for the excellent job he'd done with her.

"It was no job, Herr Weiss. Sarah's a good girl," Vater said.

"What is this 'herr' business? It's Friedrich, please," he said, loud and jocular.

She caught Herr Weiss's wink as he leaned toward Vater and, half covering his mouth, turned down the volume to ask, "So, my friend, what's it like with the little Juden?"

"I'm not Juden, I'm Auschwitz." It came out as a growl she tried to swallow.

But Herr Weiss's ears were sharp.

"Speak up," he commanded.

"I'm not Juden, I'm Auschwitz," she repeated, bolder than she felt.

Vater held his breath. Mutter lowered her eyes and smiled. Herr Weiss smiled, too.

"Same, same, little bird," he said. And with that, the important-looking man took his leave.

She packed as the brothers scrambled about. Sarah had not yet finished the Grimms' stories, so the brothers were not yet finished with Sarah. "One more," one said. "One more," the other parroted. When she said they were too old for stories, they cried like babies.

She'd never seen anything so fine as the valise she was given, gold leaf filling the channels of the letters of their name, now hers. Into it she put her three dresses, the hems let all the way out. Undergarments. Nightgown. A sky-blue sweater Mutter had knit and boiled in a pot on the stove to keep her warm as toast when the weather turned. A picture of the family wearing the same sky-blue sweaters. The scrap of paper that went wherever she went.

The valise was small, but all that was hers did not begin to fill it.

The man would return in the morning. Down the hall, Mutter wept. Sarah guessed they hadn't planned to love her. Herr Vogelmann, worn out from the family's petitioning, insisted over and over that he was doing what was best for the girl. Soon she'd be sixteen, and then what? "Do you think we can give her a dowry or find her a job?" he asked. His well-to-do friend, on the other hand, could take care of her. *Excellent* care. He'd promised to pay for a school uniform. And books. *It's the best thing, it's the best thing,* Vater repeated over and over, but something weighed on him. She could tell by the way he didn't call her *liebling* or look her in the eye, even the next morning as she walked out his door for the last time.

"Are we now animals like all the rest?" Sarah heard her mutter of eight years cry to her husband.

"In this house, we are all Survivors!" he answered. And there was truth to it.

1961

Herr Weiss's attic was a box made of wood. Heavy beams supported the tall, pitched ceiling. There was a lamp on a nightstand by the bed and two thin eiderdowns whose feathers had lost their loft. At the side of the bed lay a circular rug on which Sarah had knelt every evening for four years. Herr Weiss was an exacting teacher, and with a firm hand he bent her head into the angle of modesty most pleasing to those who answered the prayers of motherless girls. He handed her the little prayer book he kept in the top dresser drawer by his own bed for her to read from, though she knew it by heart,

I am small

then laid himself down on her bed, making the sounds she closed her eyes on,

My heart is clean

everything, even the floor beneath her bare knees, shaking with it.

Holding the prayer pose, she waited until his chest sank and the room filled with cigar breath and he patted the side of the bed and parted the front tails of his shirt and again put his large hand on her head, this time guiding it down to the little saucer waiting, though there was no saucer, just his night's milk, cupped for her to lap from the base of his belly, colorless as frost on a windowpane, slippery, flavorless, familiar.

And in it lives only Jesus.

Sarah had no prayers of her own. She had dreams. Not the kind that made you stupid with hope but the kind that bloomed in dark attics and made you know things you shouldn't, like that no ground is so firm it will remain underfoot forever.

When the families of Celle awoke to their new order, she alone was prepared. It happened on a summer Sunday. August thirteenth. First, she prepared the Weisses' breakfast. While their tea steeped, she prepared herself.

She was no thief. She gathered what she'd come with—a valise monogramed in gold, a portrait of a family called Vogelmann, a crumpled scrap of paper—the only thing attesting to her Before. In exchange for the clothes on her back, she left one of the seventeen Deutsche Marks she'd earned over the previous four years doing chores for neighbors, the same neighbors who would claim no surprise over her sudden departure, telling Weiss he was lucky to be rid of her, a girl who stared at the floor when spoken to and never returned a smile.

What she had of her own to give, the braid that tickled her back, she cut off at the root with Frau Weiss's meat shears, Frau Vogelmann's tortoiseshell clasp biting its frizzled end. This she left in the top dresser drawer by Weiss's bed. Wiry as a horse's tail, it had been harder to scissor through than she'd expected.

She knew it wouldn't bring much at market but told herself it was fair enough compensation for the little prayer book she suddenly couldn't bear to leave behind.

In the parlor, the gentleman of the house and his wife, like every villager, were in front of their radio, teary and desperate for the staticky report to tell them it wasn't true, that their beloved capital had *not* been desecrated, sliced through the heart by an impenetrable wall, and neither noticed Sarah, her chopped hair, or the breakfast tray she'd brought them—tea, strong and sweet, and yesterday's biscuits—or her exit to the broadcast's severing blows, a symphony of opportunity to her ears.

Berlin was an idea that lived in the East. She didn't know which way was East and trusted no one enough to ask. She trusted only her feet. Putting one down, the other followed. She walked for some time before reaching a crossroads where an arrow-shaped sign said *Berlin, 284 km*. She looked back over her shoulder. Celle was no longer in sight. In every direction, the sky and road were deserted. She looked down and wondered where she might be now if she had started on the other foot. Two-hundred-eighty-four kilometers was an idea that broke her in two, the old and the new. How far away it was, how far she'd already come—in time, in distance—were mysteries. A small voice whispered, *Be a good girl. Turn back. They'll be wanting supper soon.* She looked at the arrow-shaped sign and again at her feet, the right then the left, trying to decide which first step would allow the miracle of her journey to continue. But miracles were not made of decisions, rather, in this instance, of five soldiers in a jeep who spotted what they thought was a lady, in possible distress, and stopped to ask where she was headed. Sarah pointed to the sign above her head. The driver smiled big. "Hop on board," he said. "We're goin' your way." At their insistence, she squeezed into the front seat between the driver and one of his mates.

The soldiers were crew-cut, straight-backed, and well-scrubbed. They drove fast and all spoke at the same time. From their jabbering, she gleaned the words "lady" and "wall," "big" and "city." It was an English she recognized, the American kind that flooded the Weisses' parlor night after night. Over the airwaves, it sounded loud, loose, and boastful. In person, the same.

They raced through the north German plains. With the wind whipping at her newly bobbed hair, the knobby tires kicking up clouds of dust, and the strong American shoulders bolstering her on either side, it felt like flying. So when the driver suddenly swerved to a stop at the side of the road, her first thought was that his wings had given out. The second, that he was done with her. He could see she was worried. Up ahead was Helmstedt, he explained. Their first checkpoint. Once they passed through, they'd be in enemy territory all the way to Berlin. That meant no stopping. Not for anything. He'd seen a citizen hauled away just for pissing out his car window. The other soldiers laughed. "They won't mess with a bunch of uniforms like us," he assured her. "But a pretty lady like you is sure to get their attention, and believe you me, you don't want to get the attention of the East German guards. So, you'll have to ride in the boot for a while. *If* you don't mind." He sucked the side of his cheek like he was nursing a sore tooth, but she didn't mind. He threw a tarp over her for good measure, and she didn't mind that either. He'd called her pretty. Pretty was an idea that lived nowhere in her, but under cover, it was easier to pretend.

When the jeep stopped again, she was unveiled and returned to her seat of honor. Up front, she saw that where they were was nothing like where they'd been. The sky was cluttered and close, the road thick with cars and trucks and buses. In the modest homes sprouting like weeds along the autobahn, she saw a prelude to Berlin. Further on, they gave way to bigger buildings, bigger than Celle's biggest, hunched together, new walls jutting from ancient foundations, tall and smooth-faced, every empty lot sounding progress, hammers and saws at full throttle, men with rags tied around their noses and mouths shoveling the shale of their pasts into the backs of trucks to be hauled away, and people, so many people. *But where is your Wall?* she wanted to shout, the soldiers grumbling about what a mixed-up world it was. Five men in a jeep sent to save Germany, sworn enemy of the past, from Russia, sworn enemy for life. The Nazis were bad news, but the Reds, these five agreed, were far worse. Sarah wondered how it was possible for a great curtain of iron to hide in plain sight. The driver, free of all wonder, steered them onto Friedrichstraße, entering the stream of vehicles on the way to the city's center. They inched along until the road split and the traffic came to a standstill.

"Guess this is as good a time as any," the driver said, slamming the jeep into neutral and turning to their passenger. "Auf Wiedersehen," he added with polite finality.

Sarah was confused. There was no wall. No stone or concrete or steel anywhere. On the island separating Friedrichstraße's two legs, there was only a wooden shack, roughly built, slapped with paint, hardly bigger than the Weisses' outhouse. Maybe the Americans had made a wrong turn. Maybe all along they'd been up to no good.

A man posted at the shack's door waved furiously at the line of cars. One inched ahead, zigzagging through a maze of barbed wire. The Jeep, in gear, lurched forward a meter or two. Along the walkway, people had made their own line. It moved slower than the cars. The people looked tired and anxious. The barbs of the barricade caught the sun. The people shut their eyes to its radiance. Sarah felt it burn away her mounting panic and then understood. This *was* the wall. They *were* in the right place. The Americans were leaving her behind.

"No, no, no," she pleaded. "Me . . . with you."

"We're gentleman, me and the fellows, not idiots," he snapped. "It's a one-way ticket from here, you know. Cross over and there's no coming back. I'm talking life with that Commie mob, always a defector, never allowed a thought, a word of your own. Is that what you want?"

In their green jeep, dressed in identical green, they looked and sounded so much alike she couldn't tell one from another. She didn't know how to tell them what she wanted but knew that leaving the jeep and taking her place at the end of the people's line would show them. With a shrug of their meaty shoulders, the driver and his pals continued on as if they couldn't have cared less.

Perhaps they hadn't cared. They were her first Americans, so Sarah couldn't have known what they held dear. If they'd been more like the Shvartze Mark, she would've offered her bag of Deutsche Marks to pay for her passage. If they had been more like Teacher, she would have smiled wider and raised her hand higher. If they had been more like the Committee members, she would have made promises, knowing they'd be forgotten by morning. If they'd been more like Herr Weiss, she would have gotten down on her knees and prayed with them. But the Americans didn't want her money or smiles or obedience or bent knees. They only wanted her to see the world they saw. A price she couldn't pay.

Then, at the crossing from West to East Berlin, Sarah met a man who, unlike the Americans, was a gentleman *and* an idiot. A sweet, sweet idiot ready to give everything for the everything he asked of her, a price she paid on the spot. His eyes were transparent as glass. He smiled at a comrade, showing off the gap between his front teeth, and quickly covered his mouth with his hand. As if he could hide the light he contained. He was nothing but light. He was a beacon. A love. A Russian soldier. A *Soviet* soldier, he would remind her again and again.

They had three days together. When it ended, she wasn't surprised. From the moment she saw him and understood what a heart is for, she knew it couldn't last. In fact, when the blade came down on their union, her only surprise was that there was anything left to learn about being alone. She discovered this standing between a pair of Russian guards as they waited for her to board the airplane that would take her away. The guards whose responsibility she'd been for three days wanted nothing more to do with her. She understood. She'd brought an end to a comrade's promising career. "You people," they said. "Trouble just follows wherever you go." They hated having to deliver his letter but owed him that much.

The airplane was boxier than the ones in the newsreels, more like a large bus with wings. The Russians left her to climb its metal staircase on her own. She began with her left foot. Inside, there was moaning and weeping and the misery of babies who had no idea what they wanted but knew they weren't getting it. She eyed the door. There was no reason to expect her love would come charging through, but Sarah nursed her expectations until the door shut and the winged bus lurched forward. All gripped their seat handles and prayed to God. All but Sarah, who suspected He'd already made His decision.

She didn't remember being told their destination and didn't ask. Trouble would have a harder time following if not told where it was headed. She opened her letter. There were many pages, and she was a slow reader, but by the time the wheels of the bus touched ground, she had read it three times.

August 15, 1961

Love of my life, piteously short as it turns out, this wasn't our plan, you pressing on, only a tale of our imaginary future to warm you, me failing you, my courage deserting me when you most needed it. But I keep asking myself, if any other outcome had been possible, how would I have missed it?

I write on behalf of a truer story to be told, that of a girl who searched for a Russian hero and the miserable poet who found her first. How arrogant I must sound. Calling myself a poet without a poem to my name, always thinking I had so much time, hating myself for wasting it, until I met you. You, the epic poem I was waiting to write.

But I won't lock you to my memory with a chain of pretty words. They are for the little one growing inside you. Now you think I've lost my mind. And maybe I have, but I beg you, though there is little to my story that sets me apart, if this fool's dream turns out to be real, if he is real, let these words find him.

I was three when the devils began pawing at Moscow's gates, too young to know a siren's warning from a wailing mother's despair, that poor woman already dying, my father at the Front, never to return. Alone, hungry, raised by the State, conscripted before I'd had my first vodka, a remnant torn from one cloth and hastily stitched onto another. There were millions of us. But finding someone whose frayed edges so perfectly matched mine made me one in a million.

I hate the Americans for seeing you first, thinking they could be your champions, warning you of the darkness, the strangeness you were bound for, as if strangeness wasn't your birthright. But I feel for them, too. What torture it must have been watching you pass from their side to mine.

I remember how pathetic you thought it, our Wall. Secretly I agreed, though it loomed large over us all. The temperature climbed steadily throughout the afternoon. The windowless room was suffocating, but you were unfazed. Your dark eyes fixed on a spot none of us could see, your black hair a tangled ruff, your prim yellow dress buttoned to the throat, a sweater the exact shade of the August sky. You perched on the edge of that gray steel chair like an exotic bird at home in the heat.

I was summoned because you claimed not to be German yet spoke the language like a native. I was struck by your stillness, your lack of apprehension. Portraits of dead leaders hung above our heads. You did not ask who they were, who I was, why you were being detained or by what authority. It was as if for you this day was passing no differently than any other.

I introduced myself and addressed you by your surname, Fraulein Vogel. Vogelmann, you corrected, but my German was good enough to know that Vogelmann means one who catches birds, and you, my love, were a bird meant to fly. Wanting you all to myself, I locked the door of our interrogation room and waited until finally you confided your wish to become a real Russian. I asked why, and you said it was because we were your true liberators. The rest, imposters.

I was tempted to let you through. I had that power, but it was pointless. You'd never find work, and without a job, you'd never afford a flat, and if you managed to find a willing landlord, you'd both soon regret ever meeting. Your only hope was to marry a Russian. Then marry me, you said, as if joining one person to another was as simple as getting a shoeshine. And isn't it, I found myself thinking. I was free, unattached. If you were my wife, everything would be yours—my name, my citizenship, my Moscow, my country. Except you could never become my wife without papers of your own. In the old days, your little bankroll would have bought you passable documents. But in the face of the penalties ushered in with the Wall, even the Black Market had grown principles, and I could never ask a comrade to look the other way. I was proud of the incorruptible social contract we shared. I couldn't bear any of them knowing how willing I was to tear it to pieces.

The hours advanced, you grew fretful, and once everyone was asleep at their posts, we slipped away. I carried your valise. You were reluctant to part with it but knew chivalry was all I had left to give.

Though the town was closed for the night, a tattoo shop at the end of a dark alley remained open, and the flicker of its neon sign telegraphed its solution, one so preposterous I thought it just might work. I'd heard

Jewish families were able to "repatriate" to Israel. Good riddance, being my government's sentiment. But there's more than one way to be a family, I told you and got down on one knee to ask if you'd be my sister. You laughed, which got me laughing, too, but eventually we came to our senses. If only you were Jewish, you said with a rueful sigh. I can be, I told you, rolling up my sleeve, baring my forearm. I would get a tattoo. We both would. Of course, it wasn't that simple. I'd be living with a lie and you with an eternal reminder of that place. But without a word, you took the valise, opened it, pulled out a scrap of paper, and showed me the string of numbers written on it. You'd never forget where you came from, you told me. Reminder or not.

The tattooist was a mean little cuss in a suit worn to a shine and dingy cotton gloves that once were white. Switching on his headlamp, he asked us what we wanted. You handed him the slip of paper, and we watched the color drain from his face. He was GDR, and no little farmer could bust into his shop and call him a fascist. I suspected my uniform made him nervous, but in the end, only a rich man could turn away two paying customers.

Watching him stab away at you weakened my resolve. A good Communist? Israel? A girl I'd known for hours? What was I thinking? But in those hours, I'd seen your soul. And scheiße, why not Israel? What was Zionism but another army of the downtrodden? What was the desert but Siberia without snow? Suddenly I couldn't wait to trade the linden for the smell of orange trees growing in a backyard and endless hot sun and one more guttural language to make our own. If leaving everything behind meant the end of me, it also meant the beginning of us. As he wiped your arm clean, I laid mine down. A-120240, I told him, and he despised me for it, but I didn't care.

The night nearly done, I walked you to my flat. Everyone there was asleep or passed out. We sat on my bed surrounded by the snoring unconscious, and you smiled again, a sweetness that vanished as quickly as it appeared, and, holding a book you'd pulled from your valise, asked, shall we pray now? Proletariat don't pray, I laughed, although maybe in our case it would have been a good idea. I kissed you, covering your mouth with mine, but your eyes remained open, watchful, and you felt so cold that I pulled away. Were you angry, I wondered? Did you hate me for marking you as no one else had, pulling you into a hellhole of lies? I couldn't risk asking.

You watched me undress. You did the same and lay beside me, so close I could see the down of your lip in the wan eastern light, only the little book of prayers between us.

I lowered myself onto you, into you, my chest expanding with the sounds I'd learned to swallow for fear of waking my comrades (yes, there'd been other fräuleins). You seemed only curious, not fearful, as we made maps of each other's bodies. After, I poured vodka and taught you to take it down without inhaling the fumes so that someday we might drink all night without losing our heads. And I taught you to smoke, which you quickly took to, dragging long and hard, while our plan cooked up light as a soufflé. I put my papers to your cigarette's ash, and we watched them burn.

So, this is what it feels like to be no one, I said. You said I'd get used to it, and I kissed your strand of numbers, only hours old and yet looking like you'd been born with them, smooth and dry, the indigo already fading around the edges. The pinpricks along my arm showed beads of blood, but we were together, of one mind. Man and wife, I said. Sister and brother, you corrected. Together we had faced the German guards of Auschwitz. Now only the German guards of East Berlin stood between us and Norway, Spain, or whatever country allowed passage to the land of your people. I have no people, you said. You will, I promised. It was then I knew my seed would take hold in you. I ached to tell you, but in a matter of hours, we would need to act like brother and sister, and how could you do that if you knew?

There is nothing more fearsome than men born with discipline but no heart, the GDR in a nutshell. Facing them, I felt sorrow for every other soul who had. They demanded our papers, and I told them we had none. We are Jews, I said. And I said it proud.

You are family? they asked, unmoved. We nodded. They looked suspicious. Every feature of my face had been drawn from the Russian steppes. We rolled up our sleeves to show off our tattoos. One guard grabbed your arm, another mine, and without a word, they marched us into separate rooms. My hands shake wondering what was done to you. The one in charge pulled my trousers to my ankles, and there I stood, trembling with anger, flagrantly uncut.

I told them everything, and believing I was a paperless Russian, not a paperless German, they immediately put me in the custody of my uniformed brothers. My only comfort was that you would be, too. You were Auschwitz, after all, a Pole, and because of us, the Germans would never hurt you again.

I must say, my former comrades showed more mercy than I deserved. Since what I'd done, I'd done for love, they let me know where we erred. It wasn't, as I'd assumed, the Russian blood weeping from my tattoo or the telltale foreskin. In that camp, every group of prisoners bore unique codes, and I wore the numbers of a woman.

I was at peace as they left me to dress, untended, uncuffed in a windowless room, the gift of my leather belt coiled on the table. I felt you being carried away, like a little bird nesting in the belly of a bigger one, my son, our little poet—humor me—nesting in yours.

Tell him you didn't love me for my mind or the grit and vodka mixing in my veins, certainly not for the strength of my convictions or the breadth of my shoulders, woefully inadequate to the task, or the cut of my jaw or the poems I talked of writing and dedicating to you, or even for the devious nature that finagled your second liberation. Tell him the truth, that you loved the flavor of my sweat, that's what you said anyway, leaning into me and closing your eyes so you could take more in with each breath.

The world will tell him that it takes time to know a person. You tell him they're wrong, that it takes an instant to know another and that the remainder of the life two people share is spent undoing that knowledge. Tell him I'm glad we didn't get that chance. Tell him how much can happen in a single day, and that on this day, someone died wearing his mother's brand and that he would die all over again not to disappoint her, that he would've killed to save her, but there was nothing he could do to save himself.

Our great Pushkin wrote these words knowing I wouldn't . . .

I loved you; even now I may confess,
Some embers of my love their fire retain;
But do not let it cause you more distress,
I do not want to sadden you again.

Instead, dearest, enjoy the desert sand between your toes and pick an orange for me every day. There will always be better poets than I, but who of them could craft a better ending for our tale than your lover, your scribe, your Sasha?

A lady waited on the tarmac of the recently opened Leonardo da Vinci Aeroporto. A bus with wings had flown them from East Berlin to Brussels to Toulouse to Rome. Sarah wanted only to stay put and fly on but followed the rest of the stupefied off the plane.

The lady stood with her chin up, shoulders back, and right arm raised in formal salute, partly in deference to their completed passage, partly in defense of the Mediterranean sun that had turned this place the color of toast. There on behalf of the Jewish Immigrant Resettlement Program—JIRP, she called it—she spoke of its important work and the twenty-five years she had spent moving Abraham's flock around the globe. She acknowledged their need to be heard. She called them brave and asked that they form a line. She wanted to meet them all, her audience of passengers on the run, still heaving from the turbulence. There was always turbulence.

Sarah was bored of lines but did as she was told and waited her turn, breakfasting on the honied morning air, the soft Roman breezes, currents of petrol, and refugee murmurings. When her turn came and the JIRP lady bestowed an energetic handshake and earnest assurance that soon *home* would no longer be a concept but a place, Sarah tried her best to believe. Her hands, her feet, her underarms, and undergarments were sorely in need of a wash.

On a proper bus with no wings, they made their way into the city. It was still early, but the office where they were to be processed was already jam-packed. There were no windows to open, no places to sit. Asked how long they'd been waiting, one of the earlier arrivals said, "Too long." Someone unwrapped a salami to a round of curses, it stunk up the room so. Midday, JIRP staffers brought around baskets of bread and cheese and syrupy black coffee. The cheese was rank, but Sarah was glad for the bread, tearing off a hunk to calm her stomach. After lunch, the snores of upright sleepers crumpling in on themselves swept the room. One by one, they were shaken awake and led to another room. It was nearly the end of the day when she learned the signora would see her.

Signora, the JIRP lady, was deep into her file when Sarah entered. "Ah, Mrs. Vogel, I've looked forward to this," the woman said, peering over the top of her reading glasses. "Is English all right?" she asked. Her vowels were broad like an American's, her tone polite and clipped like a Brit's. Sarah said English would be fine. The woman had kind eyes of an unmemorable color and a perpetual smile, a little V nesting in the V of her pointed chin. When something really pleased her, the smile expanded, revealing ivory-colored teeth, nicely shaped but with an inward tilt. She extended her hand across her desk for Sarah to shake a second time.

"Excellent. Sit, sit. I know it's been a long day, but I have the form riiiiiight"—flipping, flipping—"here! Just a few blanks to fill before it goes in my outbox. Ready?" she said, smiling at her new client. "Please state your full name for me."

"Sarah Vogel."

"Date of birth?"

Sarah sat silent.

"Date of birth?" the JIRP lady asked again, looking up from the form.

"They said I was six when I came."

"Ah, and I have here that was 1948, so shall we say 1942?

Sarah shrugged.

"And I'll need a birthday. Does Liberation Day suit you?"

"It suits."

"April fifteenth it is. Religious affiliation. Juden?"

Sarah shrugged, adding a nod.

"Good enough. And for your temporary housing assignment, do you require Jewish roommates?"

Sarah thought about it for a moment before shaking her head.

"Is that a no?"

"*Nein*. No," Sarah's voice sharpened.

"Do you require a kosher kitchen, a mikvah, or a location within walking distance of a synagogue?"

Again, Sarah had no answer. The JIRP lady peered up over her eyeglasses.

"Do you know what any of those things are?"

Sarah shook her head.

"Tell me something, Mrs. Vogel," the JIRP lady said. "Do you know anything about being Jewish?"

Sarah regarded the woman with suspicion. She recognized the help being offered but along her way had learned two principal rules of survival—how to spread her legs to make water without anyone knowing and how never, *ever*, to give anything away.

Experienced with the reticent, the JIRP lady put down her pen, signaling that the form was on hold. They'd now be talking strictly woman to woman.

"Do you *want* to be Jewish, Sarah?"

"I think I do," she said with a hesitant nod. No one had ever suggested it could be her choice.

"And why is that?

"To be chosen?"

"Do you know what Jews were chosen for?"

"To be reminders, no?"

"Reminders of what?"

"How good it is not to be chosen?"

"All right then," the JIRP lady said, her little V of a smile widening as she reached for the stamp to seal the deal on her last case of the day. "All I need is your nationality and we're done."

Sarah stared dumbly.

"You don't know where you're from, Mrs. Vogel?"

It was a small opening, but Sarah seized what she feared might be her only opportunity to tell the sad, sad story her poet-lover had made her memorize in the event they were separated, some of it true, most not—the tragic loss of her family, friends, home, everything taken by the wretched fascists, and just when she thought there was nothing left to live for, the man of her dreams, an honorable soldier of the United Soviet Socialist Republic, made her his wife, and they'd thought the dark days were over, but the fascists were there too, waiting in the shadows to snatch him. Now, on her own, what could she do but pray that the JIRP people could help her find a place with no shadows, a place like Israel, the land of promise for her people, even more so for her and her husband. Sarah could tell that her passionate plea for aliyah, delivered exactly as rehearsed, was taking effect but couldn't resist mentioning that her husband, Viktor Aleksandr, whom everyone called Sasha, was so in love with the sun that it hurt to think of him slaving away in Siberia, so if they could do anything at all, they should please hurry and do it because she needed him, she and . . . pat to the stomach, alluding to the non-existent baby whose existence she suddenly wanted more than anything, a boy if there was any justice left in the world . . . and she could've gone on about her husband's eyes of melted ice, his beguiling manner of parking the tip of his thumb in the gap between his front teeth when beset by deep thoughts, but it wasn't looking like it would be necessary.

Sarah had seen all kinds of crying—the mewling of the shamed, the wailing of the angry, the shuddering of the frightened—but she'd never seen this kind. Soft and silent. Lady crying, she figured. A clock somewhere in the room erased several moments from the day, and the JIRP lady sighed. Dabbing her damp eyes with a hankie she kept tucked in the wristband of her watch, she pulled a compact from her pocketbook and fixed her face. The golden clamshell spattered the sun's last rays around the room. Sarah thought it the most beautiful thing she'd ever seen, but before she could grab it to make the light dance herself, the JIRP lady snapped the clamshell shut, dropped it back into her pocket and, sighing again, pulled another form from her files.

"I'll be needing a little more information, now that you'll be staying on with us."

"Staying?" Sarah said, forgetting about the golden compact.

"Of course, dear. It's too difficult a journey for someone in your condition," the JIRP lady said, impulsively reaching across the desk to take her client's hand. Sarah pulled away, cursing herself for straying from the original story. There'd been no baby in the version Viktor Aleksandr had made her recite so many times she could do it in her sleep. Now she'd gone and made a mockery of his dream.

Staring into the JIRP lady's kind, gullible eyes, Sarah pushed up the sleeve of her dress and showed off her bare arm to let her numbers do some persuading.

The JIRP lady teared up again, but she'd spent too many years moving heaven and earth for girls like this not to know when her hands were tied. She tapped wrist to wrist, demonstrating the constraints of her binding.

"I can see you're a fighter, dear. I am, too, and I won't stop until we get this done."

"When will that be?" Sarah asked.

"When the time is right."

A trip to Israel, a golden trinket that could make light dance, a chain of promises knotted together with lies, an eternal love you'd never see again, and a stranger who used your name as if she'd known you all your life. There was a lump in her throat that couldn't be swallowed. When you want something that you don't deserve, you shouldn't be surprised to lose it. Sarah felt something wet splash her arm. *What kind of crying was this*, she wondered?

She was assigned temporary lodging in the Campo de' Fiori near the old Jewish ghetto where she'd share an apartment with three women who worked at a factory that made zippers. By her second day in Rome, Sarah worked there, too. For their own protection, JIRP banked each client's earnings, from which they'd get a weekly stipend, adjusted according to their circumstances. Single girls received the least but would leave with the most. Like a dowry, they were told. An awfully stingy dowry, they said. They could've stayed in the Old Country if all they'd wanted was to work long hours for no pay and a deadbeat husband. It didn't help that the factory was situated near a famous film lot and the girls they encountered on their commute dressed like they should be *in* the movies, not cleaning up after them. Her roommates found it humiliating, but when it came to clothes, Sarah didn't know fancy from plain. All that mattered was having bread to dip in her morning coffee, more bread with a slice of cheese for lunch, and a bowl of macaroni with a little red wine for dinner. Now and then a tomato, a peach, sucked down with such greediness it frightened her. First you fall in love with the native fruit. Next thing you know, you're calling it home, like her roommates, who thought Sarah a fool for wanting to leave a place where women carried fine leather handbags for one where they carried Uzis.

She wasn't happy that the cost of the broom she needed to clean the factory floor was deducted from her first week's stipend. But at the end of each day, half of which she spent sweeping around the feet of the young women working the line and half of which she spent plucking bits of bias tape and zipper teeth from the dusty piles, the broom was all hers. She called it Charlotte Berger and groomed it like a pet, bringing it home every night, sweeping around the wardrobes and under the beds, before bath time and after every meal, when and wherever dust threatened to settle, until her irritated roommates sent her out to attack the hallway and staircase, vestibule, front stoop, and even a patch of sidewalk in front of their building. Her thoroughness did not escape the attention of the mamma of the house, an elderly woman who lived on *primo piano* and asked if Sarah might like to sweep her floors for two lire a day. Sarah would have done it for free, but she loved the weight of the coins the signora slipped into her pocket on Sunday afternoons.

If one day differed from any other, she couldn't say. She worked and swept her way through them all. The sameness was interrupted only on Wednesdays when the JIRP lady came to check on her, giving Sarah an opportunity to ask if everything was moving in the right direction. Nothing seemed to be moving in any direction, but she wouldn't complain. She figured the JIRP lady had enough pests in her life, and the *pasta en brodo* she brought for their lunch soothed Sarah's newly finicky stomach. Wednesdays became the scaffolding of her routine.

Many Wednesdays had passed by the time the floor manager appeared at the assembly room's door and called Sarah's name. The floor manager was a formidable woman, one of the rare JIRPers to settle in Rome and make something of herself, a stickler for rules. Sarah couldn't think of any rules she had broken but knew nothing good ever came from the floor manager knowing your name. *So, this is it*, she thought. They'd seen the mistake they'd made, taking her in, trusting her, and would now send her back to Germany where she belonged.

But no one was sending her anywhere. A sewer had gotten her papers and gone off to the States, leaving an empty seat, which the manager needed filled. Though others had been there longer and had more experience—Sarah didn't even know how to sew—she saw something of herself in the girl, hard-working, diligent, able to keep her nose out of other people's business, qualities she held in high esteem.

"You'll need a pinafore, but your increased stipend should cover it." The floor manager, tall and imperious in her black-rimmed glasses and wide-shouldered suit, tapped her wristwatch, signaling that her benevolence had reached its time limit. All Sarah had to do was say yes. Instead, she threw up on the poor woman's shoes.

Another girl took the vacant seat, and the vomiting continued. Sarah was beset by constant hunger and a corresponding disgust with food, which sent her running to the WC during every meal. The other girls warned her that bad things happened to skinny girls who refused to eat, but whatever Sarah choked down came back up. Fearing it was contagious, her flatmates issued an ultimatum—get fixed or get out. They also gave her the name of a *dottore*, a gray-haired lady with sharp button eyes known to favor instinct over training and renowned throughout the ghetto for her magical healing powers. Sarah met her in the kosher butcher's back room and reluctantly opened her paper sack to show the cash she'd brought with her. Before she knew it, those bony hands upon her, a verdict was delivered. She'd be a mother come May.

"It was only a story," Sarah cried. "Please, check again."

The *dottore* advised her that the story was only beginning. Of course, if it was a different outcome she wanted, they could talk. "There is still time," the *dottore* added.

Time for what? she wondered. Getting rid of it? From inside of her? She had no more intention of doing that than of having the thing.

"Pray it's a boy, then," the *dottore* said. "You'll need someone to take care of you."

Sarah told the girls only that she'd been fixed and was careful to keep up her hours at the factory, as always working through lunch, which she couldn't keep down anyway. Learning to throw up more quietly helped keep it secret.

And then the sickness passed, her strength returned, and with so little else changed, she began wondering if it wasn't the *dottore* who'd been telling stories. She hadn't seemed the devious sort, but wasn't that the thing about the devious? All Sarah knew was that her strength had come back, her appetite raged, she was taking the stairs two at a time, and in those scant moments she had to herself, she was revisited by the feeling she'd had between her legs the night Viktor Aleksandr, her Sasha, had given weight to her unnamed parts. Stranger still, an unfamiliar sense of peace had her smiling at storekeepers, coworkers, neighbors, and even her flatmates, the same ones who damned her treacherous heart when she began to show in December.

She could forget about Israel, her flatmates told her. No country would have her now. Not with some Commie brat filling her belly. They were not pitiless but had their own welfare to consider. Sarah couldn't hide that bump for long, and then the factory would dump her. She could say goodbye to the sweeping, too. No work meant no rent coming their way, and then what? What a position she'd put them in. What a stubborn, stubborn girl she'd been.

But stubbornness was her friend. Though becoming a sewer was no longer in her future, the floor manager had put her on the assembly line, where she continued working through lunch, except on Wednesdays when the JIRP lady's big bowl of brodo brought her close to believing in God. More work awaited her at home, where she now swept the second, third, and fourth floors of the ancient complex, a place that stayed wonderfully cool in summer but turned rotten with cold in the mild Mediterranean winter, by which time she felt the baby everywhere—in the cradle below her belly, in the small of her back, and down the back of her thighs to her swelling ankles. But she was an incubator, not an invalid, and to prove it, she kept up her sweeping and took on a little scrubbing, dusting, and mending to boot. Her savings were gone. If there was any work to be done, she would do it.

1962

She lost her water between the second and third floors. In case she thought she could pretend any longer, the first contraction encircled her like a rope trying to cut her in two. Once her breath returned and she put everything in its place, drying her reddened hands and shutting off the lights, she went to the corner where she caught a trolley to the hospital and was wheeled directly to birthing, a cold, steel-clad room with bays divided by curtains. Through chattering teeth, Sarah requested a blanket. The nurse disappeared for what seemed an eternity but finally returned, blanket in hand, no payment asked.

As the intervals between the vice-like cinching of her mid-section shortened, Sarah bit deep into the heel of her thumb. Another nurse passed on her way to check bed charts and take temperatures, and Sarah grabbed hold of her hand to say, "It's coming. *Now*." The nurse took Sarah's temperature, shaking the mercury down the slender glass wand with the flick of her wrist before slipping it under Sarah's tongue and helping her onto a gurney. "Your first?" she shouted over the howl of mothers-to-be. Sarah nodded. "Just relax. Let your knees fall apart. Good girl. The doctor will be here in a minute."

It was a long minute, and by the time the doctor reached her gurney, the baby's scalp was showing. Believing her now, they moved quickly. Above their masks, their eyes looked grave. Everything wanted out of her. Sarah feared she would defecate and her shit would poison or suffocate the baby, not to mention what it would do to the table and her attendants' pristine uniforms. She felt her face open, every pore, the holes of her nose, the mouth, every orifice stretching, and though it seemed a great wind was escaping, nothing came out. "What's wrong with her?" she heard the doctor say. "Let it out, Mrs. *Woogel*, let it out."

"*Vogel*," she screamed, her voice but a gust.

When it was finished—the weight extracted, the cord cut, the detritus kneaded from her loosened belly, her forehead and legs swabbed—a baby was smacked to life. Sarah, as helpless as she'd ever been, asked to see it, her boy, the son his father had earned, quietly growing stronger with each breath.

"Here she is, Mrs. Woogel," said one of the nurses.

She.

It was April fifteenth. A birthday real enough to stitch the two of them together. It had come three-and-a-half weeks early. Too early. Small but alive.

How a lie becomes truth.

"It's a girl, Mrs. Woogel," said one of the nurses.

"And she's perfect," added the other.

And truth a lie.

1963

After two years and much resistance, Sarah surrendered to life's simple pleasures. The JIRP lady's kindness and healing broth. The slick-haired *mammoni* and waistless widows animating the ancient boulevards. Motherhood. She had a baby now, pretty enough to stop strangers on the street with her pale blonde hair and arresting blue eyes. A beauty from the start, people said, and so good she never cried. It had taken a while, but Sarah had fallen in love with her. She'd fallen in love with it all. Just in time.

In faraway headquarters, some unknown higher-up had decided consolidation was the way to JIRP efficiency, consolidating the Rome office right out of existence and forcing its head into retirement. The JIRP lady, now Dorotea to her, lost her staff and most of the office furniture but forged ahead with her work up to her last day when she closed the file on her last case. The Vogel girls were going to Israel. A party was in order. It would be a small affair, just the three of them, but in addition to her Wednesday soup, there'd be fresh-picked tomatoes and fried artichokes, cake and other confections, a nice Prosecco for the big girls, Aranciata for the little one.

It was another fine Roman fall, and only a death as big as John Fitzgerald Kennedy's could put a damper on things. For two days, the bells had been ringing through the streets like weeping widows, and the Pope, in English, spoke reverentially about Jack, his brother in faith and soldier *in nomine Patris*, et cetera. Dorotea brought in her own television set, lugging it up three floors to the office so together they might watch the funeral of America's first Catholic president. It sat on her desk crowned by telescoping rabbit ears and connected to the wall by a web of electrical cords. It took some knob-twisting to calm the jittery scroll of black, gray, and white, but soon, from across the sea, came the slow hammer of Chopin's "Funeral March."

"No one puts a hero in the ground like a Pole," Dorotea sniffed as she fiddled with the rabbit ears. The bubbly wine tasted of tears.

They watched the procession. The lone veiled woman in black, her precious children, all the white horses and the dark one that was saddled but riderless, the crowd, God's heart heavy with drumbeat, an army of people on foot and in cars advancing on the stark white dome of the Capitol, the solemnity of their progress underscored by the stark, flattened quality of the newscasters' narration. If there was anything to this thing called destiny, Sarah suddenly saw she'd gotten it wrong. Hers was pointing West, not East. America called to her, not Israel. Dorotea sighed and said it was a lovely dream.

"Do I look like I'm sleeping?" Sarah asked.

"Well, no . . . I mean, I understand you *want* to go to America, everybody does, but . . ."

"Then you'll help me?"

Dorotea reached to lower the television's volume. A rage she'd been sitting on for years was about to hatch. There'd been too many of them, dropping their desperation in her lap, begging, demanding, swearing they'd stop. However long it took, whatever roommate or job they were given, they'd be glad for. Liars. They were never glad or thankful or patient. Only disappointed. In her! Over the years her skin had thickened, but she'd let Sarah get under it. She'd become a mother to her, the little one called her *Bubbe*, but the time for quiet understanding was over. Dorotea shook the tears from her eyes and let the girl have it. Was she out of her mind? Did she not understand? Everything was done. Their work of two years, *her* work of two years. Done! The papers were stamped. The plane was leaving first thing in the morning, and if they weren't on it, there'd be hell to pay.

Sarah asked how much hell was charging these days.

"That's not funny," Dorotea wailed. Jobs may end, but you couldn't retire feelings.

Sarah fingered the numbers on her arm and lit a cigarette. Dorotea was past caring.

"What about your husband?" she demanded. "Being with him meant everything to you."

"There is no husband," Sarah said, the words riding a plume of smoke.

"Don't say that, Sarah. There's always hope."

"But there never was no husband," she said. "I made him up."

Dorotea looked as if she'd been punched. "All that talk . . . your love, and the sun on your face, the sand between your toes . . . Heaven, you called it. You made it all up?"

How could she tell her friend that she hadn't made it up, she'd given up? The face, the touch, the worry, each day skidding further from reach. The love once tethered to the inscription on her arm drifting away like a cloud from one of his Gitanes. And even if the heaven part were true, she never believed she'd be let in. But a country that could reel with shock over the death of a soldier, where the dead were hard to forget because they had names *and* faces . . . in a country like that, who needed sun or sand or even a husband?

Also, the Kennedy children had a little Russian puppy. Pushinka.

It was Dorotea's last bit of matchmaking. Her disappointment in Sarah ran deep, but retiring or not, she was still a professional, practiced at putting her feelings aside. The calls began that Monday, and over the next several days, she refiled their applications; obtained replacement papers, passports, and visas; bought winter coats for both mother and daughter (she couldn't have them going off to America looking like refugees); booked their passage to New York; and, in a volley of telegrams with a counterpart in the States, secured them a spot with a houseful of Jewish girls from the Eastern Bloc in a place called Queens. Thursday evening, she drove Sarah and Sasha to the airport. They had only one valise to bring.

In two years, the sleepy Leonardo da Vinci Aeroporto had grown into a full-fledged international hub, its runways crowded with jet planes readying themselves for transatlantic flights. Civilians were no longer allowed on the tarmac, so their goodbyes were said at the gate. Swaying, clinging tight, Sarah had the irrational thought that if only they could stay like that—holding on until both she and her child had a chance to grow into who they were meant to be—they, the world they were leaving, and the world they were going to would be better off. It was Dorotea who let go, pressing her gold compact into Sarah's hand, the only gift she could think of that was too useless to be taken for charity.

In flight, picturing Dorotea alone and blue in her darkened house at the end of their hectic week, Sarah felt a vague, unnamable sadness. The child on her lap seemed to wrestle with it, too, and to calm her, Sarah read her favorite fairytale, the one about the hero who wanted to be a poet. Her daughter promptly fell asleep, but Sarah always had to finish. It was a good ending. The right one. So right it made her wonder what had stopped her from sharing it with Dorotea. The truth wasn't much worse than the lies she'd told, and it might have lessened the hurt she caused. Maybe she could send it to her from America. It might be too late, but she could try. No, she wouldn't *try*, she'd do it. It would be her first act of mercy in the new world.

A vow forgotten the minute the wheels touched ground.

No one waited at Idlewild to greet mother and child, only a man in uniform, unimpressed by how far they'd come or how far they had to go but in a hurry to stamp their passports and send them along. When Sarah asked if he could point them toward their new home, he told her he never heard a no place called Ka-veens, and in New York, people found their own way.

Sarah left the terminal with her small arsenal of English words, leather valise, and child in tow. Outside, she took her first gulp of the city's exhaust-laden air and followed the sidewalk to its end. There, a man wearing a flight jacket and cap, cigarette tucked behind his ear, called her Doll and told her it must be her lucky day. He and his copter were on their way to Wall Street. He'd bring them along for just ten bucks. "Bucks" was not in her arsenal but sensing she didn't have a spare ten of anything, he immediately lowered the price. When she didn't jump at six, he told her heck, he'd do it for free, no use sitting around growing roots. Nothing scared folks away faster than a dead president.

His copter was a clumsy-looking machine that inspired no confidence. With its bulbous body, stubby tail, and single propeller that sat like a dinner plate instead of upright like on real planes, she doubted they'd ever get airborne. But as they lifted off the pad, straight up and sideways, she felt curiously at home, like *she* was doing the flying, not the aircraft. "See, Saskela? All the sky and water in the world? It belongs to America. And so do we."

Sailing into the city over a river rough and gray, the pilot shouted the names of buildings they passed. She couldn't hear a thing over the enveloping *whomp-whomp-whomp*, but it made no difference to her.

They landed at the end of a long pier. The air smelled of fish and gasoline. Handing her a small coin, the pilot said the R train would get her where she was going, which was almost back to where they'd started. He shrugged over what he called the crazy long-and-shortcuts of life and gave her a two-finger salute before climbing into his machine and heading up and away.

The cold sliced at the back of her neck. Her fingers were losing feeling. Dorotea had been an angel buying them coats, but they'd needed hats and mufflers and gloves, too. Carrying the baby and her valise, Sarah walked toward the thicket of towering buildings, each a veritable castle. There were no train tracks in sight. She didn't know which way to turn, and she didn't know how to ask directions of the people she passed. It was new, this frightened feeling. It smelled of spoiled onions. Sniffing the warm wool bunched under her arm confirmed it was coming from her. A man in a black topcoat and fedora stopped and offered assistance. When she didn't answer, he offered again. His face was kind, but she knew to be careful of men in black hats, Polish men, German men, Italian men, and yes, even American men, who could put a price on the moon and make you think it was a good deal. She had money. Dorotea had exchanged Sarah's bag of lire for an anemic stack of American dollars, but Sarah would sooner have parted with an arm than give up a single bill for what he was selling. And why did she think he was selling anything at all? Because a gentleman would have tipped his hat and continued on his way. A gentleman would have left her some dignity. That's how she knew he was Black Market. The Schvarts Mark left nothing. This one was daring, though, conducting business out in the open, people everywhere. And just as she thought, *Maybe this is how they do things in America*, he offered his arm like she was his lady friend, and next thing she knew, she was clutching his coat lapels and sobbing about how she hated the cold and being lost, and here she was colder and more lost than she'd ever been. To her surprise, the man with the tear-soaked lapels happened to be quite familiar with the borough called Queens.

For a penniless girl to buzz like an insect across the sky and land in a city where kindness ran like rain in the gutters, where men in black hats weren't men in black hats, where the air was thick but free . . . she'd heard rumors that America was the birthplace of miracles, but now she knew it for a fact.

She'd heard about its people, too. They were brave and brash. They could become something from nothing. And in those somethings was bred a chronic fear of fortune's reversal, making them strong but also skeptical. And now she could add helpful to the list because without them, she'd never have found the R train or Corona, Queens, or the apartment complex that was bigger than the village she grew up in, with its own parks and shops, a post office, and even its own streets weaving around the buildings, all identically brick-clad and dotted with hundreds of metal windows. So big it was a globe unto itself, each building named for a destination its inhabitants could only dream of visiting—Shangri La, Avalon, Amsterdam. So big she would circle for an hour before landing in front of Building #16, as per Dorotea's instructions, only to discover that Building #16, an address she'd traveled so far to reach, was a place called Rome.

And they said Americans were not an ironic people.

Life

1963

Monday morning, Sarah Vogel reported to work at Rivlin & Son, Purveyors of Buttons, Zippers, & Passementerie, in the heart of the Garment District. Soon she'd be living like a queen, according to Jane, the roommate who'd pulled the strings that got her the job. "Pillow talk" is what Jane called cooing into the ear of her beau, the "& Son" mentioned on the sign painted before his birth by a hopeful father, the senior Rivlin with forty years of experience in trimmings. What other girl with an accent thick as Sarah's was lucky enough to have a commute that got her home for dinner with $8.80 in her pocket, $8.80 *a day*, one day off with pay at Christmas (the goyim's great gift to her people), a divan stuffed with feathers for sleeping, and roommates who'd babysit now and then for a few shekels? No matter how many times Jane asked, Sarah failed to answer satisfactorily. She always had her rent but ran habitually short on gratitude.

And with so much to be grateful for. A spacious apartment perched on the highway with no buildings to block the morning light. The nonstop rush of cars her roommates likened to the lull of tides, constant, soothing, and better than any sleeping pill. Sarah gathered they'd been to the ocean. A sophisticated group, it seemed. Jane (née Channah) and her friends Gertie (née Gittel) and Malcah (née Malcah, Hebrew for queen, and she was sticking with it). Their one bedroom fit only two twins, but the three of them took turns, Jane and Gertie (also on the Rivlin payroll) working days Monday through Friday, Malcah answering a higher calling working nights making challah for the Tri-State Jews. They all worked hard, but Jane had ambitions. Already she'd climbed from sweeper to stocker to receptionist to merchandise manager—perfecting the nasal accent of her adopted city, keeping a few *Yiddishe* phrases in reserve for the senior Rivlin's benefit—and hoped to make office manager by year's end, unless Solly Rivlin, the boss's only son and future owner of Rivlin & Son, Purveyors of Buttons, Zippers, & Passementerie, remembered he had a backbone and beat that deadline with a marriage proposal.

Sarah had no ambitions but knew her way around a zipper and moved quickly from cleaner to stocker. It was tedious work—counting, sorting, and labeling, recounting, sorting, and labeling—but there were no deadlines and little oversight, and at the end of her half-hour train ride, she had steam enough left for a second job cleaning up after the rambunctious young attending the complex's nursery school (a job she found on her own) for $3 a night and a promised spot for Sasha, whenever she started making in the potty, which Sarah prayed would be soon.

She'd return to find Sasha asleep on Gertie's bed, sprinkled with challah crumbs, and Gertie on the divan deep into some show. *Andy Griffith*, *Red Skelton*, one for every weeknight. Sarah would watch, too, laughing when Gertie laughed until the program ended and baby *and* divan were hers again. Then Jane would rattle the door, announcing her return from one of her after-work classes on dictation, cooking lumpless hollandaise, or crafting the perfect thank-you note—bettering herself was her passion. It being pleasanter avoiding such random encounters, Sarah learned to feign sleep.

1964

At least twice a week, Solly and Jane dined at the Fifty-Seventh Street automat, the fare preferable to his mother's—dry, rubbery, and tasting of the Old Country, his estimation of everything in her life. He'd never left the split-level he'd been born into, ate whatever she served without comment, and though truly fond of the woman found her embarrassingly quaint. He was no easier on his father, making the business of notions the butt of his more cutting jokes.

"You should be a comedian," his friends would tell him, fostering the belief that a career in stand-up might be in his cards.

"Everyone's a comedian," his father grumbled upon hearing his son's plan to hit the road.

Solly was short and holding onto his baby fat well into his twenties. He wore thick glasses and by midday sported a five o'clock shadow. College hadn't been his thing. He was more interested in marching off to wherever Negroes weren't allowed to use water fountains or hitching cross-country with a guitar he couldn't play. Rivlin Senior, known around the office as Señor, was somewhat sympathetic. He'd played mandolin when he was young and knew what it meant to have a *bissel* talent. "But life, it comes along with a vengeance," he warned his boy. "You don't wanna wind up in buttons and bows, you gotta do more than dream. You gotta work, you gotta plan, you gotta lay a foundation." But for the son of a Rivlin, Rivlin's was too sweet a gig to fret about the future. He had a bank account, a roof over his head, and parents too afraid of answers to ask questions.

In the meantime there was Jane, who filled out a sweater nicely and brought a bit of pizazz to his wholesale/retail world. And when, at the end of a date, she'd come in extra close for a goodnight kiss, pressing the top of her thigh into his crotch, he'd almost forget his promise to his papa not to fool around with any of their girls, not even the Jewish ones, especially not the Jewish ones with families left behind in those forlornly out-of-the-way parts of the world. Fortunately, the situation never allowed for more than a kiss and a quick feel before she'd be skipping down the subway stairs and out of sight, leaving him to adjust the wood in his pants and move on to the rest of his evening with a clean conscience. A little Ellington, some Jack on the rocks à la Dean Martin, a girl on a barstool to kiss away the taste of the last, and a ride he wouldn't remember back to Whitestone, just this side of Long Island.

When asked what it was about Solly, Jane always cited his gentlemanliness. It wasn't every day a girl from nowhere found a fella that respectful, and in return, she kept her nose out of his business. She knew Señor started his days at the Kaddish factory down the street from the office, earning himself a second nickname, the Minyan Maker, and while she treasured the picture of a caring son spending Shabbos in Whitestone with his father, a man so devout he supported not one but two temples, she would not be surprised to learn that Solly rarely set foot in either. So what? In the big picture, there was a landlord getting his rent regular, a boyfriend learning that bad girls were fun but good girls were forever, and a family named Rivlin who could keep being Rivlins as long as the stream of skittish immigrants desperate for work kept flowing their way. All because of her.

And how was she thanked? By her latest foundling throwing herself at Solly's feet.

Jane couldn't get what any guy, let alone hers, saw in Sarah Vogel. No meat on her bones. No bosom to speak of. And, okay, she'd learned the rudiments of proper hygiene but never spent a nickel on a lipstick and wouldn't know how to use one if she did. But there was a look. Hungry and humiliated. Skeptical and dangerous. Though Jane was younger by several years, prettier, and at this point thoroughly American, she couldn't compete. Like it was her fault Hitler pooped out before she was born. And if she had wound up in the Camps? Well, she wouldn't go throwing it in people's faces. Jane was a peacekeeper, not a riler. It was in the interest of peacekeeping that she'd filed away her suspicions, and filed they would stay so long as the source of the trouble kept her mitts off her man.

If Solly ever spoke to her, Sarah didn't remember. She had enough on her mind managing her daily earnings, the $8.80 from Rivlin's and the $3 from the nursery school, a day and a night's earnings from which Sarah paid her daily rent of $2.40, $1 to each babysitter, 30¢ for the subway, 50¢ for coffee and a pretzel, and $2 toward the eventual nursery school tuition deposited directly into her brown paper bag. This left her $18.20 a week for whatever else they wanted or needed, which sounded like a lot until broken down to the $2.60 a day she'd spend on the pint of sour cream Sasha liked so much, schnitzel, sliced ham, a sour pickle—halved and buttered—milk, a box of Cheerios, and diapers, still with the diapers. Everywhere in and around the building called Rome, Sarah watched people taking part in a thing they called life. *Have dinner out tonight,* it teased. *Get your girl a library card. Take her to the zoo, for crying out loud.* It refused to understand that the version of life she'd been allowed was circumscribed by $2.60 a day. One guaranteeing that $2.60 only for the day completed, the next day in the hands of a boss who didn't know her name and a tyrannical roommate who arched a plucked eyebrow at her every move.

Sarah and Solly were not friends They were not co-workers. It was only the way Jane looked at Solly whenever she caught him looking at Little Miss Auschwitz that got people talking.

December. Fat men in matted white beards. Dwarves in green tights. Brownies with flashcubes. Tongue-singeing cocoa and sequin-sized marshmallows. Icicles that never melted. The slap of wet galoshes on terrazzo floors. The dogginess of wet wool. Hatchets to be buried. No sourpusses allowed. For the roommates, Christmas was a season all its own, and they were hell-bent on making believers of the Vogels.

The child, until then only tolerated but now their holiday mascot, gave them license to partake of the many pleasures they'd missed out on as kids. The windows on Fifth Avenue, pots of poinsettias, visiting Santa—the line stretching clear across Thirty-Fourth Street, every youngster in that line straining to pull free of their adult, wanting to run and throw things, to gobble all the sweets they could connive from any future allotment they imagined coming to them, to assert themselves. Only Sasha was content in her mother's arms, weightless, burrowing her head into her chest, dubious of the pageantry. Jane praised her model behavior, promising it would not go unnoticed by the big man but warning that she'd better speak up when Santa asked what she wanted lest he forget all about her.

But if the child had any wants, she didn't yet have words for them, and when eventually their group made it to the head of the line and Santa hoisted her onto his lap, she could only stare into his great, white beard, nodding away every question he asked.

They splurged on a cab ride home. Sasha slept the whole way, a candy cane stuck to her cheek. She asked for it first thing the next morning and began wailing when Sarah explained she'd thrown it away.

Jane was at the door, arms crossed, foot tapping, saying a candy-cane tummy was all that was wrong.

It was not like her child, though. Sarah pressed her lips to Sasha's forehead. It was dry and fiery, but Jane was leaving. Against her better judgment, Sarah left too.

By lunchtime, Malcah was at Rivkin's handing off her charge. She wasn't paid enough to be no nurse, she said. Sasha was delirious. The commotion drew & Son from his office. Sarah's face was ashen, the baby's flame-red. Not knowing what else to do, Solly told her to get her things, he was taking them to the hospital. Even Jane could see the child was in terrible straits and held her tongue.

The wait. The paper-pale child. This fellow from work, nearly a stranger, interpreting for her. The hurried doctors. The harried nurses. The foreign words. Sasha. Surgery. Straight from the doctor's mouth. Seconded by her boss's son. Doctors lied, but why would Solly?

"Sasha needs surgery," his words strangely drawn out. "The appendix, it's a tiny thing, a *bupkis*, you know? She goes to sleep, they cut, they sew her up. Good as new." A crowd was gathering. "Tell Mama you'll be fine, Sasha, and you'll get allllllll the ice cream you want. Doesn't that sound nice?" Imploring the twin sets of eyes glaring at him and still not shutting his mouth. People staring. Fingers tapping lips, a unanimous *shushhhh* against the tide of talk, all for a child who'd never needed shushing before, who'd endured a beating before letting loose the squall bottled up in her newborn lungs, who, back from the delivery room, wrapped tight as a deli sandwich, had to be invited to the tit, never grabbing. This child who'd never made her mother miss a day of work. Slung across Sarah's narrow chest or strapped to her back, or, once she could stand on her own, suckered to the woman's stockinged leg, clinging with all her strength. There'd been no fever, no rashes, no whooping cough, no mumps, measles, or rubella to interfere with what counted. Work. The first thing she'd reached for was a zipper tab. Zippers were in Sasha's blood, and she'd always known better than to whine or laugh or even wonder aloud because she was her little bird and none of them, least of all Solly Rivlin, had the strength to pull them apart, not unless one of them let go, and one must have, or maybe both. There was a doctor, two muscle-bound orderlies, a trio of nurses, a whole team organized against her efforts to hold on to the quiet while she caught up on everything she hadn't done to avoid this moment. And Solly kept talking. That is, until her palm breached the space between them, stinging his soft cheek. The slap was unintentional. She'd only wanted to stop his slow-motion narration of the calamity coming at them full throttle. To prove to him, and everyone, that she understood why, just not *why*. To show that the mother was not a child. But it was indeed a slap. There were witnesses.

The hospital staff gave them a moment. Solly begged to know what she wanted of him. And what could she say? It was for a father to hoist the woeful bundle onto the gurney, to stop the mother from charging after it, to spare her the details, to smoke his Gitanes, flaunting hospital rules and suffocating her panic in one aromatic cloud. Solly wasn't that father. Solly wasn't anything.

The nurses directed them to the waiting room. The surgery went quickly. Sasha pinked up nicely in Recovery. The attending pulled up her hospital gown to show off his work. Three stitches. A triumph of minimalism swabbed in traffic-cone orange and knotted with black thread. "She'll heal fast as a kitten, Mrs. Vogel." He bragged how he'd tied the scalpel to his fingers to keep the incision tiny, all for a future full of bikinis. Sarah did not return his smile. A nurse covered the girl and took her vitals. "Snip, snip," the doctor said, scissoring his fingers on the way out.

They were discharged the next day. Solly showed up in a taxi and took them home. He sat up front holding the flowers he'd brought for their little patient and talking sports with the driver. Sarah sat in back, Sasha curled in a ball on her lap. She moaned as they bumped over the curb into Rome's roundabout. "Hush *mamaleh*," Sarah said, taking her from the cab, carrying her to the building's entrance, patting her pockets for the keys she'd left at Rivlin's. A resident on his way out held the door for them. She thanked him and let the door slam shut, stranding Solly on the sidewalk, his taxi gone, not another in sight.

Upstairs, sour-mouthed and keyless, Sarah knocked to be let in, which Jane did without a word.

They were to stay put for several days, doctor's orders. Sarah took on the business of minding her own daughter with trepidation, but the time passed quickly, lounging on the divan, inventing new snacks and impractical hairdos, and poring over board books in which A was for Anteater and X, not Z, was for Xylophone. With the sprout of Sasha's ponytail tickling her cheek, Sarah succumbed to this thing called play, wondering what had taken her so long.

Christmas bought them one more day. A birthday so big it shut down the world. So big it brought Solly Rivlin to the front door, straight from the house of his bris and bar mitzvah still bedecked with Chanukah bunting, his arms loaded with a pint-sized tree, a doll that cried real tears for the convalescent, and a turkey breast roasted off the bone from a kosher deli in Whitestone. When Jane had invited him for dinner several times and he had declined. When it would be her first time receiving her beau at home and she hadn't bothered to fix her hair the way she knew he liked it. When he didn't notice . . . "Where should I put it?" Solly asked, a goofy grin stretched ear to ear. Sarah waited for the door to be slammed in his face, but Jane, with little inflection and a smile that didn't reach her eyes, told him he could put *it* wherever he liked, though what he planned to do with a tree that had no stand, she couldn't say. Solly stood felled and frozen in the doorway.

"Oh, for goodness sake," Jane said, reaching for his bundles. "If you're going to come in, come in."

Sasha was down for a nap, her unopened gifts piled in a corner of the room, Santa's load too much for her. Solly added his doll to the pile. The roommates added his food to the rickety card table they'd borrowed for their spread. Jane slammed around the kitchen in search of serving spoons. And Sarah counted the minutes until her boss's son, awaiting further instruction and receiving none, spit out a string of lame excuses and left.

In the holiday's drab wake, Sarah dressed for work. Remembering what happened the last time they separated, Sasha wrapped her arms around her mother's legs and wouldn't let go. With Malcah on strike (never properly thanked or paid for schlepping the kid into town) and Jane already gone (the trains extra slow the day after Christmas), Sarah had no choice but to stuff the whimpering child into her snowsuit and carry her out into the cold. Too bad if what she wanted was a mama who'd roll around on the floor with her all day. But Sarah knew her girl was content with the mama she had. *Ach*, she thought. *If only there were a board book to teach a girl to want more.*

Jane was parading a flock of new girls around the floor when Sarah punched in. "Well, well, Mrs. Vogel." Her voice a scalpel slicing through the din of Rivlin's laborers, souped up from their big day off. "Nice of you to stop by."

"Ont wawa, Mama," the child whispered.

"Not a word, little bird," Sarah whispered back.

With Sasha under the fan of her mother's skirt, the girl clinging for dear life, silent and invisible, the two went to the company water cooler. Only Jane the bloodhound suspected, meeting them at the cooler just as Solly showed up, earlier than usual, holding two cups of coffee from the corner kiosk and looking warily from woman to woman. "Why, Mr. Rivlin, how thoughtful," said Jane, eyeing the coffee. Solly, confused, relinquished neither cup, instead asking Sarah how the little one was doing.

"See for yourself," Jane said, pulling a roll of Life Savers from her pocket and luring the child from her hiding place. "Looks okay to me. Come, Sasha, let Auntie Jane find you some fun so Mama can get to work."

Sarah watched her daughter carried off to Lorraine the receptionist—recently engaged and chomping at the baby bit—and began the day's sorting and labeling, molars grinding. Solly, leaving both coffees behind, went to raid Rivlin's sample cases for the child's entertainment. Jane resumed the new girls' introduction to operations, keeping Reception in her sights.

Morning minyan broke at 8:46. At 8:56, Señor caught Lorraine in full fluster, headset askew, scribbling madly on a pile of paper, trying but failing to engage the toddler planted on her lap, the lights of her phone board blinking angrily. And at 8:57, Solly reappeared, his hands sparkling with glitter.

Jane flashed her chilliest smile.

"You know this kid?" Señor demanded, a frown cutting down to his jaw.

Jane drew closer.

"That's Sarah's . . . Mrs. Vogel's girl," his son explained, shaking glitter from his hands.

"So now we're running a kindergarten? I'll see her in my office, Solomon."

"But—"

"No buts. Bring the woman to me. NOW."

Jane relished the shock, the disapproval, the chagrin on both men's faces. Sarah Vogel wouldn't survive the day, a delightful thought, even if firing was too good for her.

As commanded, Solly delivered the summons to Sarah, and everyone stopped what they were doing to pay their respects as the two of them marched through the workroom to the boss's office. She was dismissed on the spot. Señor told her she could collect her things and see herself out. "The least you could do is let me help her," Solly whined. Sarah agreed. It was the least he could do. She had nothing to collect.

On the way out, he took her hand and led her into the supply room, a tight fit, its walls lined floor to ceiling with shelves bowing under the weight of adding machine tape, boxed staples, reinforcement rings, and the like. It was the only place where they could talk in private. He needed to explain. His father was a fair man. A man who believed in second chances. Solly was sorry for the spot she was in, but she'd see, he'd fix everything.

Footsteps silenced him, the sound of high heels on terrazzo. The joyous stride. The right foot striking harder than the left, the one Jane favored, because she bought her shoes to fit the smaller foot. She was on her way to the mailroom, a morning regimen that took her past the supply room. The door was ajar. She stopped to shut it and continued down the hall humming an unidentifiable tune, some jingle that had planted itself in her head. *Loo la loo-loo-loo.*

When she was gone, Solly released the breath he'd been holding. He felt safe in the dark, and Sarah couldn't have that. He was Jane's, and Jane needed to learn how easy it was to lose the things you thought were yours. Like Solly. But the darkness was a block of stone from which the two of them were carved. "Am I falling or floating?" he whispered. The hands that had been fumbling with his belt buckle were becoming surer at his fly, and the hem of her skirt stirred his nakedness as the knee of one bare leg nudged itself under his arm, her dainties circling the ankle of the other. Then it was she who was falling, or floating, Solly the only one there to catch her.

Their expulsion from the apartment was surprising only in its swiftness. The valise stood waiting in the hallway. The only thing missing was the only thing of consequence—Sarah's savings. The lock unchanged, she let herself in, settled Sasha on the divan, and ran to the bedroom where she quickly spotted the crumpled brown bag in the wastebasket under the vanity half-buried in used cotton balls and late-night snack wrappers, tossed away unopened but every penny accounted for. In the end, they were an uncurious lot. Sarah sat on the edge of a twin bed she'd never slept in and, as if for the first time, saw how grand a home it was, this home she'd never lived in, how grand and yet how small the others had made it feel.

On the nightstand was the pamphlet Jane studied to help her become a better girl, "Definitions You Should Know to Assist You in Determining Your Zipper Needs." Sarah took it, too.

Out on the street, heart racing, the child whimpering, she stopped to catch her breath. *What next?* she wondered. A place for her child to spend the night. A job. A cigarette. Somewhere to smoke it. Something to eat. Somewhere warm and safe to eat it. There was a diner close by. Menus thick as magazines. She let Sasha pick the booth. Sarah ordered a cup of coffee and a dish of rice pudding, extra whipped cream, two spoons. While they waited, she studied the want ads in a newspaper someone had left behind. There was a listing for a place in Kew Gardens. She liked the sound of it—Kew Gardens—and called from the diner's pay phone. A man answered and told her to come right away. She asked about the rent. They'd work it out, he said. She had the waitress wrap the rice pudding to go and flagged a passing cab.

The man from the phone buzzed them into the building. An imperious presence on the third-floor landing, he watched her climb the stairs, her two-and-a-half-year-old in one arm, the valise holding everything they owned in the other.

The tour was brief, everything visible from the doorway. He told her she was lucky. A year ago, one-bedrooms like these were going for twice the price, but since that Eye-talian girl got herself killed, thirty-three people watching from their windows and not a peep, they couldn't give them away. Handing him a stack of bills, she said maybe he was the lucky one. He snorted and dropped the keys in her hand.

They'd live at the back of the building, staring at the backs of three other buildings, but it was quiet, it was furnished, and it was theirs. She tested the lights, flipping them on and off, Sasha laughing as their shadows danced across the wood floor. They sat at their new table and chairs and polished off the rice pudding. *They'd had worse dinners,* Sarah thought and set to work unpacking. For a while, Sasha was content sitting on the floor of the closet, handing clothes to her mother one piece at a time, jangling the hangers until finding a better amusement, a compact with the heft of real gold drawn from a side pocket of the valise. She toyed with the jewel-like clasp until it opened and a puff of powder filled the room-sized closet with its scent of undue effort, of Dorotea, a woman who may have saved their lives but could never have come up with a place this fine.

1969

With the door closed on zippers and trim, Sarah answered a listing for a job on the custodial staff of Queens College—an expansive commuter school in the least glamorous borough of the most glamorous city anywhere—and spent the next five years dressed in coveralls and orthopedic shoes buffing beige linoleum floors, swabbing mint green walls, and plucking spent sanitary napkins from the bins of a dozen bathroom stalls. Nothing disgusted her. Her supervisor said she'd been made for the job. High praise, she'd thought, until that summer of greatness when a man's walk on the moon showed everyone how small they were and how giant they might be. It wasn't an astronaut that set her straight, though. It was a man of human-sized leaps, more pedant than pioneer, a professor she noticed loitering in her hallway one day, blowing on his take-out coffee like there was such a thing as spare time. She passed him a dozen times before he noticed, stepping into the path of her machine to say hello, taking her in, the name on her security badge, the numbers on her arm.

"Do you know what an anomaly you are?" he said, leaning in so close she could smell the coffee on his breath.

"What is that?" she asked.

"Something that has no right to be where it is but is."

"And where is it you think I have no right to be?"

"Oh, I don't know," he said, his voice softening. "In that uniform? My life?"

Her machine sputtered. It was a chore restarting it once it stalled, and there were more hallways waiting. She said she had to go. He said she should stay. He found her foreignness intriguing, begged her to let him guess where she was from. It was a game he liked to play. Accents were his thing, and he was stumped by hers—the German tainted with Polish, the overlay of telly British, the heavy bass line of gulag. After he'd told her how heartily he approved of the intensity of her gaze, after she'd told him about the daughter she had to pick up on her way home, like she was the one who had something to confess, he told her how attracted he was to intelligent women.

Her eyes narrowed.

"Most women would take that as a compliment."

"Only the ones who aren't so smart."

"Which isn't you, obviously. What are you doing being a maid, anyway?" Like they'd asked how much of a dummy she was and she'd lied to get the job.

She ran her fingers over the name on the card he handed her, David H. Bloom, Dean of Humanities, Professor of Russian Literature. She wondered what the *H* was for but didn't ask. His eyes, watery blue, peered at her from over his half glasses. His brown hair curled over his collar, the long sideburns showing a validating touch of gray, the beard connecting to his mustache similarly touched, his mouth a soft island of surprise.

"This job you're not too smart for?" she asked, flicking the edge of the card.

"Far from it," he said. "But seriously, I think maybe I could do something for you. Stop by . . . if you're interested."

At the urging of her neighbor, Gerri Capogrosso—self-described busybody and amateur shrink—she did stop by. "*Maybe* he can do something for you?" Gerri had said. "Honey, *that's* the kinda maybe a girl like you can't pass up." And she was right. Sarah left Bloom's office with a new job filing and answering phones for the Dean of Humanities. It came with a respectable salary, her own desk, and the luxurious start time of nine a.m.

She slept with him immediately. Russian blood flowed on both sides of his family. His eyes seemed always to smile, and if any work were to get done, he needed to clear a path to it. He locked the door and drew the blinds. They used his desk. He was slow, thorough, generous with his touch. When they finished, he made a note for her to stock up on rubbers—for *both* their sakes—and then kissed her, not like her first Russian, as if his life depended on it, but sweet enough to send her to her desk with the thought of him teasing her lips for the rest of the day.

That first time was special. Also, the second, when he told her he used to dream of making love to a Survivor. Even after their appointments became just another of her daily duties—the wrangling of students, the mid-morning pot of coffee, the afternoon shtup—for him, each thirty minutes he booked was transformative. Sarah was a window to the soul of one of the world's great tragedies. Tragedy was his métier.

The sex was good—*splendid* (his word)—and though the remuneration was far from brilliant, the respect and vacations were ample, the daycare provided was affordable, and the birth control the clinic doled out was, astonishingly, free. But the jewel in this new crown was the tuition the college covered for its full-time employees, and when it came to the subject of education, Professor David H. Bloom, Dean of Humanities, her boss and lover, was bullish. "That's money in the bank you're flushing down the toilet," he lectured. "Dammit, a girl as smart as you should have a degree. Remake yourself."

"Only beds get remade," she said.

"You're so beautiful." He sighed.

"So you say."

"Because it's true. You're beautiful. Terribly beautiful. Unbelievably beautiful."

"And what happened to smart?"

"Okay, don't go to school." He laughed, raising his hands in a gesture of surrender. "I'm not sure I could stand you getting any smarter than you already are."

School wasn't for her. But Sasha, she was like something raw in a bowl, a twist of dough waiting to rise. College? That money in the bank he mentioned at every opportunity? It would go down no toilets.

Sarah would have slept with him regardless, but it was nice having reasons.

Thanksgiving came on the heels of her professional upgrade. She'd never gotten used to being paid to do nothing. During her time on Custodial, she'd worked through all the days set aside for old wars and dead presidents, students furloughed, offices shuttered, Sasha along for company, TV dinners waiting at home, Swanson's three-course specials, starting with the peach cobbler and working their way back to the Salisbury steak. What could the holidays of others mean to them?

On Thanksgiving Eve, she learned what they meant to others. The corridors emptied, the afternoon's lovemaking finished, her cigarette ember the only light in the dusky room, their clothes piled at the foot of his desk. She knelt to retrieve hers—the worn underwear, the gray flannel skirt that brushed her shins, the white cotton blouse ironed that morning. Swiveling back and forth, naked in his leather chair, staring her down, the hair on his forehead, shoulders, chest, and belly damp and matted, he asked about her plans for the holiday. She told him she had none, though they'd accepted an invitation to Gerri's. She didn't know why she lied. There was no reason to.

"Then it's settled. You and Sasha will come to us." How at ease he was mixing the intimacies of their bodies with the casual chitchat of co-workers.

"That's a terrible idea," she said, buttoning her blouse to the throat.

"But the wife's terrible idea, not mine. Nothing makes her happier than giving some lost soul a seat at the table. This year, it's you."

The wife was a fact he'd never bothered to hide. Her name was Kit, but Bloom called her the landing lights on his runway, the Guinevere to his Lancelot. Together, they'd turned their home into a citified Round Table, only the crème de la crème allowed. He'd pour drinks. She'd serve dinner. He'd pick some bookish fight (would, for instance, a modern-day Tolstoy have his precious Pierre enlist or run off to Canada?), and when things got too heated, she'd dish out dessert. There wasn't an argument a slice of her pound cake couldn't settle. Out of her league when it came to highbrow literature, Kit Bloom knew what dangerous terrain she sent her man to every day, each new crop of ingenues eager to bathe in his sagacity, hair untended, bellbottoms dragging, Twiggy eyes behind wire rims, ready to trounce him on any subject of his liking. Even the best of men tripped up now and then, and he was far from the best of men, but she wasn't afraid of a little flirting. It kept them both at their fighting weight.

Sarah wasn't familiar enough with the word "marriage" to have qualms about breaking one up, but Mrs. Bloom called the office daily and was always kind, asking about Sasha, laughing about the hapless husband who needed two women to keep both shoes tied. Being included in the joke smacked of friendship, something Sarah had never had with a woman and not an unpleasant thought, though a friend, she was beginning to think, might be someone whose husband you *weren't* sleeping with.

"We should stop," she said. "For *her* sake."

"It's precisely for *her* sake we shouldn't," he countered. "Don't you see? You're my test." He doubted he deserved Kit, but she proved her love every day. And now he'd proved his. They could withstand anything. Even Sarah. "If you really care about her, you'll be a good sport and come." He zipped his trousers, gathered some work for the long weekend ahead, and kissed Sarah goodbye.

Gerri handled the change of plans well. She knew better than anyone that a working girl don't say no to no boss.

The Blooms lived on a quiet, treeless street in a brick double-decker shouldered on either side by identical neighbors, each securely fenced in wrought iron, only the filigree varying. Not a pushcart in sight, only the prevailing neatness of rolled-down garage doors, skinny strips of blacktop, and small squares of lawn like welcome mats at the foot of every cement stoop. Not what she'd expected of her bohemian boss.

Sarah rang the doorbell and waited, anxious about handing off the caviar and Polish vodka she and Sasha had bought on their way over. An offering meant to impress the professor.

But it was the missus, Kit Bloom, who opened the door, a look of surprise instantly brightening to recognition. "Sarah, you're here! I must've lost track of the time, but how good to finally meet you. Come in! And this must be Sasha. Ooh, those blue eyes . . . no wonder David's so crazy about you. And that reminds me—my apologies, on his behalf. I can't believe he waited 'til the last minute to ask you. He can be so rude, but I'm happy you could make it. Thanksgiving's my favorite holiday. What a beast, though. So much to do, so little help, and David—well, I don't need to tell you. He's as useful as a scratched record. Hire in, he always tells me. Like you can hire in tradition. Honestly, it drives me nuts the way he's always telling me to cut corners when he knows darn well he didn't marry a corner-cutter. But this year, I'm taking his advice. Let's see how he likes that . . ."

She stood a head taller than Sarah, hair like spun gold, lanky as a teenage boy in a body-hugging turtleneck and ironed jeans. The picture Bloom kept on his desk didn't do her justice. Sarah felt trapped in their chilly foyer, its walls papered in a dizzying mod print, listening to the loveliest of women rant about the man they shared, dressed like a crazy person in a suite of clashing paisleys she'd let her seven-year-old pick out, skirt dusting the slate floor, a crocheted shawl draping her shoulders like yesterday's curtains. But Kit, unfazed, ranted on, mostly about the kids, who weren't much more help than her husband. "I mean, I tried to make a game of it—they used to love games—but when children don't feel like playing, what's a mother to do but put on a smile, send them to the mall with their father, and pray they don't pig out at the food court? And then I dug in. Burned through my list so fast I started in on the Thanksgiving project we talk about every year but never get to, gathering all the nice things we no longer use for people who have so much less to be thankful for, like the homeless, or, I don't know, maybe a children's hospital. With them out of my hair, I purged my little heart out. Hit every room in the house. I was tying up the last of the bags when the buzzer buzzed, and, well, here you are," she said, her smile as genuine as ever. "I think early birds are the most trustworthy people, don't you?" Fat black garbage bags lined the floor of the foyer.

"I'm cold, Ma," Sasha whimpered into the folds of Sarah's skirt, as if she hadn't been warned that she'd be better off in the nearly new corduroys and matching sweater they'd gotten from consignment. *That's what you get for crying over a party dress*, she would've screamed if not for the professor's wife and what she might think of a mother so cowed by tears she'd let her child have her way, a child who, given the choice, had made the wrong one and was now a froth of pink, bare-legged and shivering, only a cotton shrug to ward off November's bluster, her thumb parked in the gap between her two front teeth, a nervous habit inherited from the father Sasha'd never known, that and the pin-straight hair now desperately trying to hold the curls she'd spent the morning winding around her fingers because she'd wanted to look pretty, her saucer eyes begging to know why her ma never let her be pretty.

Not my job, Sarah wanted to shout, instead spreading open her shawl to wrap the girl in motherly warmth. But too late, Sasha's interest had already shifted to their hostess, Kit, on her knees rummaging through one of the garbage bags—a trove of naked Barbies, flowery bath salts, mismatched socks—mumbling as she dug, until finally getting her hands on what she was after: a wooly coat of loden green, never worn and almost Sasha's size. Kit sat back on her heels as Sarah helped the girl try it on.

"Like it was made for you," Kit said, beaming. Sasha, too, though the wool was so stiff her arms wouldn't bend.

Wonderful, Sarah thought. *Now you know what a good ma is like.*

"My God, have we taken hostages?" Bloom's voice boomed. He had a block of butter in each hand, his face ruddy from the cold, his joy uncontainable, his children stacked behind him. "In, in. Everyone in," he shouted. And they would have done just that but for the cry their eldest, Cacky, released.

"Mooooooom, that girl's wearing my coat!"

Sasha's eyes were clear blue saucers rimmed in pink.

"Take it off, *mamaleh*," Sarah whispered.

"Don't you dare," Kit ordered. Then to Cacky, through clenched teeth, "It's way too small on you, and you wouldn't wear it when it fit."

"Which doesn't give you the right to go around messing with my things."

"You know, you're absolutely right. Oh, but wait . . . I buy everything around here, so technically they're *my* things I'm messing with."

"You mean *Dad's* things. Because *technically*, it's *his* money. *You* don't even have a job."

"Enough," Bloom bellowed, a thunderclap out of a cloudless sky. Sarah was impressed. With a single snarl, the child had brought the barometric pressure to prestorm levels, turned her mother to stone, and set her father on fire. The poor man looked stricken by his outsized response, but in their stunned silence, he pulled himself together and pushed his children inside.

"Jesus, it smells good," he said, inhaling deeply, his cheerier tone and brisk hand-rubbing relaying his willingness to forgive and forget, if they were.

In contrast to his office—a forest of heavy brown pieces he called antiques but were merely old—everything here was black and white and rigorously modern. A tautly upholstered living room set, salt-and-pepper shag carpeting, Lucite tables, a few throw pillows for color. The jazzy cool was tempered by the aroma of roasting meat and a brisk percussion of radiators. Bloom flung his jacket over the back of a chair. The buttons of his shirt pulled across his midsection. *Has he always had that paunch?* Sarah wondered.

"Boys, outside. Cacky, take Sasha to your room."

"She's not going anywhere until she apologizes, David."

"C'mon Kitten," he said in the whispery voice he sometimes used on Sarah. "It's Thanksgiving. Can't you give her a break?"

Apparently, when he called her Kitten, she could do anything.

"Just make sure no one kills anyone," she said, retreating to the safety of her kitchen. *A sensible woman*, Sarah thought.

Cacky kicked off her shoes and was about to nestle into the sofa with a magazine.

"Go," Bloom ordered, pointing to the stairs. "And take Sasha with you." His tone was gruff, but the fire was out.

Cacky threw her magazine on the coffee table and stomped off. Sasha, terrified, followed.

"You know that coat was supposed to be for some homeless kid who actually needs it," the queen bee sniped on their way up the stairs.

"That's my sweet girl," Bloom called after them.

Then he and Sarah were alone. He said he hoped she'd had no trouble finding the place. She told him his directions were perfect and it was nice finally meeting his family.

"Listen to us, polite as strangers," Bloom sighed.

"In your house, that's what we are."

"Then don't think of it as my house. I barely do. The house, the kids, my job, my worldview, my liquor cabinet . . . she's shaped everything I have. Everything but you, Sarah."

She'd been naked with the man but never felt so exposed.

In the kitchen, a one-woman band played her pots and pans with a wooden spoon. At the front door, new arrivals hammered at the buzzer, funneling into line as they entered. Kit's parents from Long Island, Grant and Catherine Miller. Her sister, Dr. Caroline D. Miller, from Manhattan. A couple from next door with their three kids. And Vincent O'Malley, a professor-friend of Bloom's from Oregon. Sarah fell in behind them. She was glad Gerri had told her about hostess gifts, how much forgiveness a good one could buy a girl like her, but everyone else had brought something handmade or homegrown in comely wrappings. Even the visiting professor, whose simple bouquet looked more special in its cone of colorful tissue paper. Sarah's had set her back a week's salary, but without a ribbon or card it looked as common as a bag of groceries. She never got anything right.

But Kit was a lady as well as a hostess. "Isn't this different," she said, pulling the tin of caviar from the bag, examining it carefully, her thumb rubbing a spot of rust from its lid.

"We've never been to a real Thanksgiving," Sarah said, like that explained anything.

"I love it, but you better not go to this much trouble next time," Kit said.

The words "next time" rang with promise, but it wasn't forgiveness Sarah heard, only the insinuation of how much more she might need forgiven. Another thing Gerri had gotten wrong.

Squalls of activity separated the day's lulls. A fizz over Kit's tray of snacks. A stirring over Bloom's tray of cocktails. From a corner of the room, Sarah surveilled the scene. Sasha with the other children sprawled at the foot of the TV, elbows sunk into the carpet, upturned faces rinsed in bluish light. Grandad a frowzy old king in the only armchair. Caroline perched provocatively on its matching ottoman. The neighbors at either end of the sofa, their eldest and Cacky cross-legged on the loveseat. Only the visiting professor found nowhere to light. His day-dreamy gaze, drifting from Caroline to the girl in the corner who'd gone from invisible to unavoidable in the blink of an eye. Unlike Kit, who'd been raised to own every room she entered, Sarah hated being noticed. And here was Vincent O'Malley plying her with questions, driving all eyes her way. Where she was from, how long she'd been in America, what she thought of New York, of Queens, how a single mother in a foreign land with a full-time job and no family to lean on had managed not to lose her mind.

"How indeed?" asked Caroline, twisting around on the ottoman, curious to see who'd stolen the attention of the man she'd been dodging.

"Maybe a person holds onto a mind when there's nothing else to hold on to," Sarah answered.

"Hear that, Caroline?" Grant said. "Just like a good quarterback. Ball lands in his arms and what does he do, stop and think about it? Hell no. He sees an opening and runs."

"He would, being a simple-minded thug playing a purposeless game, cheered on by childish fans."

Bloom, sweeping through the living room with a second round, took offense. "Those're highly trained athletes, okay? Built like tanks, fast as Corvettes, fearless, heroic . . ."

"It's entertainment, David, not war."

"*That's* entertainment," Bloom said, pointing to the televised parade of cartoon characters floating down Central Park West. "Actually, that's not even entertainment . . . I don't know what that is."

"Tradition?" Grant offered.

"What the hell . . . heck . . . does giant Pooh have to do with Plymouth Rock?" Bloom protested, at which point the televised parade was overridden by the roar of football fans and the kids' screams of revolt.

"Freddie loves giant Pooh," said Kit on her sweep through the living room to clear away the snacks. "And turn it back, David. You don't even like football."

"It wasn't me."

"Well, it didn't switch itself."

"Guilty," Grant Miller confessed, waving the plastic doohickey the kids called The Changer.

"You know the rules, Daddy. No football until after dinner."

"Damn thing'll be over by then," he muttered.

"Grandad meant to say 'darn,' kids," Bloom said.

Sarah felt the backwash of regret. This place of blue-faced children and gland-puckering drinks and smart people arguing the merits of a game played by men the size of cattle. This was no place for them. But *was* there such a place? Had she felt right anywhere but in the arms of men? Long after forgetting his face, she felt the strength of Viktor Aleksandr's hold. And Bloom, when he scooped her up, along with Sasha, made her feel almost deserving of his shelter and solace. Mightn't his Kitten say the same? That her true home was not a collection of rooms with the life decorated out of them but the scoop of the arms of this man she seemed to love enough to overlook his more disappointing aspects?

"I knew it." Kit giggled in Sarah's ear, dimpled chin grazing her shoulder, pointing to their girls. "Already best friends." Sarah felt her smile. "Good kids, aren't they? Hungry little monsters, though. Lucky I have another bag of chips stashed. Hon?" Kit called to Bloom. "Can you mix us another pitcher of Cranberry Cheer, please? And use Sarah's stuff. I'm opening the CA-VEE-AR!"

"Fish eggs and football, what'll they think of next?" said Bloom as he went to work on the Cheer, using the vodka instead of the recipe's rye. Sarah watched the magenta haze filter through the ice and spirits, a science experiment gone awry. Regretting not buying a cheaper vodka, she followed her hostess through the swinging door into her kitchen, the visiting professor following.

"To us," Kit said, raising her glass for a group clink. She seemed practiced at this cocktail thing, downing a healthy swig that sent her into a brisk shimmy.

Vincent leaned into Sarah. "I've always wanted to go to Poland," he said, low so only she would hear. "Any tips?"

"I don't remember much about it," she said, looking to Kit, who was arm-deep in a cabinet and searching for that last bag of chips when she spotted Sasha nudging her way through the swinging door.

"Well, hey there, Sash," Kit said.

"What's wrong?" Sarah asked. There was always something wrong.

"You're fine, right? And just in time to help," Kit said, tossing her the bag.

Sasha poured the chips into the big wooden bowl Kit put out for her.

"Now," Kit said, kneeling to look her right in the eye. "You bring these out to the kids, and you'll be my hero for life."

Sasha nodded her solemn oath, a grin spreading across her face as she hugged the bowl to her chest and headed to the living room where David, on his third glass of Cheer, tangled with Caroline, whose PhD had gotten her a lowly adjunct position at Barnard while her brother-in-law with only a masters was already a tenured professor at a public college. From the kitchen, Sarah watched the rush of kids, desperate for more, nearly swallow her child, and then the timer's ding signaled that the real star of the day, the toddler-size turkey, was done. Vincent hoisted it from the oven to the kitchen table. With everything waiting under warming tents, the last minute neared. Only the carving remained. That being Bloom's domain, Sarah and Vincent were dismissed.

Sarah said she could use a cigarette. Vincent said he could, too.

Outside, he sheepishly admitted he'd lied. He had no cigarettes. He didn't even smoke. Never in his life.

"It's all right," she told him, pulling a pack from her pocket.

The wind had picked up, and she went through several matches before Vincent cupped his hands around hers, allowing the flame to catch. She closed her eyes and took a long draw.

"Could I bum one?" His request a cumulus cloud in the cold air.

"So you do smoke?" Squinting on the exhale, her cloud mingling with his.

"No, but you make it look so good."

His decision, he was a grown man. And not bad looking. Tidier than Bloom. Plus, all that obedient hair. Presentable, Gerri would call him, by which she'd mean single. "I'm told it's a bad habit," she said, handing him the pack. He took one and smiled. But before he had the chance to light up, Kit called to them, her voice a bell. "It's show time."

Sarah stubbed out her cigarette. Vincent pocketed his.

"What have you two been up to?" Bloom demanded, tying himself into a frilly apron, his carving knife ready.

"Just having a smoke out back," Vincent said.

But Bloom, immersed in moving the turkey from the counter to the table, had stopped listening. "And where the hell were the place cards, Kit?"

"We're streamlining this year, hon. Remember?"

Vincent had taken off his glasses, fogged from the kitchen's heat. He was less attractive without them, his eyes too small for his head. But still presentable, Sarah thought.

"It was a total free-for-all, but don't worry, they're all gathered around the table like good little pilgrims. And I snagged Vincent a seat next to Caroline."

Vincent stepped closer to Sarah. Both Blooms noticed.

"David, Vince is our guest. He can sit where he likes."

"Then he better like sitting next to Caroline. That was the deal. It was your idea."

"And if Vince is interested in someone else?" Kit said, her smile sly.

"Who else would he be interested in?"

"I don't know . . . the only other available woman here? Who's looking very pretty, I might add." Her smile sweetened as it landed on Sarah.

"Sarah?" Bloom said.

"Yes, Sarah. Why, don't you think she looks pretty?"

"Do *I* think . . . of course not."

"Wow. Your face just turned the color of Cranberry Cheer." Kit wiped the edge of the stuffing bowl.

"It's a goddamn steam bath in here."

"So, which is it?"

"Hand me the thingy over there, will you?"

"Pretty? Not pretty?" Handing him the carving fork, Kit double-hitched her eyebrows, showing Sarah how much she enjoyed torturing her husband.

"I plead the Fifth."

"But don't you think they're kind of cute together?"

"Stop it, Kit. You're embarrassing yourself. And them."

"So-rry," she said, though Bloom had it wrong. Far from embarrassed, Kit was tickled. And Vince was proud. Sarah was desperate to roll back the clock and start the day over at Gerri's.

Bloom flipped the switch of the electric knife and attacked the bird with such force he sent a drumstick flying. Vincent's quick reflexes saved it from the floor.

"Good catch," Kit said.

"Is he okay?" Vincent whispered.

"Oh, sure. Carving is his art. Right, babe?" The evil look she shot her husband went unheeded. The slices of meat were piling up. "Be an angel, Vince, and take the gravy bowl to the table. And you, Sarah, grab the rolls and sweet potatoes. We'll be out in a minute with the rest."

Once the platters, tureens, and baskets appeared, Grant said grace. The house wine, a chocolatey red, was poured. The turkey passed. The sides followed. Vince looked down in the dumps seated by Caroline, his bid for Sarah's attention ignored. Sarah only had eyes for Sasha and her new friends, happily unsupervised at the kids' end of the table playing a game involving forks and knives. Conversation had given way to the serious task of eating when Bloom noisily pushed himself to his feet. The Cheer had caught up with him. Weaving in place, he topped off his glass and raised it high above his head.

"On behalf of feckless scholars everywhere, present company included," a drop of wine quivering at the lip of his glass, "I stand before you on metaphorically bended knee, thankful for . . . well, you," waving his glass toward Kit and Sarah, the drop holding fast. "You beautiful girls who work until the work is done, never calling us out for the useless asses we are. Why you do it is one of life's great mysteries." The stubborn drop still clinging, Bloom shook it free and slumped back into his chair, all eyes on the crimson dot seeping into the beautiful white cloth.

Kit broke the spell. "Nice job, hon. Guess we'll be sticking to white next year. Seconds anyone?"

Bloom, sobered on Kit's pie and coffee, was dispatched on his final errand of the day, driving the remaining guests home. First Vincent to his sublet and then Caroline to the subway. Sarah said she'd take the bus from there, but Bloom was adamant. "The wife wants me to see you to your door, I see you to your door."

"Whatever the wife wants," she said darkly.

He kept his mouth shut, hands on the wheel, and eyes trained on the white center line. Sasha was asleep in the back. There was no traffic, but they hit every red light. One long enough to invite Bloom's complaint. "A little full of himself, wouldn't you say?"

"You mean Vince? I wouldn't say that. I wouldn't say that at all."

"Well, sure, he was all over you, *your Vince*. But a dick to my sister-in-law. And to be clear, it was Kit who thought they'd be perfect together."

"Caroline barely looked at him all day."

"He was out of his league." Bloom smirked.

Sarah stared out the car window.

"Tell me I'm wrong."

She couldn't. Bloom wasn't wrong, he was jealous. And why? Because a man he deemed his inferior had made her smile. His own wife had never withheld a smile from anyone, deserving or not. And yes, Sarah was stingier with hers so they meant more, but *her Vince* had worked for it. Far from apologetic, she'd enjoyed his flirting. Enjoyed being the object of his desire. Almost as much as she was enjoying Bloom's pain.

"Come up," she told him when they got to the apartment.

He carried Sasha upstairs and set her on the couch. She stretched and moaned as her mother pulled her arms from her new coat and removed her shoes. Then Sarah led Bloom to her room.

The bed was perfectly made and draped to the floor in pink chenille, a lone touch of color. On the nightstand was a small lamp, white, the shade molded from the same plastic as the base; a gold compact; a leather-bound book with a German title; and an instruction manual with an illustration of a zipper on the cover. There was a cream-colored rug by the bed. Nothing on the bureau, no jewelry, no pictures. Above it hung an unframed mirror. The window—a dark void in the clean, white wall—looked out at a fortress of windowless brick. She'd seen no need for curtains.

Bloom lay on the bed, she next to him. He kissed her forehead, her cheeks, her neck, her mouth, his ardor wiping the evening's slate clean.

After, they dressed and moved Sasha from the couch to her place in Sarah's bed. Bloom's reminder that he wouldn't be missed. Standing at the door, he took a last look around. He'd never seen so empty a home. She'd never made love on so full a stomach.

On her way back to her daughter, Sarah noticed the loden green coat lying on the floor, picked it up, and folded it into a neat cube. Monday, she'd leave it at her bus stop where it might find that homeless kid who actually needed it.

1972

Sasha was ten the first time she grew out of a pair of shoes. They'd always worn out before they got too small. Kit, now *Aunt* Kit, promised a shopping spree. Girl time, she called it. They'd go to Gertz's, Jamaica's finest. It was the Fourth of July weekend, and everything would be on sale. The sky was the limit. Kit sent over a stack of Cacky's *Seventeen* magazines for her to study, dog-earing the pages featuring a particularly pretty teen model becoming famous for her gap-toothed smile. *How 'bout that?* Kit had written on her scented stationery. *You're so in!* Sasha blushed as her thumb found the empty space between her front teeth.

They had a date for eleven o'clock. Kit was always punctual, and because the woman Sasha babysat for on Saturday mornings was always late, she begged her mother to call and say she was sick.

"What, you can't tell a lie good as me? And don't give me those big bowls of sad soup. The world won't end if Mrs. Bloom has to wait a few minutes," said the woman determined to ruin her daughter's life.

On Saturday, Sasha squared her stance and informed her client that she'd be leaving at ten and there'd be no one to blame but herself if her kid drank Mr. Clean from under the kitchen sink. The startled mother not only heeded her warning but returned fifteen minutes early. Sasha ran all the way home.

The windows along Broadway were gussied up for the holiday. In comparison, Sasha's looked undressed. Her mother leaned out of one. Aunt Gerri out of the other. Two old birds scanning their turf. They'd been at it ever since the Vogels moved streetside. Sarah always watching for her daughter and Aunt Gerri just watching, the two of them yakking away, window to window, broadcasting everything, even private stuff, to the neighborhood. Like there wasn't a phone to pick up or a door to knock on. And Aunt Gerri could project. Sasha heard her shouting from a block away.

"Was it Mrs. Professor who ran to the super soon as she heard the Yanitelli boy got himself busted for peddling to a narc and gave his father a stroke on the spot so the rest of them had to run off in the night, leaving behind two bedrooms, a suite of perfectly good furniture, *and* groceries? Was it Mrs. Professor who nagged you to ask for a raise so there'd be no more sharing a bed with a child? Who, by the way, is no child no more. No, but she got no problem coming around in her big boat of an auto*mo*bile to stop the world from spinning because she thinks she can do better for your girl than us!"

And as one aunt, a smoker and no spring chicken, ran out of steam, Sasha's only other aunt pulled up in her big boat of an auto*mo*bile. It was eleven on the dot. The car door opened. "Summer Wind" played on the car radio. Kit got out, sandaled feet first, legs lean and bare, her gauzy blouse and long, crocheted vest revealing only a suggestion of the print miniskirt underneath, her hair pulled into a low ponytail, a few straying wisps. Big Jackie O. sunglasses, like she'd stepped from the pages of *Seventeen*. Sasha threw her arms around Kit's waist, nearly tackling her to the ground.

Sarah *yoo-hoo*ed for her to come up and change into something nice for shopping. Sasha, who'd expended her daily allotment of fierceness, bit her lip and began to wish some infirmity upon her mother. Heartburn, an aching corn. Nothing fatal, just uncomfortable enough to ground her for the day. But Kit shouted back that Sasha looked perfect and Sarah had better hurry down if she didn't want them leaving without her. Gerri raised a single witchy eyebrow at that. She'd never cared for the professor's wife.

Since Sasha got carsick, she sat up front with Kit. Sarah straddled the hump in back. A twist of a key magically raised the windows and shot cold air through the dashboard vents. Air conditioning! Blowing in her face. In a *car*. Heaven.

Then they pushed through the revolving doors of Gertz's. She felt like a Disney princess entering an enchanted castle decorated with her favorite things. The air was perfumed and so cold you could try on snowsuits in July. Smiles everywhere.

They rode the escalator to the shoe department and were welcomed by a man in a blue suit. Kit told him they were looking for back-to-school shoes, sturdy but stylish. He had Sasha stand straight and tall while he measured her feet, turning her pink by calling her petite, and then went to see what he could rustle up in her size. Kit said it was the salesclerks who kept her loyal to Gertz's, all so polite, well-dressed, knowledgeable. Theirs returned with a tower of boxes opened for their inspection, shoes swaddled like twin baby dolls in their cardboard cradles. Scooting close, he patted the spot on his thigh where he wanted Sasha to put her bare foot, took a ped from his jacket pocket, and stretched the skin-colored nylon from toe to heel. His hands were warm. After guiding her foot into the shoe, he pulled the laces tight and tied a perfect bow. His lips pursed as he poked and squeezed around the front of the shoe.

"Nothing worse than a tight toe box," he said.

"It does feel a little tight," Sasha told him, not knowing what a toe box was but hating the dull, brown shoes.

He suggested they try a bigger size. To Sasha's relief, Kit told him not to bother. "Too boring," she said, sending him off for a pair he swore they couldn't resist. It was an update of the classic Buster Brown saddle—the white part in black velvet, the vest in black patent leather. Just in. She'd be the first to try them on.

"Oh yeah," came Kit's most kittenish cry, the clerk responding with a smug smile.

The shoes were heavy and stiff. Sasha felt like a statue wearing its pedestal.

"You sure are lucky to have a mom with such good taste," the clerk said.

Kit quickly corrected him, pointing to the real mom, but it was too late. Sasha tried to hide her delight but wasn't fooling anyone. She'd give all the new shoes in the world for this beautiful, pleasant American woman to be her mom, and Sarah couldn't blame her.

"So, what do you think?" Kit asked the real mother solicitously.

"Nice," Sarah said. "For a funeral maybe." She mumbled the second part for her daughter's ears only.

"*I* like them," Sasha said. She wasn't as convinced as she sounded, but she knew her ma would be her ma good or bad. She wasn't sure she could say the same of a pretend aunt.

Kit had him wrap them up. At the register, both women reached for their wallets. Sarah insisted she'd pay for the shoes. Kit insisted harder.

Sasha was in a daze riding home from Gertz's, Kit going on about how jealous she'd make the kids at school. Even Sarah was convinced her girl had friends she couldn't wait to show off to.

As they pulled up to the apartment, Sarah figured a little groveling, a quick embrace, and they'd be done, but Kit asked if they'd mind her coming up for a pit stop.

"You don't need to get back to the family?" Sarah asked.

"Ma," her daughter groaned. "She wants to come up, let her come up."

Sasha led the way.

Sarah was relieved they'd left no underwear on the floor or crusty dishes in the sink. A person could eat off her spic-and-span floors, but it couldn't compare to the home Kit had made. A place that felt owned, not merely occupied. And yet Kit, refreshed from her pit stop, had nothing but compliments for Sarah. She loved the kitchen curtains and matching dish-towels Sarah had found at Goodwill. Loved the fruit bowl on the kitchen table that filled the apartment with the smell of oranges. And loved the picture Sasha had drawn when she was small, taped to the refrigerator so long ago Sarah hardly noticed it anymore. It was all so homey. So neat. What a job she'd done. Considering... *Considering what?* Sarah wondered but didn't ask. Instead, after almost not letting the woman up to pee, she giggled like a girl and offered her guest a glass of the lemonade Sasha had made for the sidewalk stand she'd wanted to set up for the holiday weekend before the shopping trip was planned. Sarah hated to see all that lemonade go to waste. Kit said lemonade would hit the spot.

Sasha found it strange, the two of them talking like friends, the only fully grown women in her life, aside from Gerri and the teacher who'd be out of her life come June. Even stranger to realize they were about the same age. Kit felt more like a big sister; her mother'd been old for as long as she could remember. Kit gave the impression of being taller but stood only an inch or so above her mother. Neither had wrinkles or veiny hands. But with all they had in common, Sasha could only see what made them different. Kit was an open book, fun-loving, kind. Sarah was impossible to read, judgmental, and rude.

"Nice and tart," Kit said after finishing her drink. She told Sarah how lucky she was to have such an enterprising daughter. Cacky thought money grew on her own personal tree. And hadn't David mentioned something about babysitting? That the professor talked to Kit about her when she wasn't there opened a life for Sasha outside of their apartment. She felt herself expanding, and then her mother had to go and ruin everything.

"Turns out she loves babies. Who knew?" Sarah laughed.

"You're the one who doesn't love babies," Sasha pouted.

"I love *my* baby. How many more should I love?" Sarah asked.

"Well, a sister might've been nice," Sasha said. "Or a brother."

"And who'd be the papa of this sister or brother?" Sarah asked.

"What do you mean, who?" Sasha said, looking to Kit for confirmation. Kit, her aunt, her role model, her friend, who'd have the perfect words to explain the obvious and wipe the sneer off Sarah's face. But Kit said nothing, staring past the Vogels to the picture of the family on the refrigerator door that said it all. Any seven-year-old might have drawn it, but Kit had raised enough kids to know the proper lineup—man, woman, child, everyone in their place, tallest to smallest, a daisy chain of balled hands—and Sasha's was all wrong. The man in the middle, his balled hands hanging at his sides, connected to no one. To his right stood a child with two dots for eyes, a straight line for a mouth, and no nose. To his left a woman with hair like a scouring pad. The man was short. On the end of a comically big nose was a pair of half-round spectacles, a bushy mustache and beard hiding his mouth. He resembled an intelligent scarecrow. An intelligent, professorial scarecrow who sparked simultaneous recognition in both women. Sasha, too, who in that moment understood there never would be a baby of the Vogel-Bloom variety to bring the ends of their circle together, cementing the new natural order that she'd thought all along *b'shert*, and not because her mother didn't love babies but because it was wrong and even worse, because Sasha had gone and made it *their* wrong.

Kit rose to her feet, a wild look in her eyes. Sarah asked if she'd care for another glass of lemonade. In those exact words, *Would you care for another glass of lemonade*? One polite housewife casually torpedoing the life of another, and Kit managed a no thank you before darting from the apartment.

Sasha was crushed, sure she'd never see her again, but Kit was too much of a lady to drop them just like that. Or maybe cutting them off would've made it too real for her. Or maybe she felt safer keeping them in her sights. Whatever the reason, the hand-me-downs, homework help, and holiday invitations kept coming, but Sasha knew things would never be the same. The Blooms and Vogels could still call themselves friends, but they were no longer family. Meanwhile, Sarah's affair with her boss simmered on.

1975

During midterms, the Queens College lit department called a cleanup session for all non-proctoring staff. Participation being voluntary, the tenured opted out. All but Bloom. He was there early and grinning like a fool when Sarah arrived. Not in the play clothes he'd been picturing but the coveralls and orthopedics that reeked of her Before.

"What?" she asked, watching his smile wash away in a cascade of disappointment.

"Nothing."

But it was never nothing. "It's the uniform, no?"

"Yes, the uniform. But why, Sarah? After all we did to get you out of it."

"It's for cleaning. We're cleaning. What did you think I'd wear?"

"I don't know. I just wanted . . ."

"What? What did you want?" Always wanting. Every note of praise hedged by his need for more.

"I wanted to know who you are when no one's around. To see a glimmer of your true style."

"What style? I have no style."

"Nonsense. Everyone does. It's what a person's about."

"Primping and shopping and being fussed over at the beauty parlor?"

"Like my wife?"

"That's not what I said . . ."

"It's what you meant. Why not say it? Kit's a fusser. She's pampered and wears makeup, okay? Not every day, but she'll do herself up for a party. Because she likes looking nice. That's *her* style. But tell me, Sarah, who's the vain one here? The woman who puts on a little makeup to feel better about going out into the world or the one who thinks she doesn't need it?"

He took a deep breath. This was not what he'd wanted. They'd come to restore, not disrupt the order in their world. He took a class syllabus from the top of a pile. It was three semesters old. "What do you think?" he said. "Keep or toss?"

"Are you saying you'd like me better in makeup?"

He sighed and looked up from his paperwork. "No, Sarah. I would hate you in makeup."

His words, kind but stopping short of tender, put more than the argument to rest, and for the remains of the morning, they cleaned, Sarah deciding the fate of every folder, While-You-Were-Out message, Boss-of-the-Year mug, and collection of pens it held. Save, toss. Save, toss. Letters from adoring students, academic awards saved. Mimeographed tests, a pair of unclaimed shoes, tossed. The windows were opened, the air let in. The leather-bound tomes of the world's august authors returned to alphabetical order. By noon, the tossing and saving was done, and the place smelled like a lemon grove.

At home, Sarah ate leftovers for lunch. By Monday, the disinfectant would have evaporated, dust would dull the sheen of their desks, and the first packets of soy sauce would begin repopulating the drawers. The predictability supported the pretense that nothing had changed. But she knew she'd be scheduling no more afternoon meetings, and for Sarah, that meant everything had changed.

By the end of the same morning, Sasha had bled through the seat of her Levi button-fly bells, the ones she'd whined, begged, and bartered for. The ones her mother, thriftiest woman in the world, had paid full price for. The ones she'd barely torn the tags from before trotting them off to school.

She'd missed the movie explaining the monthly disruption endured by all girls everywhere—Sarah had lost the permission slip for her to attend and told Sasha to tell her teacher that if it was only her permission they needed, they had it, and next time they'd still have it, so they might as well stop asking—but once the sensation of warmth began spreading beneath her, she knew. She was halfway through algebra, and her life was ending.

Between classes, a visit to the school nurse got her a pad, a note excusing her from the rest of the day's classes, and instructions for *Mom* to give her two Tylenol if she started cramping.

Walking home—drenched in shame, a sweatshirt scavenged from the Lost and Found tied around her waist and leaching the dampness from her bottom—Sasha swore she would die before telling *Mom* anything.

Before her mother got home, she cleaned herself up and buried the incriminating evidence. After supper, Sarah discovered the jeans in the trash and figured it out. It didn't take a genius to recognize the elegant symmetry of the moment, her daughter donning the cloak of womanhood just as she'd shed hers. Sasha caught in her first lie, too. But was she lying or protecting her privacy? Did a mother's right to the truth prevail over a daughter's right to secrets? Lie, secret—either way, it would be her first, and how much nicer it sounded, *Sasha's first secret*. If judging be needed, let them judge Sarah for choosing silence over worry and fixing a *glezl tey* with a spoon of raspberry jam because it always made Sasha feel better and she was still her good girl even if now biologically a woman. Those jeans were a shame, though. They could've been saved.

1978

Sasha had asked about Sarah's tattoo only once, when she was young enough to be curious and old enough to realize that mothers don't all come with numbers. Sarah sloughed it off, calling it her passport to freedom, Hitler's little gift. *How special she must be*, Sasha had thought, *getting a present from so famous a man*. She was sixteen when she learned Hitler had similarly gifted millions. It was in her high school auditorium, she and the entire student body gathered in the dark for a screening of a made-for-television miniseries called *Holocaust*.

"Show of hands," the vice principal called out. "How many here have heard of the Holocaust?"

Most of the students were too busy horsing around with their friends to comply. Sasha was embarrassed for the three who did. Like it was possible *not* to have heard of the stupid war and Hitler's gang of Nazi hoodlums. Although to be fair, the word "holocaust" had only recently popped up on their vocabulary list.

The vice principal's description of the show they were about to see included more customary vocab words, like "gripping" and "illuminating," and a warning that some might find the content upsetting. Anyone who wanted would be excused, no questions asked.

"Pussies," one of the jocks snorted from the back of the auditorium.

No one left. Like anyone would pick a boring study hall over a homework-free romp in the dark. But four mornings of made-for-television sobriety made Sasha regret mastering the signature that gave her the permission to do anything she pleased.

After, the cafeteria was eerily quiet, nothing but lunch trays rattling along the steam table's metal rails, like the sound of the Camps, which made Sasha mad. Mad at her stupid self for having thought her mother could've been the only one, mad at her mother for letting her believe, all this time, that her father was the hero of their story, mad at school for showing her how sad she should be when all she felt was mad, so mad she wished Sarah had died with the others. Not really, but now that Sarah had an excuse for being different, Sasha no longer had one for hating her. And who can a girl be safer hating than her ma?

Somewhere at the end of the line, a boy sneezed. It wasn't a real sneeze, more an unleashing of frustration, the *ah ah ahhh . . . choo*, loud and exaggerated. The responding laughter encouraged others to join in, each adding his own emphasis to the final syllable, so that by the time it reached the boy behind her, no amount of clowning could disguise its ugly message, *ah ah ahhh . . . Jew . . .* and she snapped, whipping around to face the boy, and without any thought other than to shut his big fat trap, raised her tray high over her head and slammed it down on his. The thrill of retribution was intense but short-lived. The trickle of blood from the gash got her victim's pals howling and her sent to the principal's office.

Her mother arrived soon after, baffled by the charges the secretary had relayed over the phone. "*My* Sasha? Are you sure?" Apparently, her Sasha had left no room for doubt.

Sarah, arms crossed, wanted to know since when television had replaced teachers. The principal patiently explained that the series had great educational merit. They'd seen it as "an opportunity to show the students what *really* happened, you know, back then. And yes, it was difficult material, the Holocaust was a tragedy, but they proved up to it . . . with exceptions," she said, staring down the girl in the hot seat.

"Why?" Sarah asked her daughter, getting only a wordless shrug in return.

"The boy needed five stitches," the principal added.

"So, this television show that was supposed to be good for the children wasn't so good?"

Sasha winced at the word "children."

"I understand you want to make the best case for your daughter. The experts say our youth are especially vulnerable to what they see and hear coming out of Hollywood, and frankly, I don't know what else could account for an assault of this nature by a student with so flawless a record. But you tell me, Mrs. Vogel. How can a person in my position condone such an act of violence?"

"I don't know," Sarah said, uncrossing her arms so her numbers wouldn't be missed. "I'm just a mother but seems to me people in your position find a way."

The principal blanched, a stammering apology followed, and for her act of bravery in the face of "prejudice," Sasha received a hearty commendation.

Mother and daughter caught a city bus home.

"Are we Jewish?" Sasha asked after several stops.

Sarah, high on vindication, had been replaying it all, the meeting, the turned tables, the triumphant exit, the words *we* and *Jewish* registering but not breaking through.

"Ma, are we Jewish?" Sasha asked again, bringing Sarah back to her bucket seat.

"What? Did someone say something? I knew it. What's his name? Tell me so I can kill the anti-semitten bastard."

"Calm down, Ma. It's a yes or no question." Shouting in public, even on an empty bus, topped Sasha's list of humiliations.

"Yes. No. Does it really matter?"

"Knowing what we are? Yes, it really matters."

"Saskela, we're alive. That's what we are."

But at sixteen, alive wasn't enough of a thing to be.

1979

The change in Sasha happened fast but not overnight as her mother liked to believe. There were signs. A bathroom floor covered with pale blonde hair. The rest of it dyed purple. Speaking in monosyllables. There was the week she came home with two holes in one ear; the one she came home with a surprisingly substantial bosom; then the one she stopped speaking entirely. It was an aggressive silence, most noticeable during their meals, tortuous half hours spent pushing food around her plate, pretending to chew, and once excused, holing up in her bedroom, door locked, ears plugged, nodding the night away to music only she could hear.

Gerri called it a phase, but by the start of senior year, it was official. Sasha and her purple-haired friends were full-fledged punks, which Sarah chose to see as a good sign, her daughter having friends, even if they did spend every weekend at some place called CBGB and occasionally cut class when there was an extra hot lineup for a midweek show. What did CBGB know from school nights?

To the real deals the infamous club pulled in, they were a bunch of babies in dog collars, their fishnets drawn on with Sharpies. But the bands were loud and jangly, their lyrics banal and clumsy, and whatever they thought of their audience, they lit up a path right out of the borough and away from the cushiness of the girls' homes, and if it was scary panhandling for subway fare and a slice, it was exciting, too.

They talked about dropping out, moving to the city, starting a band. And they did start one. Improper Fractions, they called it. Though it ran aground soon after the naming. They all wanted lead, and none knew a sharp from a flat.

On the Wednesday before Thanksgiving break, the principal nabbed Sasha for wearing an unlawful T-shirt to school. The tee was tight and clingy, but it was the hand-printed logo stretching across the bust that drew the principal's ire—Kikes & Kockettes, a statement on its own, but also the name of the next pretend band she planned to start. The principal was new to the post and to Sasha Vogel, but a quick scan of her file revealed a good girl on a steep decline. Was she looking to leave high school with the reputation of a troublemaker? he asked.

"I prefer provocateur," she told him.

He said he'd let her know after the break what they'd do with her and called her mother to pick her up. Weary of the demands this new creature was imposing on her life, Sarah told him to do what he had to do. *She* wouldn't be leaving her office until leaving time.

The principal sent Sasha home on her own.

"Get it over with" was the greeting Sarah received as she walked in the door that night.

"Get what over with?"

"I know you're mad."

"Me? Mad?" Her daughter, still wearing the offending tee, sprawled the length of the divan, her spiked hair stabbing the cushions. "It's your life."

"It'll go on my record if I'm suspended."

"I know."

"Which won't look good for getting into college."

"It won't."

Both knew Bloom was waiting in the wings, ready to pull the strings to get her into Queens, if necessary. All she had to do was graduate. Only yesterday, that seemed a given.

"At least we know what you *won't* be wearing to Kit and David's this year." Sarah laughed, hoping to bring the conversation to safer ground.

"Who said I'm going to Kit and David's?"

Was there no safer ground anymore?

"We always go for Thanksgiving. I told them we're coming."

"You should've asked me first. And why do *you* want to go?" Sasha jabbed like a fighter. "It's not like you're friends anymore."

"Don't say that," Sarah said, her voice rising. "Why would you say that?"

"Oh my God," Sasha groaned. "Are you blind or just stupid?"

"You tell me, you're so smart all of a sudden."

There was a well-timed knock at the door. It was Gerri. She must have heard them shouting or she would have walked right in.

Sasha went to her room, loaded the turntable, and cranked the volume, but nothing could compete with those harpies once they got going. Even when they were on the same side.

In this case, her mother didn't seem to care about her going to the Blooms, only that she be taught the importance of commitment. And Gerri agreed, in principle.

"She needs teaching? I'll teach her. D'Agostino's for two. Just her and me. Allll the trimmings."

Knowing neither woman would be happy until they made her do the thing she least wanted, Sasha put on her trashiest clothes, painted her face, teased her hair, grabbed her fake ID, and walked right out the front door, the two biddies staring after her.

She took the train to Manhattan and bluffed her way into an East Village joint she'd heard about where a boy she had an instant crush on paid her way in and told her to go to the bar if she wanted a beer, which was too expensive, but the pills—blue ones, black ones—were plentiful, easy to swallow, and free, and the music pounced like an ambush, and the light show was radioactive, and people matted together on the dance floor, and the object of her crush took her to the bathroom and bent her over the sink, and she wasn't sure if she said or thought *I don't want to*, but who could tell the difference between saying and thinking, or if it was the music or the grind of porcelain, or if crashing on a sofa that hemorrhaged stuffing and smelled of cat was better than going home to relieve the suffering of a pair of old birds in wait. Whatever. She'd never tell anyone how she got pregnant. Or ask about her ma's Thanksgiving with the Blooms.

1980

At the age of thirty-seven, worry had caught up with Sarah. Sasha's morning sickness was bad and stayed that way longer than it should have. Every day, she threatened to quit school.

Coca-Cola was the only thing that would stay down, and sugary sodas had just been banned from the cafeteria. Sarah took her to a doctor.

"People have babies all the time," said the silver-haired ob-gyn whose belly strained at the buttons of his white coat.

"People, sure. Not *my* baby," she told him. He encouraged her to reach out to her circle of family and friends. A challenging circle to plot.

There was Gerri, burning candles for them, and though there weren't enough candles in the city to burn away a misfortune the size of the Vogels', Sarah knew she would stand by her, by them both, by the eventual three of them, if only to show the neighbors how magnanimous she could be. Sarah would never hear the end of it.

There was Bloom, who received the news with characteristic gusto, picking Sarah up off her feet and waltzing her around the office, a lapse he begged her to forgive. They hadn't touched in several years, but he was dying for someone to call him Grandpa and Cacky wasn't even close to thinking about kids. Only he could rub Sarah's nose in disgrace and make it seem like a good thing.

There was Kit. True, as Sasha had bluntly noted, they weren't friends anymore. Truer that they'd never been friends. Yet as cooled off to Sarah as she'd become, who but Kit would care that Sasha had curled into a ball on the couch and stopped eating or communicating or going to school or band practice or anything? Who else would understand that however impetuous and impractical it may be, this baby was turning Sarah goofy with joy? And with Sasha tumbling into a deep well of helplessness, knowing the more her mother did for her the more helpless she'd feel, and the more helpless she felt the more Coke she'd drink, and the more Coke she drank the more television she'd watch, and the more television she watched the tighter her little ball became, even while her mother kept stopping at school for homework she'd never look at and the diner for rice pudding she'd never touch . . . who else but Kit would understand it's the useless things we do that remind us to breathe?

Not the school counselor, who remained irrepressibly optimistic about Sasha's chances of getting a college degree *and* having some sort of life but for the time being could only pass along the school's referral list of therapists.

Sarah made an appointment with one specializing in family matters. Their family of two arrived early. Sarah found it fishy that they were the only customers in the waiting room.

The doctor spent thirty-five minutes alone with Sasha, Sarah flipping through old *Ms.* magazines, certain she'd be told that her daughter's downward slide was unstoppable, they were doomed, and it was all her fault. But the actual prognosis was worse, the doctor pronouncing the patient's emotional state "perfectly within the range of normal."

"You can't give her a pill or something?" Sarah asked.

"An anti-depressant *might* help, uh . . ."

"Sasha," Sarah reminded him.

"Yes, Sasha . . . *if* she were depressed. But as it is, all I can prescribe is time and patience. And perhaps some weekly sessions of talk therapy . . . if you're interested." The doctor buzzed reception. Their time was up.

Gerri offered a more direct approach.

"A week's pay for a few minutes of hocus-pocus? It's a baby she's got in her, not cancer. All you gotta do is get her back to school so she graduates. Then you and me, we'll see what's what."

Who needed a therapist? Or Kit Bloom? If Sasha guzzled Coke for the duration, it was fine by her.

The baby came on August sixteenth. The ob-gyn was on vacation. His answering service assured them there was a bank of fine doctors on call. Sarah packed a bag and called a cab to take them to the hospital. The delivery was smooth. The baby, a girl, was small but perfect. Amazing how it just slips right out when they're young and resilient, one of the nurses said.

Young and resilient as she was, a low-grade fever kept Sasha in the hospital for two nights. Dehydration the probable cause. The nurse brought pitchers of ice water, which she wouldn't touch so Sarah smuggled in a cold can of Coke. *That* she drank. Bloom and Kit showed up—she with polite congratulations and a basket of baby clothes, he with typical grandstanding flair and a big bunch of balloons. Gerri came with flowers and a bear wearing a *Hug Me* T-shirt.

Soon they were discharged, and a nurse came to wheel her daughter, holding *her* daughter and the balloons, to the hospital's portico. From there, they were on their own. The nurse told them they could keep the wheelchair until a taxi showed up. The sidewalk had been washed clean by an early morning downpour. The smell of blacktop rose from the parking lot. There, under the clearing sky, Sarah made two decisions: One, they would call the baby Malcah (because what little girl doesn't deserve to be a queen?), and two, she would do whatever it took to put Sasha back together.

It was bold, asking for leave to stay home with someone else's baby, but Sarah had no recourse. Sasha never came around. If anything, she got worse. Sleeping on the divan—day, night—like she didn't have a bedroom of her own.

"Everyone gets the squat and push blues," Gerri counseled. "You don't remember is all."

"I remember plenty. I was scared, not blue."

"Same difference."

"Does she worry about losing a job if she's late, even once? Is she up all night shushing and rocking so they're not thrown out on the street? And what a crier, this one. I can't leave the house in the morning without my heart breaking."

"So, stay home. Take a leave of absence. People do these days."

"Like I can afford to lose my job," Sarah said.

"With all you got on the professor, he should give you the leave and throw in a bonus."

Sarah didn't have the stomach for blackmail but couldn't trust her daughter to minister to the baby's most basic needs. And she was missing so much. Every gurgle, every smile another first.

"Hey, who's gonna fire you for asking?"

As Gerri suspected, no blackmail was required. Bloom had waited a long time to prove his dedication, his worth, his *menschlichkeit*, and presented her case to the college's review committee as if it'd been his idea all along. Sarah Vogel hadn't missed a day of work in ten years, he argued. She'd accrued enough vacation and sick days to last her another ten. The least this valued employee deserved was her requested three months off, *with pay*. Surprisingly, the reviewers agreed.

They spent several weeks indoors, safe from the ever-present array of outdoor hostilities—exhaust-ridden air, honking horns, pigeon shit, dog shit, the shit of vagrants. But with the first cool breath of fall, Sarah strapped the baby to her chest and headed to a nearby park. It was protected by a sturdy-looking gate and rimmed in tall maples that danced with the gentlest breeze. Only small children and caregivers allowed. With two bottles of formula, a pacifier, and a twenty for emergencies, she felt organized, fit, and filled with disdain for the platoon of young mommies and nannies from the neighborhood, their doll-sized strollers straining under the weight of provisions: sunblock, hats, diapers, wipes, rash-smothering creams, rattles, plush toys, band-aids, baby Tylenol, picnic blankets, ergonomic bottles, juice boxes, Goldfish-stuffed Ziplocs for the toddlers, Kahlúa-laced slushies for their mothers.

By the end of the day—the Snugli's straps cutting into her hips, both bottles emptied, and Malcah's only diaper soaked through—Sarah knew she'd be joining the stroller brigade.

She found a big, boxy Silver Cross at Goodwill. It was old-fashioned and mildewy but sturdier than any she'd seen in the park. And the price was right.

Her building super, Al, who always watched out for her, offered to hose it down, plump its flattened tires, and clear a space outside the front door where it could be parked. Sarah wasn't happy about leaving it untended. "Lady," Al the Super said, "no one's gonna mess with this tank, but you wanna schlepp it up and down the stairs every time the kid needs some fresh air, it's your back."

She left it in his hands and thanked him for his trouble.

Upstairs, her daughter was on the couch napping. Sarah couldn't wait to tell her all about the new carriage and gave her shoulder a shake. Sasha half-opened her eyes, rolled over, and fell back to sleep.

After dinner, Sarah went down to check on things and found the Silver Cross parked where she'd left it, clean from its shower, only a hint of mildew remaining.

The next morning, she took her new tank for a spin. Under the navy-blue canopy, her little queen lay sheltered from everything but her own dreams. Sarah felt invincible. She made a mental note to pick up a bottle of schnapps for Al the Super on the way home. And maybe a bicycle lock, just in case.

It took Bloom showing up at the door for Sarah to realize she missed him. His amends for not coming earlier included a bottle of Stoli for her, another bear for Malcah, a family-size bag of M&Ms for Sasha, and profuse apologies for his dereliction of duty. He'd been busy. Lots of departmental changes. He wouldn't bore them with office talk. She'd be back at her desk soon enough. "But Sarah, my God you look good." He stared. The baby was cradled in the crook of her arm. "I guess I've never seen this side of you before."

"What side is that?" Sarah asked, shifting the baby to her left arm, trying to remember what she'd missed about him.

"The mothery side."

"And which is my unmothery side?"

"Okay, that was insensitive, but the way you are with her . . . well, it's a beautiful thing. Right, Sasha?"

They were at the kitchen table, Sarah gazing at Malcah, Bloom gazing at her, Sasha sorting the M&Ms into color piles and processing the truth Bloom had nailed, that Sarah had never looked at *her* like she was the baby Jesus or come running at her every sniffle or narrated her way through the day in that gooey warble that made her sound like a crazy woman.

"Boy, though, she's your spitting image," Bloom said. Like it was a compliment.

Sasha shrugged. "That's what they say. I don't see it."

"You will. One day I could swear Cacky's her mother's twin and the next it's like I'm looking in the mirror."

"Yeah, well, there's just me, so . . ."

The professor looked crestfallen. *Serves you right,* Sasha thought. Feeling so pleased with himself. Thinking he'd saved her from sleeping her life away on the couch. Like it was possible to sleep in a room next to a gurgling, snuffling baby. Like it was any business of his where she slept or when she needed a break from it all. She wouldn't allow Bloom the satisfaction of thinking he'd fixed her. The last thing she needed was for her mother to think she was fixed (whatever that meant) and up to tackling her stupid to-do list, the college applications and job interviews, next steps, and mommy-and-me classes . . . future shit. As she played with her color-coded mounds of M&Ms, crushing candies one at a time, then sucking the coating from her thumb, it occurred to Sasha that as much as her mother wanted her grandbaby to stay a baby was how much she wanted her daughter to grow up, and that, she could assure everyone, wouldn't be happening any time soon.

"Why are you here anyway?" she asked the professor, looking up from her emerald green thumb.

"Sasha? David's our friend."

"More than friends," Bloom added. "We're family, kiddo."

Sasha smirked. "But we're not, though, David. Can we stop pretending?"

"That's enough. Nobody talks like that in this house." Sarah's fury had tightened into a harsh whisper. God forbid she should wake the baby Jesus.

"Well, okay then . . . *Mother*," Sasha said and marched to the door.

"Where do you think you're going?"

"Out."

What could it matter if a slammed door woke the kid? She had a grandmother happy to rock her back to sleep, and Sasha had a craving for pizza.

It was time for Bloom to leave as well. Sarah, cradling the baby, walked him to the door.

"We are friends, aren't we, Sarah?" Bloom whispered.

"Nobody can say we're not."

"There was so much more I should've done."

"Look, my girl hasn't left the house since the baby came. Tonight, you made a miracle."

He laughed and gave her a peck on both cheeks. He was no miracle man but headed down the hallway, his old swagger regained.

It was the end of a long day. An even longer evening lay ahead. Weary of the bouncing and swaying, Sarah let the baby cry herself to sleep, got into her nightgown, and curled up on the couch to await her daughter's return.

Beyond pestering range, Sasha took the opportunity to get stoned for the first time in forever. Who could fault her? Someone had shown up at the pizzeria with weed, weed laced with angel dust, a legend of a drug she'd've had to be some kind of nun to pass up. Two hits were enough to ignite the walls of the place and, once she could pull herself out of her chair, light a way home for her and her friends. All of them guys. One pretty mouthy. The others, no mouths at all. And they weren't really friends. Just the freaks who'd gotten her high, by then a high on its third or fourth bloom.

Out on the street, the moon was a klieg light. She could see the way home with her eyes shut. The entourage of stoners followed, eyes wide open. It occurred to her that there were many possible reasons why. None of them good.

Don't let them see where you live, she told herself. *DON'T. STOP. WALKING.* But as she neared the apartment building housing her sleeping mother and child, she couldn't *not* stop.

"Uh, I'll see you guys around," she said, hoping to convey how little she cared.

"Uh, no you won't," said the mouthy one, detecting beneath her nonchalance something he knew could be twisted into fear. "We're coming with you."

"No, you're not," she said.

One tried stuffing himself into Sarah's Silver Cross, which squealed like a beaten animal. The others laughed. The mouthy one moved closer. "Yeah, we are."

"Look, my mother's up there and she's old." Why hadn't she stayed on the couch?

"Yeah, but see . . ." He moved closer still. "We wanna, so we are." Which might've been the last word on the subject had a man not appeared in the vestibule. Or maybe he'd been there all along, staring at them through the door's window of wired glass, an impassive hulk holding a garbage bag in each hand. It was Al the Super, on the job in the middle of the night.

"Forget your key, Miss Vogel?" he shouted through the closed door.

Sasha nodded. She didn't like Al the Super but was glad to see him.

"Come on, then," he said, dropping his bags and opening the door just enough to let her through. The others tried to push in after her.

"Not you," he barked at the mouthy one. Al was stronger than he looked and hadn't had any angel dust. Only a Bud or two, judging by his breath.

On the other side of the door, Mouthy put his hands up like Al was a cop, not the hired help. "Ain't looking for trouble, man."

"You don't leave now, you found it, *man*. And you," Al shouted at the one half in and half out of the Silver Cross. "Get your ass outta that buggy. NOW."

The squealing stopped. The pack loped off to refresh their high. On the safe side of the door, there was only the buzz of fluorescence.

"You okay?" Al asked.

Sasha nodded and left him to his work.

Once in the apartment, she felt her way around, sneaking past her sleeping mother to the room with the crib that held her sleeping daughter. Within the cave-like darkness, Malcah was a human glow stick. Drool slumped like a strand of pearls from her rosebud mouth. She was the most beautiful thing Sasha had ever seen, and she stood there watching until the night ended and her daughter turned back into a regular baby, still beautiful but in the dull light of a city morning, no longer fluorescing.

Sarah woke feeling like she'd spent the night in someone else's bathwater. She didn't know how long she'd been dozing, only that Malcah should be crying and wasn't.

She was surprised to find Sasha in the bedroom clutching the rail of the crib, singing softly . . . *loo la loo* . . . her mothery side loosed.

"It's all right to touch her, you know," Sarah said, wanting her daughter to have this moment alone with her baby, wanting as much to be part of it.

"That'll wake her," Sasha mumbled.

"She's yours to wake."

"But I don't want to."

"What *do* you want?"

Sasha laughed. "You're asking now?"

"When else?"

"Like maybe seven thousand times since I was born."

"And tell me, Saskela, those seven thousand times, who was asking what I wanted?"

Sasha sighed in surrender, leaning over the rail into the crib. "Why weren't you the boy you were supposed to be?"

"What kind of talk is that?" Sarah said, stepping into the room. "A boy, a girl. What does it matter? It's your baby."

Sasha turned to face her mother. Her eyes were glassy, the pupils big as dimes.

"All Papa wanted was a boy, and you and me, all we do is disappoint."

"Sasha . . ."

"I'm tired, Ma. Let it go." She pushed past Sarah.

With the creak of sofa springs, the baby stirred.

Sarah clutched the crib rail, afraid to let go, afraid her will was the only thing powering the rise and fall of the baby's chest, the rhythmic flexing of those tiny fingers. But then, she was always afraid of the wrong things. She'd never worried about drugs, for instance, though everyone else had. For good reason. She'd seen the kids wandering the streets, staring dully into the air. None of them drank anymore. Too bad. Drink made you loud and sloppy but mostly kept to evening hours and left you sorry the next day. Drugs left people unmoored, doddering around no matter the hour like old people tickled by their own forgetfulness. She'd felt shame for their parents. She should've saved some for herself.

The baby would be up soon. No use going back to bed. She boiled water to warm a bottle and make a cup of instant coffee. Standing at the counter, she savored the moment on her own.

Malcah's pre-cry sputtering hurried her back to the bedroom. She fed, washed, and dressed her, packed their things, and blew a kiss to Sasha, whose back was turned, dead to the world. Or pretending to be.

Outside, the air was fresh and kind. Malcah settled in for the ride, squawking as the first rays of morning sun fell across her face. Unfolding the carriage hood didn't help. It took Sarah a moment to see why. The bonnet's pleats were in tatters. Someone had taken a knife to her Silver Cross.

She ran all the way home and unleashed her panic on Al the Super. "You said it would be safe," she cried, panting as she raised the hood.

"The bastards," Al cursed.

"What bastards? You saw them?"

"No ma'am. Musta been on my break is all I can think."

"Who would do such a thing?"

"I'll tell you who. Some dirty, drugged-up, punked-out, no-good kids is who." How close he was to ratting out that wild daughter and those crap friends of hers. "These streets, Mrs. Vogel? They're a misery."

Gerri Eyes-on-the-Street Capogrosso was even less helpful. She'd slept through the night and bet Al the Super had done the same. She'd never trusted him or his bad advice. But Sarah was starting to think he was the only one to trust. Maybe, like he said, it was these streets they couldn't trust. Maybe it was time to find better ones.

1981

Who knew a house could be bought sight unseen, five hundred miles away, in a small town surrounded by the gentle hills of Ohio's farmland?

As the realtor's pictures indicated, the little ranch was not new but had all the modern conveniences. Two telephones—one anchored to the wall in the kitchen, one on a shelf in the hallway between the two bedrooms—a refrigerator/freezer; a roomy electric range and dishwasher, both excellent for storing pots and pans; air conditioners set into the walls of the master bedroom and living room; speckled gray wall-to-wall carpeting throughout; a parqueted foyer; two baths, one a cake batter yellow with a tub *and* a shower, the other egg-yolk yellow, with a sink only big enough for hands. Behind the house was a patio laid with stone, a backyard that was part of a blanket of backyards, a paved driveway that led into the garage that led into the house, a front yard where a patch of clover had gone to flower, and a basement where she found a lawnmower and a plastic jug of gasoline. The tract included 374 other houses that looked the same.

The realtor called it a steal at $32,500. The owners had bought into one of the area's newer tracts and were eager to move. After seventeen years of scrimping, Sarah's savings, which took an evening to count and recount, amounted to $33,958. The next morning, she wired the cash to the seller's bank. Nothing in her life had been easier. The remaining balance would be enough to set up house. And the job Bloom had gotten her—their reason for being there—meant she could start saving right away. She heard it rained a lot in Ohio.

Poor Bloom. If Gerri was devastated, he was abject. They'd survived the end of their affair and reached a plateau of comfort. Knowing they'd soon say goodbye for good seemed only to rekindle his hunger for her. Not for the sex part, just for them. But she needed to be somewhere Sasha could come to love her again, somewhere Malcah could be safe, and he rose to the occasion, doing all he could to ease their exit and ensure Sasha could still go to college. The baby, too, if Sarah stuck it out.

She refused his offer of airfare. She'd already bought train tickets, and planes got hijacked.

"Jesus, Sarah, what are the chances? One in a million?"

"You always say I'm one in a million."

"But trains take forever."

"This trip will take the time it takes," she told him. "I think it will be relaxing."

There was nothing left for him to do but drive them to Penn Station. His wife sent her best wishes but didn't come along.

"You'll write, yes?" he asked.

Sarah nodded.

"No, you won't," he said.

How thoroughly he knew her was a sweet kind of pain.

She never got the chance to tell him, but the trip was awful. The train's rocking wasn't at all relaxing. Sasha slept the whole way, and the baby never stopped crying, Sarah curled around her, pumping her full of formula while half-dreaming a familiar strangeness of sound and rhythm and closeness. They arrived at their new address in a shock of early morning light, unprepared for the relentless vastness outside, the empty vastness within.

There was plenty to unpack but nowhere to put anything. She'd left their furniture (the *Yanitellis'* furniture) behind, figuring a bag full of blankets and pillows could tide them over until she figured out what they'd need. A 1975 Rambler parked in a driveway three doors down had a *for sale* sign taped to the windshield, and Sarah bought it, no questions asked. Before the baby, Sasha had gotten her driver's license, and that afternoon, Sarah had her drive them to the bank so she could open her first checking account. She'd brought every document she had: their freshly minted citizenship papers, a letter from her new boss at Kent State, her lien-free deed.

"All's I need is your money, ma'am," the teller told her.

"This is all of it," Sarah said, handing over her rubber-banded roll. "It'll be safe?"

"Sure will, but it goes fast when you're starting out in a new place, and a lot of our customers find a home equity loan helpful," the teller said without losing count.

Sarah had no interest in owing anyone anything, but two men in suits were already headed their way, and it didn't take them long to wear her down. Who said a bank was *anyone* anyway? Besides, her granddaughter deserved a nice place to grow up in, a place with curtains, beds, sofas, and lamps. Sarah signed on their dotted line and walked out of the bank with a stack of temporary checks, a booklet for recording each loan payment, and the name of a straight-arrow furniture dealer known for friendly prices and layaway plans, though Sarah would be laying nothing away.

The next day, she parked herself on her front stoop and waited for the truck. It came right on time. She'd paid for curbside delivery, but the wiry driver and his burly helper, taking pity on a single mother, pulled out their white gloves and moved everything in and around until it was exactly the way she wanted—her splurge of a new queen in the master bedroom for Sasha—she'd be needing her sleep—and the crib and twin bed in the smaller bedroom so Sarah could stay with the baby for the time being

Waking to their first furnished morning, she carried Malcah to their new kitchen, strapped her into her new Kanga-Rock-a-Roo, and, to the optimistic sound of perking coffee, congratulated herself for getting this one thing right.

Malcah, in seeming agreement, gurgled something Sarah identified as a word. If her ears weren't deceiving her, that word was "Ma."

"Yes," Sarah cooed with delight. "We're so clever this morning. Again, dolly. Mama." She took the pot from the burner and poured herself a cup, repeating, "Ma . . . ma."

"Ma . . . ma," came the tiny creature's reward.

"That's it. Mama, Ma-ma," Sarah trilled, lifting her from the Kanga-Rock-a-Roo and running with her to wake the young woman whose rightful name the baby had mastered. But the room was empty, the bed made. Sarah was confused. Was it not morning? Had they not planned to take Malcah to meet her pediatrician? Had Sasha ever made a bed?

But it hadn't been *made*, the bed was never slept in. On it lay a letter written in bright turquoise ink.

Ma, it began.

Last night I was thinking about elementary school and the girls in my class who had all these gods to pray to for a Cricket doll or a 100 on a spelling test. Remember? I asked which god was ours so I wouldn't waste a prayer on the wrong one, and you said, Open your eyes, Saskela, you see any room for God in this place? And you were so right. There was never room for anyone but the two of us. Now there are three, and even in Ohio, where there's nothing but room, I couldn't sleep wondering if we'd ever all fit.

Remember the shoes Kit bought me? Those black velvet things I said I loved? Well, I only said that to please her. Truth is I hated them. I tried to sneak out of the house in my Keds the first day of school, but you caught me. No one noticed—me or them—but I was embarrassed. They were so big and indestructible, I was sure I'd be stuck wearing them forever, so I started dragging my feet until I wore a bald spot on each toe, and you went crazy, remember? Making me go back to Gertz's with you to call out the salesclerk for pawning off inferior merchandise on a hard-working woman who may have had an accent, but her money sure didn't. And he made the mistake of blaming it on me, and you yelled so loud they had to call the manager, who thought a new pair would make you shut up and go away, but you set him straight. I should take more bum shoes from you? You took my arm and marched us right out of there. I wanted to die on the spot, but Ma, I was proud, too. I didn't say it then because I was so pissed. I knew you were fucking the professor way before I knew what fucking was. I just never knew there was anything wrong with it. I mean to any kid fucking is gross and generally wrong, but if you had to fuck someone, it never occurred to me that fucking David Bloom would be any wronger than fucking anyone else in the world. He was part of our us. Because of him, there was always a place for me to draw or read or just stare out the window. And because of him there was Kit. Beautiful Kit. The solution to every problem, a smile as warm as the sun, part of our us, so when you tore her to pieces and thought you'd fix it with a glass of lemonade? I don't know, maybe I was just pissed for being such an idiot, believing that mothers might do terrible things sometimes but never lie, and then you went and let me catch you in a whopper. And Kit, who'd never been anything but nice to us. You should've done better, Ma.

But same goes for me, so I won't lie. I'm pissed, but not about Kit anymore. You made me believe my father was a giant, and here I am, still believing in giants, which of course don't exist, except for maybe you, bigger than life, maybe too big for life. But you never showered me with things I didn't need or fluffed me up with fairy tales. You fought for me and would've died for me and understood that eventually I'd outgrow you, like a pair of shoes. But I had to leave before that happened. Before Malcah made me her champion because I'm not ready for that and not sure I ever will be.

Love her in your way. Tell her the story of her Russian grandfather, but tell her yours, too. Teach her that the customer is always right and that she is always the customer. Tell her to always start with the peach cobbler so she won't ever be too full for the good things in life. Let her know that someday she'll have to stand on her own two feet, and it's never too soon to start.

If you're lucky, our little queen will hate me enough not to have to hate you.

—Sasha

I'll need my own driver's license was Sarah's first thought. And then a tornado started drilling its way from the top of her cloud-packed skull to the silty bottom of her bowels, annihilating all thought. Sarah carried the baby to the kitchen to check the yard for signs of life. She wanted more than signs. She wanted Sasha. She'd move them back to New York if that's what it took. She'd never again mention college or jobs. She'd only wanted more for her daughter, but who should know better than her that the more you get, the more there is to lose? Malcah gurgled unintelligibly, a tiny hand on the place where the tornado churned hardest. It didn't make sense, a sky so blue, the earth under siege.

She dialed the Blooms. Kit answered. They hadn't seen or heard from Sasha. They'd call if they did. Kit was certain everything would be fine. *Our Sasha's a good girl*, she said. The bubbly certainty coating the possessive got Sarah counting the nights, seventeen years of them, spent in fear of losing her. And now she was gone. There was a baby, though, to feed and amuse and put to sleep, and Sarah moved through the tasks singing her song with no words. When finally she closed her eyes, her greatest fear realized, worry now useless, the relief she allowed herself for that night only worked like a drug. In the morning, she went to the police. She didn't show them the letter, afraid they wouldn't look hard enough for a runaway. Afraid of what they'd do if they found her. At some point during the interview with her assigned officer, Sarah began feeling like *she* was the criminal.

1982

That spring, spent from her day assisting the very driven dean of Women's Studies at Kent State University, Sarah received a collect call that included little information and long silences but proved the girl she'd lost knew how to call home and wasn't dead in a gutter.

1983

By the next spring, noticing a whole hour could now pass without a thought of her lost girl, Sarah began to face facts. Though Sasha would remain a permanent resident of her head and heart, a forever weight on her shoulders and limbs, it was possible she'd never see her again.

There'd been no word from the Blooms in over a year, and she was *sure* she'd never see them again. Her letter to Gerri had come back "Addressee Unknown." Dead in the ground, living the life on Miami Beach, or, more likely, warehoused in a nursing home. She knew Bloom's friend Glory (short for Gloria) Hall, now her boss, had been told only that her new hire was a single mother, no mention of the child's name or age—she'd written the recommendation letter. The neighbors had never met Sasha, nor had the grocer, nor the replacement for the teller who'd been so helpful when they first arrived. The police had stopped answering the worried mother's calls. And who but Sarah was around to answer when the baby said her first word, *Mama*

That winter, she packed away the tangible evidence of Sasha Vogel's existence—the picture of her on Santa's lap, the stick figure family, the Kikes & Kockettes T-shirt, the immunization record—and began adoption proceedings.

The following fall, she sent Malcah Vogel to kindergarten as her own.

1989

By the time she arrived at the gym to pick up Malcah from dance class and meet a man unlike any other, they'd been in their "new" home for eight years. Long enough for people to stop asking about the Big Apple, how she could have stood it, how she could have left it. No more did she have to explain that whatever she dropped fell to the ground in Stow like it had in Kew Gardens. There was an office here as there was there, also files and Rolodexes and people to tell her what to do. Only the teller was new. Here it was a professor of feminist studies, not a young woman but younger than Sarah, no fan of dead men's tales, and committed to the proposition that all workers are created equal. She was paid more not because she was the boss but because she sent her assistants to the library for books, not to the dry cleaners for laundry. There was still a large personality to manage. The uncomplicated friendship with that large personality might be new, but it would not have been forged if there wasn't still a living to be made.

Sometime within those eight years, Sarah became a citizen of Ohio, though hers was still the only accent in a sea of plain-talking folk, their home the lone holdout in a neighborhood covered in twinkling lights throughout December. There were still drawings to tape to the refrigerator and sweaty brows to mop; tears over homework followed by fits of little-girl chuckles followed by gloom, snowfall, and rain. The collections were new. Milk cartons with cheery mugshots of children gone in the blink of an eye, so many cartons rinsed, air-dried, and arranged on the kitchen counter. Photos of mass weddings clipped from newspapers, hundreds of devout brides, any one of whom could be the daughter whose name was never spoken. A stash of silver dollars for Ohio's tooth fairy to leave in place of the baby teeth she'd find tucked under Malcah's pillow. And if the hole in her chest had been emptied of fear, the dread replacing it touched everything in view, from the brilliant summer sun to the solemn Midwest winter.

But then, on a stormy Thursday in September, in the gymnasium of their children's school, a man named Walter Fields made her feel like a beauty, and *that* was new. Viktor Aleksandr would have said she'd been one all along, and David Bloom would have concurred, but Walter Fields was the first she believed. He wasn't a poet or Russian or prone to hyperbole. When she made light of his compliments, he'd tell her men were easy liars, but mirrors were far less agile. And slowly, she began to see what he saw—the lift to her chin, the bit of chisel to her cheek, an invigorated spread to her narrow shoulders. It was a kind of new that would never feel normal. The once ugly were always prepared for its return.

The children, Malcah and Robbie, were enrolled in the same ballroom dancing class. Theirs were the only parents who'd never met. The rest not only knew each other but, decades earlier, on Thursdays after school, had gathered at the same gymnasium performing the identical weekly exercise. Styles were different—the boys in bow ties, the girls in white gloves—but the same teacher was there shaking her tambourine and pairing up her flock with the same disregard for height, temperament, or halitosis, and making the leftover girls dance with each other so if ever they were invited to thread their arms through a man's embrace, they could at least do a decent box step. The mothers agreed it was torture, but they'd endured, and it was now their duty to see that their offspring endure the same.

Walter and his wife, Jan, divorced when Robbie was five. She'd automatically taken charge of extracurriculars, and he was okay with that, happy to wait for the meaty conversations they'd have once his son grew up. But Robbie not only grew up, he grew away. Now they struggled for anything to talk about, teaching Walter that waiting must never be mistaken for a course of action, and if he wanted to be part of the boy's life, he needed to step up to the plate. Give me a job, he'd begged his ex. His reward was dance duty.

Pickup was at four, but he arrived every Thursday by half past three, always with a book in hand. He found reading in public one of life's great pleasures *and* a message that he was a man without time for idle gossip. Message received.

He never imagined a woman could provide greater diversion than his books, but the moment Sarah pushed her way through the steel doors, he was a goner. Hair you could lose your fingers in, an accent you could cut with a knife, a voice so gunked with nicotine that he wanted to take her in his arms and save her from herself. She was part gypsy, part Buddhist nun, at once scrubbed and adorned, her skirt sweeping the polished blonde wood, her feet in strappy sandals, dirt under the toenails, a crocheted satchel dangling from her shoulder. She put a hand over her eyes, studying the jagged line of children waiting for the music to start their last dance, and then scowled at the grand arch of ceiling, its high-wattage light redundant in the wash of afternoon sun. Her bare arms were sinewy. Even from a distance, he could read the signature that told him she was a Survivor. The word evoked a larger person, but she reminded him of a tiny bird he'd once watched flit about an airport terminal, an explorer both panicked and marvelously oblivious to the restless travelers below.

"Walter Fields," he said, extending his hand. Her hand lost in his, she gave her name.

"Well, Sarah Vogel, join me in the viewing stands?"

Lightly cupping her elbow, he guided her to the metal bleachers where they sat shoulder to shoulder.

"That one's mine," he said, pointing at a boy wearing a worried look. "Robbie."

"Handsome," she said.

"And yours?"

"There," she said, pointing to Malcah in her swirling skirt and open-toed sandals.

"Ah," he said, staring at Sarah. "Lovely."

It was true, she realized. It had taken someone else to see, but indeed, Malcah had a beauty all her own. Small like Sarah, but more delicate than meager. Eyes like Sarah's, but more curious than skeptical. Hair like Sarah's, but a dark frame of tender waves rather than a wiry wilderness to hide behind. The blueprint of the original was there in her face. But all her own was that skin, cream poured fresh from a pitcher, and the pink teardrop of gum lodged in the opening between her two front teeth, inheritance from another mother.

The last dance was a waltz. Sarah tapped her foot to the beat. The children mouthed *one*, two, three, *one*, two, three and hurried their steps across the polished floor, stiff-armed, wooden-legged. The top of Malcah's partner's head came only to her shoulder. *Poor boy*, Sarah thought. Malcah was no amazon.

The music reached its crescendo, prompting the leads to spin their partners, which they did with youthful gallantry. Malcah ducked to pass under her boy's arm, skirt fluttering. Sarah knew she'd never hear the end of it—the other girls' skirts were too snug to flutter.

When it was over, the dancers rushed to lobby their parents for play dates. Malcah had no friends and couldn't get away fast enough. Robbie did but always went for ice cream with his dad after dance class, just the two of them, a tradition he'd thought was sacrosanct, until his dad went and asked the Vogels to come along.

They walked through the rain to their cars, Walter's umbrella big enough for them all. Sarah had never been to the ice cream parlor. "Follow me," Walter said.

Malcah knew they were on a road that dead-ended in humiliation, but what could she do? She was only a kid.

At the ice cream parlor, Malcah slid in next to Sarah on one side of the booth, Robbie and Walter on the other. The kids looked everywhere but at each other. The adults, nowhere else.

Walter was amazed they'd worked at the same place for nine years without crossing paths. Sarah wasn't. For her, the world was as big as it was small. For him, a theology professor, there was mystery in everything. Why not coincidence? That anyone would pay tuition to learn about God was her idea of mystery.

"If it helps," he said, smiling, "I'm an atheist. Teaching about God keeps me ahead of the competition."

"Even worse," she said, returning his smile.

Malcah, only ten, knew they were flirting and was horrified. This man with his shaggy brow and freckled hands and reading glasses that wouldn't sit straight on his nose. Everything about him was old except his teeth, which were so large and straight and white she was sure he must take them out at night. Probably why he smiled so much. Sarah's teeth were small and blunt. Normally, she hid them, but for him she smiled like a fool.

Walter ordered coffee for the adults and sundaes for everyone. When their order came, even Malcah lifted her chin off her fists. Sarah pushed the cherry on the top to the side for later, dipped her spoon into the whipped cream and, in small scoops, mined her way to the nuts, then the chocolate, and finally the vanilla ice cream melting at the bottom of the dish. Walter bit the cherry off its stem and dug through all four layers, each spoonful a composite of the whole.

In no time, Walter's head, heart, and stomach were full. Unused to commanding the attention of a beautiful woman, especially one as reserved as Sarah Vogel, he talked enough for them both, as if he couldn't go one step further without her knowing his theories on life, which held that all students were created equal and endowed with equal opportunity to override that equality; that until women, like men, were allowed to die for their country, there would be no equality; that country was a family, and a family was always worth living for; that marriage should be a sacred thing, not a legality; that whether or not God exists, the need for God is undeniable; that you can only do what you're able to do, but you're always able to do more; and that knowing another is a thing best done eye to eye.

Over ice cream, Sarah learned Professor Fields was a man of strongly held positions and a gentleman who knew how to pick up a tab.

After the ice cream and goodbyes, after she'd buckled into her seat and remembered she had no idea where she was, after he came back out into the pouring rain and knocked on her window to see if everything was okay and found her in tears, clueless about which way to turn out of the parking lot, he scratched his ear and asked, "How long have you lived here?"

"Long enough," she moaned.

"Follow me, then," he said.

And follow she did, first to the ex's house and then to hers. Walter walked them to the door. Under the shelter of his big umbrella, she cursed herself for being such an idiot, maps being infuriatingly conceptual, landmarks bewilderingly personal. He was charmed by this chink of incompetence in her otherwise tough exterior.

He seemed in no hurry to return to his studio apartment on campus, so Sarah asked him in for coffee. Knowing the endless appetite grownups had for the stuff—they'd each had three refills at the ice cream parlor—Malcah requested permission to hang out next door until dinner and, in a first, was sent off with no third degree about homework or chores.

Few gentlemen expected a lady to sleep with them on a first rendezvous, in broad daylight, only temporarily free of kids. Which was why Sarah did.

It was like being new at it all over again, it had been so long. Same for him. They were sticky from the sundaes. She closed the bedroom blinds. Together they folded down the pink chenille spread. Sitting on either side of the bed, they removed their shoes but nothing else. He unzipped his trousers, she lifted her skirt, he rolled on top of her, and their love was made. And it felt like that—that love was being made, not arrived at or worked on or swept under the rug. If she'd ever considered it no more than a fleeting sensation, this proved her wrong. This thing being built in her bed felt as solid as concrete. Which was strong but not unsinkable, she reminded herself.

He was moved by the simplicity of her furnishings. It could've been some roadside motel, the sheets tucked tight, every footprint Hoovered from the wall-to-wall carpet, only the yellowing grout between the bathroom tiles showed history. He imagined a King James Bible in the nightstand drawer, ownerless as the room itself, never opened. He entertained and dismissed the suspicion that it was calculated, a carefully constructed diorama of invisibility, as if the woman he planned on courting, A-120239, could remain anywhere unnoticed. The indigo tattoo, now a carbon copy of itself, screamed *who needs decoration?* Not this woman, this exotic here in Ohio's bland lands.

She was moved by the extravagance of his need. Already possessing every word in the world, needing hers, too. Needing to know her blood type, her astrological sign, what music soothed her. She was tempted to tell him about her missing girl, the sum of all her words, but didn't. Not that afternoon, that night, or the next morning. At first, she didn't know how. And then it was too late.

Having grown up within the window of Sarah's celibacy, Malcah found no symmetry, only oddness, in their new triad. Robbie might have provided some balance but wasn't there much and no fun when he was. Malcah never understood why he was so mopey. She'd have given anything to have what he had. A young mom who made cupcakes for the class on his birthday, shopped at the Gap, and would have immediately taken her boy to an orthodontist if you could park a bus between his front teeth. A father, barely in the picture, buying whatever Robbie desired when he was. Like all the normal kids who had double everything, from parents to Guess jeans.

At least Sarah didn't look her age. Not like Walter, who was grandpa-old, or what Sarah called "distinguished." Dashing, in his own quiet way. A regular Gary Cooper, Sarah swore, keeping her up past bedtime one night to watch *Love in the Afternoon* so she'd see.

The movie was okay, but Malcah didn't see. Not the dash, anyway. The marbled hands, lumbering gait, and nose hair, yes. That both men were equally dreary in black and white as in color, yes. As much as she understood their attraction for their junior partners, the reciprocated attraction made her want to barf. If stale looks and kisses were all the Hollywood-perfect could count on, what hope had a perfectly ordinary soon-to-be teen?

She hated Walter. For wearing his years so badly. For pretending to be content footing their sundae bill and then spending the night doing whatever adults do after sending the kids to bed. For his pancake breakfasts too delicious to boycott. And she hated Sarah. For letting him sing in the shower. For laughing at her pleas for privacy. For signing her up for dance class in the first place. Dance class was where Malcah's problems had begun.

When reasoning, bartering, and tears failed, Malcah resorted to the only tool she had left. Silence.

"Why not let her quit?" Walter asked two weeks into Malcah's vigil.

Sarah glowered. She'd paid for the class—in full—and he knew it.

"Not that ballroom dancing isn't an excellent career option these days," he added.

Her glower deepened, the sarcasm new.

"A girl should learn to finish the things she starts," she said. There were other lessons she wasn't at liberty to discuss with a man who was only her lover. Filial gratitude, for one. The mother whose womb you crawled from may have no choice but to love you, but the mothers you find along your way, they who've *chosen* to love you, should never be taken for granted.

"Learn to give a little on the small things, is all I'm saying."

"Being rude to you, a guest in our home, is no small thing."

"And yet so easily remedied. Marry me and I won't be a guest anymore. I'll be a father. *Her* father."

"Walter. My darling. We're practically strangers."

"Sarah, my darling, you've always been a mystery but never a stranger."

The adults were growing short with each other, a sign that her protest was working, but there was also evidence to the contrary. Walter's toothbrush and razor had found a permanent place on the bathroom sink. His newspaper and magazine subscriptions—everything from *The New York Times* to *The Christian Science Journal*—came directly to their house. And her mother had gotten very good at pretending her daughter had become invisible.

Still, it was finding Sarah on her knees heaving violently into the toilet one morning that toppled Malcah's wall of silence. "What's wrong?" she cried, terrified as the woman who'd never been sick a day in Malcah's life lifted her head from the porcelain rim, wiped her mouth on her sleeve, and swore she was fine. *Liar* was all Malcah could think. Sarah looked like she was about to die.

The actual wall that toppled that day was in Berlin. At about dinnertime in Ohio, around midnight in Germany, the East reunited with the West. All week, camera crews had been capturing the frenzy, but Sarah had been too distracted to notice. Now, bilious as ever, she couldn't pull herself away. The footage was alternatingly confusing and alienating. It had been her home for three days and she recognized nothing. *Her* Iron Curtain—that bramble of wire ready to chew a young man to death, a little fun for the East German guards—was gone, concrete in its place. Covered in graffiti, it seemed a wall like any other, hardly a big deal. But of course, it was a big deal. Big enough for Walter to break his rule and watch TV during dinner because he knew this moment, coming to them live and unedited, wouldn't wait for them to finish their chops.

So they watched, plates on their laps, cheek by jowl on the living room sofa, Walter jovial from the spontaneity of it all, Malcah picking at her food, Sarah pretending all was well.

High above the line of soldiers dressed in sepia drear, hundreds of young people in sweatshirts and dungarees sat atop the Wall like they owned it, sneakered feet dangling against the spray-painted cartoons, holding sledgehammers and pickaxes they'd brought from home. Soon enough, there'd be cranes coming to do in ten minutes what would take a man dozens of hours. But it wasn't efficiency they were after, these people in wait their whole lives for proof that a better world lay beyond their Wall. They were out to destroy. And destroy they did, chopping and carving off bits of masonry, mementos to tuck away for yet-to-be-born grandchildren who'd never understand the logic of halving a city, separating business from customer, family from family. The guards looked on, defanged by orders not to shoot, not to *do* anything.

The cameras rolled through dinner and beyond. The chanting hypnotic, the eventfulness monotonous. The fat of the meat congealing on their plates roiled Sarah's stomach. When she could hold out no longer, she excused herself and ran to find relief, Walter glued to the set, Malcah staring like one of those portraits whose eyes follow wherever you go.

Locking the powder room door behind her, she settled on the toilet, peed on a stick, and confirmed what she already knew. She wasn't dying; she was pregnant.

Thanksgiving was upon them, and Sarah, prepregnancy, had decided it was time to give hosting a whirl. Hers would be a scaled-down version of the Blooms', less formal, more intimate, the guests outnumbering the dishes served, but nevertheless, as Kit had said, it was a beast of a holiday . . . in any condition.

Glory arrived first, armed with store-bought pumpkin pie and two bottles of Beaujolais Nouveau, wearing the words *Post-Menopausal and Nostalgic for Choice* plastered across the bosom of a T-shirt she'd bought off the back of a spry, silver-haired feminist at the National March on Washington. She also brought the much younger feminist she'd met waiting in line for the porta-potty, a redhead with ivory skin, gorgeous even wearing old-man spectacles and her hair in a tight bun. Her mannish blazer smelled faintly of mothballs, the shoulders were overly padded, and the rolled-up sleeves revealed rips in the lining, but her name was Chloe and Malcah was sure that no one so cool had ever crossed their threshold.

After loading the hi-fi with *Appalachian Spring*, *Sketches of Spain*, and Mantovani's *Music from The Films,* Walter turned his attention to the assembly of family and friends. The centerpiece he'd bought was too big for the table, the Butterball's skin never crisped, and the cranberry log showed ridges from the can, but it was his turn to have Robbie and though obsessed with Chloe, Malcah wasn't completely ignoring the boy. And with plenty of booze to keep the adults happy, there was no one to care if the kids stole a sip for themselves. Life was good.

Sarah, too, was having a good day, eating whatever she wanted, children behaving, and conversation flowing in a way that was inclusive but not demanding. Blessedly, there was no football to argue over, but in the after-dessert lull, Glory, a born instigator, had to bring up the March, waving it like a flag in Walter's face. She often tangled with him, but this time it seemed all about impressing her date. Chloe was fifteen years Glory's junior but every bit as opinionated, particularly about her recent experiences, both self- and mission-affirming but for the unexpectedly large and vehement cast of religionists who'd turned out to counter-protest.

"They wanted to burn us at the stake. Just for being pro-abortion," she complained.

Malcah sat up straighter, eager to be included in "us."

"Is that what we are now?" asked Walter, rising to the bait. "*Pro*-abortion?"

"You know I meant to say pro-choice."

"And if you'd said what you *meant* to say, they couldn't have rebranded their cause with your slip of the tongue. You know what they say about love and war and all."

"You don't support a woman's right to choose?"

"I absolutely support her right to choose. And her right not to see it as a choice."

"And one more crosses to God's side," Chloe said, pinning her host to the mat.

But Walter had experience with the young and fierce. "I didn't peg you for a believer," he said.

"What I *believe*," she said, having experience with the old and smug, "is that religion's a crutch. But go on. Give me your God defense. I know it's coming."

"See, that's why I love my job. I don't have to defend God, only explain Him."

"*Him*?" she asked, further boggled by his gross assumptions.

"Either God created man or man created God. If the former, we can certainly debate His holy gender. But if the latter, answer me this. Do you think man—and I mean *man*—in all his glorious impotence, would have had the balls to assign omnipotence to a female? More to the point, why even care about the sex of a mere contrivance?"

Sarah had never gotten used to this thing smart people called fun but left them to it. They were ready for more coffee, and she needed to throw up. Morning sickness, ha! Hers came any time it pleased.

In the kitchen, she put the pot under the tap to fill and took a swig of ginger ale.

Glory snuck up behind her. "You haven't told him, have you?" she said, giving Sarah such a start the bottle dropped from her hands.

"How did you know?" she asked. The pot survived, but she'd chipped a dinner plate someone left in the sink.

"You haven't touched your vodka, my pie turned you a shit shade of green, and there's a smidge of puke on the toilet seat that I'm quite sure isn't mine."

"You won't tell anyone, will you?" Sarah stared at the plate, noting the power the smallest blemish holds over the whole.

"Your secret's safe, but I'm curious to know what you're going to do about it."

"Do I have a choice?"

"When you work for the dean of Women's Studies, you do."

But Sarah had no faith in the viability of choice. Orphaned, frozen, malnourished, heartbroken once and then again. How much easier to think there'd never been any choice at all than to live with the consequences of consistently bad ones. And what of this baby's choices, to be born or not to be born, to come out a girl instead of a boy, a boy instead of a girl, to favor beauty over character, to have waited for a younger father, a more generous mother? Only one thing was certain. Whether any of them had ever had a choice to make, that time was over.

In the aftermath of their first family Thanksgiving—the dishes done—Sarah told Walter and Malcah they'd be setting another place at the table next year. They were having a baby.

Walter laughed, a one-off guffaw that worked its way into a side-stitching roar.

"This is not funny," Malcah cried.

To those in Walter's world who thought it hilarious that he was applying for Social Security and becoming a father at the same time, he said: "I couldn't have made a better choice if she'd given me one!"

1990

New Year's Day. Resolution #1: This time, do *everything* right.

Sarah learned the importance of iron in diet and in will, weighed the odds of a child from a forty-eight-year-old egg ever learning to tie its shoes, and researched every condition their combination of genes might harbor.

Walter bought her books—Brazelton, Spock, *What to Expect When You're Expecting*—and she read about muscle memory, worrying her muscles remembered nothing; Braxton-Hicks, fearing she wouldn't know real labor from false; and second-trimester bliss, waving in his face the case against making life-changing decisions—like getting married or adopting your partner's daughter—until after your baby's born and your hormones have settled.

She heard sex wouldn't hurt the baby and was glad. All she wanted was sex. Sex and sour cream scooped with her finger standing at the refrigerator's open door.

She heard about hemorrhoids, varicose veins, and weeping nipples, and got them all. She spent a lot of time with doctors. At her age, she needed many. All men, none who knew her name without opening her chart but knew her insides better than she did. They called it a miracle baby (in case she didn't already know), tested for Tay-Sachs and Down syndrome and spina bifida, and warned her to stay away from kitty litter. She'd never touched a cat but added toxoplasmosis to her worries. Of course, passing their tests guaranteed nothing with preeclampsia, gestational diabetes, and a possible breech delivery waiting in the wings.

"Alone" was a word for which she had no more use. Glory claimed her days, except those she took to stay home with Malcah, whose list of ailments had begun to draw her teachers' concern. But Sarah knew the girl needed this time with her. A rival was on its way. She could almost hear the theme of that shark movie pumping through the house.

Walter claimed her nights, reading his baby bedtime stories from *The Odyssey*, *Le Morte D'Arthur*, and the Bible (both Testaments). A learned baby his would be if he had any say.

Even in the bathroom, there was the thing inside keeping her company.

How were these never pleasures before? How were they never burdens?

In the third trimester, hard knobs began roving the globe of her belly like a tongue poking around its mouth. A feeling both complex and mystifying. No telling an elbow from a foot. She didn't remember Sasha kicking. Had she forgotten? How could she have forgotten? Or had that one just understood the imprudence of making her presence known?

Walter signed them up for a birthing class at the college. Half the age of Abraham and Sarah, he and his Sarah were twice the age of their fellow expectant parents. Colorful rugs and supportive pillows were strewn about for the couples' comfort. Walter's knees cracked as he knelt to sit on theirs and made a soft hammock with his body in which Sarah nestled. The exercises were strenuous and made her wonder how she'd managed to get this far in life without knowing how to breathe. As the group met on Thursdays, the kids were finally granted their pardon from dance. Now Robbie walked Malcah home from school and helped himself to a bag of Fig Newtons and a quart of milk while they sat on the couch that Mrs. Vogel called a divan and did their homework to reruns of *Teenage Mutant Ninja Turtles* that Professor Fields called stultifying.

Sarah gained twenty pounds, all in her middle. Women told her she was lucky the baby was taking the weight, but when she looked in the mirror it was not luck she saw, it was arms and legs like toothpicks and the belly of a Biafran. It would take more than muscle memory to push out a twenty-pounder.

Ohioans made a big deal over the end of elementary school, and she reached the any-day-now point just in time for it. At home, Malcah cuddled up to eavesdrop on her future sister (she was sure it was a girl) but in public gave Sarah the cold shoulder. Anyone who'd gotten through fifth grade knew how babies got made, and the tie-dyed tent her mother wore to graduation didn't hide the vomitous nature of the deed any more than Malcah's cap and gown hid her shame.

The gym was hot. The event long. There were plenty of awards. None for Malcah, but Robbie snagged a bunch. "Never you mind," said Walter, who held a special place in his heart for the late bloomer. The later it bloomed, the longer the flower lasted being the theory. Sarah wasn't convinced but still had much to learn about gardening.

By petits fours and punch, Walter could no longer contain the pride, excitement, and surprise he'd planned as the climax to this excellent day. The kids perked up, their idea of a proper surprise being rollerblades, tickets to the Salt-N-Pepa concert coming to Cleveland that summer, or anything that came disguised in gaudy paper and bows. But there wasn't enough ribbon in the world for the surprise coming their way. Walter had bought a house. Or rather had made an offer on one. Someone's old home that could be *their* new home if Sarah would only sign on the dotted line. Sarah was even less enthusiastic than the kids, but they all drove to Hudson to humor him.

Far from grand, the 1930s Craftsman-Tudor hybrid bore the pedigree of the region's most venerable architect. It was a standard floorplan—dining room off the kitchen, study off the living room, enough bedrooms on the second floor for everyone, a full cellar with laundry room, two towering oaks holding the slope of the front yard, and an uninterrupted lawn big enough for barbecues and badminton out back.

Walter sent the graduates off to explore while he and Sarah talked business at the kitchen table. He handed her the contract that for him explained everything but for her was a bunch of mumbo jumbo without a single provision for a new baby on its way, the friends Malcah would have to leave, or the new school she'd have to attend.

"But the Hudson schools are the best," Walter reasoned. Robbie was starting Western Reserve Academy in the fall, and with the money they'd save living together, they could send Malcah, too. It was the best of the best. A ticket into any college in the country. Jan would vouch for it. Jan was an alum.

"Look," he concluded. "You don't have to marry me, but please, Sarah, let me do this." On the condition that Malcah could continue at public school, she did.

They moved on the longest day of the year and spent three full days unpacking. It took all their strength to make their way through the meadow of emptied boxes, fall into their bed, and turn on *The Tonight Show*.

Her water broke halfway through the opening monologue. Walter was out cold. Sarah, with hours of contractions ahead of her, wanted to stay in the storm's eye for as long as possible—just her and Johnny and Ed McMahon—but there were sheets to change, calls to be made, a bag to pack, a partner to wake, a plan to be followed.

For all they did and did not do, the baby was born that morning, complication-free.

Too quickly, she was taken away to be cleaned, weighed, and swaddled. Sarah was wheeled into a double. Though there was no sign of another occupant, Walter drew the curtain between the beds. He seemed anxious. There was something he needed to say but he didn't know how. *Bully for you, first day of the rest of our lives, anything that doesn't kill you makes you stronger* . . . Wisely, he kept all that to himself, kissed the top of her head, and went off to fetch Malcah, who was home with Glory.

The nurse returned with the baby, ready for her first meal. *This* Sarah's muscles remembered. The tiny thing laid her hand on Sarah's breast, crooked her pinkie, found the nipple, and sucked, dainty as a lady taking tea. The nurse smiled approvingly. It was the most basic of instincts and yet many newborns needed to be taught. Not this one, eyes large and pensive, mouth working steadily, faintly drawn brows wrinkled in puzzlement, as if knowing this woman was her mother, just not what else a mother was for. Sarah watched the glossy lids struggle to stay open—there was much more to glean from the figure hovering above—and then slide shut. Sarah had never felt so in love or more alone. For months she'd breathed and eaten and dreamt for the two of them, she and her little traveler, and now the miraculous creature breathed, ate, and dreamt on her own. How did you go back to being *just* a mother, no more than a spectator in your child's life, when for a time you'd been her universe?

There was a quick succession of knocks at the door, an *Oh, Daddy*, giggling, and then Malcah and Walter swept in. *When had he become Daddy*? Sarah wondered. Whatever the joke, she wanted in on it, but the lidocaine was wearing off, the stitches tightening, and her visitors, hushed by the portrait of peace they'd walked in on, were now tiptoeing toward her crane-like bed like supplicants to a shrine. She pitied Walter, not yet knowing a father was the most he'd ever be. Malcah, too, who hadn't yet loved anyone as much as she loved herself. Walter pulled some bills from his wallet, thinking she'd get a kick out of taking herself to the cafeteria for breakfast like a big girl, but Malcah, tall as a grown woman, wanted only to curl up on Sarah's lap, a lap she'd never had to share. Sarah petted her like she did whenever Malcah came to her, happy or sad, needing to be held, even now that she was too big for cuddling. Sarah wanted to think there was room for everyone, but how many can one lap hold?

"You're the bravest person I know," Walter whispered, both girls softly snoring. Sarah smiled at the compliment from this man who, from their first sundae, had only wanted to do for her, would've done her labor if he could have.

"What's she like?" he said, gazing adoringly at his child.

"We've only just met," Sarah laughed, straining her stitches.

"She's already three hours old. What color are her eyes? Dark, like yours?"

The face was as familiar as her own, but the eyes wouldn't stay put. Flecks of tree bark in winter? The sheen of a particular Italian olive Walter loved? A lake gone flat at dusk? He wanted particulars, not poetry. His house was already rife with vagaries—and no matter whose name was on the deed, it was *his* house. Likewise, this daughter he was so keen to know. An eye color, a biographical through line, a name on a birth certificate. A few blanks on a form were all that remained to make her his. What could make this baby hers?

"She has . . . her grandmother's eyes," Sarah said, the only straw within grasp.

"Wait. Did you say grandmother?" Walter's double take conveyed confusion. "You had a mother?"

"People do," she shrugged. Her lie emboldened by possibility. It was an inheritable trait, after all. The genes of several grandmothers swam in that pool, and she hadn't said which. The grandmother she picked was at worst half a lie, and what grist for her husband's insatiable curiosity. His questions sprouted like leaves on the new family tree she'd just planted for him, and her answers flowed forth.

"She was a beauty. Her skin was fair, her hair fine and always coming loose from the bun at her neck. When she held me it was like being in a featherbed. And she was tall. Unusually tall." So clear, so specific, she wondered if she was no longer inventing.

"More," he said, rapt.

"Her plum dumplings melted in the mouth. She filled the house with music, singing all day long. And she read to me every night. Stories from the Bible."

"So she wasn't a heathen like you." The picture of a woman lighting Sabbath candles made his eyes glisten.

"God was not unwelcome in our home." For his sake she could let the woman be a good Jew.

"You're remarkable, Sarah. So young to remember so much."

How easily the tale was going down. It smacked of Dorotea. She'd fed her so many lies she'd finally had no choice but to leave. She didn't want to have to leave Walter, but she was too far in to turn back.

"Some things are harder to forget than remember," she said.

"Like when the Germans came?"

"Yes. We used to play hide and seek. I don't remember but it's possible we played with them, too, though there wasn't a hiding space big enough for a woman who had to duck to enter a room. One who could walk barefoot in the snow and call the cold her friend. One who could know the ache of hunger and still show off the apples in her cheeks when she smiled. When they found her, she must have been holding me so close they never knew they were taking me, too."

"And your Papa?"

Sarah shook off the question. A father was superfluous. Only a mama could've taught her the art of survival. How to hold her breath when there was no air, suck rags when there was no food, prepare for the After sure to come. Only a mama would know there'd never be an end to giving up and no use crying about it. That she'd have to keep her head down, ask for nothing, and deprive herself today of what she was bound to need more of tomorrow. Wherever she went, this mama would say, she should speak the language and remember that every so often, a plant needs its roots trimmed, the dirt shaken loose, lest it die in its own pot. Life is short, this mama knew. But life is long, too, and even the littlest bird learns to fly from the nest. Sometimes before it's ready. And so, Sarah flew. Without the help of any papa.

Walter nodded vigorously, swallowing the story whole. None of it added up, but he was too besotted for math.

"Tell me her name, Sarah."

This was her chance to come clean before he fell any further in love with them. But he wanted a name, not a confession. And she gave him one. Ruth. She'd never met a Ruth Vogel, but it sounded right. With six million turned to ash, who could say that among them wasn't a single Ruth Vogel with a little Sarah to call her Mama? And if there were a *real* Ruth Vogel alive and well in Tel Aviv or Montreal or even in Ohio, could she object to another? Or if this Ruth Vogel were dead with nobody left to say kaddish or speak her name, in blessed memory, wouldn't that make it a good lie? A mitzvah, even?

The nurse returned with the forms that would make Baby Girl Fields *theirs*. Both Malcah and the baby stretched their limbs as they awoke. Walter looked up from the clipboard and walked around the bed to be closer to his wife. He had an idea. "Love?" he whispered. "Let's call her Ruth."

"Maybe, Walter. It's a nice name."

"But this needs to be decided now. I want our daughter to come home with a name, and this one would be a gift, to her and your mother."

"Then let her be Ruth if you think a dead woman will care."

"Ruth Vogel-Fields," he shouted with a triumphant clap that startled his little one. "Don't cry, Ruthie." His voice climbed octaves. "You are my Ruthie. Yes, you are."

"You said we could call her Izzy," Malcah pouted, rubbing sleep from her eyes.

Isaac if a boy (after the son who'd made the first Sarah laugh), and yes, Izzy if a girl, was what they'd discussed. But that was before they knew she'd have Ruth's eyes, Walter explained.

"Who the heck is Ruth?" Malcah asked.

"Your grandma, sweetheart." A falsetto only a baby could stand.

"What grandma?" she demanded with a degree of insolence that yanked Sarah from her dreamy love state and split her heart in two.

Full up on men's unmeetable need for love and stories, Sarah relinquished the delicious warmth in her arms to Walter and handed what was left of her heart to Malcah.

1991

On the brink of fifty, watching her youngest take her first wobbly steps toward her first birthday cake, Sarah could finally admit life was good. It had come with an adjustment period, this goodness, this ease that a woman like her could only view with suspicion. But once the children were tucked in and they took their last sips of after-dinner coffee and put the cups in the kitchen sink and pleased each other under the covers, after allowing Walter to finish another chapter of his book, turn out his light, and succumb to the heavy, even flow of breath that described the slumber of a contented man, Sarah found herself staring into the dark and saying, soft as a prayer, "*alles gut.*"

Alles gut. Reassurance that took its time to settle in but eventually, chanted nightly, surpassed wishful thinking and became an accurate assessment. Sarah had survived the trauma of birth and brought home a baby no one could help but love. How proud she would have been, the grandma Walter called booby, his *goyishe* take on *bubbe* that never failed to make his girls laugh. How good it was that she could laugh at him and he at her, this man who'd paid for their new home but understood she'd never feel *at* home without paying him back for her half. How good that they both enjoyed their jobs, honorable vocations allowing them to provide for the family they'd basted together. A family that shrugged off most middle-class, middle-American mores but accepted that a father took care of his family, his clearest jurisdiction being over his wife. A wife took care of the children. And the children took care of each other, bigs looking after smalls, the pecking order of care. Recognizing that this was the natural order of life, Sarah said "yes" to the man who'd finally stopped asking.

They married at the house on a spectacular afternoon, their guests seated outdoors under a canopy of bronzing trees and perfect sky. Sarah wondered why so few waited to wed until there were children to witness the promises being made. How much harder it would be to break them.

A Buddhist friend from the theology department officiated, and after one last haiku, the groom stomped on a glass he'd wrapped in a napkin. "This is for Ruth Vogel," he whispered to his wife before the stomping. He thought it a tribute to Sarah's heritage, to the family that in a year had multiplied in number and strength. Sarah thought it a waste of a perfectly good glass.

Glory, their miracle baby's godmother, toasted the groom for taking only three years to wear the woman down. But Sarah didn't feel worn. She felt new, sharpened on the whetstone of the past. Walter, her whetstone for everything ahead. More than stable, he was fundamental. No pushover, he was unconditionally willing. His happiness was contagious, and she opened herself to its infection.

1993

Walter pulled a chair onto the newspaper Sarah had spread over the kitchen floor. She took off his glasses, then he took off his shirt and sat down. She wrapped a towel around his bare shoulders. For her, going to the barber was a waste of good money. For him, having her hands ruffle his hair was bliss. The tug of each clump between her fingers. The *shrrrp* of scissor blades. The feathery ends covering the towel like a dusting of snow.

"Where are the girls?" he asked.

"The big one's in her room doing homework. The little one's saving the big one from boredom."

Walter laughed and closed his eyes. The television was on. In addition to the computer, he'd bought a color set small enough to fit on the kitchen counter. Nowadays he liked a little news before dinner, though every night it was the same. Russia and America making overtures of friendship. Cape Towners taking to the streets. Hairspray eating through the ozone layer like moths on cashmere. Sarah half-listening. But tonight, two stories caught her attention. The first about the pope evicting nuns from a convent they ran on the grounds of Auschwitz, an act he'd hoped would gain him favor with the Jews but managed only to anger his Polish countrymen. The second about a pile of shoes recovered from that same killing camp and shipped to America for installation in the new Holocaust Memorial opening that weekend. Her hometown mentioned twice in one evening. A bona fide milestone. Sarah snipped up and around Walter's ear.

At the top of the hour, following a rash of commercials, the evening anchor's comforting baritone flooded the kitchen. He was not, as usual, seated at his glass-topped desk with the map of the world behind him but standing on a sidewalk in Washington, mike in hand, backed by the Holocaust Memorial, a block of white limestone cut from the April sky. Having only ever seen him from the waist up, Sarah was surprised to find he was quite short. A voice like his belonged to a taller fellow. Then again, the memorial on everyone's mind was big enough to dwarf a giant.

His critique of the building was thorough and glowing, only touching on the brewing controversy over its $190 million price tag. "Extravagant?" he asked. "Maybe. But thirty-some dollars per victim sounds like a bargain when you consider what it would've cost to save the poor devils." It was the shoes of those "poor devils" that had moved him in a way he thought no longer possible. "Come see for yourselves," he challenged those watching from their living rooms, where it was safe to wonder if they were real or mere props. "Inhale the fumes of old leather and decaying rubber. Think what it would've been like to step from *your* shoes and never make it back for them. You won't come out the same person you went in," he promised.

Sarah turned off the set and resumed her work accompanied by a symphony of ticking appliances.

"We should go," Walter said after a few moments. For him, quiet was something to be disrupted.

"Go where?" she asked, snipping up and around Walter's other ear.

"To the opening in Washington. Would you like that?"

"Maybe," she said, hoping that would put an end to it.

Brief as it was, the exchange drew Malcah from her room. She could hear a pin drop from two floors away if that pin had anything to do with her, and this one had everything to do with her. The house she'd once considered a palace had grown small and tight. In it, nothing ever happened or changed, and after a long winter cooped up with her parents and sister, she was desperate for newness, even if it meant being cooped up in some hotel with those same parents and sister.

"Can we? Can we go, Ma?" Ruthie, at her side, nodded solemnly.

"Maybe," Sarah said again.

"Great. Your maybes always mean no," Malcah said.

She had a point. "Maybe" was Sarah's safe place. "Maybe" fended off arguments. Like Walter's—that it would be easy, they'd make a holiday of it, take off school, throw some things in the car, be there by noon, the kids had never been to the White House or the Smithsonian and what an opportunity for them to learn about where she was from. As if she'd come from a place of white columns, pedestrian thoroughfares, and showcases doused in museum lighting. As if she'd come from a place anyone wanted to see. As if she wasn't already comfortable with where she'd arrived.

"It's a long way to go for a pile of old shoes is all I'm saying."

"See?" Malcah shouted. "She never lets us go anywhere."

Walter did his best to defuse the conversation. Kindness was in order, he told his step-daughter. They'd go another time. And it would have been reasonable for Sarah to take the small win and move on, but it was three against one, a majority she couldn't let stand.

"No, no, no," Sarah said, voice rising. "She wants to go to Washington so bad, let her go. All of you. Go stand in line and spend a fortune to get into a museum more crowded with the dead than the living. A little quiet around here will be a relief." She pulled one last hank from the crown of her husband's head and with a savage *shrrrp* cut clean to the scalp.

She dropped the scissors and quickly checked for blood. There was none, to her relief. He wasn't hurt. Oblivious, more like it, murmuring his thanks, fingering the bare patch she'd carved into the crown of his head, the slight tremor in those fingers skewing him older and more vulnerable than a husband of hers should be. His hair thin and wet, the groove his spectacles carved into the bridge of his nose. On his cheek, a copse of white whiskers the razor had missed. One minute, freshly groomed. The next, pathetically shorn.

Ruthie, too young to see old, left her sister's side and scampered into Sarah's arms. "Don't worry," Sarah whispered. "Daddy's hair will grow back someday."

But Malcah saw. Her former enemy turned protector, the backbone of the family diminished, the glue holding them together dissolving right in front of her eyes. A father, aging exponentially and doing nothing to hide it. Her disappointment in him was palpable.

1997

The pulling away. The protracted silences. The barbs hurled in response to innocuous questions. This time Sarah read every sign and was still helpless to do anything. The worry approached unbearable at night when, with the weight of her husband lying in bed at her side, she would stare at the ceiling and wonder—that urge to escape, to be invisible, to be nothing, was it in the blood? She would've been better off counting sheep. But the girl wasn't staging a rebellion; she was pissed.

Unlike either of her mothers, Malcah wanted to ascend, not escape. Be a star, not some hobo. But in three and a half years of die-hard effort, she'd failed to make cheerleading, be nominated for class president, or dance in a dark gymnasium under a cloud of twinkling fairy lights with a boy she could stand being seen with. In all the ways that counted, her high school career had been a total bust. And to save herself from a serious funk, she turned her ire on those doing the counting. The beauty queens and heartthrobs, the state champs and prodigies . . . the big fish born to lord over the little fish. *To hell with big fish and their pathetic ponds*, she thought. To hell with cheerleaders, high jumps, and cheerleader moms. To hell with the crushes she'd suffered, that sad succession of boys from the popular crowd who could make a girl grieve without ever knowing her name. To hell with teachers, college advisors, and pep talks. Best time of her life. Right. A girl like her couldn't help but pick the right path to some plummy job yielding loads of respect, moolah, and long-term contentedness. God, she hoped they were wrong. It was a messier path she craved. A landmine here, quicksand there. A detour from expectations. A loosening of the bands tightening around her chest so the panic could flow freely. She wanted to be seen as troubled, not merely confused. As if a Survivor's daughter had a right to troubles of her own. As if a theologian's daughter had a right to anything but the right path. And about Walter, the weirdness of him being her top ally just when she didn't want one. To hell with him, too, for thinking can-do spirit was all a girl needed to stay afloat. For calling her gap tooth fetching and then taking her to get braces—over her mother's objections—letting her believe it would make a difference when he knew the most perfect smile ever wouldn't change a thing. And for granting every favor she asked, including signing the permission slip for the class trip to New York City containing a curious advisory warning: anyone hoping for a glimpse of Eloise at the Plaza was SOL. For four days they'd be seekers, lovers, travelers . . . no tourists allowed. Pack light, they were instructed. A pair of broken-in tennis shoes and a load of questions were all they'd need.

"Just what the doctor ordered," Walter said.

"Doctors don't know everything," Sarah grumbled, annoyed about yet another decision made behind her back. She hadn't yet recovered from the orthodontics incident, and this time her objections were valid. The city *was* a dangerous place. They didn't have to believe her; it was always in the papers. And what an extravagant expense for a couple with two kids on the brink of college, another not far behind. All because the girl was bored? Oh, to be bored.

A hunter's moon presided over their first evening in New York, a place as frenetic as Ohio was still. Day or night, everything moved. On the river, sailboats and ferries and tugboats and cruise ships gliding in and out of the harbor, skirting the Statue of Liberty. On land, people strolling and jogging, cycling and taxying, those cleaning up after their dogs and those that didn't, the lowest caste of city dweller. There were brownstones coming down, skyscrapers going up. The fruit of gingkoes slicking the soles of shoes. Men layered in winter coats begging for spare change. Men bare-chested and muscle-bound wrestling on the river's piers. Fish twitching with life on beds of ice, pickles bobbing in barrels of vinegar, cow halves hanging from hooks, the air carrying currents of garbage, ocean brine, and boiled nuts. Graffitied subway cars looping endlessly from Harlem to the seaport. Everyone in head-to-toe black stepping into traffic as if rules no longer existed, or never had, not for them. And looming in the distance, a set of twin towers that could point a girl's way from any corner of town.

On their last night of it, bathing in the incandescence of Times Square, they encountered a band of boys in Yankees sweats. Cool and cocky, they descended like a cloud of mosquitos, yammering about all the things they'd like to do to them. The girls returned insults that rang with annoyance, but their tittering laughter told a different story. Only a week before, Malcah would have stood with the titterers, but the City—its people, its views—had opened her eyes. She'd hated being a little fish, but here she didn't have to put up with it. Here they were all little fish—the rich, the poor, the beautiful, the ugly—a league of millions swimming together in this enormous pond where she now swam too, her heart a giant moon bobbing in its current. *So, this is love*, she thought, feeling right for maybe the first time ever, this new watery realm a dazzle of colors she couldn't name. An elusive palette that wouldn't survive the return flight.

Back at the Cleveland Hopkins Airport, awash in primaries, secondaries, and a few select tertiaries, the girls huddled. Their goodbyes were teary, their promises of forever friendship sincere. Yet watching their bags come round the carousel, Malcah had the sinking feeling that a headful of snobby notions and a shared taste for café con leche wouldn't be enough to hold them to it, that once home, they'd return to their tiny pond and tiny ways.

"Ma," she said as they walked to the parking garage. "I *think* I want to be an artist." Though it was a statement of pride, of jubilance, she sounded more miserable than ever. It was the outcome Sarah had predicted, but for once, being right brought her no pleasure, only more sleepless nights to stare at the ceiling and worry about what each next day might bring. Would it be the one when another of her girls came home with purple hair? Would it be the one she didn't come home at all?

But as if in defiance of her mother's fatalism, Malcah did come home each next day, loading up on milk and cookies and sitting down to the college brochures piling up on the kitchen table.

Thursdays, Robbie joined her. Private school let out earlier than public, so he'd be there waiting on Malcah's stoop like an abandoned puppy. The sound he made with each gulp of milk. The way he shielded his work, like he feared she'd cheat off his college essay, like she'd need to. His bad breath. All of it tiresome. But while nothing prevented her from holing up in her room and tackling her own essay in private, she never did. In their countless Thursdays together, they'd survived dance class, their parents' courtship, and the birth of a half sibling. College was their last stand, and though it was hard to admit, she'd rather do it with him than without.

Until the Thursday he stood on her stoop waving his fat envelope in the air, wearing a Columbia-blue sweatshirt and a stupid grin. He was in.

"Can you believe it?" he squawked. He sounded like such an idiot when he got excited.

Of course she believed it. Columbia had been his first and only choice for as long as she'd known him. Columbia ranked in the top ten and gave out the Pulitzer Prize, which he planned to win, mostly to the *New York Times,* where he planned to intern. "My boy's going to be one of those smart-ass newspapermen," Walter would boast. And it was no pipe dream. He was a shoo-in for valedictorian. A Midwesterner with a 5.0, a manic list of extracurriculars, and a high-contributing alum for a mother? The only surprise was how quickly it happened, though she should have guessed he'd apply early decision, he was that certain of his chances. Which burned her. For the kid of two KSU staffers, the only certainty was KSU.

As her thumbnail searched for the gap that no longer separated her front teeth, she wondered how it had all been such a breeze for him. She was so conflicted, so dubious that the choices she was about to make were *hers* to make, so menaced by the specter of adulthood hovering in the distance. She'd never been taught to dream. Never dared order anything off the menu. Then came New York, a smorgasbord of such delight she'd lost her taste for anything else. Meanwhile, Robbie danced from foot to foot like he'd just found the answer to life's most crucial question (or else had to pee really bad), unaware of how it would make her feel, standing by while he took the lead, ready to fly solo when she was not. The indignity of being outflanked by a nerd. The indignity of knowing *he*'d be going off to the city *she* loved. If he'd ever cared about New York, he never showed it. Never even asked about her trip, the one thing reminding her that she was alive. And oh, the indignity of being jealous *of Robbie*, who, if their fortunes were reversed, would be genuinely happy for her. But their fortunes would stay put, and she'd be forever sidelined, a perennial late bloomer watching another's petals unfurl.

"No congrats?" he asked, her silence chastening.

"Congrats," she said flatly.

Missing her sarcasm or choosing to ignore it, he followed her inside.

"I could help, you know." He watched her dole out the cookies.

"Why would I need your help?" she asked.

"You're smart, your grades are good. Scores are weak, but I bet you interview great."

"Not helping."

"The point is . . ."

"No, Robbie, the point is, Kent State is free, close, and good enough. Ask my mother. She'll tell you."

"But is that where you want to go?"

"Absolutely not."

"Then where?"

"I don't know," she said with a heavy sigh. "Somewhere. Anywhere."

"Somewhere, anywhere's worse than nowhere at all," he groaned. "You've got a million brochures sitting on your kitchen table. Where do you want to go? Don't think. Spit it out."

"New York," she shouted. "All right? Fucking New York."

"Awesome," he said, nodding. "We can work with fucking New York. Barnard and Columbia might be a reach for you, but nothing wrong with NYU. It's way downtown, but it has cool professors and all the culture of an Ivy without the actual Ivy. We'll pick six more, for backup."

"Seven applications at fifty bucks a pop? Are you paying?"

"No. But there's always Dad."

"Maybe for you. I can't ask him for one more favor. I promised myself."

"You still don't get it? The man lives to do favors. Don't be stupid. Ask."

Robbie was right. Her prospects were not terrible. The list of colleges over which she'd agonized showed no more strategy than a child's letter to Santa, but she could do better. She *would* do better. He was right about the money, too. Her mother wouldn't budge. The house had put her in enough debt to her husband. And she'd made it known that if her daughter wanted to be an artist, she could stay home and be one for free. But Malcah was pretty sure Walter would do no less for a daughter than for a son. He'd spent his career preaching that college was the God-given right of every young person, or at least a parent-given right. He'd be happy to sign all the checks and guardian forms she needed. Happier still to keep their secret.

1998

Coming home to a burst of yellow crocus one day, Sarah discovered the newest collusion to transpire behind her back. Her daughter was in tears having been accepted to NYU's Gallatin School of Individualized Study with an offer too small to foot the bill but too big to turn down without serious pain.

"What should I do, Ma?" she sobbed, her plaintive cry landing like stone.

"Ask your father," Sarah said. "I have dinner to make."

May. Graduation? Commencement? Tomato, tomahto, but ceremony aside, what they'd been saying was coming true. Everything *was* ahead of her. Malcah felt lighter. She could breathe again. Laugh, even. What remained of school, in the attendance-taking-report-card sense, she'd do eyes shut. The presents tumbled in—pencil/pen sets, Starbucks gift cards, Hallmark cards holding hundred-dollar bills. This was a time for gratitude. Thank you notes were due. An ode warranted. To everything and everyone contributing to her well-being:

1. The Ohio sunshine, shrinking violet of the Midwest
2. Charles Horner, *Mister* Horner to the under-eighteen crowd, a dick of an English teacher who marked her work with his scarlet C^3 (Carelessness Clobbers Clarity) until she learned to use a dictionary
3. Homecoming King Reese Abbot, first to signal her place as a small fish, now bound for Princeton where he'd be a king in a sea of crowns
4. Her half-sister Ruthie, obsessed with knowing which half of her was Malcah's
5. Her Ma, who believed change, too, could be survived
6. The father she didn't know who'd set her free by giving her nothing
7. The father she knew who'd given her more than she could ever repay
8. Robbie, who'd made her understand it wasn't her life but her aspirations that sucked, then asked her to prom
9. And to her, Malcah, for saying yes

Robbie arrived at the Vogel-Fields home in a rented tux. Malcah met him at the door in her own version of a tux, pearl-gray and form-fitting, paired with strappy high heels to make it less office-y. He'd brought her a purple orchid in a plastic box. The orchid ruined the vibe, but it was sweet of him, and she held out her hand for him to slide the elastic band over her wrist. Walter snapped pictures.

At the hall, dancing underway, she hung her jacket on the back of a chair and allowed her date to escort her to the dance floor. Her silvery tube top sparkled under the fairy lights. Robbie didn't know where to put his hands. Malcah stepped on his foot. They could've been back in the fifth grade, except the girls now dressed like Disney princesses and the music was so loud no one cared if they had nothing to say.

When it was over, he walked her home and at the door gave her a brotherly peck on the cheek. She responded with an unsisterly kiss on the mouth. *A little something to remember her by*, she thought, feeling charitable and ready for bed. But Robbie wasn't satisfied. He wanted an invitation to her prom, too. A quid pro quo, he called it. She owed him.

"Fine," she said, fighting the urge to punch him in the cummerbund. "But don't expect to have fun."

The next weekend, dressed in the same suit (minus the corsage), she attended her prom with Robbie the Step. She couldn't have paid him less attention if he'd been a full-fledged brother. And when finally he got the message and went home on his own, she and a posse of new friends danced until their hairdos collapsed and feet blistered over.

She didn't see him much after that. His mother got him an internship at a law firm in Cincinnati. Malcah took a job at the local library. She didn't miss his company exactly, but with no more Robbie to spurn, Thursdays stopped being Thursdays.

Her life in New York began with a seven-and-a-half-hour trip, much of it idling on the George Washington Bridge. As the car lurched across the Hudson River, Sarah caught a glimpse of her girls in the visor mirror. Ruthie sound asleep, her head on Malcah's lap. Malcah, in her biggest, darkest sunglasses, staring out the window, subtracting every mile driven from those ahead. She was happy. Sarah was glad of that but wondered, did that happiness have to come at the expense of her own?

Traffic was slow going along the West Side Highway down to Greenwich Village, but the directions AAA had sent were spot on. Much of lower Fifth Avenue was cordoned off for NYU families, and the lineup of vehicles hugged the curb as the passengers waited for the next dolly to free up. Miraculously, the one they snagged had working wheels. Once it was loaded with everything Malcah had felt she couldn't live without, Walter drove off to find a suitable place to read away the wait time.

It was August. New York was hot as hell. The dorm, a repurposed hotel with casement windows and no air conditioning, even hotter. With only one working elevator, the wait was long.

They'd been told the rooms were minuscule. Malcah's was a triple and could have done with less furniture, but Sarah'd seen smaller. She crawled over the bed they'd claimed—the only one with a window—for a view of Malcah's new world, Eleventh Street, where the houses stood like distinguished dowagers in a receiving line. You could eat off the sidewalks, they were so clean. This was not a place she remembered. This was not a place she'd ever known. Despite the heat, she felt a chill wrap around her shoulders.

Malcah arranged her computer, gel pens, and journals on her desk and gave Ruthie a box of pushpins to hang the posters she'd brought. They giggled while Sarah scooted around them, folding jeans and unwrapping the extra-long twin sheet sets she'd special-ordered.

Once the roommates showed up and everyone settled in, the three of them went to find Walter. He was parked a few blocks away, engrossed in a student newspaper, perspiring from every orifice and desperate to get to the hotel he'd booked so they could shower, have one last dinner together, and enjoy a good night's sleep before the next day's departure. But his plan was thrown out the window with Sarah's announcement that she now wanted to head home straight away. She blamed the heat, the traffic, fatigue, but the truth was, for as long as she'd lived there, she was never able to love this city. Malcah, however, was in the throes of a grand infatuation. The sooner they left her to it, the better.

They said goodbye on the sidewalk. Ruthie first, tears flying as she threw her arms around her sister's waist in a monkey cling no human could loosen. Malcah told her she could sleep in her room and listen to all her CDs and Walter promised her the front seat all the way home, but Sarah knew the only way to her baby's heart was the promise of a Happy Meal. It was embarrassing how quickly she skipped to the car.

Walter dispensed some final advice: "One. Don't skip class. Two. Make sure your professors know your name. And three. Everyone swears they do their best work under pressure. Don't believe them. Stay ahead of things." Malcah hugged him hard.

Only Sarah was left. She and Malcah held on to each other like two frightened animals.

"Mama," Ruthie called from the car. "McDonald's. Remember?"

"*Gotenu*, the Nuggets won't fly away," Sarah shouted, wiping her eyes.

Malcah laughed. "*Mc*Nuggets, Ma. Wait, are you crying?"

Sarah wrapped her arms around Malcah for one last hug.

"Don't let trouble find you, dolly. That's all I ask."

"I'll try, but you know trouble's not just in New York."

"I know," Sarah said, feeling the subject was debatable.

She kept her eyes on the rearview mirror as they pulled away. This time *she* was doing the leaving. Malcah was the one being left. How small she looked planted there on the sidewalk, growing smaller and smaller. And then nothing.

The next day, Ruthie moved into Malcah's room.

The house was running smoothly, Sarah acclimating to parenting an only child, Walter patting himself on the back for the little genius they were raising, when the little genius brought home a note from the school librarian saying that Ruth Vogel-Fields would need written permission before borrowing any more books.

"Nonsense," he bellowed when he saw which book had provoked the rule. "We're talking Anne Frank, not *The Story of O.*"

He wasted no time scheduling a meeting. The absurdity of such censorship could only be communicated in person. He brought Ruthie with him.

"We don't censor students, we protect them," said the librarian. "Ruthie's been interested in the Holocaust lately, and we're concerned that the subject matter might be, you know, a bit dark for an eight-year-old."

"An eight-year-old who tests like a seventh-grader," he reminded her.

"Ruthie is an exceptional reader, but being able to read the words doesn't mean a child is ready to digest their content."

"But it's not just the dark stuff. It's reading she's into. Fantasy, adventure, anything with animals. Tell her, Ruthie."

"My favorites are *White Fang* and *Shiloh*. And of course, *Beautiful Joe*."

"See?" he said, challenging the librarian who refrained from mentioning the parallel between tortured animals and tortured people, stamped the inside cover of the Diary, and handed it to the child, signaling the laissez-faire position she'd be taking henceforth.

The ebullience of his win—for freedom, for literature, for his daughter—deflated as he watched a new collection take shape on Ruthie's nightstand. Memoirs of camp survivors, second-hand accounts of eyewitnesses, journalists, and historians. The endless inventory of atrocities and corroborating pictures. Terrible pictures. One pinned to her bulletin board, a page torn from its book. "What's this?" Walter cried. Defacing public property? The librarian would have a field day.

"It's Grandma Ruth, Daddy."

"Sweetheart, no. It isn't."

"But she looks just like Mama."

His heart sank. There was a resemblance, and although no one could prove this withered smudge of coal was the talented and tenacious grandmother of her dreams, no one could prove it wasn't.

Then, early one Sunday, enjoying a moment alone while making coffee, Sarah still in bed, Ruthie next door having slept over with friends, the neighbor called and demanded he pick up his daughter *right away*. An assortment of disasters playing in his head, he ran to the neighbor's house and found her waiting, arms in a knot, jaws clamped shut. Lined up before her were Ruthie, the neighbor's girl, and two others, all dejected and staring at the ground. "Where's your wife?" the neighbor demanded.

"She's not feeling well," he said, the wife in question eavesdropping at the bedroom window.

"That's funny, I'm feeling a little sick myself," the neighbor snapped. "Show him, girls." They pulled up the sleeves of their matching pink nightgowns and displayed the numbers inscribed in ballpoint blue on the insides of their arms. "I don't know what kind of rules you have or don't have in your house, and it's none of my business, but Concentration Camp is *not* a game we play here."

Not a word passed between them as they walked back to their house. Ruthie went directly to her room. Walter found Sarah in the kitchen, sipping coffee, stifling a smile.

"This is not funny," he said.

"It's a little funny," Sarah said. "They're eight. What do they know?"

"That's the problem. They should know. Ruthie, anyway. Promise me you'll talk to her."

"Me? What can I say? It was so long ago."

"Tell her the Holocaust isn't a dress-up game. That real numbers don't wash off in the shower. Tell her she's strong. That surviving is in her blood. Tell her your truth, Sarah."

"You want her to think I survived because I was strong? And what does that make the others? No Walter, that is your truth, not mine."

"Sarah, please. We're on the same side. All I want is for Ruthie to know who she is."

"She knows better than us. But go on and tell her your stories. I'm going back to bed."

That night, Walter began tutoring Ruthie in the ways of her people. Because Sarah would never be able to put words to her daily triumph over weakness. Because the worry the school librarian planted in his head had only grown now that he understood how the young and impressionable need a little light to balance the dark. Because he had to believe that strength can be learned as well as inherited.

At the end of their first lesson, he tucked Ruthie in and went to Sarah with what *he'd* learned. Yes, the chapter of history their child found so fascinating was among the darker ones, but if a five-thousand-year track record of marvel couldn't brighten her outlook, he didn't know what would.

The next day, he took his daughter to buy a silver-plated frame for the now-official portrait of Grandma Ruth. Its place of honor on the girl's dresser brought Malcah to tears of laughter when she first saw it, and every time after.

2000

The new century, which smoked like a bucket of dry ice, did not break the world's computers as everyone feared but did lob a non-technological threat at Walter and his girls. Sarah was diagnosed with ductal carcinoma in situ. If you had to get cancer, this was the one to get, the doctor said. She could take a wait-and-see approach. If the bad cells stayed put, he explained, she could live to be a hundred. He'd seen it happen.

"And if I don't want to wait and see?"

"We do surgery. That would mean prophylactic removal of all breast tissue."

Walter was not interested in choices. He wanted to be told what to do, but the doctor stuck to his professionally non-committal guns. It was up to Sarah, who had no appetite for uncertainty and wanted the mastectomy. But only if you make it a *double*, she said, symmetry suddenly of paramount importance. And it would have to wait until summer. Walter was on board with all but the waiting part. Why give it time to spread, he reasoned, tormented by the thought of losing her. But the doctor sided with his patient, assuring Walter that it was no emergency and disrupting the family's schedule might make things even more stressful for Sarah.

Her last stipulation was that no one be told. She couldn't bear being treated like a sick person, everyone pretending to be cheerful through the months ahead. "A little privacy is all I ask," she told Walter, who was quick to point out that as a mother, he was fairly certain she'd lost the right to privacy. And as daughters, Malcah and Ruthie had earned the right to know.

In a rare occurrence, he won.

They called Malcah, Walter on the kitchen phone, Sarah on the bedroom extension.

There were so many rings Sarah was about to hang up when she heard Malcah's voice. "What's wrong?" she asked, breathless from her sprint to catch the call. Family called on Sundays. It being Wednesday, both parents should have been at their respective offices.

Though caught off guard, Malcah took the news remarkably well and without hesitation promised to come home. Sarah protested. Just the other week, Malcah had told them about the publishing job she'd lined up for the summer. This would ruin everything.

"It's not a job, it's an unpaid internship, and I want to help."

"Of course you do," Walter said. "The surgery's June twentieth."

"Come, don't come," Sarah added. "It's your life."

"Yeah, Ma, it is."

The cancer was eradicated in a surgery performed a few weeks before Ruthie's tenth birthday, and the reconstruction was beautiful. At least that's what everyone said. It would be days before the bandages came off and Sarah could see for herself. Replacing the nipples was a simple procedure. A pinch of skin tied off like a balloon and tattooed with a blush of color. "The doctor's a real artist," they said. "No thank you," she said.

After, she was like an animal that had wounds to lick but nowhere to do so. Taking care of her family now meant letting her family take care of her. But thanks to Malcah, this newly competent young woman who redirected Ruthie's and Walter's coddling without being asked and knew how to give the garden a good spritz when it was dry, Sarah relaxed into her convalescence, doing laps around the backyard to rebuild her strength, starting with one and after a few days, two, then upping it to three, then four, arm in arm with this daughter turned friend, listening to Malcah's favorite poets, plugged into the same Discman, a single set of earphones between them. It was like reading the girl's mind. Some of the poets were household names, some unknown, at least to Sarah. Some rhymers, some not. All women because Malcah planned to join their ranks one day, and who would read her if she didn't read them? Though it was news, this literary path her daughter had chosen, Sarah was quick to answer, "I will."

The thought of "one day" plugging in to a contraption of her own and listening to her girl reading the poems she'd written fueled Sarah's progress. They'd upped their laps to twelve when Malcah mentioned she was thinking of finishing her internship while there was still one to finish. "But only if you're ready, Ma," she said.

Ready or not, she knew Malcah no longer needed her permission to do anything—it was her blessing she sought, which Sarah gave, no strings attached.

After sending Malcah back to the city she now called home, she settled in for a summer of waiting for Sunday phone calls and getting used to the new breasts someone else might as well have been wearing for all the response they gave Walter's touch.

2001

It made no sense that in a matter of hours, the Fieldses would be Manhattan-bound for Malcah's farewell to NYU when it had been only a minute, granted the world's longest minute, since dropping her off for the start of her adventure.

"Definitely one of the smoother adventures," Walter said

And for the Ohioans, mostly, things had gone smoothly.

For Malcah, too. Mostly. By the end of her junior year, she'd devoured all the meaty classes her BA offered—preposterous courses like Reading Ulysses Backwards; Men and their Sirens/Women and their Mirrors; The Gall of American Poetry from Whitman to Pound—leaving her with a heap of required credits for what should have been her grand finale. She slept through Statistics 101, Anthropology 101, and Modern Dance and performed the basic tasks of her TA and publishing house gigs on autopilot.

Her nights were another story. Those, she spent combing the city for poetry slams, waiting hours for a turn at the mike, chickening out when her name was called, and running home to stuff her computer with the words she'd stolen from those who hadn't.

Over winter break on a barhop through the East Village, she signed up for a spot at The Spoken Word Cafe. There was a boy sitting at a table up front, decidedly alone, his beer untouched. This time when her name was called, she grabbed her moment and delivered a brisk rant about the cloistered existence within the walls of academia. It was over-the-top, but his gaze never left her. After, he bought her a beer, told her he'd found her take on senior burnout "quite accurate," and assured her she'd get through it—everyone did.

He was only two years older, a two-year gap she'd never close, which might've been a sticking point, except that he was right, she did get through it, and now he was her boyfriend and she was graduating with the residual angst of a racehorse detained at a starting gate that wouldn't open and honors enough to make her parents proud. She'd kept them in the dark about the burnout, as well as the boyfriend. From the start, her mother had predicted this chapter of her life would not end well, her father that it would read like a marvelous fairy tale. They were both wrong, but why spoil it for them?

This time the family drove from Hudson directly to the Lower East Side. They left at dawn and with only two stops to gas up and relieve themselves, they arrived at the apartment Malcah and her boyfriend shared in time for lunch. They hadn't heard much about the boyfriend, only that his name was Robert, which had caused Walter a pang of regret on Robbie's behalf. "Not a bad block, is it? Enough trees to give it some charm, not enough to hide the bandits," he joked.

They rang the bell and Malcah leaned out her window to throw them a key tied up in a sock, which Ruthie found hilarious. Walter wrestled the key out and unlocked the front and inner doors. The rise of the stair caused him trepidation. He knew he needn't worry about Sarah—the doctor had twice declared her fixed—but worry had become his go-to expression of love.

The handrails sweated. The dungeon-gray hallways were dimly lit. Ruthie ran ahead and was already in her sister's arms, lifted clean off the ground, when their parents reached them. The boy was there too. After hugs and handshakes, they were welcomed into the apartment. "Careful there," Robert warned, pointing to a loose corner of chewed linoleum. "We think the last tenant had a dog. At least, we hope it was a dog." They could tell from the delivery it was a line he used a lot.

Malcah and Robert wore horn-rimmed glasses that looked too big and pants that looked too small. He called himself a nerd. She called him a genius. Maybe he was. He could have been speaking a foreign language as far as Sarah and Walter could tell. Only Ruthie seemed to follow Robert's ramble on his recent history, his design degree, his futile attempts to find a place in that design world, accepting that he'd never find an affordable apartment on a freelancer's salary, and finally deciding to take a job as a JavaScript coder for an e-learning company downtown. "It's a real gig," he said. "Monday to Friday. Benefits." The world of SCORM, ADL, and LMSs had freed Malcah to pursue her art.

"Hear that, Sarah?" Walter beamed. "We raised an artist."

Their bed sat on milk crates. Lining the wall were more crates filled with books. Ruthie sat cross-legged in a corner consuming a volume of Adrienne Rich poems. "Good stuff," Walter said, taking it from her. "In a decade or so."

"Daddy, content screening?" Malcah exclaimed in mock horror.

"This library could be lethal in the wrong hands," he said, finding an open space for the Rich and browsing respectfully through the other titles. *The Second Sex*, *Alice in Wonderland*, a fat one by a chap he'd never heard of with three names, *Illuminations*, Anne Carson, *Patti Smith Complete*, Joseph Campbell, Marx, *The Teachings of Don Juan*, which Walter pulled from the shelf. "Oh boy. I committed this one to memory when I was your age. Does it hold up?" he asked. Robert confessed they hadn't yet gotten to it.

"Who's hungry?" Malcah asked. Robert raised his hand. He was short, with the build of an out-of-shape wrestler. "She's ruining me," he said, pinching the roll circling his waist.

They pulled mismatched chairs from other parts of the room to the table. Malcah spooned out homemade pasta with pesto and they dug in. All agreed it was delicious. Even Ruthie, tasting basil for the first time. "She couldn't boil water, now she's the Julia Child of hotplates," Sarah said of the cook.

Once lunch was finished and the plates were cleared, Malcah announced she had a surprise for her sister. She'd be taking her on a tour of the city.

"With Mama and Daddy?" Ruthie asked.

"I think something like the Empire State Building is more their speed."

"And what's wrong with the Empire State Building?" asked Walter.

"Nothing, if you want to be a tourist. So Ruthie, what'll it be? Tourist or traveler?" Whatever else she'd become, Ruthie would always remember that once she'd chosen traveler.

For her, Malcah's city was proof that heaven was a man-made construct worthy of her aspiration. Walter, a hopeless tourist circling the observation deck of what was once the tallest building in the world, drew comfort from the fact that every stroke of genius is forced to bow to its successor. For Sarah, a middle-aged woman just learning she was afraid of heights, it was a miracle that the sky and earth could change places so swiftly and not pitch her over the edge.

The family arrived early for Sunday's Commencement and snagged good seats. Robert joined them under the big tent the school had pitched for the occasion. He didn't mind that Walter kept calling him Robbie. The real Robbie had also planned to be there but at the last minute had bailed saying he had too much to do for his own graduation a week away. Walter suspected his son was still too in love with Malcah to watch another boy hoot and holler as she walked.

Which, judging by the length of the speaker list, wouldn't be for hours. Sarah had trouble sitting still in even ideal conditions, and as the crowd filled in, she felt claustrophobic, the folding chairs hard on her bottom. She told Walter she needed to step out for some air.

"But it's about to start," he said.

"You'll miss her, Mama," Ruthie whined.

"I won't miss a thing," Sarah promised, hurrying out into the tumult of Bryant Park.

Under the London plane trees, boom boxes competed, the homeless staked out benches, tourists clutched their wallets, graduates' families snapped pictures before rushing to their seats, and students milled about in deep-purple gowns, waiting for the last possible moment to make their entrance. Sarah bummed a cigarette off one of them. She hadn't smoked in ages, but the urge was overwhelming. She held the smoke in her chest for as long as she could letting it billow out of her like a cloud as a troupe of baldies with topknots and orange war paint invaded the park, their robes clashing with the graduates' finery, finger cymbals dinging, chanting Hare Krishna, an exhalation full of saffron-colored bliss. One of them reminded her of Sasha. Something about the way her shoulders folded in as if she was trying to disappear. A guise of cynicism masking a core of naivete. The girl was far too young to be her daughter. And yet.

They floated by. Sarah dropped the cigarette and followed them around the tent and out onto Forty-Second Street, past the shoulder of the library building and onto Fifth Avenue where she picked up the pace, hoping to catch sight of her face or hear her voice. The voice is the last thing to age. But a bus pushing itself into the crosswalk cut her off. The library steps rose behind her. She climbed them to look over the heads of the hot dog–munching sun worshippers, but it was too late. The sound of cymbals lingered, but the revelers were out of sight. There would be no reunion today. A relief, really. What if it had been Sasha? Had she thought she could drag her back to meet the family and catch up over lunch?

She ran back to the tent. An usher, staring impassively, blocked her way. She was flustered, panting. She heard music, the main event in progress, the honor-giving underway, but he had his orders. No stragglers. Especially unticketed stragglers. "Don't you have a grandmother?" she asked. "Please, the ticket's inside. I'll bring it back to show you . . ." Hardened as he was, he did have a grandmother, one younger than this lady, and let her through.

Hurdling the knees of peeved strangers, she pushed her way to the vacant spot at the center of the row. Ruthie's worried face instantly brightened. For Walter, anger had overtaken worry. "What the hell, Sarah," he whispered as harshly as she deserved. Her forehead and cheeks were painted with sweat. He handed her his handkerchief, which she pressed to her face. The litany of names, one after another, ran together until the name they awaited jumped out clear as a bell, though the Malcah Vogel-Fields who walked the stage like she owned it seemed barely theirs. Sarah trembled at the sight of her.

They'd planned to leave after lunch. The car was packed and ready to go but on the pretense of needing provisions for the trip home, Walter asked Robert if he'd help them find the closest deli.

"Daddy thinks we need a moment alone?" Malcah asked.

Sarah nodded.

"Do we?"

"You tell me. This boy, he's for good?"

"So far. Do you like him, Ma?"

"I will if I have reason to.

"I don't know. Some days, I'm sure we'll be together forever. Others, I can't see us lasting the week."

"He knows?"

"He says he can only stomach my optimism because of its bleak underside. He's devoted. For better or worse. Like Daddy is to you."

Devotion, hmm. Sarah doubted she'd ever given as much as she'd received but decided this might be her chance to pay it forward.

"You know your old room is waiting for you. Ruthie would give it up in a second to have you back."

Malcah laughed. "It's tempting but tell Ruthie the room is hers. Ohio's home, but I need to be homeless for a while. I need to stay hungry."

"Hungry for what?"

"I don't know. Everything. But words, mostly. I can't get enough of them."

"We don't have them in Ohio?" Sarah attempted a smile.

"Not like here. New York's a department store of words."

"Come back to us, dolly. I want to do for you . . . for just a little longer."

"I have to do for myself now, Ma. You know that. Anyway, by next week, I'll be bussing tables somewhere snooty and safe, so stop worrying. Okay?"

Sarah was overcome with a powerful need to hold Malcah in her arms again, but the city seemed inhospitable to public displays of affection. It was up to Malcah, who knew these streets and the strangers who wouldn't look twice if you were seizing in the gutter, to reach for her mother. They hugged, rocking back and forth until Sarah remembered to give her the stack of twenties she'd brought along, crisp from the bank and wrapped in a brown paper bag. "Buy yourself some good words, *mamaleh*," Sarah whispered. "Buy a few for me, too."

For the length of Manhattan, Ruthie's head whipped right and left, recording every detail of this place she couldn't stand to leave. Halfway across the George Washington Bridge, she surrendered to sleep.

"Look at her, Sarah," Walter said. "She's exhausted. I am too, but it was worth every minute, don't you think?"

Sarah didn't answer, convinced she heard orange togas flapping in the wind and trying to unconvince herself that instinct was stronger than reason.

"Something wrong, darling?" Walter asked.

"No, darling," she said. "Everything's fine."

But he wasn't letting her off so easy. There was still a long drive ahead. Talk was the only thing that kept Walter awake, and all he wanted to talk about was Robert and Malcah.

"You saw it, too. Right? How much he loves her. Maybe too much? He hardly let her out of his sight. Is that healthy? At their age? And how great does she look? Like all she needed was his permission to turn into a stunner. I hope she doesn't break the guy's heart. She does seem in love, though. Don't you think? With him, that tenement, their little corner of grunge, the city, herself, every word she writes, every acronym he utters. She's love on legs. But it's a good life she's making there, don't you think?"

"There isn't a better life to be made."

"But that smell in the hallways . . ."

"Like someone forgot they'd put a pot of cabbage up to boil?"

"That one . . . but I guess love has to be stronger than anything these days . . . even boiled cabbage."

In case he had more to say, she turned on the radio to the opera station that would keep him busy for the remaining three hundred miles.

Soon after her twenty-second birthday, Malcah learned a poem of hers would be appearing in an anthology put out by one of those hand-bound, unprofitable presses. She knew how many before her had published only to disappear behind the heavy veil of obscurity. She knew it could happen to her, too, that she was no more deserving of fame than any of them. She knew it but didn't believe it.

A disbelief that went everywhere she went. On the occasional trip home. Bedding down with Robert. At each of her jobs. Until one exquisite September morning, while laying out the silverware for another breakfast shift but thinking only about her anthology's launch that evening, she perished in a restaurant in the sky, every window framing the unfathomable blue beyond.

Walter and Sarah heard the news about the attack on New York along with everyone else. It was a day before it became *their* news. Planes had stopped flying, all roads and bridges were closed, but Walter tried his best to get them there, as if there was still a "there" to get to.

Weeks later, a box came. It was from the boyfriend. It sat for days until Walter found the courage to open it. There was a note to Sarah from Robert saying he was devastated. He'd re-homed the cat they'd adopted and rented a car to drive to the West Coast in search of new scenery and maybe a job. He thought they'd want copies of Malcah's anthology. Her poem was on page sixteen.

Primer

I learned to read on my mother's arm
fingering a fairy tale inscribed there
in characters describing no subjects or verbs
a lone vowel, no consonants
a growl born in the back of the throat
a plot that lay flat as a fish
until flexed
then growing big as a whale
a great blue
or a killer, smaller, fiercer
the last of a kind surfing the waves
humming to herself
a tune that to another, if there were another, would be so
    familiar
and if there were an other but there was too much sea
for her song to ever reach it
would she care?

This is Malcah Vogel-Fields's publishing debut. Born in Queens and raised in the Midwest, she returned to the city to attend New York University. She lives with her boyfriend and cat and enjoys working at Windows on the World atop the Twin Towers where the "stars are only an arm's length away." We think she might just be one of them.

In this After, even a smudge of Before had been scrubbed from earth's dirty face. In this After, no Before existed. Each moment survived on its own, sanitized, freed from all others. Every voice an accusation. Walter's. Glory's. *She hasn't cried. She's withdrawn, shut down, bottled up. She'll explode with grief if she doesn't find release.* They talked about talk being medicine. The best, according to Glory. "Then why won't she talk to me?" Walter asked no one.

Her arms hung limp at her side, the why-nots turning to sweat in her fists. And he—her insufferably trusting husband, infuriatingly optimistic, everyone's hero—wondered why, he and his carte blanche world, giving praise, opening doors, fixing the girl's teeth, taking her side, paying for it all, running to the pharmacy for numbing gel whenever she cried from the aching, treating her to sweet corn and ribs when they came off, the damn braces, closing the gap, erasing the last of her mother's mark from her smile, and for what?

AFTER

Beginnings

Early one morning, the first of a new year, under a sky of seamless gray, a baby girl is born into a home tight to winter's winds, its walls papered in love, its bills paid in full every month.

2020

If having everything she needed hadn't stopped her from wanting more, Moll couldn't be blamed. The scars of trauma she'd never known crowded the deep end of her gene pool. Clean your plate, they nagged. Grab what you can. What was ahead, the inevitable? It was never good. She needed no first-hand experience to know this was true.

When she was still a premonition, the couple she'd train to be her family had begun auditing their world, a beautiful conglomerate of good fortune, a fortress as strong and stable as a pyramid. God, a sun-spewing eyeball at the top; below Him, a charismatic rabbi, the go-to guy for the Modern Orthodox of the Upper West Side; directly below him, the couple, a match for the ages who occupied as little room as possible so that their future little heathen would have the space to spread his or her wings. He or she, it made no difference, but their hearts and apartment could accommodate only one.

Below this trio, this troika, this tripod of faith were the grands, one set in Chicago, one in Ohio. Then came their colleagues in law and social work, the teachers who would foster their little one for lengthening portions of each day, their friends and acquaintances. Next the doormen, housekeepers, bankers, and postmen. Then an assortment of political leaders and celebrities they knew more about than was comfortable. And finally, the strangers—ones they remembered from chance sightings, those indistinguishable from the cityscape they inhabited, and the utterly faceless, voiceless homeless that the tenth-floor dwellers passed with their breath held.

This was the architecture of her life. Its centerpiece, a collection of rooms they called home, a corner unit with windows overlooking Riverside Park and the Hudson River. Sometimes it felt like the castle of a sprawling kingdom, only the ramparts of the Palisades standing between them and the great western front. Other times it felt small, like a fishbowl, the kind a child wins with the lucky toss of a ping pong ball, its lone, bagged captive an unearthly shade of orange but losing its luster in the plummeting pH levels.

She began her term on the planet, a term most predicted would succeed her predecessors by a decade, innately aware of a place called Ground Zero, only eight miles south of her nursery's window.

The couple followed the protocol of the day. No bumpers, no pillows, no blankets, no padded cover to soften the unyielding mattress. Pooh-pooh, they said to crib death, laying her on her back though there wasn't a night she didn't wind up in the warm well between them, their giant king a kind of paradise. They scheduled twenty minutes of tummy time several times a day to prevent pancake head and strengthen her core though her muscles never stopped working no matter the position. She was always in motion. She *was* motion. A relentless fidgeter. She refused pacifiers and bottles. The tit was her only comfort, though she fidgeted there, too, thumbs nimbly swiping the silken skin of her mama's breast, the first of many touchscreens to animate her world. She wriggled free of the snuggest swaddle, howled between farts and burps, and slithered until she could stand upright at the coffee table, swaying, banging, humming as loud as she could, angry she couldn't yet run, furious that nobody spoke her language, wailing in protest over the accident of her birth, being born into privilege at a time when privilege was universally despised, though better than the alternative, which she, the daughter of a Survivor's daughter, remembered cellularly. The scars.

She'd known only the couple for an entire year, though the word "knowing" was an overstatement. She knew the physical contours of the bubble they'd constructed and that her role within it was to fascinate. Which she obliged with every gas-driven smile and an attention span that allowed her to identify words on shop signs before she knew what those words meant. Other kids dreamt of becoming doctors and firemen. She dreamt of being a genius.

I'll remember this and every moment after, she'd sworn on her way through the birth canal, but the memories she most treasured had been mined from the family's albums. Like the one of the couple, their inquisitive eyes peering over the accordion of baby blue that covered their noses and hid their smiles. For a full year, it was only the three of them. A year she might as well have spent in utero. Outside was a blip, a maze of manholes and potholes, a gulp of prickly air on the way home from the hospital. And then the door slammed on the three of them and on New York's entire population. Some stayed put, passing the time cutting tea towels into homemade masks. Those who could abandoned the city, opting for the slow descent into upstate sloppiness. The couple could but didn't. Running away didn't sit right with them, though their moral code stretched to include a car parked in the garage beneath their building, allowing them an occasional respite from urban vigilance and returning them to a now-familiar land of mask-filled gutters, people waiting to be buried, and the smell of 77 percent alcohol permeating the air. By the time she learned that it wasn't meant to be like this, that it had been a hundred years since a sniffle caused panic of this proportion, Covid-19 was just another fact of life. Like traffic or engineered beef.

In quarantine's quiet corner, she learned the couple's names. Mama, Dada. She learned to negotiate for treats before giving in to their demands. She learned to answer to Moll, as Mama and Dada sometimes answered to Ruth and Noah. She learned that her Chicago grands, Henriette and Josef, were pragmatic, efficient, and fiercely loyal. Josef was a mensch, and Henriette was said to love the sound of her own voice, making her hard to take but easy to love. She learned that her Ohio grands were trickier. Moll spent a total of six weeks with Grandpa Walter, two per summer for the summers of '22, '23, and '24. He passed before they made it to another. The reverberations of his boundless love outlasted any memory of his face. She didn't have to remember Grandma Sarah, who'd stuck around. She was like Henriette only in reverse. Of her they said a stone was more emotive, which made her an easy companion but an effort to love, and Moll learned it was incumbent upon her to make the effort.

Someday she would venture beyond the apartment walls to experience the world's manifold characters and plotlines firsthand. Until then, her mother's stories entertained her. Ruth Fields, *Doctor* Ruth Fields, was a licensed psychologist with a PhD in social work. Her specialty, families in need. Her modus operandi, keeping the facts of a family's life from interfering with the truth of its stories. Stories were her stock-in-trade.

Her father had stories, too. His were lessons drawn from the Bible or some bearded rebbe fluent in allegory, all in praise of *Hashem*, whose real name was never used. For all the nuance of his telling, the plots were slim. Like the one where *Hashem* paused after a hard week's work, took stock of His Creation and thought, *something is amiss*, setting Him immediately to work on a magnificent clay pot that He filled with Divine Light, a source of never-ending sustenance for any who inhabited His realm. Upon receiving this gift, the world became perfect. Alas, He'd chosen the clay of mortals to make this pot, and the force of divinity pushing at its walls burst it into a million shards that scattered across the universe. Thousands of years later, their People were still hunting for those shards, praying for the day the last one was found, the pot repaired, and perfection reigned again . . . or something to that effect.

Moll was eight when she asked why *Hashem*, if He knew everything, didn't make a better pot. The *if* troubled Noah but having come to accept such thoughtfulness from his only child, he answered in kind. "If things didn't break, nothing would need repairing. And then what would be the point of our lives?"

He regarded it a father's duty to teach her that something could be true without being real, but her mother was no teacher. Her stories were like the precious portrait miniatures Moll grew up to see hanging at the Met, the subjects tightly framed, without backdrop or context, pure essence captured with grace and economy, each complete unto itself.

And Moll ate them up, the ones about the young woman she was named after, Saint Malcah and her fiery demise. The baby teeth her Ohio grandmother wrapped in tissue, saving them for the day she'd plant them in a sand-filled casket. The ghost swimming under the coats of new paint in the room that became Ruthie's when she was eleven. "Ruthie" was a childish version of her mama's name, but it had been a child who woke to the news that just like that, she was half of nothing, a child whose mother had been put under a spell that lasted until Ruthie forgot how to need a mother.

For Noah, such stories were the shards of a broken family awaiting repair; for Ruth, a collection of scraps to be stowed in her drawer of widowed socks; for Moll, an inheritance, a jigsaw puzzle without a straight-edged piece in the box.

2008

The day Ruthie Vogel-Fields—collector of stray socks, single child, half of nothing—told her parents she'd accepted a spot in the honors program at Kent State University, it was as if someone flipped a switch and took the house off life support. By her account, the windows were thrown open, the rugs beaten, all muzzles removed.

Her father was quietly disappointed. He'd pictured her somewhere stimulating and edgy. Kenyon or Oberlin, maybe. Somewhere close, but not so close they'd bump shoulders on the way to class. He was troubled that she might be settling on their account. But he pushed his misgivings aside when he saw Sarah come to life, rising with the sun again, out in the garden, a steaming cup of coffee in hand, singing. His mourning dove done with mourning.

"Isn't it great having the old girl back?" he said to his daughter one morning, both of them watching her mother, smiling, gloveless, tickling the spring finery—her work. And Ruthie wondered how Walter had gotten it so wrong. This wasn't "back." This was uncharted territory. A place where Sarah didn't fear the evening news and conversation didn't stop when she entered the room. She wanted in on conversations now, asking questions, listening to answers. She even thanked her daughter for the sensible, *safe* choice she'd made.

Ruthie bridled at the notion that Kent State—*four dead in O-hi-O* Kent State—could be anyone's *safe* choice. She wasn't settling. Or playing it safe. She had a plan. Living at home would cost nothing and offer no distractions, allowing the kind of course load that would let her graduate a semester early, maybe two. Meanwhile, she'd work every summer and bank every penny. While her classmates took their semesters abroad, she'd take the LSATs and submit her NYU School of Law application, hoping their pride would outweigh their fears. If she'd wanted to hurt them, she'd've taken Barnard's package and been done with it.

2009

But at the end of her freshman winter break, Sarah and Walter kicked Ruthie out of the house. For the first time in her life, she'd given them cause for worry. Though in excellent shape academically, she rarely left her room, spoke only in monosyllables, and, as far as they could tell, hadn't made a single friend. The eviction came at Glory's prompting. "Your daughter's depressed," she told them. "She should be living in the dorm like a normal college kid." Walter agreed. Sarah did not. The faculty deal covered tuition but not housing. What kind of fool, she wanted to know, would pay for a bed and lousy food eight-and-a-half miles from the bed and lousy food she had for free? "The kind that knows a smart, beautiful eighteen-year-old has no business eating dinner in front of the six o'clock news with a pair of old fogies," Glory was happy to tell her.

The move was radical, and not part of the plan, but Ruthie could've gotten on her knees and kissed her godmother's feet. Being a townie in a sea of foreigners sounded wonderful. Icing that cake were the Blackberry and used Honda Civic Walter bought to keep her connected.

Years later, her mother's packing list would become Moll's first fairy tale, recited over and over when nothing else would calm her frenetic soul. Laptop, Christmas parka, snow boots, tennis shoes, three pair of tired-looking jeans, an L.L. Bean hoodie, two wool sweaters, one white button-down shirt, three long-sleeved tees, seven pairs of white cotton underpants, one bra, a bag of socks, one bathing suit, a large bottle of Prell, three bars of Neutrogena, two bath towels, a blanket, her half-sister's set of extra-long twin sheets, and the framed picture of Grandma Ruth. As Walter carried the bags downstairs to the Honda, Ruthie took one last look around the emptied room, desolate as her mother's garden in winter. The faded rectangle on the wall where her grandmother's picture had hung, the stripped bed, the bookshelf holding the carefully curated collection of her youth . . . why did she feel like a deserter when it was *Malcah's* room she was leaving, *Malcah's* door she'd be shutting behind her. *You can't desert something that was never yours*, she told herself. But just in case, she retrieved Grandma Ruth from the last bag she'd packed and put her back on the wall where she'd hang like a sentry while she was away.

She shared a double with a girl named Lily from Mamaroneck, an exotic-sounding suburb not far from the city, filled with new-monied Jews and Italians. She was from the Jewish part, as was the girl Ruthie replaced who'd gone home for Thanksgiving and never returned. It drove Lily crazy not knowing to what misery the girl had succumbed, but she was happy to take over both sides of the closet and all but two dresser drawers. She was amused that everything of her new roommate's fit into those two drawers. Ruthie was amused that despite all she'd crammed into their cramped space, Lily wore the same thing every day—a long, black turtleneck over black leggings, a silver puffer, and Uggs with no socks. She had luxuriously long hair (requiring a lot of work), dangerously long nails (fake), and a sparkly anklet of tiny diamonds (real).

Lily was fun and generous with her stuff. "Help yourself," she told Ruthie. "All my friends do."

Ruthie went to their parties, sat in their late-night talk circles, and memorized the names of all their crushes, but feared she'd never catch up with the months of coed living they had on her. A presidential election had been settled in that time. And while she'd been curled up in her childhood bedroom transposing notes from various lecture classes, Lily had been going dorm room to dorm room signing up Democrats for Obama. She'd been recruited the first day of school and swore it changed her life. Ruthie hungered for a life-changing experience of her own but didn't know how to go about finding one. And then, on a Friday morning in the doldrums of an Ohio winter, when her only crisis of conscience should've been whether to stay in bed or attend the stupidly early class she'd scheduled, one found her.

The election and inauguration were old news. What remained of the heated contest, the posters of the big-eared hopeful from Illinois, barely registered any more. But this morning, they stopped Ruthie in her tracks. Someone with a Sharpie had drawn a toothbrush mustache on every one of them. The sight and smell of it turned her stomach. Her first instinct was to call her mother and convince her to stay home for the day, but the Blackberry's battery was in the red zone and Ruthie had no bars. (Walter's bargain plan sucked.) Then, she remembered, she'd missed last Sunday's call, which meant Sarah would be pricklier than usual, Sunday's call being the only string attached to the Blackberry. And what would be the point? Did Ruthie think a cartoon, no matter how evil, could scare off Sarah Vogel? Did she think the woman needed a lecture on slippery slopes? *She who'd been born on one?* And wasn't this bigger than anyone's mother?

It was the cry to action she'd been awaiting. After ruminating through that early class and all the rest on her schedule, she went directly to the Student Union, bought some razor blades and a spray bottle, and headed out to scrape the offending posters from the campus walls. It wasn't likely to stop the rise of fascism in Ohio, but in addition to drowning out the chorus of *sieg heils* ringing in her ears, it would be the perfect conversation starter for next Sunday's call home.

Mid-scrape, cold fusing the blade to her fingertips, Ruthie noticed a young man walking with great determination, pitched forward into the wind, like he was late for something important, suddenly stopping, as if trying to remember what that important something was, gazing in her direction but not at her, then at her, registering her act of vandalism, nodding, as if studying some inscrutable work of art, or maybe giving his approval, stroking his beard, nodding again. "Nice work," he said.

His name was Noah. He was on his way to Hillel, the Jewish campus organization, for a thing he called Shabbat and invited her to join him. There'd be dinner. Kosher but free. Not to make any assumptions—she didn't look Jewish, but what did Jewish look like anymore? And he had this feeling that he knew her. From another place maybe, a former life? Just a feeling, she assured him. She would've remembered him. The odd manner, stiff, formal. The old-man coat flapping like a cloak, a tweedy newsboy cap, the top and brim snapped together, relics dug up from a grandfather's closet. "Did I mention it's all you can eat?" he said. She tried to beg off. She was in jeans, her hands caked with paper and glue, hardly appropriate attire. "In my temple," he said, "you shine because you show up, not because you dress up." His smile was blindingly confident, and she had a feeling he'd never stop until she packed up her razor blades and followed. Which she did.

From the outside, it looked like any storefront in any strip mall, but inside, the reverence of the small coterie awaiting his arrival lent it grandeur. They called him Rabbi. When he'd said "my temple," he'd meant it. Hillel shared a long, institutional-looking corridor with several secular businesses and nonprofits, but every weekend, Rabbi Noah and his flock worked magic transforming the building's lobby into a place of worship.

Ruthie pitched in. There was the soothing clatter of folding chairs and tables, silence as the candles were lit in the last moment before sundown, and then the doors opened. Once the rush of students was seated, Rabbi Noah mounted the makeshift dais to chant the evening prayers. He had a beautiful voice, surprisingly deep and resonant. And how good he looked on his podium, friendly yet dignified in a tailored suit and sky-blue dress shirt that matched his beanie. The microphone squawked when he got too close, and he finally gave up, stepping down to walk among them, directing all to rise and turn to the open door and sing with him the L'chah

Dodi. Tonight, he explained, was about turning their eyes and hearts to the One whose gift was a new understanding of time, who completed them in and apart from time, the One who demanded nothing from them but peace and devotion. "The Sabbath is a Bride," he said, "we her welcoming partners." He was better without the mike. His voice was calm, reassuring, and quiet in a way that made people lean closer. The tactics of a pro.

It was a short service, the threads of the prayers braiding together with the smells of casseroles warming in chafing dishes. He chose a peppy tune to march them to dinner. She was the only one who didn't know the words.

He sat at the head of the table and hardly glanced her way throughout the meal. It wasn't until the sweets were passed that he finally sauntered over and asked what she thought of the evening. She told him she hadn't made up her mind. He said if she let him walk her home, he'd make it up for her. This time his smile was warmer, less confident, more honest. On their way to her dorm, she told him about Malcah. It spilled from her in a way that nothing about the evening could have forewarned, and Ruthie was mortified. But he took it all in, tears falling freely, and in front of her dorm building for all to see, he called her Ruth, his Sabbath Queen, kissed her on the lips, and made her a believer.

It was the kind of crush a girl was meant to have at fourteen. The kind that would break her heart and, in the mending, leave it stronger. But having skipped that phase, *Ruth*—she'd never be Ruthie again—was unprepared for this boy, this man who saw her off to class with a kiss, and after, was there waiting with another. Who claimed to have begun naming their children the moment he laid eyes on her. And this girl kissing him back? In public? Who was she? Was she really in love? Did she want to be? When did a person in love eat? Or sleep? Or remember to call home when remembering only came late at night wrapped in the warmth of Noah's sheets or in the early morning, watching him rock to and fro, bound in the leather straps of his tefillin, like the pork roasts Walter tied up with kitchen twine, her Blackberry recharging at an outlet too far from the bed to reach without moving. And the Sundays slipped by, at one point prompting Noah to ask if she even had parents.

"You know I do," she said, eyes narrowing. "I talk about them all the time."

"About, never *to*."

"We're not that kind of family."

"The kind that loves each other?"

"The kind that keeps tabs. The kind that sticks their noses in each other's business. My mother . . . she's a private person."

"A mother nonetheless."

Easy for him to say. Noah never had to remember to call home. Home called him. Maybe if Walter and Sarah had been more like the Koenigs, she'd have been more like Noah, patiently answering their endless parental questions and concerns, and no matter how short or long the call, ending with *I love you, too*.

"She's different, okay? Can we leave it at different?"

Her Blackberry vibrated on cue. The ringer was off, but a red light blinked with urgency. Ruth stared at the screen until it stopped, sending the message-bearer to voicemail.

"Sounds like someone wants to talk. Maybe that private mother of yours."

"Fine," she said, tapping play and holding the phone up so Noah could hear the message. But it was Walter, not Sarah, they heard. "I'll keep it short, Ruthie," he began, which made her cringe. It had been so long since they'd spoken they didn't know she was now Ruth. "I . . . uh . . ." There was a pause. "We miss your voice . . . especially your mother. And it's Sunday, so give us a call, darling." Another pause. "Okay then. Hope you're . . . hope everything's good. I know midterms are coming. Remember, by three in the morning you stop remembering anything. We, um, miss you. I guess I already said that. But, well, we do. So call. And get some sleep, honey. Okay?"

"But he sounds amazing," Noah said, his face crinkling in confusion.

"Who said he wasn't?"

Noah wisely backed down. He loved Ruth for all the right reasons—her quiet, contained demeanor, her thirst for learning, her soulful eyes, the waves of chestnut-brown hair swinging from her hastily gathered ponytail. He'd never even met the parents.

As if intent on changing that, Walter and Sarah showed up at his door that afternoon. Walter had suggested they wait to be invited, but Sarah was done with silent Sundays. They started at the dorm room they were paying for but where their daughter no longer lived, according to Lily the roommate, ratting out the second roommate to abandon her that year and the boyfriend monopolizing her time these days, Noah Koenig, a sophomore from a rich Jewish family in Chicago who, she had to say, was kind of an asshole. She'd provided his address without hesitation.

"Come in, come in," Noah said, his smile showing instant recognition and respect.

But Ruth was alarmed. Her parents weren't the dropping-in sort. She'd been sprawled on the bed, *his bed*, surrounded by books, no impropriety, both were studying and fully clothed except for the shoes parked at the door.

Sarah crossed the room and knelt at her daughter's feet. "Your father says I shouldn't worry, that when there's something wrong, we hear. But when there's something right, we should hear, too, no? Am I not interesting enough? Your father says I only need to be interest*ed*, so I'm here to tell you . . . I am. In everything about you, dolly. Also, and this is something I should've told you a long time ago." Her fingers tightened around Ruth's arms. "Losing you would be my end," she whispered so only the girl could hear. "Do you understand?"

Ruth had come up against her mother's harsher side. She'd known how mocking, caustic, and cold she could be, but this teeth-clenched, brow-pinched fury was new and clarifying. When it came to love, she'd given her mother a pass. It never seemed that she was capable of such feelings, *any* feelings, but now Ruth understood. As horrible or unlovable as she might be, her mother would love her because that's what mothers do. They give their love to a child. And what does that child do? She gives it to her father, then to a man, and then to her own child. And that child gives her love to her father, then a man, then the next child. It was the human chain. It felt heavy around her neck. Heavy yet comforting. A kind of peace that made her know she would make her call next Sunday and every Sunday after.

But closing the door on her parents, Ruth was confronted with a new, unanticipated front of fury.

"How could you keep this from me?" Noah demanded.

"Keep what, Noah?"

"I hear about your dead sister the minute we meet, and *this* is a secret? I spotted it right away, the tattoo on your mother's arm. *She* wasn't hiding anything."

"She never does."

"Don't put this on her, Ruth. Meeting a Survivor is rare enough, but in my own home? Without warning or even mention of it?"

"So I still have details to share, Noah. Don't you?"

"*This* is what you call a detail? No, my love, *this* is what makes you who you are. *This* is your nature, your character, your worldview, your true north. And, my God, you don't know how happy you've just made my parents. *This* makes you one of *us*."

In bed that night, after the fury had boiled away and he'd kissed her more tenderly than usual, two truths bled into the liminal space separating consciousness from sleep. Only fresh from the folds of anger does love come into focus, and with the addition of Noah, her *us* would grow exponentially.

2011

It was inevitable their parents would meet. An inevitability hastened by Noah's graduation.

The Koenigs doted on their son. There were two older sisters—out of the house, building their own families—but their boy was special, and they'd been anticipating this day since his birth. Henriette (Hennie to most), her thick hair smoothly coiffed, sheathed in Eileen Fisher, stood tall in low-heeled Ferragamos, imperious but kindly, a matriarch, not a queen. Josef (Yosef or Yossi to Henriette) was slight and affable with a lazy eye that made people take him for a *nebesh* (a mistake, Noah warned; in the boardroom, he was a lion). He wore a rumpled Brooks Brothers sports jacket, white button-down Oxford cloth shirt, L.L. Bean chinos, and a skull cap of Burberry plaid. Next to them, the Fieldses seemed arrogantly brandless, Sarah courteous but distant, always on the lookout for a corner to hide in, Walter a big-handed ball of warmth, grateful for the permission they'd been granted to horn in on this momentous family event.

The Fieldses assumed they'd have dinner together, but the Koenigs begged off. So many emotions, such a long drive home. And that would've been that if Ruth's father hadn't sputtered a last-minute invitation for breakfast the next morning, a quick egg scramble that would put them into the worst of Chicago's afternoon traffic, but what could the Koenigs say, their only son looking at them with those eyes? The idea didn't thrill Sarah, either, but what could she do with the boy's mother already calling them *mishpachah*?

The promised egg scramble blossomed into a full-blown brunch. French-press coffee, berries and sour cream, lox, bagels, and babka.

"Sarah, you must have been up all night preparing. I hate having put you to so much trouble."

"You didn't," Sarah said, eyeing Walter.

"My dad's the cook," Ruth interjected. "He made the babka *and* the bagels."

"Lucky you," Hennie told Sarah, then turned to her own husband. "Ach, this babka. Good as your mother's, no Yosef?"

"Just as good. But who knew you could make your own bagels?"

"Well, we get such good ones by us," said Hennie, smiling politely at her hosts.

"Still . . . homemade bagels. My hat's off to you, Walter."

The corner of Sarah's mouth curled. Reading her mind—the man's *hat* was never off—Ruth shot her a derisive look but couldn't stop her own lips from curling. It was an awkward moment, Hennie not knowing what the joke was only that her husband was the butt of it, and in return, she surprised them all by inviting Ruth to spend the summer with them. She made it sound like the idea had just come to her, but everyone knew this wasn't a woman who did anything spontaneously.

Josef, a born mediator, reminded the love of his life that their son would be interning, working late nights and weekends. "What did you call it? A special kind of hell?"

"I got through it. So will Ruth. We'll help her." To the kids, she said, "Your father and I are modern people, and these days a girl doesn't need a ring on her finger to get to know her in-laws better. Right, dear?"

"Mom," Noah said, watching Sarah pale. "I haven't even proposed."

"Oh, but you will, boychik."

Ruth smiled, coyly lowering her eyes. Hennie, with great satisfaction, told them about the graduation party she was hosting on the twenty-sixth. The whole clan would be coming, and she couldn't wait to show off her son's new friend.

"Marvelous," Walter said. "That's the day Ruthie turns twenty-one!"

She wanted to die on the spot.

Henriette turned to Noah in dismay. "And you didn't tell me? Well, then it's simple. You'll all come, right Yossi?"

Before either Josef or Walter could speak, Sarah made prayer hands and asked Henriette (she refused to call a grown woman Hennie) if she might have a word with her daughter. Alone.

The assault was swift and fierce.

"Now you're getting married, moving to Chicago, running away from school, us, and your responsibilities? He can't stand being away from you for two months, tell him to work here.

You start following him around now, you'll never stop. Your father says you're old enough to make your own decisions. Well, then, decide to celebrate this birthday right here, with your family, where you belong."

"Why are you making this such a big deal, Ma? You haven't had a birthday party for me in years."

"You never said you wanted one."

"I didn't. I mean, I never cared one way or the other."

"So now you care?"

"I'm just trying to do the right thing, Ma. Why won't you let me do the right thing?"

Ruth did summer in Chicago—Winnetka, actually—and accepting their gracious invitation proved to be the rightest thing she could do.

At the Koenigs' Tudor-style mansion, people dressed for breakfast and minded their manners. Henriette showed her how to set a table, pointing out which china went with meat and which with dairy. There was gardening, volunteering, and lunching at the club. The woman had never earned a day's wages but called everything work. Ruth, who didn't know what it was not to work, had found herself a beautiful oasis of idleness, sunning within the lush borders of their manicured yard, soaking in the guesthouse's deep clawfoot tub, and luxuriating between the percale sheets of its king-size bed.

Showing the extent of her graciousness, Henriette changed the date of Noah's graduation party so her daughter-in-law could be home for her birthday. And though Sarah surpassed any previous measure of festive, Ruth was struck by how impervious to the pleasures of housewifery her mother had always been.

At the end of her season of luxury, Ruth returned home, done with campus life. Being back in her old room, *Malcah's* room, was strange only in how familiar it felt. Like she was in high school again, Sarah *loo-la-looing* about the house, brewing her muddy coffee, tidying up, Walter calling out newspaper headlines and falling asleep in his armchair, red pen in hand, a pile of students' papers on his lap. Sarah, swathed in sweaters and still cold, lobbying to crank up the boiler for the season. Walter's rose-colored glasses making fall's leafy extravaganza rosier than ever. He'd cleared a space for Ruth in his study, but she preferred working in her bedroom where no one bothered her. She'd made it clear that Noah's late-night calls were the only interruptions she'd tolerate. Except for post-call gushing, should she encounter anyone raiding the fridge on their way to bed. The gushing always featured the Koenigs. It was the Koenigs this, the Koenigs that, until Sarah had to leave the room lest she say something she'd later regret.

Ruth graduated that December. She chose not to walk, to her father's consternation. She flew instead to Chicago to prepare for her wedding.

It had been sprung on them all. After her first Yom Kippur with the Koenigs, watching Noah raise the long twist of ram's horn to his lips, the air filling his cheeks, the mournful, pagan wail of the shofar rousing them from their stupor, all of them emptied, cleansed, trembling at the precipice of death, knowing that whether or not they'd proved themselves worthy, their lot was cast, the women bustling, the mothers, sisters, wives, and daughters laying the dining room table with a feast—challahs, borscht, pickled herring, kugels, honey cake, a spiked schlag for the coffee—and preempting the *motzi* that would allow the first longed-for bite to be taken, Noah had gotten down on one knee and, in front of everyone, declared his intention of asking Ruth's father for her hand in marriage, *if* she were agreeable. Without hesitation she assured him that it was her hand to give, so yes, she would marry him, the sooner the better. And there was cheering.

Ruth didn't call home, thinking it news best delivered face-to-face.

Her parents were waiting at the airport when she landed. She'd spent the flight practicing her speech for when that face-to-face moment came, but the diamond on her finger, a knockout, said it all. Walter couldn't have been happier, Sarah happy enough.

The next day, Henriette called with more news. She'd booked them for December twenty-fifth, the only date their synagogue, rabbi, and best kosher caterer in town had free. The photographer, florist, and orchestra were a different story, but no one doubted who'd prevail.

"The woman's a miracle worker," Walter shouted, lifting Ruth off the ground and swinging her around.

"Sure, what's Christmas to her?" Sarah said.

"What's it to you?" Walter asked, slightly out of breath.

"I don't understand the hurry is all."

"Youth, darling. Haven't you noticed? It's always in a hurry."

It took a moment for her husband's wisdom to sink in, to understand how little would be gained by stepping on the brakes and how much could be lost by trying.

"This is the one?" she asked Ruth. "You're sure."

"Very."

Sarah guessed it was time she got used to this long-distance thing.

The night before they were to marry, after countless nights sharing a bed, Noah and Ruth made love for the first time. Since they'd met, God had been coaching Noah on the benefits of chastity, how it would protect their union from the bad luck that nudges its way through the smallest seam of indiscretion, and so, no sex until they exchanged vows.

She was surprised when he knocked at her door, both families bedded down in their assigned rooms, but she'd never been opposed to a little fooling around, and the bouquet of condoms he presented made her laugh.

Unclothed, eyes open, touching and touched, she found herself beguiled by the circle of thinning hair always hidden under his kippah. Beguiled by his concern for her pleasure. Beguiled by his fluency in the language of passion. Beguiled.

After, Noah compared them to Moses's tablets, bound together, only the spine of God standing between them. Ruth wasn't sure she agreed but always enjoyed a good simile.

The ceremony took place on the bimah where Noah had become a bar mitzvah under his father's reign as president.

Through the porthole of her dressing room's door, Ruth watched her mother walk the aisle, each foot landing in syncopation with the klezmer-like beat of the music they'd chosen, the young usher at her side instead stomping *on* the beat. At the rehearsal dinner, Ruth had practiced the mincing steps she'd take on the big day, hanging on to the arm of a proud, teary father, ready to be unveiled and *given* to her betrothed. But it was her mother she now and for the first time wished to emulate, every step sure, significant, taken alone. She'd never seen her mother's solitude as independence, never imagined her a bride or lover. Her father was at her side, shifting nervously from foot to foot. Noah was already in place, expectant, anxious, stiffly bound in tux, cummerbund, and bow tie, washed of the wisdom he'd stockpiled in his time guiding others, awed by the temple's block of silence, naked as she'd ever seen him.

As the strings transitioned to the wedding march, Ruth paralyzed by indecision, the wedding planner tapped Walter's shoulder and sent the confused man down the aisle on his own. Mrs. Koenig would not be pleased. And Mrs. Koenig was paying the bills. But a wedding planner's raison d'être was to ensure the bride got her every wish, and whether she knew it or not, this one's wish was to flaunt tradition and take that aisle unencumbered, joining her love, her partner, under a chuppah dripping with flowers, held aloft by four posts, open on all sides, homage to the sturdy, welcoming home they'd someday build together.

"*This* is your moment . . . *go*," the wedding planner hissed. And Ruth stepped through the swinging door.

Noah had compared them to Moses's tablets, but seeing him now, nervous, vulnerable, she knew theirs was not the union of two pieces of stone, unmovable, punitive. More like two pieces of cloth. His silk to her wool. Each differing in qualities of strength and tension, warmth and drape, beauty and strength. *That's us*, she thought. *A garment durable enough to outlast the pine boxes we'll be buried in.*

Once Ruth and Noah were pronounced, the guests, bundled into their winter finery, made their way through snowy streets to the ballroom of the Koenigs' country club, and partied late into the night.

2012

Before the last thank-you note was mailed, they learned they were pregnant. Noah was halfway through law school. Ruth at the beginning of her own quest for an advanced degree. Hers in a psych/social work program designed for students who'd seen enough of the world to want to help others but needed a class schedule that would accommodate their working lives. She'd seen little of the world but liked the idea of flexible classes. The deposit was non-refundable.

"This wasn't the plan," Ruth sputtered between sobs.

"What plan was that?" Noah asked. Surely they'd let her defer once they heard about the baby.

"Excuse me? This program leaves time for a job. Why not a baby?"

"So we agree. It's allllll good."

He was the most unconflicted intellectual she knew. In his mind, once they decided they wanted a baby, the when and how of it became mere details. Ruth—wanting *this* baby, not *a* baby—felt herself drowning in those details. Also deeply insulted by his tone-deaf reference to hormones, her understandable despondence over waylaid plans, and his optimistic forecast that all she needed was time. Then again, if he thought time was the answer, she'd ask for it, along with his promise not to tell a soul until she was ready. "Of course," he said, though his definition of "soul" included those in their inner sphere. The corner grocer? The mailman? The registrar at the law school? All fair game, as he saw it.

Eventually, Ruth relented and let him tell his mother. Surprised at how good it felt, she told hers. That was week seven. By week eight she was jubilant. By week ten it was over.

They called it a blighted ovum. She'd been pregnant with fear, hormones, doubt, self-recrimination for that doubt, and expectation . . . everything *but* a baby. There'd been no embryo, not even a hairball to wrap her grief around. She'd *lost* nothing.

But in the devastation was Sarah's chance to prove her worth. Only she knew the solitary confinement, the humiliation of loss. It was Ruth's first real failure, and only her mother had no words, aphorisms, or advice for her. Even her father drove her crazy with his clucking. Only Sarah's frank assessment held solace. *This happened . . . what next?*

The master's program was next and thank God she hadn't deferred. Her courses and internship at the university's health clinic left no time to wallow.

2017

Ruth and Noah focused the next five years on their careers, completing their schooling, becoming licensed in their respective fields, and getting the kind of first jobs that led right into better ones. Noah had assumed they'd do their ladder-climbing in Chicago, but the offer of all offers from a top New York law firm changed everything.

The response to the news differed predictably. Noah's parents opened a bottle of champagne and put a deposit on a condo at the Plaza so they could visit as often as they liked. Sarah offered a bruised "What, Chicago wasn't long-distance enough?", and a disparaging *hmph* in regard to the Plaza. Easy for the Koenigs to trot off at their pleasure or for special events like the New York Bar Association's induction ceremony when their boychik would be anointed Noah Edward Koenig, Esq., filling his parents with enough pride to forget that his father's law firm hadn't been good enough for him.

"*We* work," Sarah said.

"*You* work for your best friend and your husband has been emeritus for a decade," Ruth countered.

Walter promised to come soon and often and successfully wrested a second to that promise from his wife. But every Sunday it was another battle, Sarah maybe'ing away invitation after invitation, pushing Ruth up against her line in the sand.

Her father's birthday fell on Passover this year. Their first in New York. She was dying to show off her new apartment and hostess skills but was done begging. "Come or don't come," she told Sarah. *They'd* celebrate Walter's eighty-fifth with or without them.

Sarah had known her youngest daughter was smart. She'd underestimated her cleverness.

Her years of sedering in Winnetka had taught Ruth the many ways in which *this* dinner party differed from all others. Everyone arrived on time. The men dined like pharaohs while the women ladled soup. Two meats were served when one sufficed. And there was the work of boxing and schlepping the chametz to the food pantry, unboxing the *pesadich* dishes, rinsing the crystal, polishing the candlesticks and Kiddush cups, and puzzling over what to cook ahead and what to save for the last minute.

For Sarah, Jew by default, it was a night no different than any other. Her praise of her daughter's apartment—the calm of the neighborhood, the view from the riverside windows, the resplendent table—sounded sincere but rehearsed. That her mother was no more comfortable in this house than her own made Ruth feel like a fool for thinking it could be otherwise.

Once the Koenigs cabbed over from the Plaza and everyone was seated, Ruth took her first full breath of the day. Noah, handsome as a prince at the head of the table, asked them to open their Haggadahs, giving Walter a minute to fawn over the

Arthur Szyks they held in their hands. Brought from Poland by Henriette's grandmother back in the '30s, these priceless first editions had been the kids' housewarming gift (the downpayment on their apartment couldn't be giftwrapped). Though Ruth had never cared for them—she'd outgrown her fascination with the dark and foreboding—she was proud of her father for recognizing their worth. Proud of Noah, too, for his flawless davening and thoughtful commentary, in English for Walter and anyone else who needed a reminder of slavery's horrors and freedom's burdens.

Noah did everything with such zeal, whether leading a service or inhaling his mother's matzah balls, feather pillows with high-density centers, just like he liked them. And as though a new weather front of gratitude had swept the table, Henriette congratulated Ruth on the brisket, so tender it melted in the mouth, Ruth thanking her mother-in-law for advising her to keep an eye on the butcher—the *schnorers* were always trying to keep the fat flaps for themselves. And upon hearing about the half-cup of sumac her daughter-in-law had added, Henriette, who'd never heard of sumac, called her a "real *balabosta*." Josef praised his children for working so hard at everything they did. "Too hard," added his beloved, who deemed every extra hour Ruth spent with her clients one less devoted to her husband. "Just how," she asked, "would they ever squeeze in babies with their schedules?" (Saying *their* but meaning *her*.)

For once, Sarah took Ruth's side. To her, children should be a surprise, not a squeeze, and she couldn't speak to Noah's schedule, but if Ruth liked working long hours for her troubled clientele, maybe they should all shut up and let her be. Henriette, not one to be *shut up*, claimed it was Noah who worried about the time Ruth was spending with strangers, sometimes more than with her own family, and when her exasperated son insisted he'd said no such thing, his mother asked since when was it a crime to worry about your daughter-in-law—*even one who'd refused to take your family's name.* At that, Noah pushed his chair from the table and headed for the door. Walter told him to stay, they'd talk it out, which made the Koenigs laugh, assuring him their son was no flight risk, it was only tradition to open the home's door at meal's end, inviting a long-dead prophet to grace their gathering, drink from the last cup of Manischewitz, and share news of the Messiah's coming. Through the opened door, Walter got a glimpse of the long, carpeted hallway, which he thought an unlikely setting for a mystical event but was betting this would be the year. "What good prophet could say we haven't earned a brighter future?"

"Ah, but *this*, my friend," said Josef waving his Haggadah, "is the only future. Take it from one who reads it every year . . . there are no plot twists. It always comes out the same."

Then why bother? Walter would have asked if Sarah hadn't chosen that moment to bring in the cake, the tall, airy thing—plush with shaved coconut—triggering a sublimely unreligious chanting of "Happy Birthday."

Ruth seemed nervous but sliced and served the cake. Once everyone had had a few bites she signaled Noah, who presented their gift, an interactive watch that doubled as a phone. Walter was over the moon with his new toy, strapping it on though it wasn't yet charged or loaded with the software that would allow him to do anything from anywhere, and he thanked the kids for dragging him into the twenty-first century.

"But enough about me," Walter said. "Let's give Josef a chance to enjoy his cake. He hasn't even touched it!"

Josef gave a sheepish shrug, leaving Ruth to explain that they'd already eaten the afikomen, which was supposed to be the last food to pass their lips.

"You didn't think you could tell me? Am I a child?" Sarah's voice rose in alarm.

"They asked to break one little rule," Josef offered. "I said, why not?"

"Here, here," said Henriette. "And isn't that the thing about us Jews? There's always next year to get it right.

Sarah froze. There it was. *Us Jews.*

"What do you mean?" asked the inquisitive gentile at the table.

"Only that we're a hopeful people. Always looking ahead," she said pleasantly.

"Hopeful, yet existential. I like that." Walter said, equally pleasant.

"Existential?" Josef said.

"Absolutely. Christians have the Afterlife to keep folks in line. All you've got is a good set of questions. And seemingly, as many answers as people in the room. The heaven you guys would have invented."

"If we'd invented heaven, we'd've had to invent hell," Noah quipped.

"We have a hell. It's called history." Josef couldn't resist.

"A history you read over and over, each time hoping your People will reach the Promised Land, knowing they won't."

Under the table, Sarah took hold of her husband's hand and squeezed.

"And you think *Hashem* should have fulfilled His promise, giving them a pass and hoping for the best?" Josef asked.

"The Christian God would have."

"Then our God is more practical," Noah said. "These existentialists you speak of lived their lives shackled, treated like animals, poisoned by self-pity. Let's face it, they were screwed up. God kept them wandering only until the last remnant of damage was cleared from the People's memory."

Sarah gave his hand a hard squeeze, preempting Walter's rebuttal. She rose and laid her fork across her half-eaten cake, prompting Hennie to do the same.

"Sit, Henriette. You've done enough. Ruthie and me, we can manage from here."

In the kitchen, the two women worked to the hiss of steaming water, the clatter of dishes. When she could no longer bear the silence, Ruth asked what was wrong.

"Tell me," her mother answered, shutting the faucet. "When you look at me, is it damage you see?"

"What are you talking about?"

"At the table. Noah said I was damaged."

"He was talking about the Jewish *people*."

"And he doesn't think I'm Jewish people?"

"Well *he* does, but *you* don't."

"He said it, Ruthie. You can't tell me he didn't."

"Ma, he respects the fact that you're . . . different. And he loves you because he knows that whatever it is that made you . . . that way . . . it's not your fault."

"But it would be better if it was my fault, no? Then he could sleep at night knowing it's not something genetic, something you could pass down to his precious children."

"He thinks no such thing. He married me, didn't he? And I'm okay, aren't I?"

"Maybe he thinks it skipped you. It does that." Her son-in-law hadn't once blamed her for the miscarriage, but there it was.

"Do you know how crazy you sound?" Ruth cried. "No one thinks you're damaged, no one thinks I'm damaged, and no one thinks there's any damage being genetically transferred to our brood of hypothetical children. Daddy loves debating with his son-in-law. It's an exchange of ideas, not an attack. You can finish up here or leave the rest for Noah and me. I'm going back to my guests. It's been a nice night, Ma. Please don't come out until you can do so without ruining it."

It was a while before Sarah returned to the table. Everyone was engaged, talking, laughing. Only Ruth recognized the off-kilter smile. Only she guessed how long it would be until a next visit.

2019

Time ticked by on Walter's miracle watch in spurts of pings and bongs, the vaguely familiar riff of a steel-drum band signaling a call from the kids, who knew he got a kick out of talking to his wrist. Knowing it made Sarah feel like a character in a James Bond movie, they made their Sunday calls to the real phone, the kitchen phone, her lifeline. No one else bothered them on the weekends, and she let Walter handle weekday callers, especially the ones selling something.

But it was the kitchen phone that startled her one morning when she was home alone, Walter off having coffee with some retired professor pals. If she'd known who was on the other end Sarah wouldn't have taken her time picking up. Lucky for her, her long-distance daughter was impervious to rudeness this morning. She'd felt a twinge in her left ovary. The kind that could only mean one thing. Ruth was pregnant.

She hadn't even told Noah. They'd promised, when/if it happened, to keep it to themselves until she started to show, but she couldn't help herself.

"It was an accident, Ma. We'd stopped thinking about kids."

"Accidents happen."

"But it's a good one, yes?"

"Nothing says an accident can't be good."

"I knew it the moment it took. Do you think that's possible?"

"Whatever a person can think up is possible, dolly."

Ruth cut the call short. She was on her way to the doctor but promised to get back to her.

Sarah hadn't digested the first call before the second came, Ruth in the doctor's waiting room telling her about the strange urge she had to laugh and cry at the same time, insisting that contrary to prevailing wisdom, one could indeed bring up children in the city. And shouldn't one? The diversity on every corner, the character-building risk chromosomed into every day, the cultural nuggets rewarding the curious, and more, but the nurse was leading her into the exam room.

Ruth called again en route to the office, asking for Sarah's discretion. "You can't tell anyone, Ma. Not Glory. Not even Daddy. No one. Because you know, everything sucks." To the driver: "No. Take Park. Madison will be nuts." Back to her mother: "The country's going to hell, you know what I'm saying?"

She did.

"People spreading lies, nothing stopping them?" Ruth hated bringing a child into a place so bereft of trust, truth, and decency. Hated the strain this tiny being would put on their fragile world through no fault of its own, hated the elitism of her harbor (yet who better to have children than good, kind, resourceful people?), hated her secret desire for a girl who was pretty and smart and content with the gender she started out with, when her baby's health was all any real mother should want. There were so many things to hate about having this child, and yet never had she wanted anything more.

"You have a good job, Ruthie. A good husband. You and the baby will be fine."

Her mother's blessing was comforting. She felt small again, but in a good way, a little girl racing to a big-girl lunch in the backseat of someone else's car, ready to ignore the political angst swirling around her and hunker down to the future she'd build for her family.

"Ma?"

"Yes?"

"Is it too much to ask? Keeping my secret?"

"Go back to work, dolly. Secrets, I'm good at." And a privilege to be asked. If something happened, another loss, someone would need to remind Ruthie and Noah that for a moment it had been more than air and dreams. She was that chosen someone. Henriette didn't even know yet. For a night or two in April, Sarah slept soundly.

Soon enough Sarah was released from her promise. The mother-to-be began calling more frequently, randomly and about the smallest things, and Sarah always ran to pick up. But in the fall, she answered a call that turned her cold. It was Noah. Noah never called. Ruth was in her fifth month. Anything could have happened.

"Is it the baby? What's wrong? Is it Ruthie? Tell me. Noah, I can hear it in your voice." Maybe it was the wiring, arthritic, mouse-nibbled—most of the time, she was amazed anyone got through.

"They're both terrific. Only Ruth's been unusually emotional about the 9/11 Memorial this year. She's never been to one, you know. Never been interested. And now, out of the blue, all she wants is to go."

"Then she should, Noah."

"But the baby kicked last night, Sarah."

"That's good, no?"

"Yes, except she's convinced herself it's a sign . . ."

Sarah listened for the words between his words.

"The first kick coming so close to the damn Memorial? I don't know, is she right? Is it a just kick or is it a sign? Is it good or bad? You tell me."

"It's good. It's good, Noah. What else can I say?"

"It's just that . . . well, Ruth needs you. I begged her to call, but she was afraid."

"Not a day in her life has that girl been afraid of me."

"It's causing you pain that scares her, Sarah. They're expecting thousands. She shouldn't be alone in a crowd like that, and she doesn't want me there. She doesn't want anyone there but you. It's only two days away, but there's still time to get here. I'll book your flight. There's one into LaGuardia leaving Cleveland in the morning. You can call me back if you need to think about it. But think fast."

She didn't have to think at all.

She owned a complete set of luggage now, the rolling kind. *What smarty-pants thought up suitcases with wheels?* she wondered. The smallest piece would hold all she'd need, but this trip begged for her old leather valise. It had been hiding under her bed, a crypt of mementos, for years. Daylight showed off its cracked leather and balding corners. One of its metal clasps snapped off in her hand. They were contemporaries, she and the bag, but the years had been kinder to her. She rested her hand on top and closed her eyes in hasty meditation before taking it to the cellar for good.

Walter, back from a walk, was happy to hear about the trip. Had she gone anywhere alone since they met? He was pleased for her *and* for Ruth. Of course he had concerns. The anniversary always took a toll. Though each got easier, surviving the next was never guaranteed. But he dodged that touchy subject with a reminder to pack her Nikes. The city was hell on feet.

Walter dropped her at one airport; Noah met her at another. Men were handy that way.

Despite the somber nature of the imminent event, her son-in-law grinned the whole way back to the apartment. He hadn't said a thing to Ruth, in case she didn't show, Sarah suspected. But here she was, and he was giddy over the big reveal.

Back at the apartment, he made tea and together they waited for Ruth's return from the office, Noah chattering on and on about his wife's love and how much she did for people never asking anything for herself, how grateful he was that he and Sarah were able to do this thing for her. For a man with so much, he sounded nervous. As well he should be. Like her mother, Ruth was not one for surprises.

And it did take her a moment to process the scene she walked in on, her mother and husband tête-à-tête over tea.

"Is it Daddy?" she cried, her eyes big and round. "Is he okay, Ma?"

"What is it with you two?" Noah said, after a kiss. "Something always has to be wrong? She came for the Memorial, Ruth. She's your date."

Ruth ran to her mother, wrapped her arms around her, and held on for a long time. They had dinner, they talked, and when invited, Sarah laid her hand on her daughter's belly to feel the kick of the fierce and determined baby on its way. They retired early. No one slept.

The morning papers put the terrorist level at orange. Breakfast talk stayed on the tinny side of cheerful. Noah, in pinstripes and skullcap, kissed them both goodbye. Ruth was amused by the fanny pack her mother buckled around her waist.

"Go on, laugh. There are thieves everywhere," Sarah warned.

"So I've heard," Ruth said, then asked her mother how she felt about taking the train. "I'd call a cab, but they've probably blockaded the area."

She assured her daughter she'd be fine. She had her Nikes.

As early as they were, they couldn't get close enough to see the stage. Several large screens cantilevered off the sides of the surrounding buildings promised everyone would see everything once there was something to see, but so far the cameras showed only the twin pools filling the spots where buildings once towered.

Ruth worried about her mother standing for so long, when it was she who needed to sit. She hardly showed, her bump still easily concealed by a loose top, but a hernia pushed at her groin and sciatica burned down the back of her leg.

The murmur accelerated as stagehands began hustling people into place—the Memorial's founders, leaders of what 9/11 charities still operated, first responders, movie stars and mayors, all the living presidents but for the one in office, and a state senator who was sixteen and on his way to Stuyvesant High the day his father, a Filipino immigrant and elevator mechanic, gave his life helping others out of the North Tower.

They each had something to say and two minutes to say it, a timeframe that left little room for creativity. Only the state senator, that grown-up sixteen-year-old, dispensed with the de rigueur praise for past martyrs to address the terrors lurking ahead. Five minutes into the speech, he was pulled from the stage and the reading of the names began.

They numbered close to three thousand. Sarah was there for only one. Hearing it would kill her and not hearing it would kill her. She begged her daughter to leave with her, but for the sake of the baby who'd soon bear the name she, too, was afraid to hear and not hear, Ruth refused. Being heard by these thousands gathered was a way for that name to be cleansed, liberated . . . loved, and nothing could drag Ruth away.

But Sarah was like water. A mosquito, a mouse, a crowd only another something to slip through. And the names were read without her, hardly a breath separating one from another. All present had their own reason to cry. Ruth now had a new one.

On the way to the airport, Noah, who always had something to say, was silent. Because of Sarah, Ruth wouldn't go to work, her face a ruin of tears. Because of Sarah, he and his wife had fought, and somehow he'd come out the villain. He hated being the villain.

He pulled up to the curb, put the car in park, and took a deep breath.

Sarah unclipped her seat belt, but Noah wasn't done.

"You let us down," he said, staring straight out the windshield. "I've been your number one defender, but all my wife wanted was for you to be there, the one person she trusted to know what she was going through. I gave you a choice, too.

If you'd said no thank you, I would've understood. But you said yes."

"I'll call, Noah. I'll apologize. She'll give me another chance."

"I know she will. She's got nothing but chances when it comes to you. She's only mad at me because I expected too much of you. That's what it's come to. But is that what you want? For Ruth to lower the bar until she stops expecting anything of you? Our expectations come tangled up with our care and love. Do you want my wife to stop caring enough to be hurt by you? Because that's where you're heading."

What she wanted was for him to stop saying *his wife*, as if that was all Ruth was. Sarah wished he hadn't been so hellbent on surprising that wife and had understood the magnitude of his ask. But her wishes had no weight.

Her former number one defender got out of the car, set her bag on the curb, and told her to have a safe trip.

He'd asked only that she be the mother his wife needed. She'd promised to do better. He said he believed her. But months later, when Ruth went into labor, it was Walter's miracle watch, not the kitchen line, Noah called.

2020

Like a great ocean liner it sat, the Upper West Side, tiers of windows overlooking the frigid Hudson. It was through one of those windows that Sarah sent her cigarette smoke while waiting for news of her grandchild's birth. Only Walter had been invited, and not because Ruth and Noah needed a ride home, their newly formed family like fresh-picked eggs in the protective carton of his backseat, but because he'd never failed them. Wanted or not, Sarah was there when her daughter waddled in holding *her* daughter, a whole day old at the start of a whole new year. Noah followed, nerves on high alert for hazards, a wrinkled rug, a drafty window. On the living room armchair, he built a throne of pillows for his sore-bottomed wife and nodded to his mother-in-law, who saw he was ready to weep—from fatigue, from joy—but instead threw his arms around her, happy she was there to see their family assembled for the first time in their home. Walter was parking the car.

Sarah hovered over mother and daughter, Ruth aware of nothing but the beautiful stranger sleeping in her arms. "This is your grandma," she whispered. "A great woman you'll want to know. And Grandma," she said, "say hello to your granddaughter Moll."

Moll. After months of thinking it was a Malcah they were making. A Malcah brought out of the shadows to remind them of the courage it took to dream . . . if it would please Sarah. "Would it?" Walter had asked. Would this Malcah be the object of grandmotherly joy or an echo of loss? She wanted to say yes, meant to say yes, but "maybe" was her answer, a stall for time that led to the reneging that made Sarah call out in her sleep, YES, so that only Walter knew how pleased she would've been.

They had their reasons. Moll was more modern, more American, easier to spell. Her Hebrew name would be Malcah. There'd be a ceremony at the temple. Noah hoped they'd both come. Said so twice.

All was not forgotten, but an olive branch had been extended. In return, Sarah gave up cigarettes.

2022

Despite everyone's intentions, it was two years before they met again. A lethal virus put the baby naming and everything else on hold. People were advised to shelter in place. Henriette and Josef, flaunting government warnings, made several trips across state lines, but the Fieldses were no scofflaws. Daily video chats kept them sated, and the steady feed of their worn, placid faces amused Moll for a while, but Ruth knew it wasn't enough. Their toddler needed all her senses engaged. A lap to sit on. She wished her parents would come to them, but only Walter was game. They were nearing August. Vacation time. The virus wasn't going anywhere, but they were shot and boostered to the max, finished with fear, and sitting on a considerable war chest of credit card points from eighteen months of online shopping. To see them, she'd have to play Mohammed to her mountain of a mother, clear her calendar, and book the flights for their first family trip home.

2024

Push mowers and ceiling fans. Sweet corn and beefsteak tomatoes. Grit ringing the tub after a day at play. Surfing the thrust and choke of the ancient Subaru her heavy-footed grandmother drove. The hideaway under her grandfather's desk. The smell of chlorine and a persistent crotch rash from sitting in wet bottoms strapped into a car seat. Summer. Ohio.

The first trip went so well—both parents rested, the child spoiled rotten—that another was planned, and another, until summering in Ohio became a foregone conclusion. Though calling it a summer was an exaggeration. They never stayed more than two weeks, but to a little girl used to measuring time in Mommy minutes, those parcels took on the stature of an entire season.

Only one summer stood out from the rest. Moll was four, old enough to file away memories of her own. Her grandmother had finally retired from the university, so she was around more than usual. A presidential campaign was in full swing, and the adults were all plotzing over a junior senator from New York whose rabble-rousing had monopolized all television viewing in her grandparents' comfortable house. The noise, the flashes of color, the constant, thudding bass woke her in the morning and quickened the pulse of her dreams at night.

Her parents would've denied her the media blitz, but her grandfather defended her right to a front-row seat for what he called "a revolution of reasonable proportion."

"You're addicted." Her grandmother sounded angrier than usual. "You want to make the child addicted too?"

"Only thing I'm addicted to is you, kiddo," he whispered in Moll's ear, his knees cracking, his stubble a rasp at her neck.

He'd bought the whole family tickets to the Akron Rubber Bowl so Moll would always remember it was her grandfather who introduced her to her first rally. Sarah bowed out, not the rallying kind. None of them were, but the appreciative hooting of the crowd-filled stadium was infectious. There was music, cotton candy, and people draped in American flags, like a county fair without animals. And it was fun. Spirited.

Having kicked up some local dust at a 9/11 memorial a few years back, the candidate, New York state senator Gabriel Flores, was a national nobody who'd slogged his way through the pack to become a contender for the highest office in the land, and all the nobodies in that land were cheering him on.

Moll, a fidgeter, climbed her parents like a human jungle gym until a boy walked onstage and sucked the restlessness right out of her. He was small but way bigger than her. That mop of dark curls, the Yankees T-shirt, baggy camp shorts, high-tops, everyone at his feet . . . she felt the need to be up there with him like an ache in her bones. Then the senator, handing over his megaphone, called the boy his daughter, Gabriella. Which was all wrong. In Moll's world, girls dressed like princesses, not baseball players. But this girl who looked like a boy, no ballplayer or princess, gave Moll goosebumps. The good kind. "What do you get when a politician promises big change?" Gabriella Flores shouted, and a thousand coins pulled from a thousand pockets rained down on the metal bleachers.

Anticipating this now-signature move, Walter had brought a canvas bag for Moll to fill with all the pennies, nickels, and dimes she could gather. The bag was so heavy he had to carry it for her. Sarah was preparing a barbecue for the kids' last night in town—hot dogs, sweet corn at the height of its season, watermelon, the works—and on the way back, the rallygoers stopped at Hudson's ice cream parlor where Moll paid for the hand-scooped tub of their favorite, Rocky Road. It was the perfect finale to their late-summer feast. The perfect finale to their stay.

The next morning, the Koenigs headed home wedged into the car with their luggage, singing along to Raffi, worrying only about Monday rush hour traffic on the GW Bridge, pleading with Moll to wave to the grandparents waving at her from the driveway, the old man she called Grandpa and the woman she used to call nothing but now called Great-Great after overhearing talk about some great grandmother and reasoning that if any grandmother was great why not all?

With them gone, Sarah tackled the breakfast dishes; Walter wiped the tears from his eyes, hopped in the shower, and whistled "Happy Days Are Here Again," a song having little to do with the meeting ahead of him but everything to do with grandfathering, one of the best reasons he'd found for having a soul. He was a man obsessed with happiness. The accumulated happiness of the work he'd put into making his home office baby-friendly. The happiness of knowing his daughter had done well for herself. The happiness of left-behind board books—the soft fur flaps, reflective ovals, and tiny cardboard doors he'd play with after Moll's departure. The happiness of those fleeting parcels of summer with all his girls home. The happiness of having a wife, a grandparent herself with so much mystery left to plumb. Happy to be the plumber at her side.

Only his son gave him pause. If he'd been there for him maybe Robbie would have accepted his prized internship at the *Times* instead of waiting and waiting at the tip of Manhattan for Malcah to rise from the rubble. Maybe he would've found himself by now. In a way, Walter lost two kids that terrible day. But it had fallen to him to be the happy one. What could he be but happy? Happy that his candidate, no sure thing, was polling well. Happy for his wife's wisdom. *What change? Talk to me when people start walking on ceilings.* Happy to be a contributing member of society, head of his family, and grateful for the small band of grad students—devotees of a study few still considered relevant—who continued to need his guidance. Happy to know the university had chosen to validate his life's work with an endowed chair, still able to peddle his bike along the dusty path to what he thought would be the final meeting of the university trustees underwriting the chair that would bear his name.

He would not have been happy with the ending written for him, collapsed on a patch of hot blacktop outside his office building, his bicycle locked in place. Most likely a heart attack, the medics said. The man *was* past ninety. At least he'd never learn about the humiliating loss his candidate would suffer, or that the chair he'd so coveted would never materialize, the trustees too lily-livered to cough up the dough for a theologian who questioned the validity of theology. Some called it a blessing. The unsuspecting Koenigs did not. They got the call on their way across a bridge, high over a river. The only way back being forward, they continued, weeping as they bumbled their way off the northbound exit, through the streets of Harlem, back over the bridge and onto the highway in reverse this time, checking into a motel room that smelled of mold and had only one bed in which the three of them slept without even changing into pajamas.

There'd be no funeral. Walter had wanted his body donated to the Cleveland Clinic. He'd looked forward to becoming some hard-working med student's lucky cadaver. But a day of sitting shiva was planned. Noah thought he would've liked that, and Sarah agreed. You couldn't send a man like Walter to cold storage without some kind of whoop-de-doo.

Robbie was the first to arrive, a forty-five-year-old stranger who could've passed for the boy Sarah had eaten sundaes with so many years ago. *What,* she wondered, *would a forty-five-year-old Malcah look like?* As if wondering the same, Robbie crumpled into her arms sobbing, unlocking the dam holding back Sarah's tears.

Ruth, her four-year-old clinging, directed the setup. The rentals came within the promised window but missing the table linens. The driver was no help. Sure, someone goofed, but he had a truck crammed with merchandise and a schedule that was heading toward overtime. So, unless they'd consider pushing their event to the end of the day . . .

"Push shiva?" she snapped. "And make our guests eat off plywood?"

"I've eaten off worse," Sarah chimed in.

"I'm handling this, Ma."

"Let the man go, Ruthie. We've got tablecloths in the cellar." Sarah had intentionally left the linens off the order—such a waste of money—and wasn't about to confess.

"I don't want you going up and down those stairs."

"I do it all the time," Sarah grumbled, taking Moll onto her lap.

"Please, Ma, today just be a grandma."

At that, Moll, longing for her own bed in her own room, staged another fit of tears.

Ruth hated the cellar, its crumbling cement floor, the low-beamed ceiling strung with cobwebs. But through the lens of adulthood, it was less creepy and more organized than she remembered. Metal shelving held Bankers Boxes with stick-on labels: Financials, Warranties, Tax Returns, Docs Awaiting Shredding, Batteries Awaiting Recycling, and, as Sarah had said, Tablecloths. The linens inside the box were yellowed and wrinkled but better than nothing.

As she pulled the box from the shelf, something flopped down into its place with a spray of dust. Sarah's old valise. So much smaller than Ruth remembered, a thing near sacred in their home, always kept close but unreachable, deep under a bed or at the top of a closet. Malcah had been brave enough to root around in it behind their mother's back but usually got caught. This would be Ruth's first unchaperoned peek.

Releasing the latch and lifting the lid unveiled an unholy mess. Like one of those kitchen drawers where people stowed their madness—wine corks awaiting another use, the little discs that stop chairs from scraping the floor. Sarah never had one of those drawers. She'd had this. A scrap of paper with a string of characters they all knew by heart; the slim book her mother refused to read to them; the manual of zipper parts covered in crayon from when Ruth mistook it for a coloring book; the golden compact, that big-girl Polly Pocket better than any toy. She curled her fingers around the cold metal. She thought about asking Sarah to give it to Moll now. It would be hers someday anyway.

But there were other things, unseen things—papers and pictures of strangers. A blue-eyed girl on Santa's lap. Some long-ago family, a man, a woman, two little boys, and a wiry-haired child with Sarah's face—it could only be Sarah—though she'd never mentioned brothers, and the woman looked nothing like Grandma Ruth. And the man? A grandfather she'd never imagined? Equally puzzling, a grouping of stick figures on yellowed construction paper, a bespectacled man, frizzy-haired woman, and little girl, "Sasha" printed in blocky letters. Paperclipped to it were several sheets of paper covered in school-girl cursive, the ink a vivid turquoise, no date, no return address, no salutation, only the lethal words *Remember, Ma?* The compact dropped from her hand. She heard voices. *Oh God, Hennie and Josef.* They'd brought the prayer books. Shiva would start in an hour. She knew she shouldn't go down this rabbit hole but didn't think she could face her family until she had. Once she read what she had to say—this girl, this Sasha, this aunt, *this sister*—she wondered if she could face them at all.

But shiva was starting in *less* than an hour. Not for the unknown she'd just lost or might wish to lose but for her father, an innocent in all of this. Unless he'd been in on it. An unthinkable thought. Her father was no liar. Which made her mother what? Moll was whimpering, Noah calling from the top of the stairs, pulling her from the basement, a place she'd never set foot again.

In her haste, she realized she'd left the box of tablecloths behind. But like her mother said, cloths, no cloths, it didn't matter. The tabletops were already covered with the neighbors' cakes and casseroles. Jan the Ex was making an entrance. Glory right behind her. The Koenigs bounced Moll in their arms. Ruth was uncharacteristically solemn. But it was her father's shiva; no one expected smiles.

Needed at his office, Noah flew home the next day but insisted his girls stay on. It would be a lonely time for Sarah, and he was sure having them around would help. Ruth blew her husband a kiss goodbye and kept manically busy for the whole week. The air in and around the house grew heavy with anger. If her mother noticed, she said nothing. Ruth wouldn't've cared if she did.

Once home, Ruth enrolled her four-and-a-half-year-old in a full-day pre-k program. Just like that, the limbo of endless TV and coin collecting were over. Her little one had a schedule. Moll loved the creative parts of school—painting with fingers, stringing necklaces of macaroni—but couldn't tolerate being creative on demand, napping, or the smell of room-temperature food kept too long in lunchboxes. The child was a dependable source of drama, but between her and work, Ruth's mind stayed too engaged to wander off into her mother's deceit.

2025

Sarah's widowed mornings were hard. Not at first, when the garden was still warm and inviting, but gradually, as the sun rose later and there was only the dreaded chill waiting for her in the kitchen.

One morning, too impatient to wait, it came up and found her in her bed. Downstairs, everything sparkled as if the night's stars had been swept from the sky into her living room. A broken window the culprit. Pulling Walter's robe tighter, her slippered feet crunched across the glass dusting the floor. There were no signs of intruders. *The wind*, she thought. These days, it pounded her house like it was waging a vendetta. Then she saw the bird lying dead on its side. "You didn't do either of us any favors today, did you, my friend?" The wind was still at it, banking the glass against the room's oak moldings. Shards of window rickracked the inside of the frame. She wiggled one and then another, but they held fast. She'd need to call in help, but for now, covering the hole was her priority.

In the cellar, toasty from the furnace, she found a box big enough for the job. As she hunted for supplies, a different kind of sparkle caught her eye. She bent down to look. It was the whatchamacallit. She couldn't find the word but recognized Dorotea's last gift.

The bulkhead door was bolted. Nobody could have gotten in. She almost wished they had. If she'd dropped it herself and couldn't remember, if she'd been sleepwalking, for instance, or wide awake but not in her right mind, *that* would be worse than burglars. The case was dented, the mirror cracked. What had it been doing lying in a pile of crumbled cement? Remembering she'd been in the middle of something, she shook her head, slipped the compact (*ha!* the word loosed from the tip of her tongue) into the robe's pocket, and headed upstairs with hammer, nails, and tape.

In the kitchen, she let Mr. Coffee do his work and dragged an old stepstool into the living room. Walter would say she had no business climbing it. But Walter wasn't there. No one was. She'd wait for business hours to call a glass man, if there still was such a thing—but for now, the cardboard and blanket she tacked to the window trim would do.

Her coffee was hot and ready to pour. She'd learned to drink it black. Now, even the smallest carton of milk soured before she got to the bottom of it. She ate her toast and soft-boiled egg over the sink. After the day's messy start, she'd have to shower and dress quickly. She had a ten o'clock. Not a year into her retirement, she'd called Glory asking for her job back. After Glory finished laughing, she'd scheduled the interview. HR protocol.

"Is it the money?" Glory asked point-blank.

Money had nothing to do with it. Sarah had taken her Social Security at sixty-two, a move everyone, even Walter, said she'd come to regret, as if she'd leave money on the table for someone else to grab. It was a paltry sum to live on but enough to direct deposit into a savings account and forget, the miniscule interest steadily compounding. She'd gotten rich on the government's dole, so no, she assured her friend, it wasn't the money. She missed her. She missed the office. Missed having a purpose.

Glory smiled sympathetically and handed Sarah a file folder full of forms.

"I can't hire you, but it's good you came in. You never filled out your retirement papers, and you know how HR feels about that," Glory said. "Bright side is now we can do it together." She had a set, too. The only relevant feminist is a young feminist, she'd learned from the youngster who'd be taking over the department she'd created. She was trying to think of it as an opportunity, a chance to write that book she'd been talking about for as long as Sarah had known her. "The package is decent. Maybe I'll hire you to help me. Just what I need, a shit typist who hates libraries . . . hey, I'm joking."

Sarah had stopped listening. In the file, stuck between uncompleted forms, was a clipping from the *Times*. The obituary of David H. Bloom of Queens, New York. The picture, small and grainy, showed a man younger than she'd ever known. What followed was the summation of a life, beginning, middle, and end. Thursday, November 27, it was dated. Bloom had died a Thanksgiving ago. Bloom was dead and she hadn't known.

"I'm so sorry, Sarah. I forgot I put it in there for you. I knew you'd want to see it. You were with him a long time."

"Ten years."

"Not as long as you and me, but long enough to be friends."

Sarah nodded, trying to concentrate on the two columns of crammed type.

Glory looked quizzically at her. "You weren't more than friends, were you?"

Had they ever been friends at all was the question.

"He watched out for me. We . . ." She remembered a coat, green and woolen, too stiff for a child's arms to bend. "*I* owe him a lot." Enough for her to have sensed he was gone.

"Good. I loved the guy, but he couldn't keep it in his pants. Even *we* had a thing . . . don't be shocked, Sarah Vogel, he wasn't my first man. We were presenting at a conference. The Rise and Fall of Feminism in Post-Soviet Russia. God, how we fought. I didn't know he was married. I didn't care. But like with you, he watched out for me. That was the turn-on. And *what* potential. I always thought if he could just grow up, David Bloom would do great things. It wasn't in the cards, I guess, but there was a good man there. Maybe not a good man, but a good mind. You and I definitely lost a good mind."

Sarah was saddened by the loss of this man and his mind, by the reminder that she'd never been his one and only, the shock that one of his many had been the only real friend she'd ever had. But the ache in her chest was for Kit, at his bedside, lighting his runway to the end, and then getting him into the *New York Times*. She wondered if Sasha knew, if this shudder from the past would be the thing that brought her back.

Glory took a bottle of vodka and two glasses from her desk drawer and made a great show of tossing the obit in the trash. "The university wouldn't approve, but what do you say we toast our dear friend and scholar?"

After downing their shots, Glory tidied up. In the only moment her back was turned, Sarah impulsively pulled the clipping from the trash to take home with her. David H. Bloom. She'd always wonder about that "H".

It felt strange walking the campus with no direction or intention in the middle of the day, students everywhere, none aware of her existence. The gray hair and slow gait made her invisible. What did the invisible have to care about? Nothing to hold them down. Gravity? *Pffft*. These half-child-half-adults only wanting to be seen? They, too, would be invisible someday, never knowing an old woman had once offered to teach them the benefits of moving through things *un*seen—crowds, trouble, anything. Eventually, they'd look in the mirror and wish they'd taken more precautions against the sun and made more trips to the dentist, had done better all around, changing the oil in their car more, stretching or at least practicing how better to occupy the hide that would someday hang from their frames. And maybe, someday, they'd wake on a chilly morning and find a dead bird of their own on the living room floor. Or go to the bank and find out the teller who'd licked her thumb while counting bills had been replaced by a machine that never made mistakes except for ones that couldn't be corrected. Or one day, the sky above them, blue as a little girl's tongue after finishing a raspberry Icee, would turn dead white and opaque as the enamel lining the lid of an old lady's canning jar. If they'd asked, she'd have told them that people don't change, they just get old. At least, in Ohio.

On the ninth of Tamuz in the year 5786, Ruth lit the yahrzeit candle Noah had bought to mark the first anniversary of her father's death. The Christian calendar wouldn't have him dead for ten more days, but according to Noah, a yahrzeit's a yahrzeit. The jelly jar, the colorless wax, the generic label. It was determinedly unmodern, so practical and poetic, so Walter Fields.

She set the candle in a dish on her desk. Her most recent promotion had come with a window, which she opened, letting in an early spring gust that snuffed the small flame that was meant to burn all week. The sob rising in her throat wouldn't be contained. The period of mourning was officially over. As a Doctor of Psychology specializing in post-traumatic stress, she knew no calendar could be the arbiter of grief but thought she was due some measure of release. Yet loneliness lingered.

It was Saturday. July. Just another Shabbat for the Koenigs. No work, no traveling to work, no striking matches, no lighting wicks, period. Laws were laws, according to Noah. *Hashem* did not leave it up to His people to decide which were the important ones, which were negotiable. *Hashem* assigned them—all 613—with a simple *do your best.*

This year, she had not done her best. Had not honored her mother with patience, trust, kindness, or truth. Had not made it easier for Sarah to spend time with her granddaughter. And when Sarah accused her of spoiling Moll, she'd raised her voice and told her she should've tried spoiling her own children once in a while. She'd stolen from her, lied, and with each Sunday lied again, answering Sarah's question, *is everything all right?*, with *everything's fine* when Ruth was not fine. She was disappointed, disgusted, and dismayed that she could have read a missing girl's letter and not said a word. That she'd kept it in her pocket through a whole day of hiking with her mother and not said a word. That she'd buried it in her underwear drawer on returning from Ohio and still said nothing, not even to her husband. Had she become her mother?

Even worse, Moll had spent too much time in daycare, a consequence of Ruth spending too much time at work—weekends, holidays—everyone worrying that she was running herself into the ground because they refused to understand that there was never enough time in a day for paperwork *and* clients, and then her higher-ups got her an intern, a gifted young woman who wanted to be just like her, down in the trenches where it counted, overworked and underpaid. She was smart, gutsy, and bragged about her research skills, which Ruth did not hesitate to test.

"Let's say you have a life-changing experience," she put to the intern the day she started. "Like, you're at summer camp and get a letter from home saying your dog died or your best friend moved and you'll never see her again, and the only person who understands is your counselor, who gives you special attention for the rest of that summer and promises to be your counselor forever, but the next summer, she doesn't come back. Maybe she goes traveling and you're crushed but have fun anyway and forget all about her. But years later she pops into your head, which you figure is a sign that you're supposed to find her. Could you show me how you'd do that?"

Knowing her way around universes and algorithms, the intern was able to find faster than show, and despite a dearth of data—a name, a birthdate from the Stone Age, a public school somewhere in Queens—she quickly had the computer spitting out Sasha Vogels from all over the place. The number in California alone sent Ruth to the restroom to pant into a paper bag. A real job stole the intern away before she could make any more headway. She offered to keep going, after hours on her own, if she liked. Ruth, who knew she'd taken things too far, assured her that wouldn't be necessary but wondered if she'd mind printing her results before taking off. The genius Googler had never used a printer but loved a challenge. The exercise ended with hugs and a voluminous list to be added to Ruth's underwear drawer.

She'd brought the list and Sasha's letter to the office on this anniversary morning. To exorcise the house, file them away with her other dead cases, or perhaps touch them to the candle's flame. But the candle had gone out, and she wouldn't try again. Not on Shabbat. Once was barely justifiable. Twice was asking for trouble.

She stopped the next sob about to break as Noah bounded down the hallway and burst into her office, straight from shul, loud and happy, Moll in tow, sharing her daddy's sabbath high. There weren't many youngsters who could sit through an entire morning service without a peep, and the attention she got came with treats.

"How 'bout I take my girls to lunch today?" he said as if it were a novel idea, though taking his girls to lunch after shul was the best part of their Saturday ritual.

"Sure," Ruth said, putting the letter and list in her purse. "If those Dum-Dums haven't ruined her appetite." All sugared up, Moll's lower lip began to quiver, which Ruth nipped in the bud by picking her up for a cuddle, an important reminder that she could still count on her daughter's trust because her daughter could still count on her. It occurred to her, scanning the restaurant menu, that a safe-deposit box would preserve her documents while keeping them out of her reach and everyone else's. On Sunday, she'd call Sarah and start a new kind of conversation, one where the words wouldn't sour on the way out of her mouth. First thing Monday, she'd stop at the bank.

Life

2038

Moll hadn't had a tantrum in fourteen years, but graduation was bringing her close.

She wasn't alone. Millions of her generation from all over the country were straggling into their high school auditoriums hung over from partying and sighing in anticipation of the tedium. Her personal claque included Ruth and Noah, already teary, and Bubbe and Zayde Koenig, both dressed to kill and beaming. No Sarah. No excuses. No big deal. Though after all those summers enduring weeks of geriatric diatribes on Ohio's weather and the health benefits of gardening, Moll couldn't help wondering what a girl had to do to get a little payback, die? Bite your tongue, her mother the mind reader was undoubtedly thinking. They weren't a superstitious bunch, but dark thoughts on happy days were strictly verboten.

A wave of tentative applause from families and guests cascaded over the students down front ready for the show to begin. A show that, in normal years, should've starred Moll. She was in the upper echelon of her class and due several awards, having made Science Nationals all four years at IHi (Manhattan's High School for Innovation). But due to the last-minute addition of a surprise keynote speaker, their time-honored program had suffered some cuts. The student orchestra's rousing but pitchy cover of "Smells Like Teen Spirit"? The top dog's speech about moms and rocky shoals? Both? A girl could hope.

At the sound of backstage rustling, audience members leaned forward in their seats and hushed as the lights dimmed, eager for the reveal of their promised surprise. But the great velvet curtain did not swing open. Instead, a thirty-foot hologram shimmered into shape against its flexing folds and identified itself as Gabriella Flores. The adults groaned, knowing all about the pain-in-the-ass activist and her "de-seat the elite" agenda. The graduates jeered, for whatever grief Flores had caused their parents, she was no movie star or tech mogul.

Flores made no apologies, jumping in with the one truth they'd been hearing all year: Graduation should mark the beginning of their lives, not the end. Everything else, she'd come to tell them, was bullshit. They *should* be worried. They *should* be confused. And angry. They had been raised on terror, financial disharmony, and fear. The diet of victims. But they needn't be victims. This commencement was an inflection point. They could choose to be agents of change, part of a new order voicing their full-throated yes to valedictorians and no to homecoming kings and queens; rejecting a future of four-hundred-dollar haircuts, four-thousand-dollar handbags, and forty-million-dollar penthouses; embracing limits to the kind of profanity one could use, the amount of property one could own, the number of marriages one could have. It would be on them to say no to tattoos and smut, high heels and fast cars, yes to a country with an org chart flat as Kansas, no to titles and promotions, and an emphatic no to dreams of growing up to be president—a hollow crown worn by a powerless figurehead. Showing off could no longer be tolerated.

The only way to keep from being judged by their covers, she warned, was to *keep those covers blank.*

She was a sheaf of tawny browns—eyes, skin, suit. Her skull a luminous globe, not a hair on her head to mar the effect. Whether by choice or affliction, no one knew. She had a larger-than-life presence but embodied the anonymity she professed. "Every tick of the clock wipes a piece of the past clean," she said in closing. "Be that tick. Scrub your way to a new order, the New Order of Modesty."

That night, 67 percent of the Class of '38, calling themselves NOOMers, wondered what they should do next, put their heads together, and decided to shave them.

Over coffee the next morning, Ruth and Noah read about the mass protest incited by a commencement speech that had bumped nerdy awardees from daises across the country. One headline named it "The Great Coup Cut of 2038."

"Wasn't she—"

"The kid from the Akron Rubber Bowl. Yes . . . all grown up."

They chuckled over the pictures of skinny-armed teens huddled like freshly shorn sheep.

"Can't tell the boys from the girls," Noah said.

"I think that's the point," Ruth said.

"Time to buy stock in sheitels?" Noah's joke, a bad one, reminded them of other shorn sheep they'd seen in pictures. Auschwitz. Dachau. Buchenwald.

"What do they think they're proving?" Noah asked.

Neither had an answer.

Nor could they believe their eyes when Moll emerged from her bedroom, one more sheep in the flock.

"What have you done?" Noah cried at the sight of his daughter's shaved scalp.

"What everyone else did," she said, rubbing against the grain of fresh stubble.

"Do you know how many have died doing what everyone else did?"

Moll reminded him of the AP history she'd taken and said she was capable of *looking* like everyone else without *being* like everyone else.

"Leave it alone, Noah," Ruth said. "Hair grows back."

Only if you let it, Moll thought, rubbing her prickly scalp. A thirty-foot-tall apparition had told her to be like water, a mouse, a whisper from the past, an ode to the future, the clock's tick forever erasing itself, forever replacing itself. She, too, remembered the Akron Rubber Bowl, marveling over a child who could command an audience, pining to be that child. It was the path she'd picked long ago. Traveling it as a NOOMer might provide the cover she needed.

2041

Moll's next graduation was equally non-conforming. She'd matriculated at the Center for Continuing Innovation two weeks after leaving its little sister, IHi. The three-year degree program discouraged shortcuts, held stars in low esteem, and drew no distinction between study and work. Her mentor, Roz Benton, demanded a professional polish to whatever her mentees touched. "Think of me as your project manager, not your teacher," she advised on day one. "Think deliverables, not homework." There'd be no orientation, no hand-holding counselors, no top of the class. Nothing but long, intense days. Moll was in heaven.

Sufficiently insulated from the world's petty problems, she barely blinked when Gabriella Flores "came out", pledging allegiance to the party of Independents and winning a House seat that rendered her moot to NOOMers nationwide. Moll, like her fellow future innovators, kept her shorn head down until the day she looked up and realized her program requirements were complete, her time within higher education's golden parentheses over. It felt like a minute. The longest minute in the world.

Half the class would take a short break and move on to one of several advanced degree programs. The rest, including Moll, sick of school and hungry for a taste of the real world, would start real jobs. The placement center had already reviewed their applications and shared them with those companies participating. Though every applicant was guaranteed *an* offer, there was only one she'd consider. Never mind that Roz, a member of that company's C-suite, had sworn there was nothing to worry about. Moll was a nervous wreck.

The allotted four tickets were all Moll needed. Two for her parents. Two for Henriette and Josef. Showing up for the family wasn't in Sarah Vogel's job description. Apparently nagging was in her mother's. For months, Ruth had been on Moll to grow her hair so she'd look normal for the pictures. Her mother asked so little of her, but Moll stuck her stand. This sleek-skulled do *was* the new normal, and the sooner her mother accepted it, the better. She caved on the light buffet Ruth planned—no principles on the line there, though her mother's idea of "light" involved six protein-filled platters, a full complement of pastries, and a cornucopia of fruit.

The morning concluded with a communal sigh of relief, everyone's wishes granted. Contract in hand, Moll hurried home to change out of her dress clothes in time to greet her parents' friends and dispense with their pesky questions before the IHi crew showed up. She'd kept in touch with only a few. The program left little time for external friendships. Moll wanted to know where they'd been and where they were going, and she'd picked up some joints for them to smoke on the fire escape, celebrating their last moment as kids. She'd only gotten high twice at the Center, both times non-inhaling and work-related, the lab having brewed a new substance for her team to test. One small dot absorbed through the skin proved instantly intoxicating, and she'd been on the team tasked with studying its commercial applications. Suspending the substance in a salve was Moll's idea. Rubbing it into the palms was her partner's. Infusing it with the scent of kumquats, the smell of happiness that filled the Koenigs' apartment at Chanukah, hers. Naming it "Kumquat," adorably suggestive, his. Putting their salved palms together, a shared instinct. Discovering that the substance induced an almost hypnotic state of telepathy between lovers, each sensing the other's wants before they did, turning the act of pleasuring into a truly reciprocal event . . . *that* was one of life's beautiful accidents. She didn't know what name it would take, or if it would make it to market. She'd left all that in the hands of the incoming class, *all but the jar she'd appropriated.*

What it was like to pre-experience an orgasm was of little interest to her *bubbe* and *zayde*, however. It was her pre-*pre*-orgasmic self they'd fallen in love with, that sylph-like creature without hips or tits. They still loved and were proud of her but already dismayed by the preteen pudge she'd picked up—along with the nail-biting, foot-tapping, knuckle-cracking, scab-picking mess she was on track to becoming—the image of her copulating while intoxicated, even under the aegis of science, would've pushed them right over the edge. When was she going to trim down? How did she plan to support herself? What would she be when she grew up? That's all they wanted to know. "Listen," growled Roz, her former mentor future boss. "This girl's on track to be one of the great hypothetical artists of her time. I'll kill her if she grows up." Henriette and Josef excused themselves without comment.

Moll had no intention of growing up. Or trimming down. Her grandparents could worry all they liked, but her future was unstoppable. She did agree with Hennie on one point. It *was* time to strike out on her own. What had always been *their* home had begun to feel like the exclusive domain of her parents, she the interloper busting in on them at inopportune moments. She'd never caught them with their pants down, but all their moments shared a quality of intimacy that no longer included her.

Good for them. And good for her. Because she'd gotten the job she wanted and, lo and behold, coming up with problems only she could solve was surprisingly lucrative. She could afford her own place and had no interest in a roommate (her mother's suggestion). What was being on your own about if not being on your own? No one to bother or be bothered by. No one to walk in on her with her pants down.

She and her fellow sardines had shared a can for three years with no fucking around (none that didn't involve the scent of kumquats). Catching up could be fun.

She found the perfect apartment at the Brill Building. Once filled with recording artists and producers, the Brill had been the hub of hip for several generations. But nobody could make cool stay where it didn't want to be, and the whole operation had gone belly-up in the first quarter of the 2000s, when it was sold to an international conglomerate and then to a particularly prescient NOOMer who'd grown up on an elderly aunt's stories of near-embalming nights at a wild hangout called the Chelsea Hotel and thought he'd try a reprise. The Brill never reached the same heights of wildness. Its residents routinely brushed shoulders with danger but a safety net of anonymity allowed them to retreat, repair, and reset no matter what shit they wandered into. The price per square foot was high, but the restriction on square footage kept the rent manageable, and with a tenant-discounted in-house gym, a top-floor bar, a food court, and a wet and dry cleaner in the basement, all open 24/7, who needed space? She worried about living in such close proximity to work—the company's new Think Tank division had moved into the Brill's ground-floor office suites—but what did it matter if the mother ship was in India or ten floors down.

There was an assortment of small luxuries she'd give up. But if she ever needed a change of clothes, someone to nag her about her hair, or reminder of what glory there was in walking room to room, naked as a baby through the rooms of her own home, she could always go home.

Moll had come late to sex. She was sixteen her first time, with a boy she'd grown up with. Nice, Jewish, their families friendly. They'd studied together since sixth grade, neither wanting much else from the other. Then, one night after hours of cramming for finals, he floated the idea. She was okay with losing her virginity to Eddie Feuer but asked for a day to think it over. "Sure," he said. "As long as you don't blab to your mom." Which made her laugh. Of course she'd tell Ruth. Moll told her everything. She was consistently nonjudgmental, open-minded, and slow to say no. If Moll thought (perhaps hoped?) that this time would be different, she was wrong. Ruth was all for it. "Anything you ever want to do, you can do right here, you know. Love is just another form of art," she told her daughter. "Poets and painters must practice, why not lovers?"

"Don't start planning the wedding," Moll said, the words "lovers" and "practice" making her gag.

"Got it. No Eddie-the-son-in-law. He's only a friend. But, see, that's what's good about it. Friends don't break your heart."

This would be good for the kids. Ruth was convinced. They were too ambitious to let passions prevail. She doubted either expected harp strings or cymbals, which meant neither would be disappointed.

"Since when are harps and cymbals not worth the risk?" Noah asked, appalled that his wife could be so cavalier about the deflowering of his only daughter.

"Then you tell her she's not welcome to experiment within the comforts of her own home, safe and protected. But don't blame me when she runs off and finds some back alley to do it in."

"Those are my only two choices? Abstinence or a back alley?"

"I think so."

"There are still back alleys?"

"Filled with Pied Pipers waiting to entrap the impressionable. At least Eddie's no Pied Piper."

"You've heard him daven, too."

"Be serious Noah. This one's smart and clean, and we know where he lives. Does it get any better than that?"

With Noah's concession, Eddie Feuer became the first of many study buddies Moll brought home for milk, cookies, and a quickie.

It was strange transitioning from high school's hedonistic heights to the program's humid microclimate of nonbinary togetherness. Knowing everyone within its puritanical corridors—by their work, dreams, and idiosyncratic proclivities—left little interest in sex (her Kumquat partner the exception). At the Brill, where no one knew anyone, mystery abounded, and everyone was interested. In Moll, especially. Which she found perplexing. She'd had plenty of boys and their boyish wants, but here there were only men. To what could she attribute their desire? The boost in stature of her new job? Something in the water? She never imagined it could be as simple as a well-shaped skull and hawk-like profile, a pleasing amount of meat on her bones and a gaze that deferred to modesty's laws but signaled a deeper dig could be worth their while. Under the sameness, she was different. Different was cool. Different was also hot. In one night at the Brill, she'd discovered a new kind of sex with a new kind of partner in a new kind of home.

She reveled in her baptism by fire at the Brill. If only her career hadn't remained so doggedly fireproof.

Ruth waited a month before paying a call. It was too soon to be missing her mother, but Moll was weirdly excited and reserved a table at one of the Brill's higher-up cafes. Ruth loved a view.

"Everything all right?" Moll asked, instantly detecting something amiss.

"Everything's great," her mother answered.

"You're sure?"

"Yes, I'm sure. Why?"

"You're kind of freaking me out with that look."

"What look? I don't have a look."

"Yeah, you do. It's that mix of adoration and worry you usually save for Daddy."

"I'm a mother. I adore and worry about my daughter, too."

"But that doesn't explain why you're downtown on a Thursday. When was the last time you played hooky?"

"Never. I missed you."

"Right, and?"

"Why are you being difficult? I had an appointment. With a doctor. But I came to hear about you?"

"You're deflecting. Why were you seeing a doctor? What did they say?"

"Nothing. Yet. He did a bunch of tests and said he'd call when the results come in."

"Mom, you don't get tests for nothing."

"And tests mean nothing without results, so like me, you'll just have to wait. But really, truly, I'm just here to catch up. It's been so long."

"I know. Kudos on the self-discipline."

"I wanted to give you time to adjust. Time on your own. Something I missed out on."

In her twenty-eight days at the Brill, Moll had slept with twenty-six men and one woman. Despite an all-nighter for work marring a perfect run, she was fully adjusted and busting to tell someone about the randy cast of unnamed characters who found, pleasured, and released one another within the exclusive ministry each night now brought. But hearing how her mother'd been deprived, she held back.

Their coffee came quickly, hot and frothy, each with a rock candy stirrer. Ruth ordered a Napoleon for the table. "And an éclair," she called after their server. Moll's eyes narrowed. Ruth rarely allowed herself sweets.

"Did I tell you about the Centennial?" Ruth asked.

"What Centennial?"

"I could've sworn . . . never mind. I'm in this group—well, it *was* a group. Now it's a commission. The hundredth anniversary of the liberation of Auschwitz isn't far off, and they're looking into what kind of event would best honor the Survivors, the few still with us. Like I don't have anything else to do. But of course your grandmother being one of them makes it especially important. I wouldn't have volunteered if Washington had won out, but lucky for me, it's going to be right here in New York. Central Park, actually. I'm on fund-raising, of all things. Me, who thought selling Girl Scout cookies to neighbors was an imposition. And this is bigger than Thin Mints. I'll be dialing up *every*one in my contacts for their contacts. So we'll see who my real friends are. Don't be surprised if I hit you up, sweetie, now that you're making the big bucks. It's the least we can do for Grandma, though, right?"

Moll had stopped listening, distracted by a man at the checkout, which did not escape Ruth's notice.

"You look wonderful, darling. Work is good?"

"So far, it's shit." The man at checkout was giving Moll the once over.

"Dramatic as ever. Talk. Tell me everything."

There wasn't much *to* tell. So far, the Think Tank was uninspiring, she uninspired, and Roz cloyingly patient. She hadn't come up with a single idea she could share with her boss . . . or anyone. Quitting while she was still ahead was an option she was considering. But knowing her mother's view of quitters, she thought it best to keep such thoughts to herself. For now, she'd be satisfied winning back the attention of the man at the register. A slight uptick of his chin said she had. The barest of nods dittoed her interest in him. He looked like he might come by their table but paid his bill and left. If Moll was disappointed, she didn't show it.

"A friend?" Ruth asked, smiling as she licked foam from her sugar wand.

"Something like that."

"Nice-looking. What's his name?"

"We never got that far."

"Okay," Ruth said, smile slipping away.

"There's that look again. Except without the adoration."

"It's nothing. I assumed you were sleeping with him."

"So?"

"Nothing."

Silence.

"You are?"

The pastries came on silver trays. Ruth speared the Napoleon, hacked it in half with the dessert fork, and brushed the crumbs into a pile.

"The server will do that, Mom."

Ruth kept pushing at the crumbs.

"Mom . . ."

"What? I get it. You're having sex with a man whose name you don't know." It was no accusation, more statement of fact. Still, her mother couldn't look at her.

"Sorry. We don't put a premium on names around here," Moll said.

"My baby's fucking strangers?"

"*Grokking* strangers."

"*That's* what they're calling it now? It's not even a real word."

Moll woke her wrist screen with a tap. "Grok, grokked, grokking," she read aloud. "Transitive verb: to understand intuitively . . ."

Ruth shoved a piece of Napoleon into her mouth. "So what am I supposed to tell your father?" she asked, shaking her head, eyes closed, chewing.

"Not my problem," she answered.

No casual observer would've detected a note of discord in their interaction. Her friends used to laugh whenever she whined about arguing with her mother. *Their* parents yelled. *That* was arguing. Ruth wasn't a yeller. She didn't have to be. Her disappointment was brutal. But it was Moll's turn to be disappointed. Any daughter who thought she could tell a mother everything was more than deluded; a daughter like that was a fucking moron. Ruth had never told *her* mother *any*thing. And they thought Moll was the family genius.

But how could she sit with what she now knew, based on the revised vision of the world she'd awoken to this past month? This one month and its incontrovertible, semi-awful, semi-wonderful truth. Her parents' love for each other; their home, the buffering zone of its pre-war walls; their dowry of faith and finances; the tolerance they exuded, if only skin-deep; the education they supervised, sparing no cost. When life turned its weaker profile to her, these were the blessings she forgot to count. In this month, she'd learned she needn't have bothered; they'd never been hers in the first place. Her education, once disbursed in year-long Big Gulps, now came in micro-doses. It had taken a month, but she'd smartened up. Each night pregnant with lessons, each morning alive with strangenesses as manifold as the strangers themselves. The idea of giving, no, opening herself to this new kind of unmanaged, unvetted intercourse, a communing not limited to sex, seemed wholly . . . no, Holy. Period. Maybe it was her father she should've been meeting for coffee on the Brill's top floor. The view wouldn't have impressed him, but he'd understand grokking.

Unfortunately, it was her mother she'd needed to tell, reassure, and educate about the many different faces of knowing someone, which Ruth needed to hear because what difference did it make if her daughter's experience was real or not? Fiction and reality constantly borrowed from each other. Grokking merely stitched the two together, embroidering around the edges for a double-strong bond. Sleeping with strangers no longer made you a masochist. It made you a child whose every morning was a birthday, every birthday becoming undone, the gift *and* the child. The irony being how old-school romantic fucking around had become, which Ruth couldn't see for all the assumptions in her way—that love was an entitlement; that it was still possible to keep a lover loving and monogamous unto death; that love meant an end to exploration, not the beginning. It further deepened Moll's disappointment to see that her mother was no better than the rest of her generation—that lapsing brigade of anyone who'd lived long enough to forget the smell and temperature of sex and yet persisted in pushing their notions of "responsible" attachment, infantile, impractical, and archaically id-based as they were. What Moll had learned, in only a month, was that grokking included love but was so much more. If done right.

There was more she would've been happy to get off her chest, but a new month loomed. A time for dedicating herself to a whole 'nother bounty of strangeness.

Their goodbyes were clipped.

2042

Iced by her mother over her penchant for anonymous sex, pressured by Roz for the next great idea, losing ground to less talented colleagues . . . so far it had not been a good year.

Rolling from the ball she'd tucked herself into, the electric crackle of her all-out limb stretch reaching the tips of her fingers and toes, still fuzzy from the half-sleep she'd nursed during six hours in the car with her parents, every wearable gadget put her monitorable functions at zero. This much was clear from the backseat of her parents' car—boredom's a bitch.

"Tell me again why we couldn't *fly* to Ohio?"

The question was rhetorical, but her parents chanted in unison, "We're going to Ohio to celebrate your grandmother on the auspicious occasion of her hundredth birthday. We're *driving* to spend quality family time together."

Their sarcasm, on the rare occasions they gave it license, irked her. "If only *she* felt the need for quality family time."

Her father sniggered.

"You can't imagine all she's been through." Ruth addressed Moll via the rearview mirror.

"Because she won't tell me. The woman's as forthcoming as a rock."

"That *woman* happens to be my mother."

"And our lady of perpetual immunity. She didn't come to my bat mitzvah or any of my graduations, or the Young Inventors of America thing when I got that award invented just for me. Not a Christmas or Jewish holiday. Not even your twenty-fifth."

"Actually she did come for your bat mitzvah."

"Really? I don't remember."

"The city holds bad memories for her."

"The city . . . and us."

"What a burden it must be, always needing the last word," said her mother before slinking down in her seat and closing her eyes on the subject, though she was the only one in the car who was truly burdened: managing a department, seeing a full caseload of patients, buffering her ultra-observant husband against an increasingly heretical world, keeping tabs on an uncommunicative mother old enough to expire any minute but showing no sign of giving in.

Moll regretted being the bitch. The ice had finally melted between them, and today, driving into the sun, about to host a surprise party for a woman whose every breath was a surprise, her mother seemed wearier than usual. Moll wasn't regretful enough to say so but would surrender the last word. "I bought a dress," she announced with spirit-lifting enthusiasm. "It's not even black."

"Much appreciated," Ruth said. "And your toast?"

"Written and rehearsed."

"That's my good girl," Ruth whispered as Noah coasted off the highway toward Bellefonte, their gas, pee, and coffee stop. Once parked, her parents went to claim a table. Moll headed to the restroom.

The sanctity of the stall was perfection, the effrontery of that perfection not lost on her, hot shit tech savant, jeans around her knees, squatting on a crapper dewy with another woman's tinkle, a view of sneakered feet scuttling across the beige tile.

Savant. What a joke. Idiot was more like it. She'd been expected to hit the ground running, but for a year now she'd only been running in place, every muscle cramping from the drag of weighty expectations. She'd heard a colleague in her cohort was already chin-deep in a floor-to-ceiling recodification of the tax system. She shouldn't have asked for pto. This was the time for Moll to step up her game, not step away to celebrate an old lady's birthday. If only Roz hadn't signed off on it. But it wasn't her job to make Moll's life easier. Just the opposite. Disappointing her mother was bad. Disappointing her mentor—a woman she owed everything, professionally and otherwise—could be fatal. Moll was sure she'd made the wrong decision by coming, equally sure there hadn't been a right one.

The toilet paper dispenser was empty. She'd have to drip dry. Sitting there, jeans down around her knees, her wrist screen brightened with an incoming post from her tax recoding colleague, Olivia Kim, PhD. Just what she needed, another doctor in her life, this one in the Pantone Color of the Month, *Affogato*, a warm mocha with a shake of cinnamon.

The piece was rough in places, overly technical in others, but its premise wasn't bad. With the supply of resources growing shorter and people lasting longer, lifespan was fast becoming the only currency stable enough to balance the planet's books.

"Imagine you've been given a credit card." And Moll did. "Now, imagine it's come with a windfall of credit, or better yet, an inheritance credited to your account before anyone's had to die." This *pre*-inheritance—they were calling it Plasma—was meant to underwrite the rest of your life. If spent too fast, it was possible to draw more from the Corporation but at a discouragingly high rate of interest. Any post-death surplus, or Easy Plasma, would be used to run the hospitals, planes, technology . . . basically everything.

There was an algorithm for determining the subject's Predicted Adjusted Lifespan (PAL), another for calculating the amount of Plasma their PAL merited, and a questionnaire for data-gathering that would soon allow Dr. Kim to run PALs on test subjects.

She was thorough. She was good. And Moll was as dry as she'd ever be.

"Shit," she said.

"Uh-huh," said a pair of feet outside her stall.

A different pair added, "Yeah, like now it's handwashing that kills, not toilet seats."

"Filth is definitely back, girl."

"Yeah, but still gross as shit."

A nugget of wisdom to think about on her walk across the dining atrium to where her parents were seated. Even windows onto a parking lot constituted a view in Ruth's book.

Their server, a true mocha marvel—Moll was continually mortified by her own pale container—brought her coffee. Black, no sugar, with a side pitcher of cream.

The coffee smelled burnt, but Moll didn't complain. The server did, though, broadcasting her woes to a sister server after being asked to pull another shift out of her ass. She was already on the verge of losing her sitter for always being late, and her washing machine was on the fritz, so if she didn't get to the laundromat tonight, her kid would have nothing to wear to school tomorrow, and maybe there'd be some hope of ever getting anything done if only there was another hour in the day. "Another hour," her colleague said. "For sure."

It was while pouring the cream, watching its delicate doily weave and sink into the depths of her mug, listening to the ordinary complaints of ordinary women, that it came to her. The Mutable Hour. It had the ring of a big idea. Why shouldn't they have another hour in the day? *Why shouldn't we all*, she wondered. How could a thousand-page tax code, a two-hundred-story skyscraper, a person's genetic map be altered, improved, taken down to the core and replaced, but time just fucking marched on? Of all the precious resources Moll's new arch enemy, Olivia Kim, PhD, cited in her adjusted lifespan scheme, it was only Time, at the crux of all efficiency, at the crux of everything, that remained tamper-proof. But tampering was Moll's thing.

A twenty-five-hour day, then. In the realm of ideas, what could be bigger? She could swear she heard a drumroll. Ruth and Noah, their eyes great and curious, seemed to hear it, too. She was dying to tell them. But it was too soon. People were undependable, always wanting more, no matter how much you gave them. Even her parents—this attorney, this psychologist/social worker—who had raised her to be a maverick but whose "help" should come labeled with risk of suffocation warnings. She knew better than to invite their questions before there were answers. If she wanted to free time from the tyranny of the circle, let it run flat in a continuum, she needed to draw, not talk. Her pad and pencils were in the car, but a graph was formulating, the packaging coming into view. She liked the idea of an empty box, as generic as possible so customers could make of their extra hour what they wanted. And what did anyone want but more time? Which was what she'd call it: More. But capped for greater emphasis. MORE. The universal answer to everyone's question of need.

"Ready?" Noah said, chair scraping terrazzo as he pushed himself from the table, hyped from the coffee.

Ahead were the Poconos. She'd lose satellite reception for much of the remaining drive. Her iPad would be useless. There was a 50 percent chance Kim's idea would blow hers out of the water, a 50 percent chance it would do the opposite, priming the company's pump for MORE. Not knowing was killing her, but it was only three days. In those three days, she had only to dig up some lipstick, give a toast thoughtful enough to make her mother kvell, and maybe squeeze a smile out of grand-mamma. By Sunday evening, she'd begin building MORE.

Sarah was happy to see them, happy having someone other than herself to talk with over dinner. But the next morning, Ruth and Noah left early on a supposed coffee run and Moll, worn out from their long drive, slept in. On her own for breakfast, Sarah put up a pot of coffee and opened the kitchen drawer by the sink where she kept important papers like her passport. It was expired but confirmed that she wouldn't really be one hundred for several days. Then again, she wasn't really Sarah Vogel. Or born on Tax Day. Maybe there was such a woman, maybe more than one, but there was nothing to say any of them were her. The signature looked like a child's. And who was this woman looking straight into the camera as if it were her shot at immortality. Who'd taken trips with a husband to a Rome filled with Communists, a Berlin reconstituted. Who'd let it expire, this mendacious document, one more number to stand in for her, one more tracking device.

And no matter how many truths to the contrary there may be, this was the day she'd be celebrated. Her daughter and Glory had planned everything. Both knew how much Sarah hated attention. She was relieved not to have to wait for August to roll around to see Ruth and the rest, but there was also something about having them, Ruth, Noah, Moll—the Koenigs—that made her sad. Something about the indivisible unit they were unaware they'd become. What's wrong with you, Sarah asked herself. Who would begrudge a daughter such happiness? Who would occupy the fourth seat at the kitchen table like she was a fifth wheel?

"Morning," the third wheel called from the back door.

Her gut twisted at the sight of her granddaughter's shaved head. No one had imagined it would stick. But they were all still bald as newborns, the boys *and* the girls. Even *down there. That* she hadn't seen for herself and didn't plan to.

Moll sipped from the mug she held, aping her grandmother's frown. Sarah couldn't help but smile, she and the little sourpuss whittled from the same block. On other trips, Moll had brought her own supply of city coffee. She didn't care for Sarah's brew.

"Too strong?" Sarah said.

"Just bitter. Like you."

"Good. Maybe it'll put some hair on that head."

"On my chest, you mean."

"Why would I want hair on your chest?"

"Beats the shit outta me, but that's where they claim the hair gets put. Where is everyone?" Moll asked, as if the day should stop in its tracks for her.

"Your mother said she had to go out. Your father went along. As usual."

The party was meant to be a surprise, the guests sworn to secrecy. But Glory had let it slip. She knew no pretense they could devise would pry Sarah from her home on a Saturday night. Only the truth—that they'd all come to honor her—would get her there, and Sarah promised to play along. She'd gladly pretend to be surprised to help her surprise party go off without a hiccup. Anymore there was nothing but hiccups. Hiccups and burps and stumbles constantly rerouting their plans. They were all so busy. Any trip for Noah meant at least one day off work as he was unable (or unwilling) to travel from sundown on Friday 'til sunset on Saturday, and a lawyer's work was so important. Ruth's social work was important, too. Who else would know how to teach the chronically unemployed to pull meaning from something other than work? And Moll's schooling, the mysterious program that consumed all twelve months of a year and now her job, her first, important, too, whatever the hell "creative containment" was. Moll had tried to explain, but how was a woman supposed to keep hold of something she couldn't touch?

"A lot has changed since you were young," Moll would say.

"Who remembers young?"

"But it's not that complicated, Gram. You know what a container is, right?"

"Like a box?"

"Exactly. I get paid to design boxes. Better boxes. The best box yet, which the company's betting is the human brain."

"And what happens when this human brain falls apart?"

"Some lucky person gets to start over. It's called play, Gram." Which brought to mind their summer of Candy Land and her excitement over playing a game with real rules until losing three times to her rule-abiding grandmother, the frustration building and building until she pushed the board, pieces and all, to the floor. Getting sent to her room, no treat, was her first punishment. That was her grandmother, a woman who didn't know how to give a child a break.

"They think you *kinder* will keep playing, cooped up in your little pens, alone, no water cooler, not even a Mr. Coffee to gather around, for the next hundred years?" Sarah asked.

"I guess there are still a few things to figure out," Moll answered.

Sarah didn't ask why the family was being so careful around her.

"You know, don't you?" Moll said.

"What? What could I know?" Pure innocence.

Moll shook her head, awakening her wrist screen to check the time and call her parents.

Neither answered, both phones ringing away in their locked car, no doubt. It drove Moll crazy that her parents got away with such thoughtlessness and she did not. Now she'd have to hunt them down.

Sarah would gladly have given her a lift to campus, but then everyone would know that she knew.

Moll found the old bike she'd used during her summers there. The garage was as clean and organized as ever. She oiled the bike chain, pumped the tires, and walked the bike down the driveway. Sarah was on the front stoop.

"I'm off to the library, Gram. Research, you know." Moll didn't know why she bothered making up a story. Her grandmother saw right through it.

"Ah, yes, I remember research. And even," Sarah said, raising her arms, eyes bright as her fingers cupped the word, "*libraries*."

Moll pedaled off to the Alumni House wondering if the town even had a library anymore.

"Why didn't you wake me?" Moll demanded of the party committee—Ruth, Noah, and Glory—already in full production mode.

"You know your mother," Noah volunteered over the ruckus. "Never wake a sleeping child."

"I'm not a child, and I wanted to help."

"You did. You kept her busy so she wouldn't wonder what we were all doing."

"Well, she knows."

Ruth and Noah groaned. Glory counted forks.

"I didn't tell her. I said I had to go to the library. Lame, I know, and she wasn't buying it. She used air quotes on me. I think. Anyway, she hundred percent knows."

"Good. Now she'll have the pleasure of anticipating." Ruth was such an optimist.

"And she won't drop dead when we jump out from behind the furniture."

For his insensitive comment, Noah was dismissed. Or spared. He'd wanted time to walk by the Hillel and see if anyone was left from the old days. He asked Moll if she wanted to come, and though time alone with her father was tempting, she stuck with the women.

Left to napkin folding, seating, and centerpiece zhuzhing, talk turned to the guests—the neighbors who Glory bet would show up in dungarees; Walter's favorite mentee and his partner, two sweet middle-agers now tenured at a college out West. A divorcee who'd let herself go. Another bringing her boyfriend, having gone straight after twenty years of strictly female companionship. "A situation your father wisely predicted," Glory told Ruth. "God, I miss that man."

"You two fought all the time."

"He was a worthy adversary."

"Funny. To me, he was almost too gentle for this world."

"Well, sure. He adored you."

"He loved me. Very much. He adored only Ma."

"Well, that woman is easier to adore than love."

"Yes. She was tough but always kind of my hero."

"After Malcah," Glory said, "some of us weren't sure she'd make it. I'd catch her sitting at her desk, holding her breath, waiting. Malcah only got to twenty-two. You were the baby, the sweet one who never made waves. You glided past twenty-two, then twenty-three, and twenty-four. She never stopped fearing her own breath. You married and had a child and knew pleasures and terrors few people encounter in a lifetime. And my dear friend was still afraid. If she didn't love you enough, you'd fly away. If she loved you too much, you'd leave anyway. Your mother survived the Holocaust, but you survived your mother. In my book, that makes *you* the hero."

Exactly, Moll felt like shouting but was afraid to break the flow moving seamlessly from the evening's dress code to the dinner seating before floating off to the question of how long, if up to them, would they choose to live. Quality was more important than quantity for Glory. She had no interest in suffering or getting her ass wiped by some apathetic, underpaid caregiver. Ruth didn't relish pain or loss of dignity but would take both in exchange for a little more time. Moll was noncommittal, which the women found amusing. What could questions of life and death matter to a girl of her age? Moll let them think that. Say the good Dr. Kim was right and she had far longer than Ruth or Glory could fathom. How could she explain that it wouldn't be enough? That the inevitable need for caregiving wasn't the ultimate indignity but that such an inadequate container had been designed in the first place. A failure she took personally considering it was her job to come up with a better one. The best one yet, she'd told her grandmother. But if death was merely a container failure, the best one yet wouldn't do. She'd need to come up with the best one ever, *no container at all.* If we were 100 percent persona, directed by the mind instead of a brain, with no container to fail, wouldn't the concept of predicted life spans, Dr. Kim's baby, be moot?

Ruth full-circled to wardrobe issues, worrying that the ruffled hem of the little black dress she'd packed might be too ingenue for their crowd, her voice already raspy with so much more of the day to go. Glory said it would be fine but was concerned that she might need a nap or a cup of tea before things got started. Ruth told her to stop worrying and focused on tenting the napkins, a job she could do seated while staring wistfully out the window. She hoped the weather would hold. Rain meant drippy umbrellas.

There was a déjà vu quality to the conversation, like a movie Moll had seen, set in the Civil War, about the camaraderie of women sitting together, ripping bed sheets and petticoats into bandages. Maybe it was the room. In their various ways, all were alums of this Alumni House, Grandpa Walter's favorite place, dusty and old yet notches above the standard event space with its wood paneling and other early-twentieth-century appointments. The oversized windows rattled with the winds but offered courtyard views. A long, boardroom-style table had been laid with seventeen settings. Every invitation had been accepted.

Much as she'd dreaded it, Sarah found the guests' chorus of *Surprise!* a succoring unanimity of comfort and love.

Another surprise was her dinner partner, a man she'd never seen before. He was younger than Sarah, barely eighty-seven, a widower, seemingly one of the KSU family, though not connected to any of the guests. Sarah assumed he'd wandered into the wrong party and was about to tell him so when Glory came up behind her whispering something about the gentleman's head of hair. Thick down to the follicles. Pure white. "A marvel at his age," Glory said, the retired feminist theorist turned matchmaker.

Music streamed from someone's phone. The man asked Sarah to dance. She'd already forgotten his name. He held her close. She could feel the lump in his pants. *More admirable than his head of hair*, she thought. His shoulder begged for her to lay her head upon it, but the song had finished, and dinner was served.

There was a choice of chicken or fish. She chose chicken, which the printed menu said had lived nearby and been killed with kindness. Passing as fish was an impervious-to-pain blend of soy and nut oil bound by flakes of seaweed that tasted a lot like cod. Sarah asked the man if he remembered when there were fish in the sea whose organs weren't filled with poison, and he stared at her as if she'd been reading his mind, his *YES* the impassioned cry of a wild goose happening upon his soulmate.

All old women were fools, but not all fools were old women.

The music stopped for the ceremonial presentation of the group gift, an all-expenses paid trip to New York for the Centennial Commission's greatly anticipated gala honoring the living Witnesses and marking the hundredth anniversary of their liberation from the killing camps. It was Ruth's cause célèbre. Sarah could feel the chill of that January gathering from three years away.

"It was their idea, Ma," Ruth said with a sweep of her arm.

"Thank you, thank you," Sarah said. And she was thankful, if not excited.

"You can't back out," Glory warned. She knew that despite Sarah's dread of wasting a free ticket, it was a distinct possibility.

"If I'm still breathing in three years . . ."

There wasn't a person there who thought she wouldn't be. She'd never taken a vitamin or run on a treadmill or cut the fat off a piece of meat. She'd never delivered a meal to a shut-in, adopted a rescue animal, or babysat so her Ruthie and son-in-law could have a break. Only a miracle accounted for her lasting this long. Why should the miracle give out now?

There was cake, a sheet as big as the table it came in on, chocolate under a shroud of ivory buttercream studded with candles. Glory swore there were 101, but no one was counting.

As the cake was cut and served, Moll took her place at the microphone. A spot bathed her in light. Everyone sat straighter in their chairs.

"To my Great-Great," she said, her glass raised. "They tell me that's what I called her when I was little, and every time I did, she'd say, 'Why? I'm not even great once, forget about twice.'" Everyone laughed. "But, when it comes to Sarah Vogel," Moll continued, "we can all agree that 'twice great' is an understatement." Someone whistled. "Right? We have in our midst a woman who never expected to see the twenty-*first* century, and here she is, barreling toward the twenty-second. I want to thank her for not giving up, or giving in, or budging on her rules or sense of civility, or lack thereof." Another laugh. "Her foresight, her utter lack of restlessness—a little something people once called patience?" And another. "And wisdom. Things change and everything stays the same?"

Sarah picked at her cake. What a graceful little liar.

"I guess you'd call it perspective," Moll continued, passing over the woman's embarrassment. "Equilibrium. Not taking things personally. It's an art. So please raise a glass to my grandmother, a tough old bird and a great, great woman, Sarah Vogel."

Everyone clapped. Some cried. Longevity was still something to gush over.

The cake had lost Sarah's interest. She was damp around the eyes, and it was hard to tell if she was moved or mad, what with the scowl that had become a permanent part of her facial topography.

"Even when she smiles, the corner of her mouth turns down," Moll whispered to her mother.

"In a lifetime of loss, the large holes between joy and happiness can fill with skepticism and mistrust," Ruth reminded her.

"So, okay, she's earned the right to scowl."

"*And* the right to be loved."

"I promise she'll always have my admiration. And respect. But how can you love someone who looks at you like she's having a tooth pulled?"

"Can't you see? You're a portrait of every minute of a life she's missed."

"By her choice."

"In your opinion."

The only one that counts, Moll thought, but this was a last word she'd keep to herself.

A few guests stuck around for cleanup. Sarah sat at the head of the emptied banquet table, a queen abandoned by her subjects. It had been too long since Ruth kissed her cheek and headed to the ladies' room promising she'd be right back to help her to the car, and when Moll came to check on her grandmother, Sarah pulled her close and whispered that her Ruthie was missing. Could she please go find her. Moll said her mother was a grownup who could take care of herself, but Sarah stopped her. "There's something wrong. I know it."

Moll was convinced the "something wrong" was in Sarah's head, but her father had looked everywhere and had also begun to worry.

Moll found Ruth in the bathroom, white as a sheet, elbows on the sink, dabbing her lips with peach-colored gloss. The tap was running.

"Mom," Moll whispered, rattled by the ghost-like face in the mirror.

"It's all over?" Ruth asked, letting go of the sink and grabbing Moll's arm for support.

"Are you dizzy, Mom? Should I call a doctor?"

"No doctors. Not a word to anyone. I'm fine. *I am fine.*"

And her daughter chose to believe her.

Sarah would spend the summer alone. It had been some time since the family joined her for their two weeks in August. But they'd come for the party and stirred the memory of how much she missed them. It would pass. There was always something to do around the place. Maybe this summer she'd start walking. Not for the exercise. For the sound her feet made as they struck the ground.

2043

Moll had thought of nothing but work since her moment in the bathroom of the Bellefonte rest stop. She knew the company was always looking for ways to increase output from a workforce already at its max, but Moll was betting her twenty-five-hour day would bring that pursuit to an end. She was sticking with MORE.

Roz grilled her every chance she got. "This MORE, this extra hour you claim is at the top of everyone's Most Wanted list. Why hasn't anyone come up with it before?" Her support was rock solid, but she had concerns.

"They were never told it was possible. That's *our* job. Two and a half minutes harvested from each existing hour and bam, the twenty-four-hour day becomes twenty-five! It could be a big win for us, Roz."

"Yes, but we're selling something no one even knows they want."

"Yes."

"Which will require an education campaign."

"Rrrrright."

To product managers, the phrase "education campaign" was like garlic to a vampire. But Moll was convinced MORE had a right to life worth any resource thrown at it and was prepared to fight for it. "Eight MORE hours will keep staff at their desks for 460.8 minutes as opposed to the 480 minutes in the current status quo, which means a twenty-minute gain in freedom . . ."

"And a twenty-minute loss in productivity," Roz added.

"More than compensated by new revenue streams—more gym memberships and movie tickets, more dinners out. Not to mention how much harder people will work, grateful to their employers for the extra hour they'll have at home with those families."

"Ah, yes, the families," Roz said. "Good for marketing pitches. Not for charming bosses." The company was the current leader in the field of Efficiency and dead set on holding that lead. "You do know they're all pricks."

Pricks that flipped for MORE. Ate it up. Even the name. More with MORE. What a slogan. The money flowed her way. Money for 3D models, regional test groups, and testimonials to be shot. Money for that education campaign and the calendaring of the rollout.

She was thrilled to have their trust. There was nothing she craved more than a deadline and meeting hers would go a long way in rectifying the failures of her first year. Roz had risked a lot for a kid who'd shaved her head at seventeen and never looked back. But the incoming data was encouraging. A clear majority of those tested wanted MORE. Moll was made a team captain. Dr. Olivia Kim was a team captain. Team captains attended weekly meetings where they put their *kops* together and let their brains storm. It was a big deal.

There was talk of awards. By the fall, Roz confirmed they weren't rumors. There was Leaper of the Year, the industry's version of the Oscar; there was the National Science Medal; and there was the Edison, Moll's personal favorite with its seven equally coveted categories. She was surprised to learn that the company had greased some palms along the way.

"Isn't that bribery?" she asked.

"It's an investment," Roz said. "We're animals, not saints."

It was a mistake going to the apartment for dinner after the bad day she'd had. Nothing on her screen was adding up, MORE's preliminary test group results were lost in the ether somewhere, and having sealed herself off from her peers and Roz—a human Geiger counter when it came to detecting her insecurities—she was sorely in need of a people fix. Her parents were just the wrong people.

Within minutes of arriving, she was spilling it all—her doubts about the product she was developing, the payola making her squeamish, the data she feared was not late but being held back to avoid raising any alarms. As always, they listened intently, lavished praise, and then began their vivisection. So brilliant, creative, destined for greatness. And MORE—so clever, so potentially important, so possibly useful. If doable. Where is the hour from? Where is it put? At the beginning of the day? At the end? Who decides? Do you buy it? If you buy it, what about the schmo who won't pay full price for anything? Is he just stuck in his twenty-four-hour day waiting for a markdown?

After cleaning up and retiring to the den to dip homemade biscotti into French press coffee, Noah walked his silent daughter to the elevator. "You can always count on us for tough love and pastries," he reminded her. "But I think you've got something going with this MORE. One small step for man, one more billable hour for mankind." The doors slid shut.

The whole way down, his words swam through her head. *One small step for man, one more billable hour for mankind.* A mantra. A battle cry. A father who found brilliance everywhere her mother found fault . . . the yin-yang of her life.

If asked, and she often was, Moll dated her fascination with creative containment to a fourth-grade assignment called My Family Tree. They'd been studying DNA. A dumbed-down version, but nevertheless a study demonstrating that life progressed with some organic rationale. This, she knew in retrospect. At the time, she knew what trees were. They were everywhere. And families. They were everywhere, too. The idea that one had anything to do with the other was revelatory. Did they expect her to believe families grew on trees, like bananas, she'd wondered. If so, what an underperforming tree hers was.

Instead of the traditional model—the vertical trunk, its branches sprouting leaves bearing the names of family members—she decided she'd draw a clock. To her fourth-grade mind, it was a logical leap. Trees were old and dependable. So were clocks. Not the kind that spat their numbers out like highway warnings but the kind that gave time a different sound depending on which room of her grandparents' house she was in. She especially liked them because clocks were round, and a circle was the first thing she'd learned to draw. Also because they'd seemed exclusive to Ohio, and thus exotic. Her classmates agreed. Her teacher did not. Not at first.

Moll had been sympathetic to her reasoning. The analog system was old-fashioned, inefficient, requiring two sweeps of the circumference each day, and what a tight fit it would be for even a small family like hers, its twelve stations leaving little room to grow. That was the point of branches and leaves, didn't Moll see? They grew systematically. Limbs off the trunk, leaves off the limbs, and so on.

"But what if the tree grew too much?" Moll asked. Riverside Park had one so big it toppled across the path she took to school. There'd been no getting around it. Besides, you didn't have to be an exceptional fourth grader to know trees took time to grow and clocks kept track of time, a thing her mother, a doctor, told her had no beginning or end, much like a circle. Her doctor mother also told her that people like to think they know what they're talking about when they talk about time in terms of years and weeks and hours and seconds, but there was so much more to it. You could slice away at time forever without getting to the smallest slice.

"But how could you possibly signify all those slices?" the teacher asked, forgetting she was talking to a fourth grader.

"I have a very pointy pencil," Moll answered.

Her drawing was a work of artistry and precision. At the top sat Sarah Vogel, alone at the midnight hour where every day began and ended. Walter was directly to her right at one o'clock; Walter's son Robbie at two; the ex, Jan, at five after; Walter's pioneering family a minute later; Ruth at three; four and five were waiting to be filled; Noah at six o'clock; seven and eight also waiting to be filled; Bubbe Koenig at nine o'clock; Zayde Koenig one minute later; Glory at ten; Great Grandma Ruth at eleven; dead Aunt Malcah a stroke before midnight.

"But Moll, where are you?" the teacher asked.

It took a moment for Moll to comprehend what she'd done, another to turn her error into intention. "I'm the clock," she said. For that, her teacher gave her an A++. The child *had* sharpened her pencil a hundred times.

The drawing kept its place of honor, framed and hanging above her mother's desk, until Ruth gave it to Moll for her room at the Brill where it continued to inspire her.

At least that was the story she'd rehearsed for the interviewer about to knock on her door. The appointment had popped up on her schedule only yesterday, leaving no time to prepare. She was pissed at the bosses for demanding she drop everything at this critical juncture to chat with a stranger but understood the need for publicity, especially with the awards coming up. And who could afford to stay pissed at the bosses? They'd wanted it at the office, but she wouldn't budge on that. Home was the only place she could talk freely.

She wished she'd gotten the names of the women at that rest stop. Introducing her muses would've been a nice touch. She thought it safe to reveal that she preferred working with her earbuds in and her screen turned off. It made key-stroking challenging but had become a necessary precaution given the proliferation of cubby-hopping-colleagues with photographic memories who had less compunction about stealing an idea than taking a sandwich from the company fridge. Maybe she'd keep that last part to herself, though. She didn't need him thinking she was crazy. In the week before the interview, bad things had already begun chipping away at her confidence.

They were small bad things at first. Team Captain Kim got the snowball rolling with the Predicted Adjusted Lifespans she'd run for each of her fellow captains, which she handed out at their weekly meeting like party favors. Fuming over the shameless stunt, wishing she'd come up with one first, Moll took hers back to her desk to read in private. Thanks to her grandmother, who shouldn't have made it to age ten let alone one hundred, Moll had been assigned one hundred thirty-three years, welcome news but also depressing once she realized she'd already burned through twenty-three of them. And then came the hand-delivered inter-office memo reporting serious slippage in the latest MORE metrics.

A situation she should've seen coming after her own sampling of the product confirmed what test subjects from three out of the four regions were experiencing, the lift of that extra hour and then the let-down. What should've pushed her to greater industry and purpose—poetic twists, productive dreams—fostered only worry. How to extend or split or spread the precious minutes, in other words, how to make more from MORE. How to bank the extra hours. Toward an extra day, maybe? An extra year? What amount of time would be enough? It was like the hour had become a vessel or cave, a place to crawl into and stay forever, safe and untouchable. She'd held out hope that she was the anomaly, but there it was in black and white. People were hooked, but yield was disappointing.

And then, the coup de grâce, her father's call with the news that Ruth had cancer, after months of knowing something was not quite right but never imagining it could be so wrong. No one got cancer anymore. Noah said doctors made mistakes all the time. He'd seek second and third opinions, alternative treatments, and she was about to offer her help when he was bumped to call waiting by an ebullient Roz, screaming that it was official, Moll was a nominee—the bloody Edisons no less—so from now on, no fooling around. And if Moll's considerable ambitions weren't enough to keep her feet to the fire, there was her father, waiting patiently for her apologetic call back, insisting she had nothing to be sorry about. What better gift could she give their Ruth in her coming battle, in *their* coming battle, than more time in the day?

"Tell me about you," said the interviewer who'd arrived late and offered no apology.

"This pretty much covers it," Moll said, handing him her fourth-grade diagram, which she now feared embarrassingly juvenile.

"And the dead aunt?" he asked after a quick tour of the clock face.

"That's Malcah, my namesake. Though on my birth certificate, I'm Moll. Malcah's Bible talk for queen and our last name, Koenig, is German for king, kind of pretentious for a family with no claim to royalty, I guess. But my Malcah died on 9/11. A personal tragedy that was either eclipsed or amplified by the national grief, I've never been able to tell. And, wow, we've never come up with a name for it, have we? 9/11. The date says it all. Like the Fourth of July, I suppose, but even that gets to be called Independence Day. Anyway, it's all history at this point. It's not like I knew her. The thing that happened to my family sets me apart, I guess. The thing that happened to my country makes me one with it. But I feel like I'm babbling. Am I babbling?"

"You're doing fine. All warmed up? Ready for the hard questions?"

Moll had been prepping her whole life for this moment, so yes, she was ready and fielded his questions, soft and hard, concerning MORE's theoretical and practical application with a perfectly delivered party line about Egyptians counting time on their knuckles and how twenty-four hours might've been enough for them, but they didn't have working mothers or rush-hour traffic or round-the-clock news to fuck their days . . . "But don't print that . . ."

"No worries," he said, then burrowed in. "So the Edisons, that's a big deal for someone your age. Especially in the Collective Disruption category. Were you surprised?"

"Will I sound like an asshole if I say no?"

"Maybe." He laughed. "But refreshingly honest. So, sticking to honest, what about Dr. Kim? Were you surprised she'd also been nominated?" He stared intently, wrist recorder on, as she lost and quickly recovered the impassive face she'd spent the morning perfecting.

"Ouch," he said, face crinkling. "You hadn't heard. We're told she's developing a product that will reassess the individual's responsibility to the corporate body. The company's never released anything to market so quickly. So tell me, what's it like being David going up against Goliath?"

"Challenging? I mean, she's our pacesetter. But I'm good at the finish line."

"A pacesetter . . . the sort that can give a team member a hand up or leave them in the dust? Would you say she'd be more apt to share the spotlight or push her peers into the shadows?"

"Maybe you should be interviewing Kim." Moll was growing wary.

"On my way there from here, but I do have a few more questions for you."

So, the dirt he'd been after was Kim's, not hers. *What an idiot*, she thought. Though he was a bigger idiot if he thought he'd ever *expose* Olivia Kim. She was dirt-free. Soulless, too. But Moll had to be careful. If she wanted to reclaim her place as this interview's subject, she'd have to rise above politics and impress him with her largesse. Kim's was the finest mind in the industry. She was honored to be in her ranks. What did it matter who won? Both represented the Company and worked for the same thing: a better, more inclusive social contract between the public and the corporations upon which it depended. Could there be any losers in a competition of this caliber? That's what she should've said.

Instead, she made an inelegant pivot. Had he heard the rumors about payola? Were they true? He said he had and believed they were. The evidence was mounting. Did anyone know how much the company had shelled out for Kim and her? If he knew, he wasn't saying. But how much would he say they were worth? Fuck it. How much was *she* worth? Daring him to put a price on her head, prompting him to ask what *she* thought she was worth. She'd proven her talent, but did she have the steel for her chosen career?

She wondered how much steel it would take to repair the damage she'd done. To her career. To her life. Everyone would see her as a rat. Lower than a whistleblower, a spineless emotional wreck. Tears would make things worse, but she couldn't stop them. She'd bet he'd never had a subject break down on him before. And she, one of the smarter ones, sensed the redirection of his interest, as if he were assessing the degree of brokenness he might be asked to mend. The dick. Her undoing had been self-inflicted, beginning long before he showed up, but if he wanted to feel responsible, she wouldn't object.

He had no more questions but said he could hang out for a while if she liked.

"And Dr. Kim?" Moll wiped her nose on her sleeve.

"She'll wait."

At the Brill, "hanging out" was stranger code for sex. With the interviewer, though they weren't technically strangers, it meant the same.

Moll volunteered the last scrapings from the bottom of her carefully hoarded, not-for-resale jar of Kumquat (a salve the interviewer had heard of but never tried). Both reached a satisfying finish, and *still* he wanted more. Had she ever been Hancocked? he asked. She hadn't. Wanted nothing to do with it. Had to mask her disgust at the thought of being tattooed with a design of his choice on the particular part of her anatomy he'd fancied. It seemed obvious that a member of a gender predisposed to ownership would feel compelled to mark his territory, like a dog peeing on the corner hydrant so other dogs would know he'd gotten there first, but it was incomprehensible that any woman would allow a man to dangle his sad invitation to "wear his autograph" as if it were a trinket she could put on and take off whenever she liked, not a stain that would outlast any memory of the moment he hoped to memorialize. Hancocking was just a new word for branding, and those who'd done it should at least have the balls to call it that.

The interviewer had been awash in a haze of gratitude (the best of Kumquat's side effects), but once recovered repeated his invitation, this time dangling a reminder of his yet-to-be-submitted interview for incentive. He'd made her cry, and he'd made her come, but a man could do all that and still ruin a girl's career. If he wanted.

So she went with him to his preferred salon—tasteful, exclusive—and sat patiently as the technician, truly an artist, poured champagne and, with a red marker, under the interviewer's direction, drew a figure eight on the bottom of her foot, her tenderest part. The needles should have come next, but in the end, she couldn't go through with it.

The marker wasn't permanent but did survive her morning shower. Sitting cross-legged on the toilet, foot in hand, she studied the "autograph," confused by the power it held over her. But in her bathroom mirror, she saw the number had shifted to its side and felt its power shift, too. 8 or ∞. It was all a matter of perspective, perspective a matter of choice. And choosing infinity over insult, Moll overrode the interviewer's raft of potentially ruinous endings and marched to the week's team meeting ready for anything.

"What is one thousand four hundred and forty?" Olivia Kim began, quickly answering her own question. "The number of minutes in a day. Divide by twenty-five, as our esteemed colleague has so cleverly done, and you get more but shorter hours."

The meetings were known for their unstructured format, but this one had an agenda—the complete and brutal makeover of MORE. It was Kim's meeting. Moll could do nothing but watch her baby go under the knife.

"But," Kim continued, "divide those by twenty and each hour stretches to seventy-two minutes."

Marketing liked it because of the even numbers; testers liked it because the fewer the hours, the more precious they became; the Company liked it because an eight-hour workday yielded a per-day productivity gain of ninety-six minutes, versus MORE's loss of twenty.

It would be years before the makeover was available to the public, but the deal was done. All held their breath as Moll collected her thoughts, forced herself to her feet, and offered her congratulations, one team captain to another, smothering the last dregs of tension.

"Thanks, but it was *your* idea," Kim demurred. "All I did was tweak it."

"And the tweaking turned it into a winner," Moll said, pleased to bring such a happy smile to the face of her *esteemed colleague*. Happy was how she wanted her. Happy was how a girl got knocked off her game.

Back in her cubby, Moll found a message from Roz inviting her for drinks after work. She figured Roz had heard about her show of maturity and wanted to talk next steps. When, over Thai basil martinis, she suggested it might be time for Moll to start looking for her next job, Moll thought she'd heard wrong. Then Roz opened her wrist screen to forward a list of companies she knew were looking.

"But the awards," Moll said. "The invitation came this morning."

"And you'll go. You're still a nominee. They can't take that from you. But did you actually think you had a chance? I told you they were pricks. They like you. They like MORE, but Moll, Kim's their winner, and we need to relocate you before they turn you into a loser."

"There aren't supposed to be any losers . . ."

"I'll write you a rec. It'll be good. Over the top."

"But Roz, my mother's dying. She has cancer."

"Aw, baby," Roz said softly. "It's a lot, I know. But you'll be fine. No one dies of cancer anymore."

The awards ceremony went on without her. The hour was a cradle rocking her to sleep, a cup of coffee wanted its pour of cream, and she had nothing to wear.

By the time the results appeared online, she'd expunged any need to appear happy for Dr. Kim.

Grief

2043

These days, any knock at Sarah's door was an irritant—a neighbor braying about the sprinkler she'd left on all night, a package meant for a different address. This knock, initiated by a pretty young woman, was no exception.

"Mrs. Vogel!" She sounded surprised to be the knocker and not the knock-ee. "Hi! I'm Daria Goldman." Her face was serious, perhaps from the weight of her cross-body bag. Big as an old-fashioned briefcase. "Outreach Director for the Survivor Registry Commission?"

"Maybe you have the wrong person? I know nothing about a Register." Sarah was old, but she had all her marbles. There were no keys in her icebox. Other things, yes, but not her keys or the lengthening list of passwords replacing them, keys not ground in a machine but forged in memory, keys that needed hints because the same thing could be remembered many ways depending on conditions as uncontrollable as a stranger's sudden appearance at the door. She remembered a taste for cigarettes and vodka, Cheerios dipped in schmaltz, a child's bangs flattened against a feverish brow, the fear of losing that child so great she sometimes found herself wishing the child away, the moment she realized she could make things happen by wishing them, her failed attempts to wish for better things. But this Register? To forget a thing, mustn't it first be remembered?

The stranger calling herself Daria Goldman looked pained. "Exactly why I'm here. We've called, written. None of our letters were returned."

"Could be they're on my husband's desk."

"All of them?"

"Depends how many you sent."

"Oh boy, Dr. Fields warned me about you," Daria Goldman said, breaking into a smile.

"*Dr*. Fields?"

"She verified the address. We were worried we had it wrong."

"You didn't."

"Did we get off on the wrong foot, Mrs. Vogel? What do you say we start over?" Without waiting for permission, she pushed the screen door open and stepped inside. "Hi, I'm Daria Goldman." Even perkier this time. "Outreach Director for the Survivor Registry Commission here to confirm that you're a true survivor of one of the world's great horrors, Hitler's concentration camps, and invite you to be part of the upcoming event commemorating the one-hundredth anniversary of their—*your*—liberation." She took a breath. "There. How'd I do?"

"A better foot, Daria Goldman, but I'm not interested in your little memorial." Sarah didn't ask if she could take Daria Goldman's coat. The girl was already too comfortable for her own good.

"Memorials are for the dead, Mrs. Vogel. That's why the Centennial's so important. We're honoring the living. *All* of them."

"I'm not the only one left?" A smile yanked at the corners of Sarah's mouth.

"Not at all. We discover more every day. Recently, we found a man whose mother went into labor on the way to Auschwitz and gave birth on Liberation Day!"

"And *that* you're counting?"

"If my supervisor says so." Daria Goldman was a giggler. "Tons of human interest. Born and liberated on the same day. The tiniest hero. Can you imagine?"

Sarah could not. It had been twenty, thirty years since the last wave of lasts. "Oldest Auschwitz Survivor Dies at 108". Her son-in-law had sent the article. An older oldest turned up a few years later. Then the cascading dominos. The last to make it through Sobibór dead at ninety-seven. The last to survive Chelmno dead of cancer at seventy-six. The last inmate from Treblinka dead at eighty-nine. Unless you considered the other last inmate from Treblinka, alive and well and living in Sweden. Then anyway. Surely no longer.

She didn't remember which was the last domino or when it fell, only that the articles with their mawkish headlines had lived in her valise long enough for the dead to have dubbed her "the last." And then this Daria Goldman came knocking, pushing her way through the door, activating her tablet, recording everything, all that Sarah was willing to give, anyway, which was only as much as she'd ever given—name, rank, serial number—and between her answers, what came to mind was the hydrangea by the kitchen door, which had outgrown its spot and needed to be moved before the summer heat prevented a successful re-root, and also Ruth, who hadn't phoned in a worryingly long time.

Daria Goldman talked on. "I *really* hope you'll change your mind, Mrs. Vogel. Most of the country is represented at this point, except Ohio."

"And I'm Ohio."

"You are. But wherever you were from, you'd be important. Dr. Fields always says, 'If my mother wants heaven and earth moved, you move it.'"

"She said that?"

Daria Goldman woke the tablet's screen and showed Sarah, the characters uploading, a slogan forming. *Accuracy and appropriateness for every honoree!* "Her words."

"You've met my Ruthie?"

"More than met," Daria said, plunking herself down in Walter's chair. "She's been the heart and brains of the operation. Such a hard worker. I don't know what we'd do without her. We were devastated to hear she was ill. Oh, God, they'll kill me for being so unprofessional. I just really care. You know?"

Maybe she shouldn't wait to go to New York, Sarah thought. They promised to tell her when. But *when* could've already come and gone.

"She'll be proud of you. Stepping up to the plate today," Daria Goldman said, signaling the interview's end. "But what about family. Ruth mentioned a grandmother. Ruth Vogel?"

"Could be," Sarah said. "Remembering is not my best thing these days. What I need, I remember. And a mother? Why would I need one now? I ask myself and have no answer, only another question . . . who needs *me* now? How do you think my Ruthie would answer? You know her so well, your Dr. Fields. Sit, Daria Goldman, I'll make tea. Or some vodka from the freezer? A sweet to help it go down easy. Ohio is so important, your Register won't mind if you stay longer, maybe long enough to tell me how to get your hardest working volunteer to call me *before* it's time to come, because after is always too late?"

"We're a Commission, Mrs. Vogel, not a Register."

"My dear, I may not sound like I understand, but I do. You push a little thing out of you, and for a while she calls you Mama. But when the little thing grows up, she'll have a little thing of her own, and if she still calls you Mama? Now that? *That* is love. Her love, not mine. Mine was there all along but hard for a child to see. Harder for a teenager. 'Mama' says love. But it's years since my little thing called me anything but Ma or Mom. Show me the place on your form and I'll write it down, that once I wanted her to be safe and successful and find good love and never suffer or die. But now? Now all I want is for her to call me Mama again, so you'll excuse me if I can't come up with a name for someone I never called anything." Sarah began to cry. It was useless to fight it—the weeping, the wailing, the keening of an animal. The only way to rid herself of it was to pour it into this vessel of a stranger holding a tablet that lit her bosom.

When it ended, Sarah's late-life tantrum, she did what she was asked, using her finger to sign on the dotted line, thinking, *Good for you, Daria Goldman, nabbing your Ohio outlier.*

But it wasn't over. Out of the big bag came a plastic box. A DNA kit, the young woman explained. "I could help you with it if you like. Or if you'd rather, do it on your own and send it in."

"This is necessary?"

"I wish it weren't, Mrs. Vogel. But you wouldn't believe the things people choose to lie about."

Sarah did believe and told her what she could do with her swabs and Ziplocs. She'd given them her story. She'd hold on to her spit, thank you very much.

She tossed Daria Goldman's calling card in the trash, but Sarah knew it wasn't over.

2044

Moll soon learned her boss had been wrong on two counts. Ruth *was* dying and the company *couldn't* fire her, even after the article revealed how sour her grapes were. (Why had she squandered the last of her Kumquat stash on that shit of an interviewer?) The nomination had raised her profile too high. Instead, they sent her to purgatory. No longer captain or even a part of a team, she became a floater. The money was less, the impermanence unsettling, and Roz no longer made eye contact. But Moll wouldn't quit.

She did leave the Brill. It had gotten too rich for her blood, she'd exhausted its supply of strangers, and the word "home" had snuck back into her vocabulary.

"You always were a kicker," Ruth said, she and her daughter inspecting the knot of sheets and blankets left after Moll's first night back in the apartment. "You'd get in bed with us, and your legs would be like two little windshield wipers. *Swish, swish, swish,*" Ruth demonstrated, moving her pointers back and forth. "Until finally I would feel this little foot hunting for the warm place under my fanny, wedging itself in. Only *then* could we all sleep."

Reminiscing was a new sport for them, one Moll was getting into.

Ruth put the back of her hand on Moll's forehead, though it was she who looked feverish. Ruth, family rock, matriarch, the kindest, most thoughtful, hardest working, and all-around best person they knew, downed but still tending to the needs of others.

Leave it to Ruth, special in so many ways, to catch a special kind of sick. Her cancer was unrelated to the one Sarah had battled years before, hence reasonably uninheritable, minimizing the reduction in Moll's PAL, little solace considering she was losing a woman who'd go a block out of her way to avoid a colony of ants parading across her usual route. Pathologically Schweitzerian she was, except when it came to the irresistible pleasures of bacon, which Ruth indulged once a year, crisp off the griddle at some out-of-the way diner frequented by no one she knew. On the way home, she'd stop for a scalding *mikvah*. She could live with the sin but not with the lingering smell she'd bring home to Noah. The day Ruth shared her secret, she and Moll laughed so hard their sides hurt.

Ruth continued working until she could no longer pretend her patients were receiving her usual 200 percent. She stuck with the Centennial Committee until the bitter end, despite Noah's nagging.

"Should you gather every Survivor in the world, it's not going to make your mother love you the way you need her to," he said.

"I'm at my finish line," his wife replied. "This is my chance to right a wrong before time runs out. And what makes you think I'm in need of love? Don't I have you for that?"

Noah took a leave from his firm but continued to teach a few classes, which got him out of the house and gave Ruth a reprieve from his misery.

Dire as their situation seemed, life in the apartment wasn't all hand-wringing. They went to movies, the Met, and strolled across Central Park to Fifth Avenue for Ruth's weekly medical appointments. She had a couple of remissions thanks to two grizzly courses of treatment, and then, as doctors predicted, the disease fought back.

Ruth thought she'd prepared herself for the tell-Sarah-when call that loomed, but the time came too fast to face, and she left the chore to Moll.

"What did you say? I want the *exact* words," Noah demanded.

He'd made peace with his mother-in-law for Ruth's sake, kept a friendly but protective distance for all their sakes, but now Sarah, who flaked out on them whenever she was needed, was about to horn in on their nest of grief when she wasn't. He was peeved. Moll got it. And she was a big girl who could take the blame for her legitimate fuck-ups. But having to defend herself for being civil to an old lady really pissed her off.

"I told her exactly what you told me," she said. "That Mom's really sick. It was her decision to come, she'd totally packed before the phone rang, so I said I'd take the day off and pick her up at the airport."

"Ridiculous. We'll hire a car service."

"She's a hundred years old. A hundred and one, for God's sake."

"Leave *Hashem* out of this, Moll. They'll have a wheelchair waiting, if she deigns to use it, and the driver will help with her bags. Just make sure she knows what to say and not say when she gets here. No snipes, no worrying us. And no tears!"

Ruth began to laugh, choking on her last bite of blintz. "Like my mother has tear ducts," she sputtered, bringing Noah to her side.

"See what you've done?" he cried to Moll, rubbing his wife's back.

"Oh my fucking God."

"*Malcah!*"

"Both of you, please. I'm fine. Noah, read your papers. Malcah, clean up. I'll be on the couch."

It took a sink full of dishes for Moll to calm down. Once they were drying and tea was poured, she apologized. "If I'd known he'd be such a freak, I would've told her to stay home."

"Your father's always been there for me. He just doesn't understand that sometimes a girl needs her mother. Even if she's no mother of the year. What you're doing is a mitzvah for us both. Now, bring him his tea and cookie and give him a goodnight kiss, please."

Twelve hours until her grandmother's touchdown at 10:53 a.m. The only thing worse than a day stuck in her cubby was a morning trekking to the airport, and Moll had been spared both. Sarah and the driver would have a forty-five-minute wait at baggage claim and another forty-five-minute ride to the Upper West Side. Bridge and highway traffic were unpredictable, but best-case scenario, she wouldn't arrive before 12:30. Ruth was now up nights and sleeping into the afternoons. Noah would head to the university by the crack of dawn. She'd have a good twelve hours to herself.

Moll shut off her bedroom lights, silenced her wrist alarm, and coasted into the luxurious twelve-hour expanse ahead, enjoying how the previous night's wrinkles and folds remembered her.

Goody, a dream, she thought, the action taking place where she slept, she and a recent lover playing themselves. She felt the breeze on her bare rump and the whiff of an actual gym coming off her lover.

From the tangle of sheets, he plucked her foot, like something from a fruit bowl he may or may not have been in the mood for.

"Tell me what you like." He studied the heel's calloused perimeter, the softer crenulations of the arch. He wanted to know what drove her wild.

A generous question with endless answers. Unable to come up with one, she left it at nothing, anything.

"Liar."

Can you blush in your sleep? she wondered, looking at him, her lids lowered, chin resting on one hiked shoulder, pouty bottom lip.

"Don't waste my time," he said, tightening his grasp.

"Then tickle, please," she said, looking over the moons of her ass, a white paler than the sheets. Her foot spasmed like a caught fish in his hand. "Easy, there. You know I can't stand pressure."

His finger drew a figure eight the length of her arch.

"Better?" His finger hovered over its sketchpad.

"Oh," she said, toes curling back, heel pressing down, pulling his canvas taut.

He traced and retraced the figure eight. There was modest enough pleasure for her, she couldn't see what was in it for him. She didn't yet know what he knew, his fingers instruments prodding deeper, her foot jerking reflexively.

"Hold still," he said. "This is about trust."

He pressed his thumbs into the ball, defended by callous and bone, then pressed below the ball, sending a tremor up her leg. *Ahhh, trust.*

"It's all here, like a road map or an electrical plan," he said, softly stroking. "I touch here"—thumbs boring tunnels of light through her unwillingness—"and a match licks the small of your back. Or here"—moving further down that vulnerable highway—"and your heart is a bird in my fist. Or here"—pressing hard into the center of the arch—"and your cunt weeps for me. The point is," he said, fingers turning to angel lips, "there's nothing I can do to you that you can't survive."

Then he went to the john, leaving her alone to mop up her weeping cunt.

When she opened her eyes, there was an old woman in his place. She was familiar, a brittle wisp perched like a bird with something wriggling in its beak, something rotten judging by her look of distaste. Or maybe it was just the look of old. The way Moll would look when she reached the end of her allotted years, making her wonder if she wanted to last that long. People still had the choice, regardless of their PAL. Geezerdom hadn't been mandated. *Yet.*

"My little queen," the old woman whispered, stroking her foot.

There was always the chance she wasn't dreaming at all.

The woman began to hum, or there was water trapped so deep in Moll's ear it wouldn't shake out.

Open eyes didn't mean she was awake.

"Great-Great?"

The old woman, her grandmother, gave Moll's foot a non-dreamlike tug.

"Wake up, dolly."

"How'd you get in?"

"Pavel, at the front desk. The one who thinks I live to speak Polish with him."

"Answer in English and he'll stop," Moll said, her eyes sticky with sleep.

"Such a nice man?"

Unwinding herself from her bedclothes, Moll checked her wrist. Barely noon. Had the woman flown non-stop to the Upper West Side?

"How about some lunch?" her grandmother asked.

"Oh my God. Not another word 'til I've had coffee."

Behind her bathroom's closed door, Moll splashed cold water on her face and sat on the toilet to check the bottom of her foot. Nothing. She *had* been dreaming. Brushing her teeth and splashing a few more handfuls of cold water on her face helped.

"Where are you putting me?" Sarah asked when Moll finished in the bathroom. Still no coffee in sight.

"It'll be crunchy with the four of us. Dad's moved into the study. I'll take the living room couch. And you'll stay in here."

"No, dolly. I'll take the couch."

"This will go easier if we both do as we're told."

"He doesn't want me in the way, does he?"

Moll shrugged.

"Then stay with me. This bed could sleep four of us."

"Very nice of you, but I'm told I kick."

"I'll kick back. Don't worry. I'll be a good guest and do as I'm told."

Sarah began putting her things in the drawer Moll had cleared for her, though she could've lived out of her suitcase for the amount of time she'd be there.

"Don't take it personally," Moll said on her way out of the room. "Peace and quiet is all he has to give, so he's convinced himself that's what she needs."

What Ruth needed, Sarah decided, was meat on her bones. The whole apartment was wasting away. She'd never been much of a cook but could pull together a respectable goulash, and with Noah teaching all day, she had nothing but time.

They lived three blocks from the market, the walk easy and direct. She spied an Austrian torte in the baker's case but left with only the things on her list. That filled two bags. Feet willing, arthritic hands less so, she grit her teeth, hailed her first driverless cab, and paid dearly for the five-minute ride.

The hunk of cow she'd bought was a lusty red. The plum tomatoes firm and fragrant. Having the kitchen all to herself, Sarah hummed away the afternoon chopping, stirring, and tasting from the pot until she was satisfied with the results. Noah and Moll had said they'd be home late. It would be just the two of them for dinner.

Unfortunately, the onions that smelled so sweet as they browned were rough on her daughter's stomach. Ruth ate as much as she could, though. For a while, there was only the sound of spoons clinking china.

"You know what I miss, Ma?" Ruth asked after reaching her limit.

"What, dolly?"

"Red wine."

"With goulash?"

"With anything. I never cared for vodka. It's like inhaling fire. But that's you, my mother the fire-eater. A good red, on the other hand . . . it's the kindling that gets the fire going, starting with the smallest flame, then roaring for a while, until finally dying down to the most delicious embers. You know what I mean?"

"Hold on."

Sarah fetched a bottle of red she'd seen hiding in the fridge. They'd kept it around for cooking, but Sarah, no connoisseur, poured them each a glass to clink. "*Za milyh dam*," she said. "To lovely women."

They grimaced with the first sip, but the second was better, and they drank until their faces flushed and their teeth turned purple.

Sarah, known for holding her spirits, felt lightheaded after one glass. Ruth, beyond lightheaded, pushed herself from the table and stood too quickly. Sarah steadied her and they walked arm in arm to the bedroom.

Sitting on the edge of her bed, Ruth asked Sarah if she remembered the picture of Grandma Ruth.

"Of course," she said. "It's sitting on the dresser in Moll's room."

"It's not her, is it?"

Sarah smiled. "You finally figured out we weren't famous enough to be in a book?"

"I've known for a long time and never told anyone. I figured you were entitled to a secret or two. Plus, having my grandmother watching over me all those years made me feel safe and I wanted that for Moll. But it's been a long time since she needed an old page from a library book to keep her safe, and now your secret's become *ours*, one we've kept so long it's turned into a lie. Do you know what that feels like, Ma, lying to someone because you're afraid of what they'll do with the truth?" The weight of a lost girl hung between them.

"*Gey schlafn*," was all she could muster.

"Oh Ma, I'm so tired of sleeping."

"If Noah comes home and finds you drunk, he'll kill me."

Sarah pulled the comforter over her shoulders and turned on the radio. There wasn't much to cleanup and the market would be open for another hour or so, enough time for her to pick up a soup chicken to make in the morning. *Nothing better than soup*, she thought, *whatever flavor can be pulled from a bird without onions*. On the way back she stopped in a wine store, first-degreeing the vintner about their best red, one that was slow to ignite but burned hot and long.

Back home, she found Ruth up but disoriented.

"Ma?" she cried.

"I'm here, *mamaleh*."

"I thought you'd run away."

"Where would I run?"

"I don't know. These drugs. They're turning my brain to mush."

"That's okay. Tomorrow I'm gonna make us some chicken soup. It goes well with mush. And this bird was blessed by an honest-to-God rabbi. But don't tell Noah. Let him worry about his kosher pots instead of you for one night. And look," she said, slowly drawing the wine bottle from the bag. "Look what I brought you."

"This must've cost a fortune," Ruth said, examining the label.

"A small one," Sarah admitted. "But we're not drinking it up in an afternoon. It's for you to keep for another time."

Ruth hugged the bottle of red to her chest.

Sarah smiled, remembering when Walter had taken their little one around the neighborhood trick-or-treating one Halloween. "You must have been five. We found you in bed the next morning holding onto your candy like the Gestapo was after it. Remember?"

"I remember being terrified you'd take it from me to give to the children who had nothing to eat."

"And where would I find such children in the middle of all those farms?" Sarah asked, wondering what other fears her child had harbored.

"I didn't think about that. It just seemed like something you'd do."

"Don't worry. There are no starving children who need your wine."

When she bent to kiss her daughter goodnight, Ruth lassoed her neck with her free arm and pulled her closer, whispering, "Mama."

By the time Noah returned from the office, his wife was out cold in the bedroom. Sarah, awake in her granddaughter's bed, heard dishes banging, then Moll loping through the apartment, then the movement of chairs, spoons against bowls, muffled conversation. "Not bad, right?" she heard the girl ask. There was only a grunt in response. Whether a grunt of derision or satisfaction Sarah couldn't tell, but she was pretty sure it was his bowl she heard being filled a second and third time.

The apartment's joints ticked. From ground level came the beat of traffic and alarms broadcasting other people's troubles. Sarah supposed you could get used to anything given the chance. At least the blackout shades worked. She only sensed the presence of her granddaughter entering the room.

"Are you asleep?" Moll asked, crawling into the bed.

"Yes."

"I thought you should know . . . it really would be fine if you stayed longer. If you want. I know how you feel about the city, but Mom would love it. She'd never ask, but I think she would, and Dad goes along with anything she wants."

"Just like you?"

"Only I make her work for it."

"More like me, then."

"Mom's been saying how much I'm like you."

"Oh dear."

"She means it as a good thing. She also thinks I should be more kind, or kind more often. I don't know."

"You did give me your bed, dolly."

"Exactly. What more could she want?"

Sarah smiled and the two shared the darkness in silence.

"Great-Great?"

Sarah's throat tightened. She'd said it again. Again meant on purpose.

"Can I ask you something?"

"Ask," Sarah whispered.

There was a long pause.

"What was left . . . after Malcah?"

"Nothing, my dear. I wish I had a better answer, but after Malcah, there was nothing."

"Because you couldn't give her your love anymore."

"Because she couldn't give me hers."

"That doesn't seem fair to Grandpa, or Mom."

"There was nothing fair about any of it. When someone you love dies, it's terrible and it's sad, but you keep on loving them. When you lose someone who loves *you*, well, there you are on your own. Waiting. Listening for a voice that can take the place of theirs. Looking for someone who witnessed the memories you shared. But the wait is for nothing because there is nothing. That's what was left after Malcah. Nothing."

That quieted Moll, but not for long.

"My mother's about to die," she said matter-of-factly. "And all I can think is, *why her?* Why not . . ."

"Me?"

"Sorry. I'm so sorry. I didn't mean . . . that was cruel."

"I understand. That it's her makes no sense."

"You know what makes even less sense? That I could be so much like someone I barely know."

As Moll's breath deepened, she felt the drape of her grandmother's arm. Neither had enough to be losing so much. Moll's fingers grazed Sarah's numbers, her thumb knowing just where to stroke, back and forth, the way a baby finds a frayed patch of something to twiddle. Now it was Sarah whose eyes wouldn't close. *Could* she stay? There was no cat to feed. No milk curdling in the refrigerator. Only a garden to go dry, but gardens rebound. She *could* stay. She could stay, she could stay, she could stay.

After a night of deep sleep, Moll swung her legs out of bed, ready for the day. The air seemed cleansed after their talk, and she felt good. Even better knowing the old woman had taken her invitation no more seriously than it was intended. Her father would have killed her.

She passed Sarah in the hallway, hand and forehead pressed to Ruth's door, chanting her goodbyes . . . *auf wiedersehen, do svidaniya, pożegnalny, addio*. She let her be. There were a hundred ways to say it but none strong enough to stop a plane.

In her empty house, Sarah sat on the living room couch and turned on the TV. It was early, but she drifted right off, waking only long enough to turn off the set and trudge to her bedroom. Tonight, she would sleep between her own sheets. Tomorrow, she'd unpack and begin the wait for next Sunday's call.

It came on Saturday. They were nearing the end of another summer, and though she knew better, she picked up the receiver fully expecting to hear Ruth's voice. *We're on our way, another fifty miles and we'll be home.*

Of course it wasn't Ruth. It was Henriette. The importance of what she'd called to say did not escape Sarah, but as she stared out her window, the everyday celebration of morning in full swing, she was struck by the courage of its celebrants, walking their dogs, on the way to the store, or going back to work after an unusually hot weekend, as if the world being turned upside down did not include them.

Ruth's death hit hard, but at least Moll saw it coming. Her father's death was an out-and-out ambush. The authorities called it accidental, but Noah Koenig was a man of purpose. He'd made sure the love of his life died in her own bed, as she'd wanted. He'd followed Jewish *and* New York City law, submitting the paperwork that let her be buried in a pine box instead of being burned to ash. His attention to ritual bordered on obsessive—rending every lapel in his closet, covering the mirrors, refusing to utter a prayer without a complete minyan. There was the whiskey he downed, three shots after each kaddish. But he sat the full seven days before uncovering the mirrors and sending Sarah and his parents back to their homes. He'd blown Moll a kiss and called her Malcah on his way out the door to work that morning. What accident waits for shiva to end and family to leave to wreak its havoc?

Because her father was righteous, or because it was too painful to consider the alternative, she convinced herself that a few whiskey shots with a former student who'd come by to pay his respects had caused Noah to lose count of how many of Ruth's Nembutal he swallowed before laying his head on his desk for good.

After, the former student had called. He had little to add. Only that he never knew a man could be so religious *and* so intelligent until meeting her father, and he hoped it offered some consolation that Professor Koenig had seemed at peace.

The fucking ironies of life, though, landing on the team designing the company's newest productivity tool, Bereave Leave, their promise to managers across the land that never again would they be left high and dry by the unscheduled loss of an employee's loved one, and to those employees the promise of three pre-calendared weeks a year to use as they pleased—mourning, a trip to Fiji, their choice. "Know the relief of scheduled grief" was her contribution. Her coworkers didn't know whether to call it good luck or bad that her Bereave Leave, her parents' deaths, *and* the height of vacation season had so perfectly aligned, but no one could accuse her of monkey business. Only monkeys with high security clearance could override Blind and Random (the program's actual name), and since the MORE debacle, Moll had zero security clearance.

She didn't know why she'd decided to spend her Bereave Leave with Sarah. But the family wagons from across Chicagoland were already circling to provide the Koenigs aid and comfort. Sarah was on her own. And in Ohio, Moll would be granted privacy, minimal acknowledgment of their shared tragedy, and the gifts of the August harvest. Just like the good old days.

Bereave Leave. Week one. A bicycle wheel with rusted spokes. A cantaloupe. A brain in a glass jar. A hypodermic full of water. She wasn't expected to bring work with her, but nobody stopped her. The cantaloupe wasn't real. Punched in at her grandfather's desk, now hers, she pushed the hypo's contents into the fake melon, plumping it up and rolling it back to its place in the grouping with every intention of completing the assignment. The company was in want of a miracle container. One for containing people as well as things. Something with the drape of skin and the toughness of rind. A container that was one with its contents. No waste for the company, nothing for consumers to throw away. Should it have its own color or take on the color of whatever it contained? Should it mimic its texture or enhance it? For the time being, they were letting her choose which questions to address. She appreciated the unusual freedom but still found the assignment tedious, the cantaloupe annoyingly fake.

Outside the window, against the scribbled sky, the figure of a crone cut the profile of a sparrow hawk. Compact. Slightly lethal. Hair like crimped wire wrestled into a bun at her neck.

Sarah Vogel, among the more quixotic forms of containment she'd ever encountered, had been hijacking her attention all morning. Studying her subject a few moments longer, Moll put pencil to paper. She began with the distinctive hook of the woman's nose, shading a sunken cheek, the clenched jaw, chin receding into the neck's sinews, narrow shoulders straining as if fighting the powerful instinct to fly, inspiring the addition of wings. Webbed. An insect's, not an angel's.

Wee cameras, nestled in two ceiling corners, craned to get a better look at what she was doing. As if she didn't know they were there. As if she hadn't been the one to activate them. Punching in, though voluntary, had committed her to a full ternion—the newly adopted three-hour unit of labor. MORE's new standard. Kim's MORE, not hers. She'd already stopped thinking of the additional minutes packed into the longer hour as extra.

Deciding the portrait was finished, she tore the page from her pad, filled her fountain pen with indigo ink, and added a caption to the lower left-hand corner, ink bleeding into the porous stock. She blew on it and dropped the sketch onto a stack of others, all so alike they could've been a printer's run of the same edition, the lower left-hand caption, A-120239, a first-rate forgery.

Her hand, loosened up, started across a fresh sheet, this one dedicated to the work for which each hour of each ternion would be modestly remunerated. So. This miracle material, this skin that performed better than skin. Should it be hard but easily replaceable, like the shell a hermit crab abandons once it grows too big? Or soft and supple, like a pair of forever pantyhose? She found it hard to care. She wasn't the first hypothetical artist called in to give shape to the Company's impossible desires. She was no longer even the youngest.

Her grandmother had resumed her work, relieved, maybe, that Moll had gone back to hers. Neither willing to give this Heartbreak Hiatus what it wanted.

Another morning. Sarah was on her knees weeding the garden. She wore an old sweater and leather gloves stiff with sweat and petrified dirt. Moll was still in bed. Every day, she slept later and later. Nothing woke her. Not the smell of coffee. Not the banging of pots. Not even a grandmother checking to see if she was still breathing, studying through the cracked door, the bedroom redecorated in wrinkled clothes and drawing supplies, the portrait of Grandma Ruth Vogel, their golem-like matriarch, a prop on a chest of drawers.

Moll finally came out and claimed a fraying lawn chair to catch the last of the pre-noon sun. Her head was uncovered. She hadn't bothered to change out of her nightclothes. Sarah didn't care for the way the shift clung to her frame, the thin cotton showing her pendulous breasts, furred armpits. Had the girl forgotten to pack her razor? There were still some of Walter's up in the medicine cabinet, but she wasn't about to bring it up.

"Jesus, Great-Great, take it off. Your sweater is making me sweat just looking at it." They were the first words the girl had uttered in two days.

"Good! My teeth chatter just looking at that *kop*," Sarah said, reaching to rub it. The girl's skin, apartment-pale up to her scalp, had already rosied under the new stubble. An encouraging sign.

"Don't look," the girl answered, batting the cold hands from her head and snagging the sleeve of her grandmother's sweater, fingers sneaking under the cuff, finding the path they'd traveled since she was a baby, eyes closed, melting the grandmother who hadn't known it was still possible.

Her arm was a keyboard the girl made her own. A regular Van Cliburn, she was. The pulse animating the numbers to be strummed.

Not a tear since she's come, Sarah thought. *Maybe she's strong. Maybe just mean like me.*

"I always expect to feel it," the girl said, opening her eyes wide. "Like one of those tree-trunk hearts with 'Sally loves Bobby' carved inside, something you don't need to see to know is there, you know?" She sounded like the air had been let out of her.

"Zelly and Bubbe? It'll never work. She's way too old for him." It was supposed to make the girl laugh, but Sarah was no comedian.

"Seriously, Great-Great. Can you feel it?"

"My numbers? Mostly I forget they're there."

"But you remember *how* they got there."

"No, dolly. Not even that."

"Hmmmm." The girl ruminated over the ring of grounds at the bottom of her cup.

"Great-Great?" Her fingers worked the digits of her grandmother's code.

"Yes?" Sarah sensed the moment nearing, Moll's tears ripe for the picking.

"Did it hurt?"

"I don't remember."

"But you'd remember if it hurt, right?"

"So many questions about an old tattoo?" *Come, curl up in my lap and have a good cry.*

"I'm thinking of getting one is all."

Sarah yanked her arm away. "When I'm in my grave."

"A-120239. What do you think?"

"The number's taken."

"But not the real estate," she teased, baby-tickling her own arm, head resting on the nylon weave of her lawn chair, spread open, a sun worshipper.

The telephone rang, loud, unignorable, but neither moved.

Moll asked if she should get it. No answer.

"Could be important."

"It isn't."

"What if I was calling?"

"You, I'd answer."

"But how would you know it was me?"

"I would know."

It rang once more and gave up. For the moment. A day hardly went by without at least one attempt from Miss Daria Goldman, the very committed young woman who was losing patience with Sarah's shilly-shallying. The anniversary teetering on the horizon was not just any anniversary, they kept trying to impress upon her, it was a *centennial.* But how could that be? A minute, or an eternity, maybe. But one hundred years? Please have your party without me, she kept telling them, to no avail.

"I don't know how you stand it," Moll said. "Losing so much. Me? Only two . . ."

"Two important ones."

"But I can't take a full breath without feeling my heart will break."

"You have a heart, it gets broken."

"We're the same now, aren't we Great-Great? Orphans."

"No, dolly, orphans have no one."

"How fast do you think hair grows in three weeks?" she asked, rubbing her scalp.

It had been a poor harvest of tears so far, but if it was what the girl needed, Sarah would sit through the mornings watching her hair grow.

Again the phone. Moll wanted to answer, but Sarah insisted it was just the the Register people.

"How can you possibly know that, Great-Great?"

"I have a very good ear."

Week two began with Moll nixing an early morning march through the park with her grandmother for a solo drive in the country.

When Moll asked for the car keys, Sarah asked where she was going. "Nowhere," Moll answered.

"That far," said Sarah. "Keys are in the car. Fill the tank on the way back."

Several hours later, Moll wound up marooned by a flat on the shoulder of some rural route skirting a town with the unfortunate name of Chagrin Falls. Nowhere, indeed. The jack was in the trunk, and she managed to pull up the car model's instruction manual (ancient as it was) on her wrist screen. Fully capable of reconfiguring a nation's workday, she couldn't budge the rusty bolts that had frozen the tire in place.

She was kicking at the tire with her sandaled foot when a truck slowed and swerved onto the shoulder behind her. Its driver had no murderous intentions. He just wanted to help.

He was a NOOMer, if only chronologically. She could see that his spirit reached further back. Shoulder-length hair. Ripped arms covered in tats. And he had a way with lug nuts, which she held while he worked.

He finished and wiped his hands on his jeans. "This tire's a temp," he said. "You should get the other one fixed or replaced as soon as you get home."

"I will."

"Where *is* home?"

"Not far. I'll be fine."

"Okay, then," he said.

This nowhere feeling better with this someone in it, she asked if she could buy him a beer to thank him. He told her no thanks were needed, but he had some cold ones back at his studio if she was thirsty.

She followed him to a reclaimed gas station on the outskirts of the town with the heart-heavy name. He was a tattoo artist. A sign in front of the building said *Jake, Ink*, the kind of cleverness she generally despised but in this case found charming.

He held the door for her.

"You're Jake?" she asked once inside.

He shrugged and cracked open the promised beers.

The place, like him, was a calculated mess. Hundreds of photographs taped to the walls, their subjects decorated from head to toe. Stacks of magazines showing the work of inkers past. A fiddle. An accordion. Charts of alphabets hanging like window shades. English, Hebrew, Cyrillic. Multi-limbed goddesses. A Mona Lisa beach towel. Plastic crosses and silvery Stars of David dangling from the pull chains of the overhead fluorescents. An assortment of infinity signs that made the bottom of her foot tingle.

She hopped onto his worktable and sipped her beer.

"This is crazy," she said.

"So I've been told."

"No, not your place. I was just talking about getting a tattoo, and here I am," she said.

"Uh-huh."

"You don't believe in fate?" she asked. Did he really not get the cosmic nature of their side-of-the-road meeting?

"I do," he said. "Show me what you got."

"What?"

"Your other tattoos. I need a melody line to find the right harmony."

"I guess this would be the melody line. I don't have any others. I've never gotten further than the thinking part."

He was skeptical. But she had proof.

"Whaddya know," he said, watching her strip down to nothing. "You really are a virgin."

"Excuse me?"

"Most of my clients are pretty marked up by your age."

"Yeah, well, I'm not one of your clients."

"You are now," he said, taking off his clothes.

They made love on his sofa.

After, she asked how much he charged.

"I usually fuck for free," he said.

"I meant for a tattoo," she said, blushing.

"*That* depends on what you have in mind." His smile hinted at a taste for torture.

She asked for a pad of paper and picked the darkest blue from a coffee can full of colored pencils to show him the letter and numbers that she wanted. She could draw them in her sleep.

"What do you think?" she asked.

"Actual size?"

"Actual in every way."

"Sure you don't want to go with a more discreet location? It's not going to sit well with a lot of people."

"I can handle it."

"Okay, then. One color, thumb and a half long. On the house cheap enough?"

And he began.

She'd heard it likened to a snakebite but hardly felt the needles. His deliciously chocolate-brown eyes were magnified by the goggles he wore. He chewed on his tongue, the tip of which poked out the side of his mouth. No chitchat. He worked steadily, stopping between pricks to swab the tiny beads of blood dotting the perforations he'd made.

She didn't look until it was finished, but as she suspected, it was good. A-120239. Like it had been peeled from Sarah's arm and grafted onto hers. Like the chill of a memory she'd never lived.

"Remember, it's a wound. Treat it that way and you'll be fine." He handed her a tube of antibacterial ointment. "And don't go around advertising it or anything."

"Will I see you again?"

"If you get that tire fixed."

Sarah was in bed when she got home. A relief, though Moll needed to talk to someone, and the fact that she'd buried that someone two weeks before made her blue. She once thought of prayer was the language of the dead. Now she thought it the language of fools. But having no other options and nothing to lose, for the first time in years, she got down on her knees and prayed.

"Dear Mom . . . wherever you are . . . I met someone today. He's different. A walking piece of art with an aversion to full sentences. I think you'd like him, but don't tell Daddy. He wouldn't understand. I'm not telling your mother either. That's all, I guess. Except for one more thing. Keep me safe. But not from him . . . keep me honest with him. Okay?"

In the bathroom, while brushing her teeth, the fool in the mirror added, *Amen*.

By the third week of Bereave Leave, Moll was in love.

How do I deserve this? she'd ponder on her drives to Chagrin. This stranger who refused to remain so, and when told she was meant to have been Malcah never called her Moll again. This attentive lover, and even more attentive listener, who gently dressed what he called *their* wound without asking what it meant, the string of numbers he'd etched into her arm, and was felled when she told him. And when she said she wanted another, leafing through his portfolio for ideas, he told her that ink was power, and *this,* wiping his thumb across the path slick with ointment, was all the power she needed. It had taken a month of strangers to open her to pleasure. Only one to turn her prudent.

He was moved when she described her family's mural of loss, sharing the many questions that plagued her. What if, instead of cancer, Ruth had been killed in a car crash? Or an earthquake had swallowed her. Or a terrorist attack had taken her and several thousand others? Would the reason for no longer having her mother change the nature of her pain? Would she miss her any more or less? Would it be easier to tolerate not having been enough for her father? Were there more and less honorable ways to die? Weren't we all, in the end, alone in missing those taken from us? Whatever answers he had were respectfully kept to himself.

Sarah suspected a boy was behind Moll's new, less tragic mien but never asked where she was spending her days and nights. The woman's lack of curiosity being the number one reason Moll had ended up in Ohio. The Koenigs had begged her to come to them. Sarah begged for nothing.

Just the thought of the Koenigs filled her with guilt. She phoned them the first Sunday of every month, which was all it took to stay on the family mailing list. There was always something—a bar mitzvah, wedding, bris—and Moll always made them beg for an RSVP. The Koenigs were the best grandparents a kid could want. She was the lousiest grandchild. Maybe she'd spend the holidays with them this year. The first dipping of apples in honey without . . . . She shook her head to empty it of all the other firsts to come.

Jake was enough of a first for now. But he was booked solid, so she'd be sticking close to home for the day.

Sarah was out walking, and when the phone began to ring, Moll skipped to the kitchen to answer it. She laughed hearing the caller was a Centennial Commission rep. The Register, as her grandmother said. The girl, sounding wary, asked for Mrs. Vogel. She hadn't expected to reach anyone, so hearing that she had the daughter of their sainted leader on the line was like winning the lottery, but within minutes, the girl's saccharine voice had Moll twisting herself up in the phone's long coil. There'd been concerns about Sarah's credibility. No record of a Sarah Vogel or Vogelmann at either Auschwitz or Bergen-Belsen had materialized. A Sarah Fogel. A Sarah Wolkmann. But neither with a number close to A-120239. There was no A-120239 anywhere, but in the interest of inclusivity and out of respect for Dr. Fields, they'd labeled the number "a-sequential" as opposed to "nonexistent." And because of her case, Daria Goldman said, all further testing had been suspended indefinitely. She thought that might please Mrs. Vogel.

"Testing?" Moll asked, the only word standing out in this shitstorm.

"DNA," Daria said. "You know, Survivor Surety. Most people have been happy to comply. It was free and all."

"Have any tested negative?"

"Sure. I've even met people who faked their tattoo . . ."

"But you don't think she . . ."

"Mrs. *Vogel*? No nononono. Why would she? Why would anyone? But I guess everyone's looking for a reason to feel special these days."

Just back from her walk, Sarah was surprised to find her granddaughter bound in telephone cord like a sacrificial lamb. Who was she talking to? she mouthed. And then she saw Moll's arm. The numbers, an enflamed version of hers.

"What have you done?" she cried.

"What have *you* done?" Moll demanded, not covering the receiver but unwinding herself from the first loop. "Your friend Daria here thinks you're a fake. Want to set her straight?" She dangled the phone between them like it was a fish on a hook. Sarah wouldn't touch it. "Suit yourself," Moll said, unwinding the rest of the way. Daria Goldman's far-off babble snuffed with the mashing of the handset into its cradle.

All Moll wanted was to be alone, but Sarah followed her up the stairs to her bedroom.

"Please, just go away," she begged.

"I can't leave you like this. Remember, dolly, you said it yourself. You and me, we're all we have."

"I was trying to make you feel better. *I* have people. People who love me. People I trust."

"Am I not one of them?"

"See? That's why it'd be best for you to leave me alone. How can I trust you when I don't even know who you are?"

"I'm your grandmother. That's all I am. If you need me to be more, tell me what to do. Anything. I'll do it."

"Anything?" Moll grabbed the black-and-white portrait, the pale face and sunken eyes preserved under glass. "Tell me who this is."

"She's no one."

"Who is she?" Moll demanded.

"I don't know," her grandmother said, the woman in the picture a complete stranger, yet so familiar.

"Sarah, who is she?"

"I don't know," she answered, Great-Great no more. There were tears now. Real ones. "I would say if I did, but it was an idea Ruthie got in her head. That's all. She was my baby. I didn't have the heart to tell her the truth."

"Don't blame this on your heart. You lied to her. Your own daughter. Oh my God, the excuses she made for you whenever you didn't show up for us. 'Oh, how she suffers,' she'd say. 'All those memories,' she'd say. 'Deep down she's good. She's just afraid to show it.' That woman gave you a lifetime pass for being a Survivor, and you took it, didn't you?"

"Your mother knew that woman wasn't anybody's grandmother and forgave me. And when have I ever called myself a Survivor?"

"You still don't understand, do you? Mom was always telling me I had Ruth Vogel's brains and Ruth Vogel's eyes. 'How could Ruth Vogel's great-granddaughter be anything but great,' she'd say. Now I find out there never was a Ruth Vogel? Did you ever even have a mother?"

"There were many women, dolly. I took a piece of each of them and gave them to your mother. She to you. Call everything else a lie but that."

Moll let the picture fall to the floor. Sarah dropped to her knees to collect the pieces.

"Don't!" Moll couldn't bear Sarah touching it. She couldn't bear touching it either but knelt next to her grandmother to brush away the fragments so she could study the picture. The paper it was printed on was flimsy as newsprint. It wasn't even a photograph. At the bottom was a caption that the frame had kept hidden. "Unidentified woman awaits delousing. German archives." On the back, a page of text, beginning and ending mid-sentence.

It was one death too many, and the tears Sarah had been awaiting finally flowed.

Moll pushed by her, charging down the stairs and out the back door, Sarah calling after her. She was scared. A new kind of scared.

Moll, too. Scared of what this lie might mean if given any more air, of what worse lies there were to uncover, of staying and not finding the words to describe her anger, of finding them and never being able to take them back.

Sarah was used to being alone, but Moll's exit was her introduction to lonely. Not even her garden brought solace, in the ruins of August showing itself for what it was. A conceit. The work of an imposter. She was not one for wishing away time but felt desperate for the cold when the birds would come to pick it clean, and she could cut it to the ground and go back to pretending.

Moll was gone. For the day or forever, she couldn't guess. There wasn't much left of her Bereave Leave anyway. She'd always said she'd head out when it was over. Sarah was now convinced she'd met someone. Hoped she had, anyway. Moll deserved someone in her life besides this sham of a grandmother, this prune of a woman to whom the girl had entrusted her need. A need more addictive than coffee, or cigarettes.

Now handed over to another. Sarah didn't know if she'd survive the withdrawal, but if Moll had found love . . . well, then she'd have to.

There was vodka in the freezer. She took the bottle and a juice glass to her husband's study. She reclaimed his desk, clearing it of Moll's things—the boxes of charcoal, the work screen, her props, real and fake—and dismantled the little cameras with their off-duty robot eyes. She found a pen and stationery and began writing. Her mind was a crowded marsh, her thoughts a swarm of weed-slithering eels. She didn't stop until they covered the page.

August 23, 2044

My dear,

You want to know who I am, and I will try to tell you. Sarah is the only name I remember, but in the time before I could talk, before I was teachable, before I knew any name at all, I remember wanting so badly to be able to read, to make sense of the things I saw, I suppose. Like the string of numbers that had no sound yet described me better than any name could. And then like magic, there was school, and I learned that letters had sounds and if you knew them you could make words. I sat in class wanting only to show the teacher how ready I was for this learning, but when he called the name Sarah, there was always another girl quicker to raise her hand. Every week it was the same, only the Sarahs were different. None of them stayed long, and I never asked where they went, but it didn't matter. In their shadow, I was already spelling and reading and writing. Then one day, the teacher called the name, and I was the only one left to answer. That was the day I became Sarah for real.

And that is a story. Grandma Ruth is another story. Everything's a story, dolly, and not all are true. It is true the violin doesn't run in your blood, but that only means you got brilliant on your own. Also true? The numbers I wear belonged to someone else. Whose I can't say, but they didn't need them anymore, and they've come in handy. Sometimes doors don't open without a nudge, you know.

Remember when I came to say goodbye, when we shared your bed and you asked why your mother, why not me, and you wouldn't look at me for wishing me away, me, a woman who'd suffered, a woman who needed handling. But you were right. It should've been me. I promised your mama that losing her would be my end and that I broke my promise shames me. That I let her go, let all my girls go without a fight shames me. That I let them go before they got to know me, before I let them know me, and that I'm still here, like a beggar begging, like a glutton gorging on time, when I've done nothing to justify what time I've had—I'm nothing but shame, Moll. A bupkis from the start. But I'm the only one left who knew my Ruthie and my Malcah and the beautiful girl whose name I've lost the right to say, my Sasha, your aunt, and you'll see, hers is the biggest story of all. You say you have people who know you and love you, but who of them can make you one with my girls? Trust me again and I will lead you to them.

Your Aunt Glory once called me the most solitary creature she ever knew, and I thought, is the woman crazy? Which she is. But me? Solitary? I can't remember spending an entire day alone in my life. Even since Walter died, he's been bumbling around after me, room to room, awake, asleep. And the others. I'd like to say I don't believe in ghosts, but the corners of my house have never emptied of them.

So, if you'll still have me, I'll come to New York. And if Daria Goldman won't bar me from it, I'll get on that stage, and when it's over and we Survivors have been counted for the last time, you can ask your questions and I'll tell you everything, the good and the bad. Or at least what memory has made of it all. This could be easier if you were in Ohio. But wherever you make your home, I promise I'll be so devoted a ghost that nothing will sweep me from its corners.

Until then, dear girl, know that you are my Moll. And me? Let me be your Sarah.

In the desk's top drawer was a well-preserved sheet of Forever stamps. Sarah printed her granddaughter's name and address on an envelope into which she folded and stuffed the letter, then licked the flap and peeled a stamp from the sheet. She doubted the postal service's idea of forever was the same as hers, but it was a breezy afternoon, and she walked her letter to the terminal in hopes of finding a human who could tell her its chances of getting anywhere.

The terminal was closed. Not for the day, for good. She was certain it had been open not so long ago. Maybe a week, maybe a year. She had no faith in the letterbox planted in the defunct parking lot. *Nothing to be done*, she thought, but then a fast-walking man in joggers and gym shoes stopped to ask if there was anything he could do for her. Only if he was going to New York

City and could deliver a letter for her, she said. He laughed and told her she was in luck—he happened to be flying there that evening and offered to be her carrier. Like one of those old-timey movies, he said, fast-walking away with her letter, leaving Sarah to wonder *which* old-timey movie and *if* the letter would make it to Moll. If it didn't, she supposed it would do as much good getting lost on a stranger's desk as her dead husband's.

She hurried home to wait for her granddaughter. Whatever Moll was planning, she'd need a change of clothes.

The days were shortening, but hours of light remained. She turned on the TV to pass the time. She felt good about her letter but worried it wouldn't be enough. She wanted another chance. She wanted another vodka, but it was upstairs, and she was too tired to make the trip. Instead she let the television put her to sleep.

She heard rumbling. Then Moll was leaning over her, shaking her arm, whispering.

"I'm going, Gram."

"Going?" Through the living room window, the bright beads of a truck's headlights stung Sarah's eyes.

"Jake . . . my friend . . . he's taking me to the airport. I came to get my stuff. And to apologize for making you worry."

"It's all right." Sarah said, smoothing herself out from her night on the sofa. "Worrying about someone is a pleasure I haven't had in some time."

The truck parked in the driveway was crimson red. Pristine. There was a man at the wheel, young but not baby-face young. This one had been shaving every morning for years.

"Have your friend come in, Moll," Sarah said. "I'll make coffee."

"Thanks, but there's no time for coffee. And I'm not Moll anymore. It's Malcah now. Jake says it suits me better."

Sarah followed as she swept through the upstairs rooms. In Walter's study, she found the tools and supplies her grandmother had boxed, rolled one of the sketches from the pile on the floor, and stretched a rubber band around the tube.

"And the rest of your pictures?" Sarah asked, following her downstairs.

"Keep them, throw them away. They're yours."

There was a man named Jake sitting in a red truck parked in her driveway waiting to take her granddaughter away. Sarah would have liked to know more but would settle for the hasty introduction she was allowed, Jake leaping from the truck to shake her hand, tall, strapping, not much to say but it seemed to Sarah he would've gladly stuck around for coffee if his girl hadn't been in such a rush. Moll tossed her bag into the truck bed, then reached for Sarah and held her tight.

"I'm not mad," she whispered. "Whatever I am, it's not mad."

"It's okay, dolly."

But Moll—Malcah, now—was not ready to let go. Her thumb felt for the faded indigo signature on the soft part of her grandmother's arm, the way she'd always done. "You know what Jake says, Great-Great? Whoever we started out as, you and me, *this* is who we are now."

Sarah, Great-Great again, nodded.

"It's so dumb it's smart, right?"

"Not so dumb."

And that was it.

Jake threw the truck into reverse and, without turning his head, swung onto Church Street. Her granddaughter rolled down her window and shouted, "Remember. If your phone rings, pick it up. It *won't* be Daria Goldman. She's done with you."

Moll, *Malcah*, Sarah thought, was not afraid of her or for her. So different from the rest of her girls. Perhaps because this one had never been hers. This one belonged only to the future. She'd sail by one hundred without batting an eye. When the rest of them no longer had eyes to bat, she'd keep going.

Though it had stayed put for a while, Sarah brought her valise from the cellar to the study. Walter's desktop was bare. A quick search turned up a roll of dental floss and a stash of pushpins. One after another, she pressed the pins into the worn oak surface and used the waxy string to weave a grid. Spearmint scented the room.

She opened the valise, took the scrap of paper bearing the name only memory could decipher, and placed it in the grid's upper-left square. Next to it, the slim volume of prayers in a language she no longer understood. "Definitions You Should Know to Assist You in Determining Your Zipper Needs," needs she hadn't felt in a long time, filled four blocks. As did the family of stick figures. As did the portrait of the family Vogelmann. As did the letter from the lover who'd vanished in a cloud of Gitanes smoke. That a life didn't fit so neatly into a grid was no surprise. Having so much proof of that life was what surprised her. The citizenship papers Bloom had insisted on. His obit rescued from the trash. A slew of newspaper clippings about the passing of Survivors, all good stories, mostly sent by her son-in-law, a reminder, maybe, should she ever think she was a special case. An envelope marked *baby teeth*. All Ruthie's. A picture of the grandchild Walter had printed from that high-performance watch the kids gave him, their first sonogram. Sarah remembered the machine thrumming and her coffee perking and him bounding down the stairs calling out, "It's a girl. Sarah. A girl." And she'd turned it every which way trying to see the thing they were calling a baby. She did the same now and still couldn't make it out, the picture *or* the girl for whom this desktop museum was being curated.

Sarah inspected her work and saw it was good. But something was missing. The valise was empty. It would all be for nothing if this story wasn't finished by the time Moll, *Malcah*, returned. Whenever that might be.

She closed the suitcase and left it standing upright on the floor by the desk. It had spent enough time in the cellar. It was part of the show now.

On the back of the study's door hung Walter's old bathrobe. She took it from the hook and wrapped herself in it, something she hadn't done in a long time. One of the pockets felt weighted down, and in it she found the golden compact, right where she'd put it that day the poor bird died on her living room floor. The satisfaction of finding a spot for the last puzzle piece immediately gave way to a paralyzing realization. Sasha's letter. That's what was missing. The compact was a paragraph. The letter was a chapter. The letter was the whole damn book. And it was gone. Unaccountably, magically gone.

August in the City. White sheets covered everything, the way servants once put their masters' summer cottages to bed at season's end. But there were no servants to shake out the linens in the dappled light. There was only Malcah Koenig. It was exactly what she'd wanted, to be alone, thinking she needed to be alone, but once alone, becoming all too aware of how alone a person could be. She allowed herself a bit more grieving, then made a list.

In the remaining four days of her Bereave Leave, she would:

1. meet with lawyers;
2. legally change her name to Malcah;
3. go to the bank to bring home the contents of her mother's secret safe-deposit box;
4. cancel her parents' accounts;
5. bag their clothing and leave it with the doorman for the Council of Jewish Women's resale shop;
6. take up the carpeting and arrange for the hardwood floors to be sanded and bleached;
7. repaint (Zen gray);
8. list the apartment;
9. return to the Tank to group-think a material as flexible, self-healing, and regenerative as skin when there already was this thing called skin;
10. quit that profitable job;
11. go to work for the Centennial Commission, a low-paying, short-term gig that would make her, officially a charity case;
12. decide whether to answer or pretend she'd never received Sarah's letter, which somehow beat her home with no postmark, a maddening underscore to Ruth's insistence that Sarah Vogel *was* worth loving despite her errors in judgment, not the least of which had been sharing such troubling disclosures with a mourning granddaughter who needed Superwoman by her side, not an old woman with a century of lies for her to shoulder;

13. put an end to mourning; and
14. call Jake the inker, *her* inker, to pledge her allegiance and recant stranger sex forever and together recite the vow they'd drafted in Ohio: *Wherever we go we'll make magic, we'll make beauty, we'll make love . . . and we'll make it loud.*

To dos.

Liberation

2045

So this is what the world wants, Sarah thought. It wants Survivors. Just not too many. And time had whittled this group to the perfect size. Thousands had come to honor her and two hundred fifty others on the anniversary of the end of Auschwitz. In the newly domed Sheep Meadow, heart of New York's greatest park, heart of the country's greatest city, the crowd was an undulating sea, at the center of which floated a circular stage, a life preserver for all two hundred and fifty-one of them. It had the air of a convention. The gaiety of workers on leave from their spouses. Everyone name-tagged. The Rosensteins, Rosenblatts, Pfeffers, and Feins. Gravitating like to like. Busy comparing numbers, knotty fingers pointing, I know you, like old friends at a high school reunion, frosted eyes sizing each other up, betting who'd given a kidney to save a stranger's life and who'd committed tax fraud, who'd run into a burning building to rescue an old woman's cat and who'd run the other way. Though that was history. The now of this After was the moment they'd been living for. The revenge of the bullied, class of '45, the thrill of vindication adding millimeters to their brittle frames, because as good or bad as they believed each other to be, limelight was the best disinfectant.

But thank God for the music, the applause, the granddaughter who'd made her come, and the rich people whose tremendous appetites for gratitude had paid for everything, this dizzying panorama so alive she could almost see sheep grazing the meadow, bleating at the roving curious, nosing the tushes of hungry tourists, the crowd stretching so far it could hold everyone she'd ever known, dead and alive. Crowds. No matter what gathered them, it was always the same. The peculiar mix of jubilance and menace, believers and non-believers, the fors and againsts, the pithy signs, the crush, the momentum of a push, accidental or intended, the camaraderie, the loneliness, a herd on alert, a stampede on hold, the oceanic swell only properly appreciated from a stage. It was her first time on one, and any lingering resistance she'd armed herself with, any regret she'd feared would follow her home, had evaporated. Whether or not she deserved to be, she was on it. And, she had to admit, it was something else.

How much better it must be from Moll's crane-high command center. *Malcah*, she had to keep reminding herself, whose hair was beginning to show, dark and curly. She'd gotten her height, her bosom from the other grandma, but fair is fair—those curls were Sarah's. The girl had no idea what a beauty she'd become, making her, in her Great-Great's estimation, even more beautiful. Jake knew, though. He hated crowds but stayed glued to his front-row spot all day, a supplicant at the foot of his queen. He was a good one, Jake. Sarah was even developing a fondness for the tattoos covering his arms. And she was sure he'd had a lot to do with Moll's decision to leave money-making and become a "charity case."

He, the freedom the move gave her, and the Register, this Centennial, that had a faith in her no corporation could rival. She asked for a budget, they provided. She asked for free rein, they gave. She asked that the tally of the lost include the Roma, the so-called deviants, and any victims of any holocaust since—so many colors and creeds the Jews didn't even have *that* market cornered anymore—and they didn't blink. But the Survivors of *this* holocaust, *the Holocaust,* were the headliners. And for them she turned the sky-like dome into a great mirror that had everyone looking up at themselves looking down on themselves. And through the middle ground she ran ribbons of digital highway lined with billboards carrying holographic messages in the languages of their post-survival. In Hungarian: *God put us to the test, and we passed.* In Polish: *God put us to the test, and we failed.* In Russian: *There is no God, but if there were, what a shit.*

Clever, thought her grandmother, watching the ticker tick away the heads of those still standing. By the end there'd be hundreds fewer.

A group at the eastern border began a solemn rendition of "Hatikva," a group from the west competing with a rousing "God Bless America." But like it or not, they all played in the same orchestra. Malcah's. With her maestro's stick she cued "Slaughter on Tenth Avenue," which had no programmatic relevance but was written by a Jew and shouted New York. It was followed by a real boy fiddling "Oyfn Pripetshik" for his real great-grandfather, a witness humming along in a far-away nursing home.

Attention waning, Malcah drew a cover of cloud over her mirror darkening the Meadow's arena and from the nethers of the stage let rise the largest Torah ever made.

Sarah had seen only one other. It was at a "shool" Walter dragged her to one Saturday morning thinking her due a reckoning with the religion of her past. He'd never needed her to be a Jew, but he needed her to be something, and being a Jew seemed a suitable something.

The service was long and undisciplined, late arrivals sliding noisily into the pews. Only when the rabbi took the Torah, their tree of life, from its ark and called the congregation to the bimah for a closer look were the beasts tamed. The ceremonial undressing and opening of the scroll, the intricate calligraphy thickly inked onto the parchment, a score of musical notes that jittered from the rabbi's mouth like a cloud of bees at a September picnic. For Sarah, it was a moment of marvel. And then it was over. With the rabbi's final incantation, the Torah was returned to its ark, the service ended, she and Walter were back home and settled in for a night of takeout Chinese and TV Westerns, and all that remained of their morning was her relief that a Sabbath could come and go without anything changing.

But that was Before. Now she was reconsidering. She'd been forgiven so much. Embracing this one wrathful God might be a step toward recompense. And here in the Sheep Meadow, as if mined from her memory bank, whole alphabets of letters sprinkled like confetti from Malcah's cloud-filled dome, many of them finding their place in a passage from the towering scroll in their midst . . . *And they said to Moses, Was it for want of graves in Egypt that you brought us to die in the wilderness?* A gust of wind carried the inebriating scent of a wilderness far from Egypt, and the people began to mix, residents with visitors, visitors with ghosts. *So they've come*, Sarah thought. Those she'd met before and those she'd be meeting for the first time. It was like looking at the horizon through a microscope; she could see pores on noses, missing teeth, and even the blood coursing through the veins of the living, ghosts like Sasha, the long-gone daughter who'd led Sarah through other crowds, a gang of kids clinging like burrs collected on a walk through a forest, her arms reaching to hoist a young woman onto her back, a beautiful twenty-two-year-old poet, the Malcah she and Sasha had shared. Surviving a Survivor had made Sasha strong. Sarah envied her.

There was Robbie, the one who loved their Malcah still, and Robert, the one who'd loved her until he could bear to love someone else.

There were Sarah's husbands, the one packed away in her valise; the other, Walter, a ghost still transfixed by what he called her mystery. And Bloom, someone else's husband but there, too, wire-rimmed glasses barely holding on to the end of his nose, his eyes shining with mirth.

There was Cacky, as tall and slim as her mother, and Kit, as stout and skeptical as hers; Gerri, the friend who'd wanted to save her and Dorotea the caseworker who had, the two of them arm in arm. And all the nameless shades, the young immigrants, remnants, and refugees she'd lived with, worked beside, and abandoned without warning, sometimes in ruthless pursuit of opportunity, but only as ruthlessly as they pursued theirs. They could haunt others if they wanted, but not her.

Only Ruthie had stayed away. But that was okay. It took trust to cavort with the living. Trust. Sarah'd broken it, and she'd fix it. Time being cooperative.

Meanwhile, surrounding her were two hundred and fifty witnesses, all committed to staying the course, lolling around in the past even while collapsing under the strain of providing the world its living proof that the Holocaust *was*. One day, one hour, one instant there'd be only one left. The last Survivor. What if it were her? And why not her? A thought that sent her running from her compatriots to join Glory and Jake on the ground where everything looked different, the past just another part of the story, every exultation, every misery, every year another chapter. One hundred of them, every day of which she'd been present, alive, remembering, differentiating—Monday from Tuesday, spring from fall. She couldn't say if it had been a good century or a bad one. If her chapter had been torn from the book, would she have missed living it, knowing it, smelling it, tasting it? Would history have written retribution into itself if there never was a Sarah Vogel? As if there ever was.

And the next hundred years? Her granddaughter's story, the end of which she was unlikely to see, especially maddening having been hooked by its promising start. But as she watched the girl, this woman conducting her opus, Sarah had a vision. It filled her, lifting her out of life's current, and the higher she was carried, the more she saw, no more ghosts, a beauty coronated, her pate fuzzed like a coconut and swathed in a rainbow-colored scarf the ends of which decorated her bare shoulder, a naked odalisque lying on Sarah's old divan, a queen gazing over her shoulder, arm draping her belly, rotund, a cradle of possibility upon which her love had tattooed the map of their colliding worlds, a map large in scope, exquisite in detail, and showing those roads they'd traveled and those left to tempt them. Some good, some not so good.

After, Malcah Koenig took the wheel of her parents' old Volvo and steered them through the tangle of streets leading to the highway and across the George Washington bridge arcing the Hudson. "Volvos never die," said the mechanic who'd made it purr again. And wouldn't her father have been pleased to see her giving it the care it deserved? Not so pleased with the vanity plates—A-120239—or the bumpers now sleeved with a century of protest stickers. "Good in the snow, too," the mechanic had said. She had a car that would weather anything, no job, and a grandmother who refused to die.

In the backseat, Jake dozed. Or pretended to. He knew conversation between the women needed no audience.

"Where do we start, *mamaleh*?"

"At the beginning," her granddaughter said, Moll, now Malcah, focused on the road ahead, intent on her assignment. "What's the first thing you remember?"

The old woman's memories were a bundle of loose threads, each with its own beginning. She pulled at one. It was long, but she pulled, one hand over the other, until an answer was in sight.

"The cold," she told her granddaughter. "In the beginning, it was cold."

It would be smooth sailing once on 80, the city's spikes giving way to a wall of Allegheny grit. The rolling hills of Ohio's farmland west and a few degrees south. The miles ahead seemed like nothing compared to the distance that hung between them, but Sarah kept her word and held nothing back. She'd burned through her allotment of broken promises.

Malcah, too, contemplated the ground they had yet to cover.

"Tell me, Great-Great," she said. "Have you warmed up yet?"

Glossary

afikomen—a piece of matzo used in the Passover seder

aliyah—literally, going up; a journey to Israel or the honor of being called to the bimah to read from the Torah

balabosta—an ideal housewife

bimah—the stage, platform, podium in a synagogue where the Torah is read

bissel—a little bit

boychik—a term of endearment for a young man

b'shert—meant to be; a version of fate but less mystical

bubbe—grandmother

bupkis—nothing, a throwaway

chametz—generally bread, but any food that is leavened and cannot be eaten during Passover

chuppah—canopy used during weddings

davening—praying, often a drone or chant with bobbing and swaying

gei gezunt—go in good health

Gotenu—God only knows

goy—the persistent "other"; "goyim", most often referring to WASPs; "goyishe", having qualities of that community, generally not a compliment

Haggadah—text of the Passover seder

Hashem—in Hebrew, literally, the Name; how to say the name of God without saying the name of God

Hatikva—The Hope, the State of Israel's national anthem

Jude, Juden (yood, yooden)—German for Jew; Jewish

Kaddish—a prayer for the dead in which death is never mentioned, recited daily by mourners during the year following a parent's or child's passing, and then on the anniversary of that death (see, yahrzeit)

Kaddish factory—synagogues established in New York City's business and industrial hubs to provide commuters a place to say Kaddish. Their heyday was in the 1930s and '40s. Many have since closed

kinder—children

kippah—skullcap, also yarmulke (plural, kippot)

knaidel, knaidlach—matzo ball

kop—head, the whole and what's inside it

mensch—an exemplary man, known for the humanity he shows others (menschlichkeit being the quality of)

meshuggana—crazy, crazy person

meydl—girl, often part of the expression "sheyna meydl" (beautiful girl)

mikvah—a ritual bath that achieves physical *and* spiritual purity

minyan—the gathering of ten men, the number required for public prayer

mishpachah—extended family, particularly in reference to in-laws

mitzvah—a good deed done out of religious duty

motzi—the short version of hamotzi, the prayer said over the breaking of bread

nebesh—a pitiful person

rebbe—a rabbi, teacher; or a spiritual leader considered to have a special connection to God

schnorer—penny-pinching, cheapskate

schvarts mark—black market

Shabbos, Shabbat—the Jewish Sabbath, from Friday sundown to Saturday sundown

sheitel—the type of wig a Hasidic woman wears after marrying

shiva—seven-day mourning period

shtetl—Jewish village

shul—synagogue or temple

teivel—devil

tefillin—phylacteries, small leather boxes containing Torah verses, strapped to the arm and head for daily prayer

yahrzeit—anniversary of a person's death (by the Hebrew calendar)

Yiddishe—Jewish

za milyh dam—a Russian toast

zayde—grandfather

Acknowledgments

Thanks to my first readers, my husband Hass, whose love, patience, and keen interest made this first publishing effort possible. My mother, who couldn't open my book for fear she wouldn't love it, cried when she finished it, and cheered me on. My brothers Steve and Ken, lifelong sources of support and inspiration. And to my daughters Dore and Olivia and their beautiful families for the privilege of letting me see the world through their eyes.

Deepest gratitude to Amy Friedman, valiant friend, writer, collaborator, activist, teacher, and editor extraordinaire, whose encouragement led me to She Writes; one of my oldest friends Christine de Lignières and one of my newest Tom Gilboy, both perceptive readers who asked the right questions; soulmates and steadfast cheerleaders Stephanie Rudolph, Susan English, and Sharona Berken; Antonia Adezio and Sheila Rabb Weidenfeld, who've mentored and encouraged for years; Makenna Goodman and Margot Dougherty who sharpened my eye and ear; Heather Schroder so generous with her advice; Tom Frick whose luminous letters prod me on; Jeffrey McDaniel, the spirited poet who ran the Sarah Lawrence Summer Program where I had the opportunity to work with Téa Obreht; the Lighthouse Writers Workshop, Denver's Litfest, that makes the most amazing writers available to those struggling with the craft they've perfected, and to one particularly magical summer session when the brilliant writer and generous reader Claire Messud inspired her workshop to continue on as a writing group—Jen Seibert Evans, Monica Vilavicencio, Patty Welze, Kate Dusto, Laura McNeil, Pete Hack, and Tom Gilboy—thank you for your marvelous insight, on your own and together.

To Barbara Stark-Nemon and Leslie Johansen Nack, veteran SWP authors who went above and beyond the call of duty helping their fellow authors and sisters learn the ropes.

To Catilin Hamilton-Summie, a gem of a publicist who was always available for handholding and support.

To Brooke Warner, Lauren Wise, Shannon Green, Cait Levin, Signe Jorgensen, designers Julie Metz and Rebecca Lown, and the rest of She Writes' incredible design and production team, who created and constantly hone the process that allows our books to shine. The homework was intense, but each assignment deepened my understanding of my own work and my respect for the industry. What an empowering journey.

To the survivors I've known, all of whom have left their mark. Four grandparents who fled their Eastern European oppressors for the safety of Ohio; my father, veteran of World War II; family and friends who suffered illnesses and the unendurable loss of parents and children; and Vera Stein Werner, my *mishpachah,* mother of my sister-in-law and friend, Karen Werner and her sister Andrea and brother Ken, who survived the Holocaust and its aftermath to begin life again in New York. Her stories, worthy of their own novel, were not mine to tell, but I confess to having borrowed a bit of her strength for my character Sarah.

And to time. Aging is the smartest thing I've ever done.

About the Author

photo credit: Erin Wik Photography

Diane Botnick was born and raised in the Midwest. She called New York City home for years, working for various organizations in support of the performing and visual arts. She and her husband currently live in Cold Spring, New York.

Looking for your next great read?

We can help!

Visit www.shewritespress.com/next-read
or scan the QR code below for a list
of our recommended titles.